P9-BJA-678

$350

COSTAS TAKTSIS

The Third Wedding

Translated from the Greek by
LESLIE FINER

 RED DUST • NEW YORK

To Carl and Jocelyn Plate

THE THIRD WEDDING
first published in Greece as
To Trito Stefani
© Costas Taktsis
© This translation Alan Ross Ltd. 1967
Published in the United States
by Red Dust Inc. 1971

Library of Congress Catalogue Card Number
79-155440
Standard Book Number 87376-018-2

Printed by: Universal Lithographers Inc.
Bound by: L. H. Jenkins Inc.

Translator's Note

This is a novel about Greek people, Greek places, Greek happenings. I have therefore made no attempt — even assuming it were possible — to translate the book in the sense of 'converting' it into a text which might originally have been written in English. The use of current English idiom stops short at obliterating the clues to custom and character which are an integral function of the Greek idiom itself.

Similarly, I have not adopted hard and fast rules in the transliteration of Greek names. Some of them, where it seemed convenient and harmless, have been changed into their English equivalents. Others not.

A difficult problem was presented by the references to customs, places, actual persons and events which, in varying degrees, are likely to be unknown to the foreign reader. It was not possible to assume an acquaintance even with important historical figures like Venizelos and Metaxas or with common features of the Athenian landscape like the ceremonial cannon on Mount Lycabettus. But to fill every possible gap in the foreign reader's knowledge about matters within the everyday experience of the Greek reader would have required a tedious succession of footnotes unsuitable in a novel. There are, in any event, very few cases in which these references are not either self-explanatory or immaterial to an appreciation of the narrative. In those few cases, I have tried to fill the gap by a very slight explanatory expansion of the original text.

L.F.

Salamis, May 1966.

Part One

1

No, really I can't, I can't stand her another moment! Dear God, why did you send me such a burden to bear? What have I done to deserve such punishment? How long must I put up with her, see her horrid face, hear her voice, how long, Oh Lord, how long? Surely there must be some misguided Christian who'd want to take her? Somebody to take this monstrous freak of nature off my hands, this souvenir her father left to avenge himself? Damn those who stopped me having the abortion!

But why am I cursing them? They're all dead now. Anyway, it's not their fault. I shouldn't have paid any attention to them. On things like that you have to make up your own mind. When she was little I used to comfort myself thinking she would change as she grew up. 'She'll change,' I said to myself, 'she'll improve. Anyway, sooner or later, she'll get married. She'll be on somebody else's back.' Well, there you are. It just shows how wrong I was. The way things are going, it looks as though she'll stay an old maid for life. And no wonder, either, with her the way she is. I hope she's satisfied, that monster Erasmia, the way she's ruined her with all that sermonizing of hers. I'd like to know what man would turn round in the street to give her a second glance, the way she dresses, the way she behaves, the way she talks. Would any normal decent man want her for the mother of his children, with those ridiculous ideas of hers, all those neurotic habits, the way she's always scratching the pimples on her face and never letting them dry up? No, she's booked to stay on the shelf, that's for sure. And, my God, I don't know who to be more sorry for, her or myself. Because, no matter what I say, blood is thicker than water, let's face it. I'm her mother, and I feel for her.

But I feel for myself, too. Every time she upsets me my ulcer drives me mad with pain. 'God made you ugly,' I tell her, 'but at least you could dress up a bit more. You never know, you might fool somebody!' But I'm afraid she's not like me, even in that. Not that I'm beautiful or anything. But I've got style. I always knew how to dress. At her age I was quite a piece. When I walked down the street you could see the men's heads turn like sunflowers following the sun — not like this ugly little lizard. Who the Hell does she take after, I'd like to know? Not me, nor her grandmother. She's nothing like her grandfather, and even less like her father. He may have been rotten to the core, and something else besides, but at least he was a man, and beautiful too — more beautiful than was good for him . . .

No, I'm no beauty, But I know how to live. There aren't many women my age as well preserved as I am. All my friends and all the girls who were at school with me have grown old. I see them in the street and I shudder. They've become grandmothers. Not because they have grandchildren — Julia hasn't any — but they've just let themselves go to seed. They've neglected themselves and grown old. The body doesn't grow old unless the heart grows old first. 'Let my daughters have the gay life,' they say, 'let my children enjoy themselves at balls and parties. I've had my day.' But they say it because their children are worth any kind of sacrifice. They don't have Maria! They don't know what it's like to have a daughter like Maria. That's why I don't blame them when they criticise me for getting married again, instead of trying to get her married off. They don't know how I weighed up all the pros and cons before I took the plunge and married Theodore. Maria, I said to myself, is like somebody drowning in the sea. If I go to save her, she'll drag me down to the bottom with her. The best thing is to save myself, at least. Give her time to grow up a bit, become more of a woman. 'Marry her off,' they all used to tell me, 'and you'll see she'll change out of all recognition.' Marry her off? Why me? Can't she find a husband for herself? Does she have to have him served up on a plate? At her age I had ten men courting me at the same time. They fussed round my skirts wherever I went. All I had to do was to lift my little finger at any one of them, and he'd come crawling on all fours to take me. I suppose you'll say: if that's how it was, how could you be so daft as to pick on Fotis. But that's another story. I'd rather not think about it. It only upsets me more than ever. Maybe, I sometimes tell myself, it was fate that I should marry him. Maybe it was God's will that I should suffer everything I suffered. Maybe I was fated to give birth to this Medusa! . . . But then again, I sometimes think it has nothing to do with God or with fate. It's my own fault and nobody else's. I was pig-headed and I insisted on having my own way. I said 'I'll marry him' and marry him I did. Out of sheer cussedness. Just because nobody in the family would hear of him. Not even my poor old father, who was always so careful about expressing an opinion. I had no intention of letting them interfere again in my affairs, poking their noses into my life like they did before. They did enough damage sticking their fingers into the pie with Aryiris. I wasn't eighteen years old any more. I was twenty-seven. I was independent and determined to do exactly as I pleased. I did. And cut my own throat!

But that's neither here nor there. Everyone is entitled to make one mistake in his life. But is that any reason why I have to pay for that one stupid mistake for ever? How long have I got to live? Ten more years? Twenty? Who knows? I might go out today and get flattened by one of those cars that charge around like Hell's bells. But even if I've only got one hour left to live, I mean to live it the way I like! There's no hope of old Galatia producing another Nina. She's deep under the ground. God, just to live without her constant nagging, to concentrate a bit, to put my mind on something more serious than the everlasting subject of Maria! Dear God, won't you ever do me that little favour! . . .

It's two or three days now since she's been fed up with Theodore. She gets her rages at intervals. She slams the door in his face. She refuses to eat with us at the same table. And when I'm alone with her, she lets loose a non-stop stream of insults against him and his whole family. And the poor man hasn't done the slightest thing to deserve it. She's jealous of me, God damn her, how else can you explain it? 'If you must have a man,' I said to her today, 'go to the park and find yourself some stud or other! The park's just down the road. Go and find yourself a G.I. or a Marine to cool your hot pants! Do I have to find him for you? When I was your age I'd not only had you, but I was getting ready to marry for the second time!' 'Go on,' I told her, 'get dressed and go out. And I swear on the bones of my father, the man I loved better than anything in this world, bring anybody you like back home with you, I don't care who or what he is, and if you tell me "this man here is my friend, my fiancé, my husband", I won't raise the slightest objection, I won't express any kind of opinion! I'll even bow to him, ten times over if need be. It's not me who's going to marry him. It won't be me in his bed. It's you who'll have to sleep with him. Just so long as he doesn't make a fool of you — and it's usually the snivelling little virgins like you who get caught — and run off after he's eaten up your dowry, leaving me with you on my back again, and this time with some little bastard child as well! Go on, get dressed,' I told her, 'and get out of my sight! And if you don't want a man — and God knows, you're so crazy you don't know yourself what you want out of life — then go and shut yourself up in a nunnery. There are still some left. Go and join Saint Miriam at Keratea! Go and be a nun like your great idol Erasmia! I suppose your father left you behind deliberately to make my life Hell? Go on, get dressed — and do what you damn well like. But watch it! I'm warning you for the last time. Don't make another scene like today's, especially in front of Theodore, or there'll be murder done in this house. I'll chop you into little pieces like mincemeat! And don't you ever dare take those photos of my father and Hecuba off the sitting-room wall again! I don't care if the frames are ugly. And I don't care if it's no longer done to hang photos on the wall. As long as I'm alive, this is *my* house. I run things here, and I'll hang any damn thing on the walls I want to, do you hear? When you get married, God willing, and set up your own house, or when I peg out, as you say, and you get my money — and the way you upset me you won't have very long to wait — you can hang cowbells on your walls, for all I care. But as long as I live, as long as my eyes are open, I want to see the photos of the people who loved me and who died, more's the pity, and left me with a shrew like you to eat me alive!' I said and went and hung the photos of papa and Hecuba back where they belonged.

When she saw what I'd done, she literally frothed at the mouth. 'Oh yes,' she said, 'we mustn't insult your old washerwoman of a mother-in-law, must we?' And I answered back: 'It's you who's the washerwoman, and you act just like one.' That's how our row started today. 'It's you who's the washerwoman,' I said. And, with one thing leading to another, it wasn't long before we were almost hitting each other. I was furious. She insults Hecuba on purpose to get me wild. You can imagine what'll happen if Theodore ever hears her call his mother a washerwoman. He'll grab her by the hair and shake her till she rattles. And who'll get upset? Theodore and me, of course. Not Maria, not on your life. She just dotes on a good bust-up, she just can't live without constant rows.

But even if it wasn't for Theodore, as long as I live I mean to see Hecuba's photo in its proper place. Not because she's my mother-in-law. What woman likes her mother-in-law? If she were alive, she wouldn't dream of letting me marry Theodore, that's certain. She may have been the best friend a woman ever had, but she'd have been no good as a mother-in-law. And I ought to know. The way her mind had become during those last years, she wasn't fit to have anything to do with other people. She wasn't the Hecuba of the old times, with her jokes, her faith in life and in people — for all that she always seemed so pessimistic. She wasn't the Hecuba you came to with all your troubles, and she'd give you the kind of advice you never got from anyone else. No, if she'd been alive at the time Theodore came back from the Middle East, it would never have crossed my mind to marry him and become her daughter-in-law. It would have been absurd. Impossible to imagine. We'd have quarrelled. To say nothing of what people would have said. How they'd have laughed at us! Even now I sometimes meet women I used to be friendly with at the time, women I haven't met for years, and and they say: 'Just fancy, Nina, did you ever imagine that one day you'd become her daughter-in-law.' And they say it so sarcastically! But I pretend not to notice. If I didn't I'd be constantly squabbling with everyone. When all's said and done, I tell myself, they're not altogether wrong. It is funny, the way things worked out. But not the way other people see it. Which of those tittle-tattle females really knew old Hecuba, or knew what a heart she had? Sometimes I wonder if I really knew her myself, in spite of everything we went through together . . . Some women found her amusing. Some turned up their noses at her, like that snob Julia. She couldn't understand how I could be so friendly with her. She never said so straight out, but in all kinds of round-about ways. 'You're so good-hearted, Nina dear,' she used to say, 'you make anybody welcome in your house. I always say so to my Lily. Lily, I say, Nina has the kindest heart in the world.' She simply couldn't understand how I could possibly prefer Hecuba's company to hers or Mrs Carouso's.

To Martha, Hecuba was like some kind of clown. I remember her telling me once: 'You're like those Emperors with their court jesters.' In spite of all her so-called book learning, even she couldn't understand the reasons why Hecuba sometimes acted like a clown—because she was so modest and humble. Hecuba loved to dramatise her life. But the more she dramatised it, the more jokes she made, always at her own expense, never at the expense of others.

As for Aunt Katie with per prudish ideas and her absurd moral principles, she regarded Hecuba as the very incarnation of the devil. And from one point of view she was right. Hecuba

14

was a devil. But on the other hand she was also a saint, and nobody can possibly know it better than I do. I followed her story to the very end, and knew what was in her heart, better even than her own children! . . .

Her children. Pfff! With the daughter I've got, I'm in a position to know that, of all God's creatures, there's probably no-one in the whole wide world who understands us less than the one who comes out of our belly. And if all that's not reason enough why I should want to see her photo, let's say it's because we went through some unforgettable times together. For I opened my heart to Hecuba, as I never did even to my own mother. When all's said and done, since she'd suffered from her own daughter and all her other children (after all, Polyxene behaved no better to her in the end than Eleni did), she was the only one of all my friends and relatives who sympathised with me from the bottom of her heart, the only one who understood and shared the grief and bitterness I felt at my wretched luck in giving birth to a child-monster! . . .

I first met her in 1937. Or rather no, it wasn't '37. It was the summer of '36, August. I remember it because it was just before the Feast of the Virgin Mary. That was the name-day of Her Highness the Grand Duchess herself, and I had to give the house a thorough cleaning, polish the parquet floors and so on. I was on the roof with Marietta. We were both in our bare feet, shaking out the velvet curtains from the parlour. It was the last job we did that day. That's enough for now, I was thinking. Tomorrow's another day. 'We'll just finish shaking these curtains out and then take a bath to cool off,' I was saying to Marietta, when we heard the little bell that tinkles every time the front gate opens. 'Go and see who it is,' I said. 'Give me the corner of the curtain and see who it is. I hope it isn't a visitor, with my hair all over the place. If it's somebody who doesn't know me he'll think I'm a gipsy or something.'

15

Poor Marietta! She gave me the corner of the curtain and jumped like a deer down on to the little balcony in front of the wash-house. From there you can see the whole way along the path from the gate to the front door. She half-closed her eyes with a suspicious look, the way she did every time she saw somebody new. I watched her and smiled. It must be some stranger, I said to myself. When Marietta screws up her face like that, it's always some stranger. That's how she was. Like a growling bulldog. She came back to the terrace and took hold of her corner of the curtain again to get on with the shaking.

I could see she had no intention of being the first to speak. I knew her ways. 'Who is it?' I said. 'Nobody.' – 'What do you mean, nobody. I heard the bell.' – 'Ooof! It's nobody, I'm telling you.' That's how she used to speak to me. 'It's Erasmia,' she finally condescended to tell me, 'with some shrew or other.'

For Marietta, Erasmia was 'nobody', just as Odysseus was for Polyphemus. So it is some stranger, I said to myself. I was right. But I had no idea who it might be. One of those queer characters Erasmia has met at holy Ephemia's place. I thought to myself, otherwise Marietta wouldn't have called her a shrew. Shrew was the name she used for any woman she didn't take a fancy to, whether she was a friend or a stranger.

The trouble was she had the habit of calling Antoni's mother 'the shrew'. It was 'the shrew' here and 'the shrew' there. It just came naturally – she was the shrew with a capital s. We'd caught the habit and we called her the shrew, too, when Antoni wasn't at home. I used to tremble at the thought that it might slip out accidentally one day when he was there. I knew he wouldn't say a word. But it would upset him very much, and he had enough troubles already, poor man, from my daughter, what with the lashing she used to give him with her tongue every now and again. Boros had told me a hundred times: 'Nina, try to stop him getting upset. His heart's in a terrible state. Look after him.' But everything I did with my care and patience my daughter undid with her tongue. If he tried to scold her, she'd say: 'Leave me alone. I don't give you the right to speak to me. You're not my father.' And that's when she was only twelve years old. She made the poor man tremble like a leaf.

We had brought Marietta from the island of Andros, one summer when we'd gone to spend our holidays with Aunt Bolena, a cousin of papa's who had a house there. Marietta was from the village of Pisomeria. And the Pisomerians, ask anyone from Andros and he'll tell you, are notorious for their lack of hospitality and their sharp tongues. Marietta was a Pisomerian and no mistake. She loved me like a faithful dog. And she respected Antoni, even if she did play him up no end. Deep down, she knew he was the master, and she was a little bit scared of him. But she had no mercy on all the others. Relatives or strangers, she led them all a merry dance. She had a nickname for everybody. Aunt Katie she called 'missus bishop'. For my Grand Duchess, it was 'the booby'. I pretended it made me angry when she said it. I didn't want to let her get above herself. But I couldn't help thinking what a good nickname it was. She's always been a booby and a booby she'll stay for the rest of her life.

But it was Erasmia she liked least of all. She just couldn't stand the sight of her. Every time she came it would turn Marietta's stomach over. And when she toted her friends along with her to show off our house to them, it was all I could do to stop Marietta turning her out. Quite often she'd tell people I was ill and couldn't see anybody. 'Go and make us some coffee,' I used to tell her. My poor mother had taught me to be hospitable to everybody, and papa always told me not to be a snob and never to condemn people before I'd got to know them a bit. And how can you get to know a person if you don't have a chat over a cup of coffee? 'Go and make us some coffee. And bring a little cherry jam,' I'd say to her. And, on her way to the kitchen, she would stand where only I could see her and make faces which meant: 'You don't catch me making

17

coffee for that lot. Who do they think they are? And jam, indeed! Not likely!' Sometimes it was quite embarrassing.

But I let her get away with it. After all, most of the time she was only saying out loud what I was thinking to myself. And then she was honest, hard-working and devoted. And there was another thing: in those years, before the war, what with unemployment and Antoni being ill all the time, we owed her ten months salary, and yet she never uttered a word of complaint. So, with all her faults, she stayed on with us. And I'd just give the visitors a wink. They all knew her, anyway, and didn't take offence. There's no harm in it, I used to tell myself. Let her think she's a member of the family and entitled to express her opinions.

'Come on, let's finish shaking out these curtains,' I said. 'I'm fed up. To hell with name-days and all the rest of the nonsense. One of these days I'm really going to put my foot down and refuse to let people through the door! . . . What's she like, this shrew of Erasmia's?', I said. I knew she wouldn't open her mouth unless I asked her a direct question. But, even then, she wasn't the type to give way easily. 'Oooff! . . . just a shrew, I'm telling you!' . . . She wasn't one for long speeches. To me she'd got used to speaking familiarly with the 'you' in the singular. She only used the less familiar plural 'you' to poor papa. If anybody had heard us who didn't know us, they'd have thought she was the mistress and I was the servant.

This time, probably for the first time ever, Marietta was wrong. Hecuba was not a shrew. She was quite unlike the ogres Erasmia insisted on dragging along with her when she came to the house, in spite of my telling her straight out not to bring strangers. (She took no notice of what I said, she had Antoni on her side.) No, old Hecuba was no shrew. My eye took her in at once. And I didn't change my mind about her, even when I discovered I had guessed right that she'd met Erasmia at holy Ephemia's place. Ah, God knows what I'd gone through, and was still going through, on account of that old fraud! . . .

Holy Ephemia was a so-called 'nun'. When she was young, she used to go round the houses selling candles, incense, bits of holy wood from the cross and books with the lives of the saints. She must have read the books and realised that it wasn't difficult to make yourself out to be a saint. So when she got old and couldn't walk any more she rented a little room near the church of St Lefteri and set herself up as a holy woman. She lived on the voluntary gifts left by the faithful (a hundred grams of sugar, fifty grams of coffee, and so on). It was her daughter-in-law — she had two sons — who, as I found out later, sold these offerings for ready cash. Her reputation rested on two things: first, she had not eaten meat for forty years; and second, she could prophesy the future.

Well, I set off to see her one day. Not to get my fortune told, mind you. I knew my fortune better than anybody — a clear dawn brings a fine day. I went to humour Antoni. Poor man, God rest his soul, he'd suddenly taken to religion in those days. When we got married he was more atheist than the devil himself. I'd never seen such a blaspheming godless man in all my born days. I don't mean to say he was godless just because he swore. There are lots of religious people who trot out an endless stream of Christ Almightys and God-damns with the greatest of ease: and there are those who set no store by religion and yet never a swear word passes their lips, like my poor father. It's a question of how you're brought up, you see. Now Antoni was neither the one nor the other. When he swore, he swore with passion, meaning every word he said. He made fun of everything to do with God and the Church. He even taunted me when I used to light the little oil-lamp — to have my sins forgiven, he used to say. He had a nerve, talking about *my* sins. Anyway, I only used to light it out of respect for the memory of my poor mother. It wasn't right, I thought, just because she was dead, to stop something we'd always done at home ever since I could remember. And, to tell the honest truth, I never really liked sleeping in the pitch darkness. I'm talking of the time before Antoni got ill.

When he had his stroke and his left leg was paralysed, he turned over his business to a cousin of his (who ended up by robbing him right and left), and we went to spend the summer at Koroni. It was the first time he went back to his village after all those years in Athens. It was I who persuaded him to go. We could have gone to Andros like we used to. But I thought the climate at Koroni might do him good. In Andros it's a bit damp. At the same time I thought it might do him good psychologically to go back, after all those years, to his old haunts where he spent his days as a child and as a young man. It'll buck him up, I thought, make him feel stronger in himself. And, as things turned out, I wasn't wrong, Except that it didn't happen quite as I expected.

Boros, his doctor in Athens, had told him to take a walk every morning to get his muscles moving. Usually, he walked up to the castle. If you've never been to Koroni, you just don't know what a beautiful landscape means. When I was a girl we used to go ever so often on excursions to Aigina, Methana, Sounion, Andros and suchlike places. But I've never seen a place to touch Koroni for sheer beauty. I hope, now that this filthy business has ended, now that we've stopped slaughtering each other, that, God willing, I'll go back there, even if it's only just once, before I close my eyes for good. We used to have a book by Athina Tarsouli with pictures from different places in the Peloponnese, and Koroni was in it. But I've no idea what happened to that book. I haven't set eyes on it for years.

The castle is Venetian. Next to one of the ruined walls there was a path going down to the sea. There was a cave there, and centuries back they'd found in the cave an ikon of the Holy Virgin painted, they said, by the Apostle Luke himself. The ikon was supposed to work miracles, like the Virgin of Tinos, and every year, on Presentation of the Virgin day, people from the nearby villages used to come to the cave to kiss the ikon. Many incurable people had become well. I found out about all this afterwards. For one thing, I liked the view from the castle.

And I usually went with him because I didn't like the idea of him going alone. (I was afraid he might slip and knock himself unconscious on a rock.) I used to take along a basket with hard-boiled eggs, cheese, tomatoes and home-baked bread, and when we reached the top we'd sit on the grass and have a picnic. Or I'd send my slob of a daughter with him, if I could dig her out of bed—she was always sleepy. 'Get up, you lazy slut,' I'd tell her, 'have you been bitten again by the tse-tse fly?' But on the day I'm talking about he didn't want her with him. 'Don't wake her up,' he said, 'I'll go by myself.' I knew what a stubborn mule he was. Once he said something he'd hardly ever change his mind. And even if he'd told me to go with him, I couldn't that day because we'd arranged with his cousin Artemis to make some home-made noodles to take back to Athens with us. We were planning to go back home after ten days or so. We'd been in Koroni more than three months, and I'd begun to be homesick for Athens. We couldn't stay on any longer. And he, too, was beginning to get fidgety. His mind was on the business. Staying on in the country was beginning to do him more harm than good.

I knew he usually got back by about eleven. 'Eleven o'clock,' I said to Artemis when I heard the church clock strike. 'Why not go and put on the coffee pot. He'll be back soon . . . ' But half-past eleven went by, and twelve o'clock and half-past twelve, and there was still no sign of Antoni. 'Run and see if he's at his cousin's place,' I said to the Grand Duchess. 'And if you don't find him there, dash round to the coffee shop in the square. He may have gone straight there!' But the little bitch began to dress up and primp herself as if she were going to a wedding. Instead of being worried like I was, she stood there in front of the mirror combing her hair as though she had all day to spare. When she got one straggly wisp of hair in place she had to go back to another and start all over again. It made me mad to see it. 'You unfeeling slut,' I screamed, 'you miserable bitch. You'll be the end of me! Haven't you got an ounce of shame in you, a little snot like you standing there for hours in front of the mirror combing your hair when I've asked you just a little favour? . . . Don't worry, my girl, I'll settle your hash when I get back!" And I just left the noodles half-done and dashed out of the house. I rushed over to his cousin's place, then to the coffee shop, then like a mad thing all over the place asking if anyone had seen him. Nobody had. He must have slipped and fallen down, I thought. He's slipped and fallen and I'll find him dead! As I hurried up towards the castle I imagined every kind of disaster, except the one that had actually happened.

I had almost reached the top, with my heart in my mouth, when I saw him coming down the hill holding his walking-stick over his head so that I could see from the distance that he was walking without a stick. 'Aren't you ashamed of your-self,' I said when he came up to me, and I burst out crying after the fright I'd had. 'Aren't you ashamed of yourself, scar-ing me out of my wits like that! Didn't you stop to think. I might have gone crazy worrying about you!" And I cried like a baby. He put his arm round my waist and we went on down the hill holding on to each other.

He didn't tell us how the 'miracle' happened. How the Tripolis and Kalamata newspapers managed to publish so many details was a second miracle. The villagers came crowd-ing into the house to see with their own eyes the man the Virgin had picked out. They touched him and stroked him to see if he was real. 'Good old mister Antoni,' I remember one of the villagers saying, 'you'll be a marathon runner yet,' and he gave him a really good kick on the knee. Artemis's front yard was suddenly full of blind men, lame men and syphilitics. It was impossible to believe that all that sickness and misery had existed in the village all the time, hidden unsuspected inside all those clean-looking freshly whitewashed houses. And when the word spread that mister Antoni was handing out money to the poor, I decided it was time to put my foot down. I took him almost by force and we packed off home to Athens. And it wasn't a week after we got back before his leg became para-lysed again, worse that it was before! . . .

2

Oh, what an unlucky life I've had, I said to myself as I climbed up towards St Lefteri's. It was bad enough that he got ill only five years after we married, just when I might have begun to take a little enjoyment from life instead of having to nurse a sick man. Now I have to put up with this as well. He's become like a religious old woman, and here I am panting up the narrow backstreets on my way to see some old religious quack, just to keep him quiet, to stop him from complaining that it was my fault he had a relapse and his business is going badly. . . . But Antoni's my husband, I told myself, I have to be patient with him.

What I really couldn't stand was Erasmia's part in all this. Erasmia was one of mama's old pupils. In the days when mama had the dressmaking salon in Sina Street, Erasmia's folk sent her from Cephalonia to stay with a married sister of hers in Athens, to help with the baby and learn dressmaking at the same time. At the beginning, she used to come only a few hours a day. But, unlike the other girls, she was quiet-spoken and hard-working, and mama took a liking to her. Gradually she began staying overnight, and finally she came to stay permanently as a kind of living-in help. That was the start of the never-ending nagging that used to go on between me and my poor mother. Erasmia poisoned our relationship. Without ever daring to admit it, even to myself, I was jealous of her. The more my mother showed her affection for her, the more I couldn't bear her. She was mean and sly, and she got on my nerves. Everthing about her irritated me. I knew she hated me, and her hate was like some kind of poison. I just had to see her sour face and, if I happened to be laughing at the time, the laugh would freeze on my lips. She hated me, the monster, because while she was working her fingers to the bone sewing beads and sequins on dresses — they were all the rage then — I was taking the air in Kifissia, or reading, or going to the cinema with my girl friends. It was still silent in those days. We used to walk out of one and go straight into another.

When she saw me wearing a low-cut dress she'd turn green with envy. And mama was so naïve she never suspected how Erasmia really felt; she thought she was a perfect model of goodness. 'What's the matter with you, dear,' she'd say, 'don't you feel well? Run around to the drapers and get ten yards of black binding. It'll do you good to get some air.' The little hypocrite had wormed her way completely into mama's confidence. Before she got down to her work, rain or shine, she'd go to St Dionysios' to light a candle. And mama, who always wanted to go to church but never found time, regarded Erasmia as the guardian angel of the house. Maybe God would condescend to save us sinners for Erasmia's sake! 'Aren't you feeling well, dear? . . .' And she'd take me into my room and pinch me black and blue, saying I was nasty and selfish and that I tyrannised the girls in the workshop.

Later poor mama got cataract and she had to stop sewing. We got rid of Erasmia for a time. She went back to Cephalonia. We sold the house in Sina Street and bought this one. But, about a year later, she came back from Cephalonia and took a room — by chance, she said — near where we lived. And she began coming to the house again. Mama asked her to come and live with us so she could spy on me. By that time she was completely blind and she needed somebody's eye to find out what went on in the house. Marietta, for all that she loved and respected her, didn't always pamper her and kowtow to her. 'Come and stay with us,' mama said one day. But Erasmia refused the invitation and took the opportunity to inject a little of her poison. 'You want me to come,' she said to mama, 'but you'd better ask Nina if she wants me, now that she's running things.' Marietta was there at the time, and she told me. Yet for various reasons I hadn't till then showed my dislike for her openly. Not out of calculating motives, as my

24

slob of a daughter says, because she did our sewing for nothing; but simply because I'd had no real reason to squabble with her. It's my nature to be patient and restrained, especially with people I don't like. I usually take no notice of them, even when they do me harm.

Just once I came near to giving her a real talking to. I'd had just about as much as I could take from her. At that time I was having my rows with Fotis, which ended in our separation. Erasmia would shut herself away in mama's room and all day long the two of them would jabber away about the arguments between me and Fotis. They came up with their verdicts — usually in favour of Fotis — and they had the cheek to try to put them into practice. Or they'd try to tell me how to bring up my daughter. They didn't want her to be a godless creature like me, they said. So they made her take after them, and they ruined her. But even then I said nothing. That was the time when, on top of the cataract, they found that poor mama also had cancer. The doctor said she had no more than a year to live, and Erasmia, it's only fair to say, stood by her, better than any nurse or daughter. She was at her bedside night and day. And when papa became ill, too, and I saw how devotedly and unselfishly she looked after him as well to the very last moment, I couldn't help being touched. I forgave her for the way she'd behaved before. I often thought I must have misjudged her, and I was sorry for it. I may have all the faults under the sun, as my daughter will tell you, but I'm not ungrateful.

In other words, at the time I married Antoni, Erasmia was more than just a close friend, she was a member of the family. When mama died, and papa went soon after, she took it on herself to act as nursemaid to the Duchess. She took her along to church, to the religious fêtes, or for walks in the park. Often I would revolt. 'Listen here,' I'd say to her, 'if you think Maria hasn't got a mother and you've decided to adopt her, there's the street! Take her and get out of here, both of you. Make her a holy hypocrite like yourself, if you like, but not in my house.

25

I don't want to know or hear anything about it!'

That's the sort of thing I used to tell her when, for one reason or another, she made me angry. But I didn't get angry very often. Most of the time I thanked my lucky stars that there was somebody to take her out and leave me to get a bit of peace and quiet at home. Now, of course, I regret it bitterly. How dearly I've paid, and I'm still paying, for those few hours of peace and quiet, only God knows. I ought to have got rid of Erasmia as soon as mama died. Then she'd have had no chance of ruining Maria; and, without Erasmia, there would have been no miracle at Koroni and no relapse in Athens. I think she was even partly to blame for his death. If Antoni had not come over all religious he would have avoided the last and probably greatest disappointment of his life, which killed him in the end.

Before he had his stroke he used to poke fun at her mercilessly about her religious fanaticism. 'Why don't you get married?' he used to say to her. 'Are you saving it for Christ?' And then he'd answer himself: 'I know why. Because he's beautiful and his feet don't smell.' And he'd burst out laughing. Erasmia would go pale and start trembling like a leaf. Even I felt sorry for her. But afterwards I realised she had no need of my pity. She enjoyed playing the part of the martyr and the Hebrew prophet by turns. She often let fly, frothing at the mouth and shooting sparks from her eyes. One day, she'd scream at him, God would punish him for his disrespect, just as he punished so-and-so and so-and-so, and she'd come out with a list of a hundred names from the Old Testament. Antoni listened and just laughed at her. But I had learned to understand what went on inside his mind, and I knew that deep down she had an effect on him, even if he would be the last to admit it. After all, he himself was really a superstitious peasant. In his bones, he was afraid of God and believed in the torments of Hell, where he had every reason to fear that he would end up. That was probably why he swore so much, I often used to think. When he fell ill, he remembered what Erasmia had said. She said nothing, but the triumph shone out of her eyes. There was no need for her to say anything. She'd injected her poison cleverly. I watched Antoni going downhill and I guessed what he must be thinking and the struggle he was having with his soul. 'Erasmia was right. I have sinned and God is punishing me,' and so on. One evening I walked into our bedroom and caught him kneeling in front of the ikons. I pretended not to see him and went out, closing the door behind me. The sight of Antoni kneeling in front of the ikons made me feel awful. I may not have much good to say about priests, but I'm not an atheist. I believe in the unknown power that rules the world. I was really moved . . . How was I to know that what seemed to be a sincere and serious mood of repentance would soon turn into a kind of comic play-acting. For Antoni's return to the bosom of Christ's Church, after we got back from Koroni, was a real theatrical performance. Erasmia greeted him like a lost sheep come back to the fold. She put her arms around him and cried like a baby. From the first night he refused to sleep in our bedroom, even though we had single beds. I put the Duchess on a divan in the sitting-room and made up his bed in the room leading off the back yard. 'You can go to a monastery, if you like,' I told him. 'Why stay here among the sins and dirt of the city? Go to Mount Athos and grow a halo . . . .'

But he didn't want to go to a monastery. He preferred to bring the monastery to my house. Through Erasmia, he got to know holy Ephemia, fanatic old-calendar priests, former priests, holy so and so from New Phaleron, and holy so and so from Brahami, and the whole lot of them began to turn up at the house. They paid hardly any attention to me. Anybody would think Erasmia was the mistress of the house, not me. I knew this state of affairs couldn't last very long. Either he'd have to change, or we would split up. Meanwhile, as I prayed to my own God to perform his miracle and deliver me from this army of holy people, I sat quiet and said nothing. The best policy, I said to myself, is to act as though I was giving in to him, otherwise we'd become complete strangers to each other. That was my attitude when I set off to meet holy Ephemia for the first time.

3

The room was off a low-class common courtyard full of dirty puddles and barefooted children with snotty noses. There was no need to ask which room was hers. The smell of incense came out to meet me as soon as I walked into the yard. I have always hated the smell of incense. Every time mama lit the little incense burner at home it used to choke me, but I had got over it a bit as the years went by. I went into the room. In one corner there was an iron bedstead, a table in the middle, chairs scattered about, an old trunk, and a rag-carpet on the floor. It was a room just like any other poor person's—except for the ikons which covered the four walls from floor to ceiling. A hundred, maybe two hundred ikons of every shape and colour: the Wakeful Virgin, the Merciful Virgin, the Virgin of the Sweet Kiss, the head of John the Baptist on a dish, the Holy Kerchief, the Presentation, the Birth of Christ, the Last Supper, the Crucifixion, the Resurrection, the All Saints, together and separately, holy martyrs and martyresses, and a whole collection of other ikons, all printed on cardboard or clumsily painted, nothing like our genuine Byzantine ikons. And, in the middle of all these ikons, hung a chart with the signs of the zodiac. God knows what that was there for!

Holy Ephemia was sitting curled up in a low armchair near her bed. She was all alone. She wore a nun's habit, with the leather belt and silver buckle, and a bonnet with a red cross. She held a knotted prayer-cord between her bony fingers. I got quite a shock. No matter how much of a skeptic you may be, it's impossible not to be impressed when you find yourself among all those ikons, and especially when you set eyes on a weird creature like that, looking more like a holy relic or an Egyptian mummy than a real live person . . .

On the day I'm talking about, Erasmia was doing some sewing in somebody else's house and couldn't come with me as we had agreed at first, but she had given me detailed instructions about what I had to do. I was to kneel down and kiss her hand, bend my head to receive her blessing, and not to speak until I was spoken to. I was quite ready to act out all this comedy, and I would have done so, but it was holy Ephemia herself who stopped me. As soon as she saw me come in, (it was as though she was expecting me — she'd been tipped off from the night before, I'd bet my life on it), she raised her hand, fixed me with tiny eyes set deep into their sockets, and with a voice which seemed to come from a deep dried-up well rather than a human throat, she said: 'Stop!' And then a deep breath. 'Stop! Your name begins with N . . . I see three rings on your fingers . . . give me some water . . .' Without saying a word I filled a glass from the earthenware jug on the table and helped her to drink it. 'I am tired,' she said, after I had wiped away the water which had dribbled down on to her chest. 'I am tired.' . . . I turned my back for a moment to put the glass on the table, and when I turned round again, she was . . . snoring!

I decided to leave. I took the packet of halva I had brought for her out of my handbag — it was Lent — and put it down on the table. Then on tiptoe I went out into the yard, and from there into the street. I breathed deeply in the fresh air and the scent of a wild lilac tree came drifting across from the opposite pavement. It was like coming back to the land of the living after a visit to Hades.

When Antoni asked me what happened I told him: 'Oh, nothing much. She told me my name begins with N and then she fell sound asleep.' He seemed quite satisfied. I didn't tell him anything about the three weddings she had 'prophesied'. It was hardly the kind of thing to tell a man with one foot in the grave. He had such blind faith in the prophesying powers of his holy woman that he'd have thought at once: 'Ah, so I'm going to die and Nina will marry for a third time!' . And, while I, poor thing, was doing everything I could, by a cunning mixture of lies and half-truths, to keep him alive, he'd have got the idea into his head that he was going to die any minute. And anyway, it didn't occur to me for a single moment that the 'prophecy' might turn out to be true. Even now I'm certain that it was a pure coincidence, or a kind of Delphic oracle. We all know those tricks. Erasmia must have spoken to her about me. When a woman has been married twice, and when her second husband is half-paralysed and has heart trouble, and she's still young, you don't have to be a Tiresias to guess the future. That's how it seems to me now, after the event. At that time I just laughed at the absurd idea that I might marry for the third time — for what else could the 'three rings' mean? But I can't say that it didn't have some influence on me. I began to be afraid that I really would lose him quickly, and I looked after him more carefully than ever. Apart from his paralysis and his bad heart, he also had high blood pressure. When a man gets ill he seems to get every disease all at once. And, in spite of trying to keep him on a strict diet, he was so greedy he used to go to the ice-box and have a secret tuck-in as soon as my back was turned. His pressure went up instead of down, and he nearly burst with the rush of blood to his head. He did blood-letting operations on himself, pushing the point of a pair of scissors up his nose and gushing half a basinful of blood . . . His leg was still half paralysed, but he'd got used to being crippled and it didn't worry him all that much. He'd take his stick and hobble down to the office or to the café. As time went on, it was more often to the café and less often to his business which, unfortunately, was also hobbling along on one leg. If business had been better, Antoni would never have let himself go downhill so much. He wasn't the kind of man to be easily depressed by illness. But the international situation was getting worse and worse: war in China, war in Abyssinia, war in Spain! . . . Everybody was saying we would soon have war in Europe. People gradually stopped investing in property. Why should we build houses, they said, if they're going to be bombed to pieces? People stopped building, Antoni's cousin continued to steal, Erasmia persuaded him to spend money on blessings, all-night prayers for his health, and charity donations to worthless creeps. Absolutely everything around us seemed to be conspiring to ruin the life we had started with high hopes six or seven years previously. Such high hopes that for a while we thought the good life would last for ever, that our excursions to Aigina, to Loutraki and Poros would never end!

About a month after I'd gone to see Holy Ephemia for the first time, we had that famous all-night prayer session at our house. That was the first time they carried her to the house in an armchair and she spoke to us 'in seven tongues'. It was about ten days after that, on the afternoon when I was shaking out the curtains on the balcony with Marietta, when Erasmia brought old Hecuba to the house. As it turned out later, she was heaven-sent, not only to rid me of Erasmia but at the same time to set in motion the wheels which, years later, were to make the holy woman's 'prophecy' come true . . .

But how was anybody to know all that at the time? That evening when she came to the house for the first time (for the second time, if we count the all-night session as the first) I had no idea that this woman would one day change my whole life. I found her quite pleasant, not like the dreadful mob that Erasmia used to drag along to the house at the time. In fact I asked her to come back again, just to irritate Erasmia. We became friends, and even the Cerberus of the house, Marietta, liked her. When she saw her coming she'd rush off without being told and make the coffee. But how could I possibly have guessed that one day she'd become my mother-in-law!

4

I don't want to blow my own trumpet: in this life you have to be humble. But the truth is that Antoni was not my kind of man. Just the same, at the time I had all those troubles with Fotis and I was left with nothing to live on, and then when mama got the cataract and had to stop dressmaking, we couldn't live on the miserable pension papa got from the University. We did have the house, it's true, and we had no rent to pay. But we couldn't eat the walls, unless we sold the house or mortgaged it. And I'd taken an oath never to touch the house, even if we were at our last gasp. Mama was so good-hearted that for years she'd supported her relatives. And then she had that good-for-nothing brother of mine who never stopped draining her of every penny she had. The result was that she hadn't managed to put a single penny aside for an emergency. There was never anything left over to put aside. The only thing she possessed was some jewellery she'd been left by her mother, and we were gradually eating our way into that. When there is illness in the house the money soon disappears. We got through the jewellery in no time at all, and we began borrowing from relatives: from uncle Hercules, from uncle Stephen and so on.

I considered taking a job, but I hadn't the slightest idea what kind of job I could do. In those days women hadn't begun to go out to work, at least no women of my class. And there was nothing except office work to do, unless I became a cook in some rich house. But I wasn't free, you see. My mother and father needed nursing like babies, and I couldn't trust them altogether to Erasmia (we'd sent Marietta back to her village for the time being). And, if they were not enough, I also had the Duchess. She was still only five or six years old. I had that ungrateful creature on my hands, and now she gives me no credit for all the sacrifices I made for her. It was quite natural that I should think about getting married. That was the opinion of my relatives, too. We owed them a lot of money, and we had to respect their views. So, although I hadn't the slightest inclination to begin my life all over again and have another man make a fool of me, I had to admit that they were right. There was no other solution. They began introducing me to prospective husbands, first an accountant, then a green-grocer — not bad-looking he was, but still a greengrocer — and finally an old man who had three houses, no family obligations, no relatives, and a case of myocarditis. But I had no intention of living on an office clerk's pittance, nor of lowering myself to be the wife of a greengrocer, nor of becoming a nurse. If I wanted to be a nurse, I could do it without getting married. At least I would keep my independence. 'Marry him,' they all said. 'He's an old man and won't live very long. You'll be left with the houses . . . .' But though I was willing to marry for money, I was not willing to speculate on an old man's death. I regarded it as a sin not against God — God has nothing to do with that kind of thing — but against myself.

So two years went by and we'd reached the end of our tether. We didn't know where the next meal was coming from. Uncle Stephen had begun to grumble, and I was forced to borrow money from my friends: from Mrs Cassimati, Mrs Carouso, and even from Erasmia. Yes, I'd sunk as low as to borrow money from Erasmia! We had taken out two mortgages on the house, and I was absolutely desperate. I used to say to myself: 'Please God, take me from this world. Stop this end-less, pointless torture. I can't stand it any more! . . .'

It was just at that time that Antoni put in an appearance. He was a widower, with a good job. He had only his mother dependent on him. I was introduced to him by a distant cousin of mama's who lived in his district. Antoni had once owned his own house, on Alexandra Avenue. But when his wife died (from leukemia) he wrote to his village and they sent him a young girl to keep house for him. In less than six months she was pregnant. I didn't know anything about that at the time;

it all came out later. When her parents heard the news, they arrived in town with an axe and very nearly made mincemeat of him. (They were from the Mani, and it's no joke when they get *their* tempers roused!) They blackmailed him into signing the house over to her. He was forced to go and live for a time with the Shrew, but he was used to keeping open house and having a woman to look after him. So he, too, was looking for someone to marry. My aunt invited us to her house one afternoon for coffee, and I saw him. When I got back home I threw myself on my bed and burst out crying. 'I'll not marry him no matter what happens,' I sobbed. 'He's just an old peasant from the backwoods. He has callouses on his hands and he has a horrible accent. He can hardly speak at all! . . . But, deep inside, I knew that wasn't why I was crying. I was crying because I realised that if I wanted to get married I couldn't possibly find a more suitable man than Antoni. I had the house, it's true. But it was mortgaged. And I wasn't a girl of twenty any more. On top of all that, I had the bitch of a daughter Fotis had left me with, and the poor man at once offered to adopt her. He would make sure she got an education and the comforts of life. At that time he was making money by the fistful. He was one of the best and busiest building contractors in Athens. As soon as we were married he not only paid off the mortgages on the house but started to make repairs which ought to have been done years before, and, while he was at it, he made all sorts of additions and alterations: he built a new wash-house on the terrace and turned the old one in the yard into a room; he pulled down the outside wall of the bedroom and made it bigger; he put in an electric cooker, one of the first to be imported into Greece at the time; and he built a bathroom (before that, we used to wash in a zinc tub in the wash-house), a bathroom with glazed tiles, porcelain fitments, mirrors and even a bidet! All the things the Duchess now takes for granted, although she insists on saying — and this is what makes me furious — that I killed her father because he couldn't afford to build me a bathroom with a bidet! But

I'm used to her tongue now, and I don't take what she says seriously. I know she's jealous of me because I had three husbands, while she's in danger of staying on the shelf. Otherwise I'd have no difficulty in answering her. I'd tell her why I threw her father out, and whether it was I who killed him or the filthy things he'd done in his life! . . .

Oh yes, I remember them all, one after the other. Every time she upsets me it all comes back to me, everything I went through in my life. It's hard to know what to remember first: all that business with Aryiris, the goings-on of Fotis, all that I suffered as long as Antoni lived, with his illnesses and later with his religious mania, and worse still when he died? I don't mean to say, like so many women, that I'm the unluckiest woman in the world. But the truth is that I've had my share of life's bitterness. What good did it do me to have three husbands, I ask you? It would have been better if I'd had one good one and lived a quiet family life like so many other women in this world. If only I'd married the man I loved, the only man I really loved — God bless him, who knows if he's alive or dead? I haven't the slightest idea. I haven't seen him ever since, even though we live in the same city, except maybe once: I was walking down Hermes Street one day during the occupation and I thought I recognised him in the distance. It seemed to be him, only much older, with a black overcoat. I almost started to hurry to catch up with him and see his face close-to; but, as they say in novels, my poor legs wouldn't obey me. It was as though my whole body was paralysed. I wanted to see him, and yet I didn't. And before I could make up my mind, he had turned a corner and disappeared. Poor Aryiris, poor Kifissia! What happy carefree years they were! All grown-up people look back nostalgically on the paradise of their childhood. They say it was a paradise even if it was sheer hell. They fondly remember the time when life was still simple and the world full of magic. But, apart from that paradise, I had a real tangible paradise, the kind that is described in the Old Testament: with trees, birds, flowers — and the serpent!

Almost every Saturday, especially in the springtime, old Alexis, uncle Markoussis' coachman, would come with a basket of fruit in season: strawberries, figs or mulberries, and in exchange, as it were, he would take me.

Uncle Markoussis had lots of nieces: the daughters of aunt Bebba, the daughters of aunt Negreponti, and so on. There is hardly anyone of them left now. The family gradually broke up over the years. But in those days there were lots of us. But of all those nieces he loved me best of all. 'If you were ten years older,' he used to say half-serious, half-joking, 'or if I was young like I used to be, I'd carry you off and let the priests shout their heads off!' Uncle Markoussis was the oldest of mama's brothers, and he'd stayed a bachelor. Nobody could understand why. When we were children we heard the grown-ups hinting about some widow or other. They talked in back-slang, thinking we didn't understand: 'Wo si id-wo?' And they'd wink at each other cunningly. It seemed that he was in-volved with the widow of an old friend. 'Why doesn't uncle Markoussis get married, mama?', I asked one day. 'Mind your own business,' she answered. None of his sisters encouraged him to get married, least of all mama. They all had their eye on the estate in Kifissia.

Uncle Markoussis' estate adjoined the Lahanas property. Old Lahanas himself was a native Kifissian, an old villager of the time when Kifissia was still a village. But his son was a well-known lawyer and mixed in the best society. He'd been elected to Parliament and was on close terms with the Drag-oumis family with whom uncle Markoussis never exchanged more than a curt good-day. This son of Lahanas had two children, a daughter of Dino's age and a son, Aryiris, who was two years older than me. What tricks we used to get up to, the two of us! Probably the most innocent of all was our pas-sion for trespassing on other people's property and stealing fruit. We had all the fruit our hearts could desire on our own land. The fruit went mouldy in the fruit bowls. But we pre-ferred the forbidden stolen fruit. We just adored escapades.

What a tomboy I was! I was full of life, not half asleep all the time like my daughter. We used to jump on the horses and ride as far as Ekali — people still had horses in those days. Or we'd ride up to Kokkinara and sit down among the thyme bushes to look down at Athens.

Aryiris was tall and fair, not like a Greek at all. Uncle Markoussis, who couldn't abide old Lahanas, said they were of Albanian stock. Sometimes I try to recall what he looked like exactly, but I can't. So many years have gone by since then. And I don't have a single photograph of him. I sent them all back. The only thing I still remember is the smell of his body mingled with the scent of the thyme. Whenever I smell that scent or see the word thyme, I remember him and it's as though we were both lying there again, stretched out on the grass, his head resting on my knees while he recited poetry. He was crazy about poetry:

> Oh, how the dream of beauty blinds our sight!
> As though but once in life we drift astray.
> The ships, the azure sea, are drunk with light.
> Embark again, and travel far away!

He used to recite poetry as though he were already an old man who had known happiness and lost it a hundred times. Poor Aryiris! Maybe the misery I caused you has been the root of all my own suffering. If only you knew how dearly I paid, and am still paying! . . . Such is life. It makes no allowances for the excuses we may have, as I had. For it was not all my fault. Uncle Markoussis had a lot to answer for. And he paid for it, too. In this life you always pay for your mistakes.

When I finished high school I wanted to study Law at the University. I was always first in my class at essays and history. Papa encouraged me. He was a progressive kind of man, and he believed in the emancipation of women. But mama, who never understood him, put it down to his low selfishness. Nobody denies that he was a womaniser, but he didn't believe in the emancipation of women because of that. 'Go on, why not let her go to the University for a year or two and get the rust out of her brain?' he used to say. But mama believed that a woman's place was in the home, and that their only mission in life was marriage and bringing up their children. Imagine having no other purpose in life than to bring up Maria! . . .

Not that I blame her altogether. All her life she had worked like a man, even harder than many men. She'd come to the conclusion that marriage was the easiest kind of work for a woman. She didn't want me to have to earn my own living. She thought that if I studied law I would stop being a woman. 'If you're going to become a suffragette,' she used to say when she saw me reading books on philosophy from papa's bookshelf, 'you'd better get out of my house.' Papa had to give way, and he advised me to do the same. I didn't want to hurt her. Her health was beginning to fail about that time from sheer over-work.

Aryiris always wanted to become a doctor. He was keen on surgery. When we were kids he used to catch frogs and mice and cut them open to show me the various organs: heart, kidneys, stomach, even the hole the frogs had for excreting. His sister Nadia and Dino couldn't bear to look. When they saw the mouse's entrails spilling out they turned pale and ran away. But I sat there with calm curiosity. Dino, who was always a tell-tale, would rush off to tell mama, and she'd shake her head sadly and say she couldn't understand how such a hard-bitten girl could have come out of her belly. But papa, who for years had been assistant director of the University's zoological museum and who had stuffed thousands of dead animals and birds in his life, would wink at me and say: 'Never mind, your mother doesn't understand those things.'

But naturally old Lahanas, who had no other son, was determined to make Aryiris a lawyer. Children today are more free than they were then to choose their own careers — if they know, unlike my daughter, what they want to do in life. In those days it was the parents who had the last word. Aryiris went to Law School. The time for pranks and games had come to an end. No more stealing forbidden fruit, no more running about like mad things, no more horse-riding (uncle Markoussis had sold his three horses and bought himself a motor car), no more holding hands in the street where anybody might see us. One afternoon a friend of mama's saw us together in the Zappeion Park and rushed off to give her the news. Mama had no idea that I was seeing Aryiris in Athens and she made a terrible scene: 'So that's why we were so anxious to become a lady lawyer, is it?' she screamed triumphantly, 'Your father wouldn't believe it when I told him, he said I was cunning and suspicious like all Greeks! . . .' From that time on she began to keep a check on where I went and what I did. Anyway, Aryiris himself wasn't as free as he used to be. The only times I managed to see him was between lectures — the University was near our house. Mama wouldn't let me go to Kifissia very often. Uncle Markoussis complained: 'You don't love me any more, you've abandoned me.' It seems he asked mama why she didn't let me go up to Kifissia, and she told him all about the love affair with Aryiris. I don't know exactly what happened. All I know is that one day he came to the house for lunch (he came more often than before since he bought the car), and after lunch he and papa went into the sitting-room and shut the door behind them. My instinct was never wrong. I knew they were talking about me and Aryiris, and my heart beat fit to burst. I knew uncle Markoussis couldn't bear the Lahanas family, but I trusted papa's judgment. Naturally, I expected the usual kind of objections, but I never imagined for a moment that he would call me into the sitting-room and tell me, in a tone of severity quite unlike him, that he forbade me ever to see Aryiris again. I began to cry and threaten to commit suicide. I insisted he told me the reason. 'I'm not a baby any more,' I said, 'I have to know why.' 'I can't tell you,' he said, 'there are some things women don't understand.' I became furious. 'So those are your fine progressive ideas, are they,' I shouted and ran out of the sitting-room. 'We'll talk about it some other time,' he said.

But there was no need for him to tell me anything. I found out from mama. She told me about it with such cruel directness that I have only forgiven her because I know how dearly it cost her in the case of her beloved son. In this world fate takes its revenge on the scoffers. 'Stop driving us mad,' she said, 'about your precious Aryiris. If you must know . . . .' And she told me, all of it. I stared at her blankly, thunderstruck. I had thought of all kinds of explanations, but not this. I cried and choked with agonised despair. Then I began to think: what if it's true? I decided to go and see Aryiris, to speak to him. But when the moment came I was so upset it was impossible to keep my voice calm. I told him bluntly that uncle Markoussis had got a man he trusted to follow him, and they found out that he had relations with a man who . . .

I didn't finish the sentence. I saw him blush and I could see he knew what I meant. I looked at him speechless, praying to God that he would tell me it was all a lie. To this day I still wonder how much of it was true. An innocent man would have laughed it off, or he would have protested furiously that he was being slandered. He'd have told me I was mad to believe them and he'd have grabbed me and given me a warm kiss. That was the only way he could have shut me up. But Aryiris just blushed. Then he turned pale. He stared straight into my eyes – I'll never forget that look as long as I live – put his hands in his pockets and walked off without saying a word. And I was left there shattered and alone, under the statue of Plato, praying that the earth would open and swallow me up.

I stopped going to Kifissia after that. Not to avoid Aryiris – on the contrary, I tried to see him again, but he avoided me – but because I didn't want to set eyes again on uncle Markoussis. I hated him. Mama grumbled and said I was tossing away a whole fortune, that he'd leave everything to aunt Bebba's daughters. But I wouldn't budge. I never spoke to him again. Besides, as it turned out after a year, it was all a lot of fuss for nothing. When he crashed into another car on the road to Sounion and died of an internal haemorrhage, they opened his will and we discovered to our amazement that the estate was mortgaged, that the famous shares mama never stopped talking about were shares in a disused silver mine, and that he had left what little he had in cash and jewellery to the widow — may he rot in hell! If it hadn't been for him, I'd be Mrs Lahanas today, rich and happy — I'm absolutely sure of it — married to the man I loved and — God forgive me for saying it — not, I hope, the mother of a child-monster like my daughter!

5

This was the time when Phaleron was becoming fashionable. New Phaleron, not Old Phaleron, which has replaced it today because all the sewers of Athens seem to end at New Phaleron and it stinks so badly you have to hold your nose when you go by. Now all those fine old villas have fallen into ruin; the theatres and cafés have closed; a whole unforgettable period of old Athens has come to an end. That's where we spent our young days. What gay crowds they were! What splendid brass bands! Then there was the casino, and the bathing beach — men and women separately at first, and then mixed bathing. The men used to go down to Phaleron in droves, not so much to swim as to study female anatomy.

We used to go down only at week-ends. Papa had his reasons for taking us to Phaleron. Poor papa! . . . He seemed to be the most innocent man in the world, yet he had two vices which were all the more passionate because his principles did not allow him to indulge them as much as he would have liked: cards and women. As he grew older, it was cards more than women. But his heart was always fluttering. He used an old saying to uncle Stephen, I remember: 'It's too bad, Stephen,' he would say, 'now that the sea's turned to yoghurt we've lost our spoons!' But all that talk about him having lovers and so on was mostly mama's imagination rather than fact. She was terribly jealous. We never found out for sure that he was having an affair with this or that woman. But while he was naturally secretive about his women friends, he took very little trouble to hide his passion for cards. He would take us to the café, order ice-cream and lemonades, pay the bill and then pretend he was going to the lavatory. Instead, he'd make a beeline for the casino and that was the last we'd see of him for hours. We all knew where he went, but we pretended not to. Mama would get into conversation with some women acquaintances.

They'd gossip about clothes and so on. We, too, would disappear in various directions. Dino would make off with two friends—the ones who ruined him in the end—and they'd meet up with some suspicious characters near the bathing huts. God alone knows what they got up to. I would go off with the Cassimatis and the Carouso girls, and we'd walk up and down the promenade, or young men of families we knew would get up from nearby tables and ask permission to dance with us. That was the time when the Argentinian tango was all the rage—'Ramona, the mission bells ring out above'—, the lights played in the water, the Phaleron breeze blew, life was wonderful.

That's how I met Fotis. He was a second officer in the merchant navy. With his gold braid and bits and pieces he was not so much handsome as manly-looking (after that business with Aryiris I was always suspicious of beautiful men). He was not tall like Aryiris. He was medium in height, with dark hair and blue eyes. God alone knows whom my ugly gipsy of a daughter takes after. We started going out together. He came to the house and asked to marry me. It was pretty well the usual kind of affair in cases of that kind. If I said I loved him, it would be a lie. Ever since the incident with Aryiris I had never been able to feel as warmly towards men as I used to. But mama was always grumbling that I would stay on the shelf. My girl friends were crazy about him and thought I was very lucky. I was flattered that he had chosen me and not the others.

Just the same, I might not have decided to marry him in the end, if they hadn't all been against him. I dug my heels in. They'd done enough damage already with their interfering over Aryiris and I was determined not to let them interfere in my life again. I wasn't eighteen any longer. I was getting on for twenty-six. I put my foot down: 'It's either Fotis or nobody,' I said. (Mama, who was never exactly a generous character, took every opportunity of reminding me of this later, after all that happened.) It was decided that he should make his next trip—he was due to leave for India and Japan—and we would get married when he came back, if we still felt we wanted to.

We were married. It was July, and it was suffocatingly hot the third night after our wedding. The sheets and pillows were soaked in perspiration. At about one in the morning I got up and went to the wash-house; I threw a few basinfuls of cold water over myself to cool off. But it was soon as bad as ever. It wasn't just the heat; there were also the damned mosquitoes. I got up twice to spray the room but nothing stopped them. Zoom, zoom, they dived like vampires and sucked your blood! About two in the morning, drugged by the heat and exhausted rather than sleepy, I heard Fotis get out of bed. 'I'm going to sleep on the terrace,' he said. 'Mmm,' I answered and closed my eyes again. But I was soon awake again. My brain was clearer. How stupid I am, I thought, why don't I go and sleep out in the cool, too? There were always two or three mattresses on the terrace. Dino never slept in his room in summer, always on the terrace. But I generally preferred my room because of the awful sun. It woke me at six and unless I went downstairs to finish my sleep, I'd be yawning all day long. I tucked my pillow under my arm, took a sheet and a blanket and went up to the terrace. In my bare feet I made no noise. I saw them in the act. Every time I think of it, I want to be sick. Without saying a word I crept down as silently as I had come, threw myself on the bed and cried all night. 'Are all men such beasts?' I asked myself again and again. But there was no answer from anywhere. If it hadn't been for what had happened with Aryiris, I don't know how I would have felt or what I would have done. But everything I had suffered in silence for so many years because of that affair made this new one seem like a huge and final disaster. I bit into my pillow to stop myself from crying out loud, 'are they all such monsters?' I asked myself, 'will any kind of hole satisfy the beasts? And as for that disgusting brother of mine, how could he?'

The more it went around in my head, the more desperate I

became. I even thought of suicide. I just could not bear the thought that I would have to face them, to look them in the eyes in the morning. 'What's the good of living?' I thought. I even got so far as to consider creeping into papa's room to take the bottle of veronal from his bedside drawer. But I didn't even have the strength to get out of bed. My body and my willpower were paralysed. What they had done seemed so monstrous that I thought I had been through a nightmare, that it wasn't real, that I hadn't even been up on the terrace, that I had seen it all in my sleep. But the reality soon came back more vividly than ever, like knives plunging into my chest.

When morning came at last, I was a shattered wreck. It was like having a corpse in the house, as though someone had died during the night, and after the first tears, however hard you try to fight off fatigue, because it seems so selfish to sleep when you have lost a loved one, in the end, no longer able to resist, you lie down on the divan (as I did when we lost poor papa), and fall into the kind of slumber which rather than refreshing you, tires you all the more; and when you open your eyes with the first light of dawn, your first thought is of the one who has died, and you say to yourself: 'From today I shall never see him walk again, never hear him speak. He's dead, dead!' . . . And everything seems dark and hopeless. Life seems unbearable . . .

When papa saw the state I was in, he knew something had happened. He looked at me, his eyebrow raised as usual with an unasked question. He was waiting for me to speak first. He never shouted like mama. I pretended not to understand. But when he saw the guilty look on the faces of Fotis and Dino he began to suspect the truth. He may not have known Fotis yet, but he knew his son. Twice they had called him to Dino's school and told him to watch out. They'd caught him in the lavatory with other boys. He was no fool, and he understood. I denied it, of course. 'Nothing's the matter,' I told him, 'what on earth are you looking at me like that for? I had a pain in my back and didn't sleep a wink all night.' And I hinted that it was some kind of woman's trouble which was no business of his. And then, when I saw he was not swallowing it, I pretended to confess the truth: that I'd had a tiff with Fotis, nothing serious, we'd soon make it up. Papa knew I was lying. He knew his daughter. He began a whispered conversation with mama. He came back to my room, closed the door, and said: 'I insist on knowing what has happened! . . . Is it what I suspect?' Naturally, I burst out in tears. That day things happened which were even worse than what had happened the night before. Every time I remember that day my heart, as Hecuba used to say, seems to crack. But, cracked and bruised as it is, my heart refuses to break once and for all and let me rest at last.

From that day Dino began to go downhill fast, and it wasn't long before he was ruined for good. He wasn't the first or the last young man with abnormal tendencies. If I didn't know it then, I know it now. Maybe he would never have been cured, but he would never have ended the way he did if papa had not turned him out of the house. And maybe mama, too, would never have got cancer.

As for the father of my dazzling daughter, he tried at first to deny everything. He had the nerve to pretend to be angry, as though he had been offended. Later he admitted it, but threw all the blame on Dino. That's the kind of coward he was, the man whose memory my daughter worships as though he were some kind of god. For naturally I wouldn't demean myself to come down to her level and tell her what kind of creature he really was. I leave her in her ignorance. That's the worst punishment she could have. Yes, that's the kind of blustering coward he was. But when he saw it was no use, since we both knew it was he who had gone up to the terrace and so it was he who must have woken up Dino, he was shameless enough to say that it was my fault: he'd been forced into doing it with my brother, he said, because I was frigid and too narrow for him. He hadn't been able, he said to make love properly and it was driving him crazy. It was a lie, of course. Unfortunately, it was a lie. I wasn't at all frigid. But even if I had been, the sod ought to have known that all inexperienced women are like that, especially when they've reached a certain age without having had relations with a man, and it was up to him to teach me. But gently. Not to treat me the way he did, as though I was one of the tarts he picked up in foreign ports, asking me to do things respectable men don't ask their wives to do even when they have been married for years! Papa became wild with anger. I had never seen him so furious before. He rushed off to get his pistol, and mama and Erasmia had to hold him back by brute force. The bastard had to pack his bags and leave. In any case, his ship was due to leave after a week. He left, and stayed away for eleven months.

During that time I gave birth to the Medusa who, for twenty-four years now has been making a fine job of continuing what her father began. You'll ask why on earth didn't you go and have an abortion? What did you want a child for? It's true, I shouldn't have had a child, and I knew it. But mama and aunt Katie were at it from morning to night: it's not the innocent babe's fault — Maria, an innocent babe! — if its father was a no good; and women who had abortions got all sorts of illnesses later, and so on, and so on. Finally, they talked me into keeping it. When he came back from his travels, he didn't care to come straight to the house, although he knew I'd accepted all the money he'd sent me (what could I do? I needed it). Instead, he sent an aunt of his round to sound me out. She wanted to let him see the baby. 'What baby?' I asked his aunt. 'Didn't he say our marriage wasn't consummated? What baby does he expect to see now?' Three days later his mother arrived. She was quite a nice woman, and she blamed her son even more than any of us did. She fell at my feet and began to cry. 'Take him back,' she said, 'he's away from home most of the time anyway.' And finally I decided to give way. He came back to the house loaded with gifts for all of us, and we pretended that nothing had happened. Even papa treated him politely, although he avoided becoming too familiar. Besides, as my mother-in-law said, most of the time he was away at sea. He sent me a cheque every month. And when he came back he came loaded down with presents. He'd stay with us for a month or two, and then off he'd go again. This sort of life lasted about six years.

Suddenly, he began to suffer from mysterious attacks of giddiness. He went to doctor after doctor, in Greece and abroad, but none of them could tell him what it was. They recommended that he should stop going to sea. He applied for a job in the shipping company's offices in the Piraeus, and the company gave it to him. Financially, it was a setback to retire so early from the sea; he had not completed enough years of service to draw his pension. But the giddy spells continued, worse even than before. And one fine morning we discovered what the mysterious ailment was: ozena, a terrible ulcer in the nostrils. His nose stank like a sewer. It was impossible to get near him, impossible to sleep in the same bed. He began using all kinds of perfumes, like a woman. As long as he was abroad most of the time and his health was good, I overlooked his faults and tolerated him. But now that he was home almost all day, and with the horrid illness he had, I began to lose my patience. No matter how good-hearted a woman may be, how ever conscious of her wifely duties, It's impossible to have a man like that near her for very long. If I'd loved him, I'd have been ready to put up with anything. But after all that had happened, what kind of love could I have for him? The bickering and squabbling began and they got worse and worse because mama and Erasmia (who always took his side) insisted on poking their noses into our quarrels. We began bringing up past history and there were bitter words between us. One day he told me I had put up with him all those years only because I needed his money to feed my father and keep him in funds for his card-playing. I became as furious as a wild-cat. I told him to pack his bags and get out. Thinking he could blackmail me into changing my mind—this was the unmanly way he always acted—he packed up not only his clothes but every single present he'd given me since our engagement. He put all the stuff into a taxi and left. When he saw that, in spite of being left without a cent, I refused to change my mind and take him back, he threatened to kill me. 'Tell him from me,' I said to his aunt, 'that I don't think he's capable of it. To kill someone you've got to be a *man!*' And I told my lawyer to start proceedings for a divorce.

I didn't have to wash all the dirty linen in public to get the divorce. The ozena was more than enough. Meanwhile, to meet the household expenses and medical bills for mama, I borrowed money from uncle Stephen. But I wasn't worried. I knew I would be getting alimony after a year at the most. When the trial was almost due to come on and he realised he had no chance of winning, he went to the doctor and asked him to close the running ulcer in his nose, no matter how. Within a week the poison got into his bloodstream, and he died. And instead of receiving alimony, I was forced to borrow more money, and more, and more . . . to feed his daughter! I can't describe what I went through those two years before I married Antoni. Of course, things changed as soon as I was married. I paid my debts to uncle Hercules and uncle Stephen; I paid off the two mortages I had been forced to take out on the house; we wrote to Marietta and brought her back from the village; we repaired the house, bought new furniture, put the Duchess into a private school, and poor Antoni even bought her a piano for thirty-five thousand drachmas because she kept grumbling that all her schoolmates had a piano at home and she was the only one who didn't. And that's not counting all the money he spent on the illnesses of mama and papa. Those are the reasons why I married Antoni, even if he was twenty years older than me. Not for bed, as that filthy bitch had the nerve to tell me today when I told her I'd sacrificed myself for my family. Antoni, for bed! Sweet Jesus, preserve us!

6

We lost mama in '35. She just faded away slowly, not so much from the cancer as from grief over what had become of Dino. It was Dino who was her cancer. I'd rather not think of the dreadful pain she suffered before she died. Sometimes I have an unpleasant feeling that I shall die of the same illness. And about a year later, less than a month after I'd stopped wearing black, I put on black clothes again for papa. He didn't get over losing her. He loved her, even if he didn't show it. He worshipped her, even if he ran after every skirt in sight, as you might say.

Men are funny creatures, not like us women. When a woman loves a man, she devotes herself to him body and soul, she worships him like a god. It is inconceivable for her that she could sleep with another man at the same time. But men are different. They can love a woman, worship her, and at the same time run after a dozen others. They're full of curiosity, everything rouses their imagination. That's the truth, even if, as a woman, I find it hard to put myself in their place. I understand it with my mind, but all my deepest instincts revolt against something which seems so monstrous. Poor papa! . . . He had a big heart. It wasn't just that he was educated, like so many other people. He was a real human being in the same way that Hecuba was a human being. I owe everything I know in life to him, and to her.

It wasn't long before we lost uncle Hercules, then aunt Panayiotta, and finally Dino. For three or four years on end I remember nothing but illnesses, funerals and memorial services. And yet those years, until the day Antoni took ill and a time of new troubles began, were perhaps the best of my life – the easiest, the most free of that constant worry I always used to have, even when there was no real reason for it. Never a week-end went by in summer without some excursion.

People still remember the parties we used to give in the winter on the slightest excuse. Sometimes I still bump into people we used to know then, people who've been lucky and don't know today how much money they have in the bank, and they say: 'Do you remember, Nina, the turkeys and roast suckling pigs we used to eat at your place?"

I didn't have my dresses made by Erasmia any more. I'd found a first-class dressmaker who worked at one of the best fashion houses in Hermes Street. Apart from two foxes, poor Antoni bought me a real Persian lamb coat, with wide sleeves, from Sistovaris, and three Bokhara carpets which I sold for a few cans of olive oil during the black days of the occupation. Apart from Marietta, I had another woman who came in to do the washing and polish the parquet, not to mention the hairdresser who came once a week without fail and on all the holidays to do my hair and give me a manicure. This was all before Hecuba's time. Hecuba met me during the years of the lean cows. The easy money stopped when Antoni fell ill. There was not as much work about as there had been, which was not Antoni's fault of course. And then the international situation made things worse. People were beginning to be afraid of war. And there was his illness, which made him all the more dependent on that crook of a cousin. And just at the time when we ought to have been making an effort to save money to avoid eating into our capital, he got this kind of Tolstoy mania: encouraged by Erasmia, he spent money right and left for charities to help people who were mostly not worth helping, and he paid the priests a small fortune for blessings and all-night prayer sessions. I was forced to cut down my own personal spending to a bare minimum to make ends meet. Fortunately, the Lord took pity on me. Whether it was because Antoni himself finally realised his mistake and decided to get rid of Erasmia and all her gang, or whether the influence of Hecuba, who began visiting us frequently, had a beneficial effect, the fact is that after that famous all-night session when holy Ephemia went into a trance and spoke in seven languages, all of them dead ones — Assyrian, Babylonian, Aramaic and so on — I suddenly had a happy feeling that something had changed for the better in our lives. The day she came to the house with Erasmia when I was shaking out the curtains on the roof, she came to thank me for my hospitality. It struck me as rather funny. Not only because I hadn't invited her myself, but because I didn't even notice her among all that crowd of strangers who packed into our house that night. But it was typical of her that we didn't speak at all about the all-night session. The conversation was all about witchcraft and coffee-cup fortune telling. Erasmia sat there listening to her, it seems for the first time, talking about witches. She was absolutely stunned. 'I didn't know you believed in all that nonsense,' she said at one point, in that abrupt way of hers. 'The coffee cup and the cards are instruments of the devil.' Hecuba was put off for a moment, but she soon recovered her poise: 'I don't know about devils or demons or whatever, Erasmia dear. All I know is that the wretched things quite often come true. As for witchcraft, well even the Church believes in that. If it didn't it wouldn't have any call to read out all those exorcisms! . . .' It's a miracle I managed to keep a straight face. God bless your heart, good woman, I thought to myself — for I didn't even know her name yet. At last, Erasmia my dear, you've found your match!

At that moment the clock began to strike seven. Hecuba jumped up like a jack-in-the-box. 'Whew!', she cried (I was to hear that 'whew!' of hers thousands of times in the years to come). 'Whew! Seven o'clock. My son will murder me! Here I sit like a fool talking about witchcraft when I ought to have been home to wake him up at six-thirty. He's on night shift at his newspaper this evening. He's incapable of waking up himself even if the guns of Mount Lycabettus go off next to his bed. I have to shake him, pull the covers off and go down on my bended knees before he'll condescend to wake up! . . .' That's how she'd spoiled the gentleman. No wonder he gets irritable now when I don't give in to his every whim! 'Stop your screaming,' I tell him sometimes when he starts shouting at me. 'I'm not your mother who trembled in her shoes as though you were some kind of god. Those days are gone, and the sooner you get used to it the better!'

Now, after fifteen years, I think back on that afternoon and I say to myself: life is so strange, we're just playthings in its hands. How could I imagine that when I asked her to come back, for no reason except to get a rise out of Erasmia, I was opening a new chapter, as they say, in the history of my life. 'You know where to find us now,' I said, 'don't wait for special invitations. Come whenever you feel like it and we'll have some coffee together.' When she'd gone, I asked Erasmia: 'What did you say her name was?' — 'Hecuba,' she replied, abruptly. — 'At last you've brought somebody worthwhile to the house!' I said. But Erasmia had already begun to have her doubts, and made no reply.

7

From then on, it was as though a window had opened in our lives to let in some light. At the beginning she didn't come very often. But we were soon on familiar terms. She began to confide her troubles and tell me the story of her life. Their house was two streets down from ours. She would rush to get through her housework and come to pass the time of day with us. She wasn't one of those women, like my good-for-nothing daughter, who could sit all day long doing nothing. 'I'm fed up with sitting, Nina,' she'd say, 'isn't there any sewing or anything I could do for you?' Hecuba was a dressmaker like poor mama. Perhaps better than mama. She'd look you up and down, judging with her eye, and, without using a tape-measure, she'd take the scissors and begin to cut. She hardly ever used a pattern and, even when she did, she never followed it exactly. She just used the patterns to get ideas: a sleeve from one, a collar from another, and so on, making her own combinations. So I'd get my old dresses out of the wardrobe – dresses I thought were beyond alteration and which I'd put by to give away – and, with a stitch here and a tuck there, she'd make them better than new. Or she'd sit darning socks for Antoni who, the truth is, had taken to her at once. When he came home and found her there, his eyes would light up. 'I've caught you!'" he'd say, 'you can't escape now. Come and play a game of whist.' He'd take the pack of cards, shuffle them in a concertina like the sharpers who play the three-card game at fairs, and they'd settle down. And since he beat her nine times out of ten, he doted on her. He'd watch that priceless expression of resigned suffering come over her face, and he'd burst out laughing. When the clock struck one, Hecuba would leave the game unfinished and jump up. 'Whew! One o'clock. My son will get home from work and the kid from school and they won't find a thing to eat (Polyxene used to eat

54

lunch at her work). I'll just pop back and fix them some spaghetti. It's nice and filling' . . . But Antoni would grab her by the shoulder and sit her back in her chair by force. 'You're not going anywhere,' he'd say, 'I won't let you. I know, you want to rush off because you're losing!' And then he'd shout for Marietta, using the thick village accent they often used as a joke when they spoke to each other: 'Hey! Marietta! I want yall run a plate of vittels over to Mrs Hecuba's son — give her the key to the door, that's right. And stick this 'ere note on the door to tell the boy to come straight round here when he gets back from school!' And he'd sit down himself and write the note. 'Now really, people, this won't do,' Hecuba would protest, 'you treat me like I was living with you. My son will kill me if he comes back and finds I'm not home again.' But next day she'd come tripping in all smiles and say: 'Guess what! My son was crazy about that moussaka of yours. "Who's this mysterious Nina who makes such good moussaka?" ' — 'Tell him to come round to have lunch with us one day and meet Antoni,' I said one afternoon. She answered like a frightened child: 'Are you serious? You don't know my son! Don't imagine he's like me. I've let myself go so much, it's a disgrace. I don't give a damn about how I look and what I do. But he still keeps to the ways he was brought up in. If he knew I sat here darning Antoni's socks he'd never let me come back . . .' From her descriptions I tried to imagine what he was like. But neither more or less than we do in the case of any other person we hear about without knowing them personally. I imagined him to be tall and thin, and certainly not bald. I never did like bald men. I always found them slightly repulsive.

8

Gradually I found out the story of her life. I doubt if there are many women who know their husband's family history in such detail. When I married Theodore I seemed to be marrying the hero of a novel I had read and re-read years before. His grandfather was a *practical* archaeologist. 'What does a practical archaeologist mean?' I asked Hecuba. 'Well, it's like this. He'd bang his stick on the ground and say "dig here". Then you'd dig and you'd find human skeletons and pots of gold coins.' To judge by his photograph, he must have been a fine dashing figure of a man. But her mother, old Pighi, while not exactly repulsive was no great beauty. 'You great thick-lips, you,' I say to Theodore when I want to tease him, 'why couldn't you take after your grandfather instead of that ugly grandmother of yours?' Hecuba insisted that her father married her mother only because she had wide hips. 'They say women with wide hips have a lot of children. And that's what my father wanted.'

He was like my grandfather. They wanted lots of children to increase the population of Greece so that we could take on the Turks, to win back the Byzantine Empire and achieve the 'Great Idea'; and also for the sheer pleasure of giving them the names of ancient Greeks. They thought this was how they could bridge the gap between ancient and modern Greece. As though the only difference was in the names! However . . . Her father's expectations were disappointed. Old Pighi's belly was constantly swollen, but she had difficulty in keeping a child, like some trees which produce a mass of fruit which falls off before it ripens. She either had miscarriages, or the child would die at birth. And even those who survived, except for Aphrodite, came to a sticky end. Lycourgos was crushed to death under a cart when the horse bolted. Themistocles trod on a rusty nail and died of tetanus. Ismini committed suicide. Achilles died of consumption. He was the spoiled child of the household. His mother loved him because he was weak and ailing, his father because, of all the boys, he was the only one who showed promise at book-learning, and he dearly wanted one of his sons to become an archaeologist. According to Hecuba, Achilles was a sleep walker. But not of the usual kind. 'He didn't go up on the roof at night, Nina,' she told me, 'he just used to prop himself up on his pillows in bed and, in the dark, he'd do his homework. When he got up in the morning he found all his algebra problems solved.' — 'Why couldn't you be a sleepwalker, too, you ugly blockhead,' I used to say to my daughter, 'and save me all that good money I throw away on tutors?' — 'So, as I was saying, he'd bring home bits of old vases and statues and pile them up on the verandah. My mother grumbled every time: "I wish you'd stop filling the house with that rubbish." — "Stop your grumbling," he'd reply, God rest his soul, "if men were like women and all women were like you, we'd still be living in caves. When our Achilles grows up he'll be an archaeologist. He'll stick the pieces together and make them just like they used to be." But he didn't live. We lost him in less than two months, from galloping consumption. My mother, who'd taken an oath that if anything were to happen to Achilles she'd follow him to the grave within forty days, kept her word: in forty days exactly, we lost her too!' 'And what happened to the vases?' — 'What vases?' — 'The vases your father brought home and piled up on the verandah, of course.' 'Oh, the vases. Well, to tell you the honest truth, I'm ashamed to say I've never thought about it. Who knows! I expect that slut Aphrodite sold them. They've gone, I suppose, along with the land she sold . . .'

Every time she paid her rent she'd come to the house with a long face. 'Bang goes another thousand! And before you can turn round it will be the first of the month again. I'm fed up with my life, damn it. Why couldn't I have a room or two of my own, instead of paying rent to those landlord bastards? It's all that slut Aphrodite's fault. But mark my words, she'll vomit it all back on that little tart Evanthia she dotes on so much . . . My father, God rest his soul, had acres and acres of land at Ambelokipi. You remember how it was then (a little dig, this, at my age), Ambelokipi was nothing but open fields, and the council sold lots for a few cents the square yard. My father was a clever man, and he knew that Athens would grow one day and that land would become valuable. So every time he had a little money to spare he'd buy an acre or two. But when our Achilles died, and then my mother, he fell into Aphrodite's hands—I'd got married in the meantime and was living in Salonika—and the dirty little dishrag managed to get him to transfer all the land to her name. She put him in a cab one day and took him to the notary, and he made the land over to her for life. Miltiades and I decided to go to court and get the arrangement overruled. But at the last minute Miltiades backed out. He must have been well greased by Aphrodite, there's no other explanation. As for us, we were simply swimming in money at that time. Who'd have thought that we'd be broke so quickly or that those scruffy fields would suddenly become gold mines? After the disaster of the Asia Minor campaign the refugees came crowding in and Venizelos took over the land to build wooden huts for them. And now Metaxas is building blocks of appartments for the mangy Turk-spawn who came over with holes in their pants and have collared all the best jobs! And that's the end of our land. We'll never get it back. Aphrodite swears black and blue that she never got any compensation. But I'll never believe her, not if they put her on the rack. She got compensation alright! And I'd take an oath she even managed to sell some of the land before it was requisitioned!' . . . and so on, and so on.

9

Her relations with her brother Miltiades were no better, even though she had him living in her house. Miltiades was a retired permanent Army officer. He'd fought at Sarantaporo, Bizani, Sangarios and so on. He'd got most of his promotions for bravery. He was the hero of the family. She had two shell cases on her mantelpiece that he'd brought back as souvenirs from the Balkan Wars. But by the time I met her the shell cases of Miltiades no longer symbolised for the family the sacred struggles of the Greek nation. They were more a reminder of the feats of Theodore when he was a boy! When he was naughty Hecuba used to lock him up in the room with the mantelpiece and the shell cases. One day they locked him up and then forgot all about him. When he suddenly wanted to pee, and nobody answered his shouts to let him out, he peed into the shell cases. Looking at him now, heavy and serious as he is, its difficult to imagine him as a boy at all, much less an unruly one. It's impossible to imagine some people as children, just as there are some children you can look at and you know at once what they'll look like when they grow old.

Miltiades was a Venizelos man. Every time Hecuba spoke about his political views she'd lower her voice instinctively. Not that there was any danger any more. Who cared in '37 and '38 if you were a Venizelist? It was just an old habit. At one time, of course, to be a Venizelist was like being a communist today. It was no joke. Once, I remember, when King Constantine returned from exile, papa almost lost his job at the University. He was a Venizelist, too. He wasn't as fanatical as some of the others, in fact he didn't much care about politics, but he voted for Venizelos because he threw a few bones to the poor. He wasn't really a man who fitted into any kind of party programme. 'What's the difference,' he used to say, 'both sides are as bad as each other for the country. What matters is to be a human being, and that's something every man has to do for himself. Whatever the regime, there will always be human beings and beasts . . .' When Kondilis held the plebiscite and brought George back to the throne, they threw Miltiades out of the Army on the grounds that he was a dangerous anti-royalist troublemaker. At that time Hecuba had come to live in Athens. She saw him disappointed and broke—his pension wasn't enough, as you might say, to keep him in cigarettes—and she suggested that he went to live with them, to save paying rent at least. But it wasn't long before they started nagging each other and then squabbling seriously. She told him to go and find a job, like all his colleagues. But Miltiades paid no attention. He hoped that things would soon change again and he would get back into the Army.

Meanwhile, he lazed around the cafés playing backgammon and muttering curses between his teeth on Metaxas and the 4th of August. Every time he walked through the hall and saw the photograph of Metaxas he'd spit ostentatiously on the floor. That was one of the reasons for their squabbles. Not that she cared about Metaxas, far from it. In her own way Hecuba was rather like my father. But Theodore was a fanatic supporter of the regime and she was afraid he'd see Miltiades spitting one day, and it would have been an impossible position for her if uncle and nephew came to blows.

She forgave him all that, just the same. What she couldn't forgive, and what finally led to the big explosion, was his passion for interfering in the way little Akis was brought up. Hecuba did not let him go and play in the streets with the other children. She made him sit and do embroidery, or she would make dolls for him and let him sit playing with the dolls. When Miltiades saw it he went wild—his sense of national pride was revolted. Greek youth to play with dolls, not with guns and war! The *Greeks* with dolls . . . he'd grab them and throw them in the dustbin. And then there would be a row of Homeric proportions, and Hecuba would come and tell me all about it in a state of high indignation.

10

Judging by his photograph (we have it in our sitting-room now) her husband was a handsome man and, like poor papa, he dressed up to the nines: hard collar, silver-grey cravat, diamond tie-pin, and so on. One day when I got to know her a little better, I remember going to her place and looking at the photographs she had on the wall. "A handsome fellow," I remarked. "Oh yes, that's how he looked when he came and asked papa to marry me. There was no bigger dandy in the whole world. He always dressed beyond his means. "Don't pay any attention," he used to tell me, "when people tell you that dress doesn't make the man. Here in Greece people judge you by what they see." So, instead of going to the University where poor old Longos wanted to send him, he had cards printed with the description 'lawyer' under his name, and he spent his time strolling up and down the road making eyes at the girls of the neighbourhood. My father's house was up in Saint Asomati street. I'll show it to you if we go by there one of these days. It had a little verandah in front with two terra-cotta caryatids. Every time I see them when I pass the house now tears come to my eyes. That's where I used to spend my afternoons. I watered the flower-pots, or sat in a chair doing some needlework. Yiannis used to live just down the road, and every time he passed by he'd say something nice to me – you know, the silly kind of things boys say to girls when they want to get round them. But I was so shy and reserved. I'd blush to the roots of my hair and rush indoors. It only made him more determined than ever. He must have said to himself: this girl is not like all the others. He arrived one day and asked my father if he could marry me. But even when we got engaged I still felt shy when I was with him. – "Mama," I remember saying to my mother one day, "I wish you wouldn't ask me to do the washing-up when Mr Longos comes." – "And why shouldn't I ask you to do the washing-up when Mr Longos comes?" – "Because I roll my sleeves up and he can see the mole on my arm" And she laughed. "Is that all you're worried about? The mole on your arm, is it? Just you wait and see what you're in for when you get married!" That's what she told me, God rest her soul. That's how innocent I was, Nina, really. Sometimes I can't believe it when I sit and think back to those days. You'd think it was impossible for a person to change so much. I'll never understand how that innocent little lamb turned into the monster I am now,' – 'Get on with you,' I'd say to her. 'You're no monster. You just like to pretend you are. What did your husband study for?' – 'The law. But he didn't have the patience to take his degree. He began doing all kinds of odd jobs – trade and that kind of thing. We lived with my mother first. Then we took a place of our own, near the Acropolis. That's where all my children were born, except for Dimitris. I had him in Salonika.' – 'And why did you go to Salonika?' – 'Well, Yiannis never really liked Athens. He was from Macedonia, you see. He couldn't take the atmosphere of old Greece. I remember when I was pregnant with Akis's mother. He arrived home one night at midnight. January it was, and cold enough to freeze the nose off your face. He wakes me up, and without a word of why or wherefore he says: "Pack a few things into a suitcase for me. I'm leaving tonight for Macedonia with Pavlos Melas. If those bastard Bulgars think they can put one over on us they've got another think coming." That was the time when the Turks were on the way out, and the Greeks and Bulgars were squabbling with each other like rival heirs round the death-bed of a rich uncle. – "And what's to become of me, Yiannis," I said, "what am I to do with the children? What about them if anything happens to you, God forbid?" – "Don't worry. Nothing's going to happen to me," he said. "I'm not such a fool as to go rushing off to get myself killed. I'm just going to have a look round and see what's happening up in Macedonia. There's no future for me here in Athens . . ." He cuddled me and kissed me and was just about ready to leave. But he changed his mind. Holding me in his arms, he turned down the light with one hand and — well, you know what men always want . . . That's how he was. Probably that's why I loved him. He was just like a god for me. Then he kissed Theodore as he lay there in his cradle, and he made off in the middle of the freezing night, with the snow thick on the ground . . . Three months later he got a Bulgarian bayonet in his hand. When he got out of hospital he came back to Athens. He stopped with us for a month, then back he went to Salonika. He started up in the timber business, chopping down trees in forests belonging to the monasteries for so much per acre. He planned to buy his own caique to transport the timber. He was making money hand over fist. But what was the good of the money to me, Nina? I didn't like living apart. Every time he came to Athens I'd say to him: "Take us back to Salonika with you, Yiannis dear, I can't go on living alone!" — "Don't be such a fool," I remember him saying the last time he came, "don't be such a fool. The situation's pretty bad. There might be a war." It was as though he knew. In less than a month the first Balkan War started. Day after day I waited for him to turn up, or write me a letter. But there was no sight or sound of my Yiannis. He was never one for writing letters. Two months went by, then three. I thought I'd go mad. That's that, I said to myself. That's the end of my husband. Either he's gone and got himself killed, or he's run off with some dishrag of a girl, which is the same thing as being dead. What was to become of me, with three children on my hands and a fourth on the way, as I'd just found out? Well, to cut a long story short, I made up my mind to go and find him. You dirty dog, I thought to myself; if you think I'm still the same old Hecuba who was shy of rolling up her sleeves, that I'll put up with you turning up whenever the fancy takes you, just to put me in the family way and then disappear, you're very sadly mistaken. You've gone too far this time, my lad. I'll show you the other side of the coin. You'll find out who Hecuba is now! . . . Without any more beating about the bush, I went straight off to the Palace and asked to see Sophia. She was still Crown Princess at that time. I was told she'd see me at a fixed time. I kissed her hand and I said: 'Your Highness, it's like this . . .'' And I told her all about it. "I want you to send me to my husband."—Don't be so daft," she says, "how do you think you can take three kids into that blazing mess. You just stay put where you are." Of course, she didn't say it exactly like that, you understand. Her Greek wasn't very good.—"Eef you no money, me help you," she said.—"I've got money," I said, "what I need is transport. And I've heard it's possible to get up there on a hospital ship. But when I went to the Red Cross to ask, they told me it all depended on Your Highness . . ." And, believe it or not, there I was two days later at the White Tower, in Salonika. Honestly, Nina, I could hardly believe I had it in me. True, the Turks by then had packed up and gone home. But tempers were still very much on edge. Our dear Bulgarian allies were taking it badly because they were too late to be first into the city. There were incidents every day, and it was more than your life was worth to go out alone at night. Every morning they'd pick up the corpses of two or three Greeks who'd been stabbed. As soon as we got off the ship, I left the children with a family who'd travelled up on the ship with us, and I set off to find the office of Papathanassiou the lawyer. I found it after a lot of trouble. And when I went in, there my loving husband was, as large as life, sprawled all over a leather armchair without a care in the world. As soon as he saw me he jumped up and burst out laughing.—"Well, I must say, I've got to hand it to you," he said, "so you managed it. I knew you would. Ha-ha-ha!" He could hardly get the words out he was laughing so much.— "Christo," he says to Papathanassiou, "let me introduce my wife. She's just what's needed to make mincemeat of all the Ivanovs! . . .' And would you believe it, Nina, he didn't so much as ask me: how have you managed all this time? How have you been feeding the children? That was the sort of man he was. Anyway, it seems that, apart from the timber business, he'd been selling supplies to the army and put a tidy bit of money aside. I persuaded him to buy a house right away, the house of a Turkish bey, complete with all the furniture. The Turks were clearing out in a great hurry, and they were selling everything they possessed for a song. That was the house my children grew up in. In great style. The sort of thing I'd never seen, or even imagined, in my father's house . . . Of course, the neighbourhood was still full of Turks. The rich ones had run off, but the poor ones had nowhere to go. Like the old proverb says: for the poor man, home is where he happens to be. They left also, after the Asia Minor disaster, when the populations were exchanged. You should have seen the way they cried. They hugged and kissed us. Yes, those Turkish so-and-sos who'd treated us like slaves for so many centuries. Well, forgive and forget, that's what I always say. To tell the honest truth, the Turks I met were all very nice people. They never let a beggar go by without giving him something. And the Turkish ladies were always very friendly, poor things. They'd invite me in for coffee in the afternoons and tell my fortune with a pack of cards. That's how I learned to do it myself. The ten of clubs would turn up every time. — "That's funny," Nairedin would say. She used to sit cross-legged smoking away like a chimney. "That's funny. I don't see you with your husband. I see another woman in his bed . . ." But I'd just laugh, I was that vain and selfcentred. I was so sure of myself. That was my mistake. I'd gotten above myself. I don't care, I used to say. I don't care if there are a hundred other women in his bed. No matter where he goes, it's me he'll come back to, me and the children. I'm the queen in his house. . . . And I didn't even take any notice when Saint Anastasia sent me a warning sign . . .'

— 'How do you mean, Saint Anastasia sent you a *warning sign?*' I asked — 'Don't laugh. I'll tell you the story and you'll see . . . One summer the old rascal sent us to spend a holiday at Valta. I took all the children with me except for Eleni who'd failed her examinations — like *your* daughter has — and had to stay in Salonika to study with a private tutor. Not that she cared! She was delighted to stay at home and act the housewife, looking after her father. She couldn't abide me because I kept her under strict control. But she simply worshipped him. At that time they still hadn't put the buses on to Valta. You had to go part of the way by horse-cab—or by caique, except that my Polyxene couldn't stand travelling by sea. Then, from a certain point, you had to go on by mule. Yiannis needed our carriage. So we hired a one-horse coach. On the way I saw a little church standing all by itself miles from anywhere—you know, like the one in the song:

> Deep in the forest, all alone
> A little church stands made of stone....

—"What church is that?", I asked the coachman.—"The church of Saint Anastasia, healer of the sick."—"And that great log hanging outside?"—"That's the bell." It seemed so funny I began laughing till I sobbed.—"Well I must say it's the funniest bell I've ever seen," I said,"couldn't they find anything better to hang up than a great lump of wood?" I nearly wet my pants laughing! . . . Well, with one thing and another, we arrived at the village where we had to take the mules. It was dark by then, and the children were dead tired with being bounced up and down in the coach for so many hours. I was just thinking that we'd have some food and I'd put them straight to bed, when the mule-driver arrived and said: "Get ready, we're going to start."—"You must be out of your mind," I told him, "didn't we just arrange to set off in the morning? What's got into you suddenly? I'm not moving an inch from here!" But at that time the countryside was still full of bandits. The mule-drivers moved in caravans for greater safety, and the other holidaymakers had decided to set off at once so as to travel in the cool of the night. If we'd stayed behind it would have meant waiting another two or three days before another group started. So, cursing all holidays and mule-drivers, I got up on my mule. Theodore, who was a big boy by now, had his own mule. We put the two little ones, Dimitris and Polyxene, together on one mule.—"Hold on tight, children," I told them.

"Mules are patient animals, but if they get angry you'll find yourselves in the ditch before you know where you are." In spite of all the driver's reassurances I set off with an uncomfortable feeling. It was pitch dark and my skin went all goosepimply as I listened to the croaking of the frogs from the swamp and the howling of the wild animals in the forest. I was sorry I'd not followed my instinct and stayed behind in the village. What would it matter if we arrived at Valta a couple of days later? We'd paid a deposit for the house and it was there waiting for us to move in. Whereas now we'd arrive at midnight, I thought to myself, and we'd have to get the owners out of their beds. Why should we put them to so much trouble? Just as these thoughts were going through my mind, little Dimitris turned round and said: "Mama, Xeni is sick!" I shouted for the mule-driver to stop the mules. I got down off my mule and felt the child's hand. She was burning with fever! "How far have we got to go?", I asked. — "Another couple of hours." I got back on my mule and held Polyxene in my arms. I held on to the saddle with one hand and held the child to me with the other.

— "There, there, my baby, don't fret," I kept on telling her. "Don't cry and break your mummy's poor heart. We're nearly there now . . ." But before we could get to Valta she'd passed into a coma. We woke up the landlady who showed us our rooms. I put the boys to sleep in one room and Polyxene in the other. Then I sent one of the sons of the house to run and call a doctor. I sat by the bedside putting cold vinegar compresses on her head, but the fever wouldn't go down. She groaned and trembled like a jelly. She could hardly catch her breath. I thought she'd die any moment. — "The doctor," I kept asking the landlady, "the doctor, why doesn't he come?" — "He's coming, he's coming," she said. But the boy came back alone. — "The doctor's away at such and such a village, he'll be back tomorrow night," he said. — I began to scream and wring my hands in a frenzy. "What about my baby," I moaned desperately, "what will happen to my baby now?" — Don't carry on like that, my love," said the landlady. "It's nothing serious. She's just tired out from the journey, she'll be as right as rain soon, you'll see!" Pfff!, I thought to myself as right as rain. These peasants! What do they know about illnesses? They don't know the difference between people and cattle. — "It's all very well saying don't carry on like that, my good woman," I told her, "what do you expect me to do? There's typhoid about and in twenty-four hours my baby may be gone for good!' And I sent her off to sleep. I hope no mother ever goes through the agonies I went through that night. I sat there by the side of her bed talking to her like a crazy thing. — "What's the matter, my love," I kept saying to her, "who's put the evil eye on you, who's trying to take my baby away from me?"

Then I got up and began to pace the room like a lioness in her cage. I had no idea what time it was. The oil in the lamp had almost burned away and the flame got lower and lower. I thought to myself: shall I wake up the landlady again or not? Then for the first time I noticed the oil-wick burning in front of the ikon in the corner of the room. I suddenly felt my knees giving way. I collapsed onto the floor sobbing and wailing. And then, believe it or not, I suddenly remembered that little church, and I began to say out loud: "Dear Saint Anastasia, Healer of Sickness! Forgive me for making fun of your bell. Make my Xeni well and I'll light a candle as tall as she is in your honour! . . ." And she listened to my prayer. Great is your loving mercy, dear Saint Anastasia! My Polyxene suddenly broke out in a sweat! The sheets were simply soaked with it! And then, as she lay there so still she might have been dead, suddenly I saw her move. She opened her eyes and said — "Mama . . . water . . ." I almost fainted I was so overjoyed. Instead of giving her the water right away, I fell down on my knees again and gave thanks to God. . . . But I'm only telling you all this because of what happened later with Saint Anastasia. Just as she saved my Polyxene from certain death, it was she who warned me that I was soon going to lose my husband. When we got back to Salonika I went to buy an ikon in her honour. I left it for forty days in the sanctuary of the Ipapanti Church, and when I took it back I gave it to a monk who often passed by the house selling candles and incense and asked him to send it to Mount Athos to have it silvered over for me. – "Have it engraved underneath," I told him, "with the words: Dedicated by Hecuba Longos". But when he brought it back I saw they had left out the "Longos". – "Where's the surname?", I asked him. He looked, then looked again, and began to make the sign of the cross. – "Lord Almighty who knows all secrets . . ." – "Never mind about the Lord," I said, "it's nothing to do with Him." Anyway, to cut a long story short, he swore to me that when they gave him the ikon the "Longos" was engraved on it. He'd seen it with his own eyes. Saint Anastasia must have rubbed it out because she wanted to tell me something, and so on and so on." – 'Don't tell me you believed him, Hecuba.' – 'Of course not! I was just as much a doubting Thomas as you are. He must have forgotten the name, I thought, and now he's trying to throw the blame on the Saint. All those monks are the same, full of cunning. But when I lost my husband a little while afterwards I remembered what had happened and I wept bitterly, just like Peter when the cock crowed thrice. That's why, from that day on, I don't dare express my opinion. Believe and don't ask questions, that's the best policy, Nina, mark my words. You may well be right to insult the nun and call her a quack. But what if she isn't? I know what you'll say, Pff! It was just a coincidence. But to me it seems a downright miracle. – "Do you think you're the only one in the world?", it was as though she was saying. "You got above yourself, my fine friend. You think no harm can possibly come to you. Well just you wait and see what you're in for! Soon you'll be just plain 'Hecuba'. And I laid my head on my pillow, like I said, and wept bitter tears. – "Dear Saint Anastasia," I cried, "you who predicted my ruin, couldn't you prevent it from happening?" But what could the poor Saint do? What could God himself do? I had been warned. It was up to me to open my eyes and take some action. But, proud as I was, I paid no heed. . . .'

11

Quite often, when we had visitors at home in the afternoon and the talk got around to unsuccessful marriages and divorces Hecuba would get excited and begin to lay down the law. She was all in favour of mutual understanding, or at least mutual toleration, between husband and wife. She was a firm believer in the injunction: whom God has joined let no man put asunder. 'There's no room,' she used to say, 'for so much as a fine hair to pass between man and wife. And nobody knows that better than me because my marriage turned out to be a failure. . . .' – 'Her first cousin turned her husband's head,' I butted in to encourage her to talk. 'Come on, Hecuba, tell us all about it. It'll pass the time. You know I never get tired of listening to you.' – 'Maybe you don't get tired of listening to me, but I'm tired of listening to myself. There are times when I hear my own voice and I feel I want to throw up . . . Yes, she turned his head, the bitch. Put a spell on him, that's what she did. One evening we'd gone to the theatre, the three of us . . . Never mind what I've come down to now. In those days I had a house with three storeys, two servants and my own coach. My husband was in trade. Known all over Salonika he was. Wherever I went there was bowing and scraping when they heard I was Mrs Longos. We were well known in the highest society. Once he even put up for Parliament. He was crazy about politics, like all men. But it was Venizelos who won the elections that time. My husband was royalist to the bone; he'd have given his right arm for Constantine. That was the time when the break between Venizelos and Constantine was just starting. Our house had become like a political debating club. All the top royalist people would get together in our parlour and jabber and discuss for hours on end. And all that food! We had to invite the peasants from the villages in for meals to make sure of their votes. In those days nobody voted for you unless they got something out of it. It made me sick to see it. Maybe I could only judge with the little mind of a woman, but I could see that no good would come from it all. I was all in favour of the King, too, but what I thought was that he ought not to get mixed up in politics. — "Really, Yianni," I used to tell him, "what's all this nonsense for? You'd do far better to leave Constantine alone and go over to Venizelos if you know which side your bread's buttered. A fat lot of good these Kings have done us anyway. What would happen, if God forbid, you were to lose your money one of these days? Do you think Constantine would give you a second thought?" But men don't have any brains. They're like little children, ready to sacrifice everything for some crackpot idea. He neglected his business and kept running off to make speeches in Halkidiki. And the things he gave to the peasants! Nothing was too good for them. But he came a cropper in the end. It was like a punishment from God. You've got money. Everyone respects you. You've got a family that worships you. And yet it's not enough. You have to be an MP, too. But then fate steps in and knocks you off your perch, as if to say: let it be a lesson to you to stick to your place in future. . . . Of course he was terribly upset. I though he'd die of frustration. He'd come to believe that there was nothing he wanted he couldn't get. To get over the shock he took me off to Vienna for a month. I'd like you to have seen what that was like. I tell you, that's the real life! The palaces, the theatres, the cafés! You've never seen anything like it. It all seems like a dream now. In other words, we didn't do badly in those days. Well, I thought to myself — cross my heart, every time I think of it I curse myself for being such an idiot — Hecuba, I thought, you've made a success of your life. You've taken a good man for a husband. It's your duty to help your relatives. . . . My sister Aphrodite was married. My brother Miltiades was an officer in the Army. They didn't need any help from me. The only member of the family I could be of some use to was a cousin, the monster I'm telling you about now. She was almost 30 and still unmarried because she had no

72

dowry. Do a good turn, Hecuba, I said to myself, and God will pay you back on the lives of your children. The world goes round, and one of these days you may have need of her yourself. So I invited her to come and stay with us for a while, so she could live in better surroundings and shake up her ideas a bit. I thought we might even find a good match for her from among my husband's friends. We'd have given her a small dowry ourselves if necessary. I'd talked it all over with Yiannis and he agreed. But she didn't need me to find a husband for her. She found one for herself. How it happened, when it all started between them, I shall never know. But I know one thing: up to that time we were the happiest couple in the world, and then suddenly we began quarrelling about the slightest thing. Yiannis was just not the same person. He'd been transformed by that Circe's witchery. The night I was telling you about, when we got back from the theatre, I went on ahead to open the front door and I tripped over some black thing in the dark. We went in and I took the lamp down off the tallboy and went out to have look. And what do you think I saw! A chicken on the doorstep, black as pitch and covered all over with threads and pins. Nobody will every make me believe that it wasn't Frosso's doing—Frosso was her name. From that night onwards, things began to go wrong. Frosso was supposed to stay two months. She stayed for six. Her mother had to fall sick before she made up her mind to go back. Unless it was all part of a deliberate plan. From that time on Yiannis seemed to be in Athens all the time.

What's going on? I asked myself. Can it be that the Turkish women were telling the truth and he's really got seriously involved with some woman? But not for a single instant did I suspect Frosso. That's how naïve and trusting I was. And that's why I landed in trouble. In this world, unfortunately, you can't trust even your own brother. That's how things stood when, by a stroke of bad luck, I was taken seriously ill. The doctor who examined me diagnosed a tumour of the womb and ordered an immediate operation. I could have had the operation quite well in Salonika. But Yiannis insisted on my going to Athens. He had it all worked out. He didn't even give me time to say good-bye to my friends. He packed me onto a train, brought me to Athens and put me in the Evangelismos Hospital. When the nurse went out of the room and left us alone – "Evi" – Evi he used to call me – "don't you think it would be a good idea to bring Frosso to stay and look after the children while you're away?" – "Bravo!", I said, "it's a very good idea. I should have thought of it myself. And, Yiannis, do try to find her some good boy. After all, you've got so many friends. She may not be much to look at, and, to tell the truth, I'm not sure she isn't a little bit cold towards men – you must have noticed it yourself. But she has her attractive side. Try to get her fixed up, even if she never thanks us for it . . ." All the time I was in hospital that Judas my aunt came to see me three times a week. She even had the nerve to bring me flowers. Finally, when I'd finished the ray treatment and I went into convalescence, I wrote to him to come and fetch me. As soon as he got my letter he caught the express train and came straight to the hospital from the station. Something snapped inside me as soon as I saw him. That's not the Yiannis I used to know. I thought to myself. There's something fishy going on. – "What's the matter with you, looking like that?", I said. – "Nothing. I'm just tired out from the journey. The couchettes were all taken and I slept all night sitting up on the seat." – "Well, thank God it's nothing more serious than that," I said, "I was beginning to think all kinds of dreadful things . . ." He got up from the chair and went over to the window, pretending to look out. It was winter, the month of February, and a strong wind was blowing. The top of the cypress tree which reached up to my window was waving back and forth like mad. Without knowing why, I felt a strange kind of melancholy, a heavy weight on my chest. In spite of all his reassurances I had a feeling something was going on. But of course there was nothing I could put my finger on. I was on the point of ringing the bell for the nurse to come and help me with my suitcase, when he turned around and, trying to sound quite natural, he said: "Oh, by the way, I forgot to tell you. I wrote to mother about your operation and she's expecting you for a fortnight or so in the village till you get properly well and put back the weight you've lost." – "What!", I said, "here was I counting the days to be with you again, like a convict waiting to get out of jail, and now you want me to go to the village. What's wrong with the summer? Why should I go rushing off to the village in the middle of winter?" – "I didn't say you had to go if you don't want to," he said. He knew how to get round me. He knew if he insisted too much I'd suspect something. – "I just thought it would do you good," he said. "Why don't you go, and I'll bring the two little ones to see their grandfather and their grannie. It won't hurt them to miss a few days at school. You know mother's always complaining that you never go to stay with her. She thinks you feel she's not good enough for you." – "Well, that's a new one," I said, "you know perfectly well it's not true. Last year I nagged you to let us go to Lithohoro and it was you who insisted that we went to Valta. If we'd gone to Lithohoro our Xeni might not have been taken ill. . . ." But I knew I couldn't refuse to go. I resigned myself to my fate. "Nurse," I called, "will you get my suitcase ready please?". And suddenly I felt disaster was about to strike. . . .

My father-in-law was waiting for us at the station. From there the village was about an hour away by mule. It had snowed the night before and a thin layer of white was on the ground. Maybe it was from feeling weak after the operation, or maybe the sudden change of climate, or maybe because I was feeling so miserable, but I was trembling like a leaf and my teeth were chattering. Yiannis got my suitcase down and kissed his father's hand. – "Dear boy," he said, "why don't you come and stay with us for two or three days?". Poor old Longos! What a saint he was! At that moment the train whistle blew. Without answering, he jumped onto the step of the carriage and shouted to me: – "Don't forget what we said!".

—He'd told me: "Don't leave the village until I come to fetch you." — "He'll come back and bring the children with him," I said to my father-in-law. But a whole month went by without sight or sound of him. I was out of my mind with worry. Instead of putting on weight I was losing more than I'd lost in hospital. And although my poor mother-in-law couldn't do enough to look after me, the house seemed dark and miserable. — "Mother," I said to her finally, "what do you advise me to do?". — "If I were you," she said, "I'd go straight back to Salonika by myself." — "And, what if he gets angry?" — "Let him!", she said. She was a dear old thing. Every time someone dies and I write the list of names of dead relatives to be remembered at the memorial service, I put her name on the paper first. . . . I arrived as it was getting dark. I took a one-horse cab and got down outside the house. As I was paying the cabbie I looked towards the front door and turned cold at what I saw: the door was closed with a padlock on the outside! I looked up and saw the shutters were tightly closed as though the house had been uninhabited for years.

—"Wait!", I shouted to the cabbie. I went and knocked on a neighbour's door. And when I found out from her what my fine husband had been up to and recovered from feeling faint, I got back in the cab and told the driver: "To the Prosecutor's house. quickly. Number 13 Evzone street . . ." I knew the Prosecutor personally. He was a royalist and had eaten at our house a dozen times at least. We were on quite familiar terms. Armenopoulos — that was his name, Armenopoulos — was a good chap. He showed me into his parlour and I threw myself at his feet. "For the dear Lord's sake," I begged, "you must help me. I've lost my husband. Please give me back my husband!". . . . And as he bent to pick me up he saw a whole pool of blood on the carpet. He called for his wife and his mother-in-law, they called an ambulance, and I was rushed off to hospital. . . . It was my friend Domna, God bless her, who told me all about it: as soon as he put me in hospital and went back to Salonika with Frosso he began to spread the rumour that I'd left him. He went to the house agents to sell the house and bought a new one in another district. He wanted to cut himself off from the past completely. He got rid of the maid. Then he sent the elder boy as a boarder to the Tsotili school and my daughter to the American girls' school. He went about acting the part of a deserted husband, shedding crocodile tears. And at the same time he slapped a divorce suit on me, claiming I had abandoned the conjugal roof and was living at an address unknown! Can you believe it! You may well wonder if such a thing is possible! Oh yes, maybe he didn't finish his law degree, but he knew all the devilish tricks and turns inside-out. And he began to serve summonses on me — where, do you think? At the house of a fortune teller called Thalia. I used to go there sometimes with Domna and get her to tell my fortune, just to pass the time, you know how it is. Naturally, she refused to accept the summonses and the filthy pig of a bailiff, who got well paid for his trouble — men, they call themselves! — would pin them to the door, serve the summons in absentia as the lawyers say, and go away. When he'd served the proper legal number of summonses that way, he went to court one day and asked for a divorce. He took two so-called witnesses with him who told the filthiest lies about me, and the divorce was granted in his favour without my being there to put my case. The very next day he married Frosso, who by that time was expecting his bastard child. Domna had gone crazy trying to find me to understand what was going on. She also believed that I'd deserted him. If only I'd written to her from the hospital we'd all have saved ourselves so much grief. But — don't laugh — I didn't write to her because I was ashamed of my spelling. When I got out of hospital, I went to see the Prosecutor again, in his office this time. "Mr Armenopoulos," I said, "after what he's done to me, I wouldn't take him back now, not if he were made of gold. But I mean to have my children back. He's no right to deprive me of my children." Armenopoulos looked at me sadly. — "Mrs Longos," he said, "there's no point in hiding the fact that I'm not very optimistic. Of course, there's already a summons out against him for bigamy and perjury. But, as you know better than anybody, he's a man with lots of money and he's in a position to pull all kinds of strings. There's nothing to stop him dragging the affair out for two or three years."—"And what about my children?"—"The children . . . the children . . ." He began fiddling with the blotting pad on his desk, moving it from one place to another. "The children . . . I really don't know what to say. Until the affair comes on for trial and his guilt can be proved, he continues to have custody of the children. That's the law . . ." To hell with you and your laws, beastly men, I thought to myself.—"And meanwhile," I said, "what do you advise me to do?"—"Find yourself a lawyer who'll take a personal interest in your case . . ." I went and found Papathanassiou. He was the best man for the job. I knew they'd quarrelled about politics and were now deadly enemies. As soon as he saw me he grabbed both my hands.—"I've heard all about it," he said, "it's the most scandalous thing on legal record. From this very moment I am entirely at your disposal and I won't take a single penny for my services . . ." On his advice, I got in touch with all my fine husband's friends, one after another, trying to get witnesses who would give evidence in my favour. But nobody wanted to get involved. They'd slip me a hundred-drachma note as though I'd come begging for charity and got rid of me with the usual kind of promises and empty words. Some of them even tried to make up to me without the slightest shame. Cynical as you please, they'd suggest that we got together. I got tired of slapping faces. There was not a single real man among the whole lot of them, nobody whose conscience revolted against such an obvious injustice! The trouble is that people are always willing to overlook your dirty deeds so long as you have power and position. Many of those very same men who used to come to our home and say kind things about my cooking, now, without the slightest sense of shame, went to Frosso's house and called her Mrs Longos. Anyone would think we'd not gone through thick and thin together, that I'd not been a devoted mother to his children. It was as though they didn't give a damn who slept with Longos at night. That's men for you. It began to look as though Armenopoulos was right. The trial was postponed again and again. At that time, the courts in Salonika worked as they used to in the days of Turkish rule. The judges didn't decide according to the law, but according to your pocket. You may well ask: what did he hope to gain from all these postponements? Well, first he thought I'd get discouraged and give up the struggle. He knew I had no money. I had to earn my keep by doing dressmaking jobs in people's houses. Secondly, he thought that as time went on and the children grew up it would be more difficult for me to keep going to court. He'd send my elder boy Theodore to see me — he'd finished by then at the Tsotili school and was getting ready to take his examinations for the Law Faculty of the University — and he'd say: — "Mama, what's done is done. Why not let bygones be bygones? People are beginning to forget the scandal. Why rake up the past and give them more food for gossip? Eleni and Polyxene are growing up now. Soon they'll be wanting to get married," and so on and so on. I knew that, logically speaking, he was right. By trying to revenge myself on him I was doing harm to my children. But however good a mother I was, that didn't stop me being a woman. And as a woman, no matter how hard I tried, it was simply impossible for me to forget. After all, remember, we were living in the same town. If he'd taken her and their little bastard kids to Athens and left me to bring up my children the way I knew they should be brought up, I might have forgotten the past. Time and distance are great healers. But for me to leave Salonika, as though I were the guilty party, as though I were some kind of outcast, that was more than I could stomach. The result was that, living all the time in the same town, the old wounds never had a chance to heal. I'd pass by their house and hear the voices of people I didn't know. I'd see the lights and hear them inside singing and having fun, and I thought I'd go mad. Occasionally, I'd meet the happy couple in the street. As soon as I saw them in the distance I'd turn round and make myself scarce. I trembled at the thought of meeting them face to face. I'd no confidence in myself. I knew I was quite capable of grabbing hold of her and tearing her to shreds with my teeth. I didn't want to cause a scandal, for my children's sake. But every day there'd be something that would remind me of the past, of his treachery, of the ruin he'd brought to my house. Dimitris, the youngest, would come and tell me: "Mama, auntie Frosso beat me again today!". If only God would strike her like she struck my children! And He will, mark my words. She used to beat the child because he came to see me. They thought I tried to turn him against them. So he had to play truant from school and come to see me on the quiet. I'd take him in my arms, and kiss and hug him, and I'd tell him: — "Be patient, my love, it won't be long before they'll pay dearly for what they've done!". I had faith in God's justice. And I'd send him back to school. — "When you get home at midday," I'd tell him, "you must tell auntie Frosso you're sorry and that you won't do it again. Playing truant from school doesn't hurt them. You're only hurting me and hurting yourself." Two years went by like that. The only thorn in their flesh, the only thing that disturbed their married happiness was my daughter Eleni. Not that she was on my side. Not on your life! From the time she was a tiny tot she could never stand me. And she hadn't changed her feelings about me. As far as she was concerned, the fault was all mine. But she loved her father as though he was her lover — God forgive me for saying so. And she was furious because he'd got entangled with Frosso before she could enjoy the pleasure of being rid of me. And being the unfeeling girl she always was, she made Frosso's life a misery. Twice she gave Frosso a good hiding. And the things she called her was nobody's business. They decided to get rid of her, and the best way, naturally, was to marry her off. Well, one day old Mrs Tavlaris, my landlord's wife, poor thing, turned up and she says to me: — "Have you heard the news?" — "What news?", I say. — "They're getting Eleni married off." — "Which Eleni?" — "Your daughter." "Well, it's about time," I said, "she's always been crazy for a man. From the time she was thirteen, she used to sit at the window making eyes at the soldiers." — "Aren't you going to ask who she's going to marry?" — "Who? — ". — "Babbis!" — "I don't know any Babbis," I said. — "You can't be serious! Babbis! You know, that knock-kneed chap who stands under his mother's window and calls her a whore!" — "Oh no!", I screamed, "not him," and I rocked my head in my hands with the shame of it. "Surely they don't intend to give my child to that dirty drug-addict!" Maybe she hated me. But a mother's still a mother, when all's said and done. When her child's in danger she doesn't stop to think: that one loves me or the other one doesn't. Well, I swallowed my pride and dignity and went to wait outside their house. When I saw him coming, smart as a young dandy as always, I went up to him, twisting my fingers together and begging him to listen: "Yianni," I said, "I'm willing to forgive and forget everything you've done. If you like we'll go together this very moment to the lawyer and I'll withdraw the summons. (How many times since then he must have cursed the hour he refused to take advantage of my offer!). "I promise you," I said, "I'll disappear from the face of the earth, I'll go away and you'll never be bothered with me again as long as you live. But in God's name, don't bring ruin on our Eleni. The man you've chosen may be from a good family, but he himself is a drunken layabout, the laughing stock of the whole neighbourhood. Eleni's not sixteen yet. Let her finish school first. . . . Yianni, are you listening to me?" He seemed to have wandered off somewhere. — "I'm listening," he said. — "Do you give me your word that you'll call it off?" — "Alright, I promise." May his soul never rest in peace. He paid for his crimes, one by one. It wasn't long before he began to suffer one disaster after another, like the seven plagues of Pharoah. God may seem to smile on sinners sometimes, but He sees to it that they get their just deserts in the end. Just when you think you've got away with it your sins catch up with you, and you pay for them all at once. Venizelos arrives in Salonika, forms a revolutionary government and brings in the British and the French. And the gentleman gets arrested for supplying German submarines. Whether it was true or not I don't know. Anyway, he gets dragged before a court-martial and sentenced to twenty years in jail. They very nearly decided to shoot him. And on top of all that, they took away his two caiques. When the war ended, he was let out of jail with all the other political prisoners and, knowing the ins and outs of trade, he began gradually building up his business again. He was paid compensation for the caiques which had sunk in the meantime. He mortgaged the house to get a working capital, and so on and so forth. But before he could begin to enjoy life again, God gives him a second smack in the eye. The bigamy affair finally caught up with him! Whether the prosecutor dug out the file himself, or whether Papathanassiou did a bit of prodding I really don't know. Anyway, although I myself had given up hope of the case ever coming on, I suddenly received a summons to go to the prosecutor's office. When the trial came on, without saying a word to me, Papathanassiou turned up with all my fine husband's enemies. People I didn't even know myself. Old Thalia came to court and gave evidence about the summonses pinned on her door. Then there was an affidavit read from his own mother who said that at the time he issued the writ against me for desertion and living at an unknown address, he himself had sent me to stay with her, and so on. To cut a long story short, they brought in a verdict of guilty against both of them. He got six months, and she got two months suspended sentence because she was pregnant again. But it wasn't the prison sentense he minded so much—he paid the equivalent fine and was let out straight away. What bothered him was the shame of it. How could he face the customers he did business with now? Without losing any time, Papathanassiou—on my instructions this time—issued a second writ for alimony and for the custody of the children who were still not of age, Dimitris and Polyxene. Theodore would soon be twenty-one, and Eleni had long been married and was expecting a baby. Two days before the trial I met him by accident in the street. He looked so worn out I almost didn't recognise him. His collar seemed several sizes too big for his neck, and for the first time in his life I saw him needing a shave. I stopped in my tracks.—"Is it really you, Yianni," I said. And I began to shake with emotion. Suddenly I felt sorry for what I'd done to him. The idea that I was partly responsible for making such a miserable wreck of the only man I'd ever loved in all my life was like a dagger in my heart. I thought of rushing off to Papathanassiou straight away and telling him to withdraw the writ.—"What's the matter with you, Yianni?", I said, "where's your spirit, where's that dashing right-hand man of Pavlos Melas? What has that little bitch done to you to bring you to this state?" . . . He smiled with a bitter irony.—"What has *she* done?" When I heard him defending her I got really mad.—"Well, anyway," he said, "if that's the way you wanted it, good luck to you. But you should have thought of our children . . ."—"Don't you dare mention the name of our children", I said. "Did you think of them at all when you broke up our marriage? Do you know that while you were in prison your mistress turned our Dimitris out into the street, and he spent his nights in wagons and got mixed up with a gang of ruffians and now he's in danger of being ruined for life? Do you know our Eleni is on the point of leaving her husband? What happened to that promise of yours to call off the marriage? Is that the kind of man you are? Phtew! I spit on your sense of honour! . . ." Without saying a word, he turned round and hurried off like a man being chased. As I found out from my Polyxene later, he went home and asked them to heat up the water for a bath. And, as he went to put his foot into the tub, he passed out on the spot. I didn't go to the funeral. Not that I didn't want to myself. No matter what he'd done to me, I still loved him. If I hadn't still loved him I'd have cocked a snook at him long before and gone straight back to Athens. But my elder daughter came and urged me with pleas and threats not go to the funeral. Her in-laws, she said, would laugh their heads off when they saw *two* widows. And so I wasn't even allowed to kiss his poor corpse. Oh, Nina dear, don't let me think about it. I get all worked up with the memory of it all, and at night I get the most horrible nightmares. . . .'

12

Whenever she told me the story of Eleni's separation, she always took her son-in-law's side. Not only because she firmly believed that marriages should be permanent ('especially when there are children to think about') and it was Eleni who had broken her marriage up, but because the way she left her husband was similar to the way her own husband had left her.

— 'How could I possibly excuse it, Nina,' she would say. 'How can I excuse the filthy bitch for throwing her husband out of his house as though he were a piece of dirt, just like her fine father did to me? I'm not saying the man didn't have his faults. He drank, and he was twenty years older than her. He wasn't exactly the kind of husband I'd dreamed of for my daughter, and, as you know, when I heard about the plan to get them married I did just about everything to break it up. But she shouldn't have behaved like that, not once she was married to him and had children by him. Babbis had his faults, but he wasn't some kind of monster. He was madly in love with her. It was up to her to change him any way she wanted, to make a new man of him. But not my daughter. Instead of helping him to stop his drinking, she made his life a misery. He had to drink more and more to forget his troubles. He'd come home from work and find the house empty and the child with dirtied pants. Tired as he was, he'd sit there cleaning up the baby. And when the fine lady got back from her outing he'd say: — "Where have you been, Eleni love?" — "Where the fancy took me," she'd reply. "It's none of your business". . . . Or he'd come home and find the little child in tears. — "What's the matter with little Apostolos, Eleni love?", he'd ask. — "I've given him a good hiding" — "What for?" — "Because I felt like it!". . . . He wouldn't say anything at the time. He was a cowardly sort of man. But he used to save it up for her. When he got back home blind drunk on a Saturday night he'd grab hold of her and beat the daylights out of her. Their house was just a little way up beyond the White Tower. It wasn't very big. Just two rooms, a kitchen, and a wash-house in the yard. But it was handy for his work. There was a widower with his two children on the upstairs floor. Hadzis was his name. That was the house their first child was born in. But it died when it was ten days old. We only just managed to call the priest in time to have it baptised. Hadzis offered to be godfather, and they became close friends from that time on. Next year she was pregnant again. It was about the time I'd served a second writ on her father for alimony. The afternoon I saw him for the last time, I was on my way back from her house. I'd gone to see her and found her in tears. — "What are you crying for?", I asked. — "I've had a row with Babbis. The dirty so-and-so, the filthy bastard!" — "What's he done?" — "You may well ask. What's he done? He's made me the laughing stock of the whole neighbourhood, that's what he's done. The bastard! And then he gives me another brat of his! I'll scratch his bloody eyes out! Tomorrow first thing I'll go and get an abortion, that's what I'll do! . . ." It was the first time I'd heard she was pregnant. She hadn't told me anything. She never told me any of her secrets. — "Listen to me, my girl," I said, "you're your own mistress and I've not the slightest desire to interfere in your family affairs. But I'd just like to give you some advice, not as a mother, but as somebody older and more experienced than you are: don't get rid of the child. Once you have the child, mark my words, everything will be milk and honey again. It will give you something to keep your mind on, and it will keep Babbis out of those dreadful tavernas of his. Children," I said, "are a blessing". — "And what about you," she says, "look at all the joy and happiness you've had because of us!". It was the first time I'd heard her speak, even in-directly, with some kind of sympathy for what I'd been through. — "If it wasn't for my children," I said," If it wasn't for thinking of my duty to bring up my children, I'd have taken a dose of poison and killed myself like my poor sister

Ismini when I found out about your father. And, I ask you, what good would it have done? No matter what we may say when we're desperate and angry, life is sweet . . ." She said nothing. And when Eleni said nothing it meant she admitted you were right. She took two dresses out of the chest and gave them to me to let out for her. And it happened just as I said it would. As soon as Akis was born, Babbis swore never to set foot in a tavern again. The bickering and squabbling between them stopped overnight. Everything was going swimmingly, and I was thanking the Almighty for listening to my prayers when the poor chap got home early one day and caught her in the act with Hadzis! Any other man in his place would have kicked her out on the spot and told her to go to the devil. But Babbis, either because he loved her or because he was thinking about the child, simply turned around and crept out of his own house like a thief who had no right to be there. He went straight to a tavern and drank himself senseless. One day – I was living at Davikos's house at the time – the door burst open and Eleni came charging in like a hurricane with the baby in her arms. She threw the baby on the bed as though it were a bundle of washing and said: – "Damn you! It was you who made me have the child! Well, if it was a child you wanted, there it is! Take it and stuff it up your skirt! I'm not having any of Babbis's brats!" – "What's the poor mite done to you, you unfeeling monster, to be thrown about like that? Do you call yourself a mother or a hyena? What's got into you to make you froth at the mouth like a mad dog?" – "I'm leaving him," she said. "I'll take myself off and disappear for good. I don't want to see anybody or be seen by anybody! I'll go street-walking for my living and get my own back on all of you! And if that drunken son-in-law of yours comes asking for me, tell him I'm no daughter of yours!" – "Get your own back on us – ?", I said, "it's yourself you'll be ruining! . . ." And with that she got up and walked out, slamming the door behind her. All the time Akis had been squealing away like a stuck pig, as though he understood what was going on and was feeling sorry for himself. As though he was saying: "What a world to get born into!" He lay there howling, and I picked him up and cuddled him and rocked him and jiggled a row of beads in front of him. But nothing worked. He just went on howling. In the end I lost my patience. I put him down on the bed and gave him two stinging ones on the backside. "Shush!", I said, and just as he was getting ready to yell his head off again, I gave him two more. He opened his eyes wide and looked straight at me, as if to say: "Well, well, this one stands no nonsense. Better keep my mouth shut in case there's more where those came from . . ." From that time on, he never cried. He'd sit on the bed with a doll and jabber away to himself. He'd laugh and chuckle away for hours on end. There wasn't a quieter baby in the whole neighbourhood. Victoria, my landlord's younger daughter, simply adored him. She'd take him upstairs after lunch and sit him on the windowsill looking out into the square, and together they'd spend hours watching the trams and cars go by. Every time a motor car passed she'd say: "There's the tram!". But our little gentleman was nobody's fool. He'd get angry and shout: "Not tam, not tam, motocar!" And when Victoria insisted he'd begin to sulk and bang his fists on the windowsill and squeeze his little lips together ready to burst into tears. Then she'd take him in her arms and caress him and say she was sorry. — "Victoria," I used to tell her, "you tell Davikos if Akis doesn't listen to his grandma, to take him to the rabbis and have them drink his blood, will you?" — "Oh no!", she'd say, "Aki is a good boy. I love him so very much! . . ." Mmm! I think she loved his uncle Dimitris even more! . . . Poor papa was quite a womaniser too in his young days, if what mama says about him is true. But, thank God, he never went to quite the lengths of Theodore's father. He loved his Galatea, oh yes, he really did. But he knew her jealous nature and he liked to tease her a bit. — 'Galatea,' he would say, 'what are you doing sitting there all the time just sewing and sewing away? Aren't you fed up with it? Women ought to walk around stark naked in the streets so we wouldn't be under their spell and could concern ourselves with more serious things!' But it made the poor thing angry. She never could see the point of his jokes. She wasn't in the least broad-minded, just like my daughter she was, always taking things the wrong way. — 'Oh yes, of course,' she'd reply, 'naturally you want them stark naked. It would make it that much easier for you to do your dirty work! . . .'

But even if it's true that he had girl friends when he was younger, it was before my time. His only fault, if you can call it a fault, was his fancy for a game of cards every now and again. But it was only because he was bored, or out of sheer desperation, just like I felt during the occupation. Mama would come out with her sarcasm: 'Hmm, now that he'd left real women alone he'd suddenly got a passion for dames on cards! . . .' But she didn't mind very much. She preferred him to play cards than to run after petticoats.

Poor papa! There was never a better man than him in the whole wide world. The only mistake he ever made in his life was to turn Dino out of the house. I admit that much. What I don't admit is that he was the only one to be blamed for Dino's ruin. Dino had really been ruined a long time before, and for that nobody was to blame except mama and her pathological devotion to him. Just as Hecuba was really responsible for the ruination of Dimitris, even if his father, and Frosso, and fate and I don't know what else may have played some part in it. Often, when I heard Hecuba speaking so enthusiastically about her Dimitris and what a handsome one he was, I couldn't help remembering mama and what she did to Dino, and it just turned my insides over.

— 'Nina,' she'd tell me over and over again, 'you should have seen what a beautiful boy he was! When you saw him dressed in his sailor's outfit you'd have thought he was a prince. People just couldn't stop talking about him. And clever! I can't tell you how sharp he was. I remember his teacher saying to me one day — "Mrs Longos," he said, "I've had thousands and thousands of children pass through my hands in my thirty years as a schoolteacher. But I've rarely seen anything like your child for sheer intelligence. But you need to be careful," he said, "he's ever so sensitive, and he's at a critical age just now . . ." But that Frosso was to blame for everything! That slimy snake, please God I may live to see her crawl on the ground like the snake she is! She left the boy short of food. She turned him out of the house and let him get mixed up with rogues and ruffians. When his father got out of jail, it's true, he brought him in off the streets. That was when he bought him his first suit of clothes with long trousers. He was as proud of them as a peacock. But when he died, everything collapsed like a house of cards. I shared the furniture and what money he left with Frosso, and she took her brats and went back to Athens. I found myself a semi-basement in a Jew's house, Victoria's father it was, and I gathered my children under my wing like a broody hen with her chicks. Not Eleni, of course; she was married, and anyway she never accepted me as a mother; but the other three. And, struggling as best as we could, we began a new life, like poor people do all over the world. Theodore gave up the university and went to work — first clerking in an office and then as a sports reporter on a newspaper. Polyxene gave up her dreams of becoming a teacher and learned to make corsets and brassieres. But Dimitris, much as I begged and cried, simply refused to finish high school, even though he had only one year to go and find himself a decent easy job like his brother. I sent him to learn a trade. The husband of a woman I knew took him in as an apprentice at his printing works. And being clever at things like that, he became a first-class technician within two or three months. But he wasn't happy about it. He considered it was beneath him to be a printer. And one day he threw his overalls at the boss and walked out. He just disappeared. As we found out later, he took himself off to Mount Athos. As you know, no woman is allowed to set foot on Mount Athos — not even a female animal. But men will be men, Nina. No matter how many oaths they may swear to cast off worldly things, the spirit may be willing but the flesh is weak. When he came back he had the nerve to bring me a hundred-drachma note. – "Take it back, you dirty so-and-so!", I screamed. "How dare you bring me your filthy sinful earnings! What's the difference, I'd like to know, you dirty beast, between the man who'll take money for fixing up a monk and a woman who sells her body to the first taker? Get out of here," I screamed at him, "and never set foot in my house again! . . ." He had a funny habit. Whenever he felt guilty, he used to smile. I knew that little trick of his. Instead of blushing and hanging his head, he just gave me a broad smile and left the house. A whole month went by before he gave any sign of life. When he finally came back, I tried to make things up. – "Dimitris, my boy," I said, "let bygones be bygones. I know it's not your fault. Frosso's to blame, and your father, and just sheer bad luck. But that's no reason to continue making the same mistakes as your elders. It's time you pulled yourself together and began thinking seriously about your future. You'll soon be eighteen. Just take an example from your brother . . ." But I could have bit my tongue off for making that mistake. It made him furious to have his brother set up as an example. – "If you're going to start that old sermon all over again," he said. . . . "Not at all," I said, "who am I to sermonise you? I'm just telling you, that's all, because Mister Michaelis has asked me a dozen times when you'll be going back to work." – "I'm not going back!" – "And why not, may I ask?" – "I'm ashamed . . ." That made me hopping mad. – "Ashamed to work, are you? Ashamed to work for your living like all honest poor people? And you're not ashamed to sell your body to the monks?" He turned red as a beetroot. He slammed the door in my face and it was two months before I saw him again. He turned up without any warning one afternoon and, without any preliminaries, as though I were some banker's daughter, he says: – "Give us a hundred drachmas!" – "A hundred drachmas," I shouted, "and where, may I ask, do you expect me to find a hundred drachmas? Do you think I'm the mint or something?" –

"Well, make it fifty, then, and I'll give it back as soon as I find a job. Cross my heart. I've been promised one as a chucker-out at a card club. As soon as I've made my pile. . . ." – "Well, well, just listen to him. Chucker-out in a club, indeed! A fine job for a member of our family! And where do you think I can find even fifty drachmas? Do you ever stop to think how poor Polyxene and I slave away here to make ends meet? (Theodore had been called up for the army at that time.) Do you expect me to go and sell myself so that you can have your pocket-money, is that what you'd like?" I said. . . . When he'd gone, I was so upset that I'd have had an attack of hysterics if I'd stayed in the house another five minutes. I got dressed and went out. It seems he must have been watching out from round the corner. As soon as I left, he went back to the house, broke the lock, and took my red woollen blanket. When I got back later that evening and found the lock smashed and the bed covers missing, I just howled and howled. When he came back I threatened him that if he didn't bring the blanket back I'd go straight to the police. I'm sorry now I didn't do it. It might have stopped him before he took the road to his ruin. But how can you go to the police about your own child? I just swallowed it and said nothing. But from that time on we didn't dare leave the house empty. He was quite capable of taking away the very beds we slept in. And, if all that wasn't enough, he got mixed up with Victoria, the landlord's daughter. Theodore never had much success with women, but Dimitris was the Don Juan of Salonika. When Davikos found out about Dimitris having an affair with his daughter he was furious. For no reason at all he would start a row with me, hoping I would be compelled to leave. He accused me of encouraging the affair because I had my eye on his house. – "Me! Want your house!", I told him, "Why, you Christ-crucifying old skinflint, if you had not one, but a dozen houses and got down on your bended knees to beg him for a son-in-law, I'd rather see my son dead that married to an anti-Christ!" . . .'

Poor mama! Every time she heard somebody bring down a

curse, she would mumble some words to herself and hold her hands over her ears. This was supposed to ward off the evil by preventing the curse from being heard. My father used to tease her about it, but she was a woman of the people, with all their habits and naïve superstitions. But this time, it seems, the antidote didn't work. The curse was heard, and it was not forgotten. Oh, I know. If poor papa were alive and heard me talking like this he'd complain that I had forgotten what he always used to tell me — that everything has a logical explanation and that there are no mysterious forces to hear or be deaf to people's curses. The truth is, no matter what my daughter says about me being the spit and image of my father, as time goes on and I get older I can see that I also take after my poor mama quite a bit.

13

'. . . If you want to know what happened to my daughter, she had got to know an oil merchant from Kalamata and they'd gone off together on a holiday to Corfu. When she finally got back to Salonika she came to the house and stayed with us for a couple of months. One day she met Babbis by accident outside Modiano's, and the silly man fell at her feet and begged her to go back to him. — "Life is hell without you," he said, "please come back to the house . . ." She was pleased as Punch about it when she came back and told me what he'd said. To begin with, she kept him dangling. But when he told her about the new law for the voluntary retirement of veteran municipal employees, and that, if he decided to retire, he would get a lump sum of forty thousand drachmas in addition to his pension, she soon realised which side her bread was buttered, and agreed to go back to him. Three months later, she was pregnant again. But this time she was determined to get rid of it, and she began taking all kinds of pills. With the bitter experience I had of the previous child, I didn't dare interfere. Let her go and do exactly what she pleases, I thought to myself. I've not the slightest desire to take the blame again. But the drugs she was taking were turning her into a skeleton. The gynaecologist who saw her told her he wouldn't be responsible for her life if she tried to have an abortion. So, whether she wanted to or not, she had to keep the baby. When her in-laws found out that Babbis was planning to leave the Town Hall they tried to stop him. It may not have been much of a job, but at least it was secure. His colleagues knew his good side and his bad side. His boss liked him. And with the mixed-up sort of life he led, he wasn't really fit for any other kind of job. At the Town Hall he knew, at least, that all he had to do was to put on his false cuffs and sit at his desk scribbling on paper, and the monthly pay-envelope would arrive no matter what happened. But there it was: he'd promised my fine daughter that he'd retire so that they could buy a house with the lump sum. When the crucial moment came to hand in his resignation, he hesitated. But Eleni put her foot down, and she got what she wanted. They bought a house at Coulé-Café with part of the money, on the road towards Seven Towers. It was a mean shabby district, and the house they bought was unfinished: it had no door frames, no windows and no plumbing. But they bought it at a bargain price from some peasant woman. Her husband had died while the house was being built, and she was in a hurry to go back to her village. With the money left over, Babbis rented a café in an arcade and began trotting round the offices with a tray, serving coffee and turkish delight — from riches to rags. They hoped that with the profits of the café they could finish building the house and make a decent living. But Babbis was not the man to keep a business going. When you've spent a whole life behind a desk with a pen in your hand, you can't change into a shopkeeper overnight. And then there was the question of his drinking. Surrounded by all those shelves full of bottles of brandy and ouzo, he was like a wolf in a sheep-pen. Not to mention his open-handed generosity. He was quite crazy, the way he gave things away. His cronies would go to the café to see him, and he'd treat them to endless rounds of ouzo without taking a cent. One day, Eleni suddenly found out from their best man that he was negotiating to sell the house. She was simply furious. She grabbed the kids in her arms and rushed off to her in-laws, weeping and wailing: "Even if you have no pity for me," she says, "at least have pity on the poor grandchildren who bear your name! . . ." It made the people worried. Not so much because they took pity on her or the children. She'd fallen out with her in-laws hundreds of times already and they'd no use for her at all. But they were worried that if Babbis did sell the house, it would be they who would suffer for it. It would be they who would have to keep Babbis and pay his rent and his debts at the taverns. So they called a family council of war straight away and compelled him to register the house in my daughter's name. They knew they could put the squeeze on him. He was a well-known drunkard, and they could easily have gone to the Prosecutor and get a declaration that he was unfit to manage his own property. So, one day they went to the notary and signed all the documents, and the very next day the poor chap got home and found the house completely empty! . . . That afternoon I was sitting in our big bedroom, which was the brightest room in the house — we'd left the Davikos house by that time — and I was darning Theodore's socks. He was supposed to be leaving for Athens in a few days to take up a sports reporting job on some newspaper, and I was getting his clothes ready. And as I sat there with my darning, sadly thinking about Theodore going away and how long it might be before I'd see him again, I suddenly heard a funny kind of knocking sound at the front door. I opened the door and there was little Akis. He'd have been about four years old at the time. — "Who brought you, child?", I asked. Not a word. She'd trained him to keep his mouth shut. If she said to him "and mind you don't say a word", he'd not open his mouth, not if you were to kill him. — "Come on in, son," I said. She must be mad, I thought to myself. She must have had to go somewhere in a hurry, and left him at the door. Or she must have had to make a visit where she couldn't take the child with her. . . . Unfortunately, even after she went back to Babbis, she still kept up her affair with the oil merchant. Not for a moment did I imagine what had actually happened. I knew that from the moment he agreed to put the house in her name they'd got along together better than ever before. In fact, on the way back from the notary the evening before they'd called in at my house to announce the glad tidings, and they were acting as lovey-dovey as you please. Babbis wanted to take her to a cinema, but she pretended she had a headache and she took him off home. She had it all planned. Her decision was made. I'll give him one last pleasant night, she must have thought, just for him to remember me by . . . She must be mad as a hatter, I thought, bringing the child and leaving him standing on the doorstep. He couldn't possibly have come such a long way all by himself. Anyway, I sat him down beside me on a cushion and I gave him a plate of walnuts and a nutcracker to keep him busy. He began cracking the nuts and eating them. Every now and again, he'd remember and give me one. I went on with my darning, until it began to get dark and I got up to heat up the food for the children who were due back soon. Suddenly I heard Babbis's voice in the street outside. He was reeling drunk: "Come on out, you filthy whore, come on out you good-for-nothing bitch! Open up or I'll tear the whole place apart!" And he began to suit the action to the word, flinging a hail of stones at the verandah window. I was simply paralysed with fright. I rushed out to open the door and there he was staring straight at me with a stone in his hand.—"What have I ever done to you, you drunken old soak, that you should call me a whore! D'you think I'm your mother? What do you want of me?"—"I'll tell you what I want. I want my wife back, that's what I want! Where's my my little wifey? Eleni, little Helen, where are you?"—"Get stuffed, sod you," I shouted back at him, "you'll made us the laughing stock of the whole neighbourhood! I'll have to move house again on your account! If you've lost your Belle Helene and you think I'm hiding here, there's the house. The door's open. Go in and search if you like!" Then I explained to him how I found the child on the doorstep. Grumbling away, he went into the house and began searching under the beds and behind the doors. And when he saw I was telling the truth, he sat down on the edge of a bed and began sobbing till he choked on his tears. It was the first time I'd ever seen a man cry like that. And just as he was going to stop, he'd catch sight of his son who was still sitting on the cushion with the nutcracker in his hand and was looking at his father as though he understood what it was all about, and it would start him off again:—"My little Apostolos," he sobbed, "my little baby, Eleni's gone and left us, son, your mother's gone and shut up our house . . ."

A few days later Theodore left for Athens. In the bus on the way back from the station I cried all the way. Good luck, my son, I said to myself, may God go with you. Dear God, I said, why does it have to be this way? Why do I have to live apart from my children? One of them's gone away. Who knows what the lad will only have to face in a town like Athens! Who'll do his washing and ironing? Who can he go to with his troubles? Who can he go and cry to and get comfort from his tears? The other one lives in the same town with us. But what's the good when we see him only once in a blue moon? Who knows where he rolls around, with what kind of scum he's throwing away his young life and his handsome looks? Those were the thoughts that went through my mind. I can't describe how low and depressed I felt during those days. I took to laying out the cards, and that damned ten of clubs kept turning up time and time again. Holy Virgin, I said to myself, what's in store for me? What bad news am I going to hear? I couldn't get Eleni out of my mind. Who knows where she's sleeping out at night, I thought, dragging that poor little baby around with her. Dear Lord, what curse is this you've brought on our family? What sin are we paying for? But the ten of clubs wasn't for Eleni. One evening, Jason, one of Dimitris' fine friends, turned up and began trying to tell me something, not straight out, but humming and hawing: — "Mrs Longos," he said, "you mustn't get upset, but something's happened to Dimitris . . ." I thought I would die before he told me straight out what it was. I thought the worst, as any mother would in the circumstances. I saw my Dimitris dead, smashed into a thousand pieces. — "For God's sake, Jason," I screamed, "speak up, tell me what's happened to him!" — "Don't go on like that, Mrs Longos. It's nothing really. Just a misunderstanding. He's been locked up in the police station since yesterday . . ." — "What!", I screamed, "my child in the police station! My Dimitris in prison!" And I began to wail and beat my hands together. I threw my coat over my shoulders and ran to the police station with Jason. I went straight into the duty officer's room and began to beg and pray: "In God's name," I said, "If you've a mother of your own who loves you, tell me there's been some mistake! Tell me you're keeping my son by mistake for somebody else. Oh, I know he's an unruly boy! He's got himself mixed up with that low card-playing lot. It's not his fault. But he couldn't possibly have done anything serious enough to be locked up." — "What's your name?" he says, quite friendly and familiar. — "Longos," I said. — "Well, Mrs Longos, I can see you're a decent sort of woman and I can understand how you feel, but there's been no mistake." And he gave a slight nod to another officer who was in the room. "Your son is mixed up in a really bad case of robbery. And the worst of all is that he refuses to tell us the names of his accomplices." He glanced over at his colleague again. "That's the way young people are today. They think it's a disgrace to give away the names of a few ruffians who deserve to be punished by the law, and yet they don't think it's a disgrace to steal! . . ." I knew perfectly well how those monsters made good pickings out of their so-called law and justice, and I'd not the slightest inclination to sit there being lectured by a lousy copper, but I sat there just the same listening to him patiently. When he finished, I said: — "Tell me Inspector" — he was only a detective sergeant but I called him Inspector to butter him up — "tell me, Inspector, what exactly happened? Maybe, as his mother, I may be able to help you. He may tell me things he refuses to tell you. But I want you to promise that you'll do everything you can to see that he gets off lightly." He told me in a few words about the robbery and sent a sergeant with me — Kalapothakis, it was, who became a friend of the family from that time on — to take me down to the cells. They called for him — Longos! Longos! — and he appeared behind the bars. As soon as he saw me he turned deathly pale. He started to smile, but the smile froze on his lips. I almost fainted clean away. — "Dimitri!", I managed to say, but I could hardly get a word out. It was the first time I'd seen him behind bars. When I recovered I began talking to him, coaxing and wheedling. Finally he gave us the names of his accomplices. When the day was fixed for the trial and we found out who the judge would be, I remembered Armenopoulous. Although I hadn't seen him for years and we were no longer on close terms, I went and threw myself at his feet once again. — "Mr Prosecutor," I said, — I didn't dare use his first name like I used to — "Mr Prosecutor, you know as well as anybody the real reasons for our ruin, you know why my son has got himself into bad company, I beg you to do what you can to get him off and save him having a criminal record!" And poor old Armeno-poulos sat down straight away and, while I waited, he wrote a letter to the judge. Our lawyer managed to slip it to him just before the trial began. With Kalapothakis helping on the one side, by giving evidence to the effect that Dimitris, while he was waiting trial, showed signs of repentance and was a well-behaved prisoner, and with the judge on the other side leaning over backwards in his favour, we tried to save him. But all our trouble was wasted. He'd repented for giving me the names of his friends and was smitten with remorse. Throughout all the trial, he didn't once turn to look at me. He did everything he could to make the worst possible impression on the court, as though he was determined to get sent to prison. When the poor judge asked him, more like a father than a judge, who organised the robbery, he threw up his head like an unruly horse and shouted: — "I did!". And it ended by all the others getting three months, while mine got four . . .

. . . I was so upset I fell ill. I had trouble with my womb again. The doctor ordered more radiation treatment. Only God knows what I suffered every time I went up the hill to visit him in jail at Seven Towers. At the beginning he refused to see me. They'd tell him, "your mother's here", and he'd say, "tell her not to come again." But when he ran short of cigarettes he began begging me to come. Two months went by. One after-noon, just as it was getting dark, I'd got back from visiting him in jail and was lying down on my bed to get my strength back, when the door suddenly burst open and Eleni came in, smiling as brightly as you please, with a ridiculous hat on her head. — "You heartless little bitch!", I screamed at her, "where have you been all this time? What have you done to that poor husband of yours? How do you think you're going to live now, alone, without anyone to provide for you?" — "I don't need any providers, thank you!" — "Maybe you don't, but what about your children? Haven't you got a thought for them? How are the poor things to get on without a father?" — "They'll manage, like orphans do all over the world!" — "Aren't you afraid of God's punishment, you unfeeling thing," I said, "do you think he'll let you get away with such a crime? Haven't you learned a lesson from what happened to your father?" — "You leave father in peace," says she, "you're not fit to let his name pass your lips!" — "Leave him in peace, indeed. Oh yes, you're his spitting image, you are. You made the poor man sign the house over to you, the house he'd worked and slaved so many years to get, and the next day you just abandon him, you cruel bitch, leaving him nothing but a bare mattress on the floor for a last laugh! What are you smiling at, you drivelling idiot, what do you find so funny? And alright," I said, "suppose you did all that. After all, you can't expect roses on a rubbish heap, but at least you could have stood by me through all my troubles. Didn't you give a damn, didn't it interest you the least little bit to find out what happened to your brother?" — "What did you expect me to do? D'you think maybe I should have offered the judge a bit of you-know-what to get him off?" — "Well, well, just listen to her. Just listen to my little daughter! Just listen to those sweet-smelling words! And what about the baby?" — "I went and left it at that smart café your boozing son-in-law runs. And, if you don't want your little grandchild over here to keep you company on dark nights, I can give him to the drunkard too. He wanted a son, didn't he? Well, now he can stuff it up his backside. I want to be free. I have my own life to live!" — "Free, indeed," I said, "is there any such thing as freedom, you little bitch? And where does your kind of freedom lead? Have you been to ask Sophitsa where her daughter wound up? Did you know Rena ended up in a whore-house?" She became furious. It hurt to hear the truth. — "Just you worry about your hoodlum of a son," she said, "and stop worrying about me." — "My hoodlum of a son," I said, "is a man, and he's got a prick. No matter what he's done, there's nobody who dares say anything to him. Is it the same with a woman?" — "The same and better!" — "I hope you're right, daughter. I hope you'll never live to repent what you're saying. After all, I'm your mother, and I have a mother's feelings, no matter what you do or say . . ." She got up and left. And, not more than ten minutes later, Babbis arrived with the baby in his arms. — "Sh — she, c-c-came, mother," he said (when he was upset and sober at the same time he stuttered terribly), "sh-she came c-c-came and l-l-left the b-b-baby on a ch-chair. Wh-wh-what sh-shall I d-do with it, m-m-mother, wh-wh-where sh-shall I t-t-take it? . . ." And suddenly, Nina my dear, I realised the man had aged at least ten years. — "Leave the baby here," I said. What was I to do, poor thing. I don't want to accuse anybody. It was just fate, I suppose . . . And suddenly I found myself nursing babies. But not for long. A month later my daughter turned up again, with another ridiculous hat on her head. — "I've come to take my kids," she says. — "And where do you think you're taking them?" — "I'll take them and throw them off the battlements of the White Tower and drown them in the sea! Is there anything else you'd like to know? . . ." '

14

Then they moved house again. They used to change houses like people change their shirts. Every incident in their lives happened in a different house. It was like the theatre, where they change the scenery for every act. How Theodore managed to become so regular in his habits is a miracle. ' . . . So, as I was saying, my elder boy was in Athens. Dimitris was away in the Air Force. The Kamara house I told you about was too big and expensive for just two women living on their own. Until we knew if Theodore would find a good job and be in a position to help us out financially, we had to make economies. So we found a cheaper place in a turning off Egnatia street: two rooms and a kitchen, no windows facing onto the street and a back yard shut in by tall houses all around. It was cool in summer and you could sleep pleasantly at siesta time. But when winter came on and it began to rain and snow, the walls, for all the landlord's assurances to the contrary, began to drip with damp. And when the weather was overcast, you could hardly see your nose. All the money we saved on the cheaper rent went on extra paraffin for the lamp. On the first floor there was a dentist, no more than about forty years old. He had an old woman who kept house for him. The landlord and his wife lived on the second floor with their child. He was a good sort, gentle and polite. But the wife was as mean-tempered as they come. From the moment I set eyes on her I was certain we would never get along together. And I was right. Less than a month after we moved in the squabbles began. One of my friends, Sophitsa, God bless her, had given us a puppy. We called it Tyke. Really Nina, you can't imagine what a clever little dog it was. It did everything but talk. My Dimitris was always fond of dogs. Every time he got leave he'd come straight home, more to play with Tyke than to see us. He'd taught her all sorts of tricks. He'd throw a slipper into

the yard and she'd go chasing it and bring it back. Or he'd say
"souza" and the little devil would get up on her hind legs and
wouldn't get down no matter what until he said the word
"down". She was better than anything you ever saw at the
circus. But that bitch of a landlady couldn't stand dogs. And
then the grumbling began: first of all she complained that the
dog had fleas, then she said it had tapeworm. "Vassili," she'd
shout to her little boy, as loud as she could to make sure I
heard, "come on upstairs away from that dirty animal or you'll
catch the tykeworm! . . ." She grumbled constantly that the
dog peed in the garden and was ruining her sunflowers. —
"Sunflowers! What sunflowers, Mrs Margaritis," I told her, "I
hope you're not serious. Or are we just standing here talking
for the sake of making conversation? Have you ever seen a ray
of sunshine in this tomb of a backyard of yours to grow a sun-
flower with?" Just so as you don't imagine, my good woman,
I said to myself, that you're the only one who can play with
words. I was determined to give as good as I got. finally
she threatened that unless I got rid of the dog she'd give it a
dose of poison. — "Just let her try, that's all," said Dimitris,
"just let her give that dog poison and she'll get what's coming
to her!" — "Just you keep that attitude to yourself, my boy,"
I told him, "I've not the slightest inclination to start trouble.
You've blotted your copy-book enough already. You just leave
things to me. I know exactly how to put her in her place at
the proper time." The proper time wasn't long coming. One
day she came out onto the back stairs and began shouting good
and proper. — "How much longer are we going to have to put
up with that filthy tyke . . ." and so on and so on. At first I
pretended not to hear. But when I realised she was determined
to make me reply, I went out into the yard and hoisted my
dressing gown up over my backside. I wasn't wearing so much
as a pair of knickers underneath. And then I let her have it:
prrrr!!! How it came out pat, just at the right moment, Nina,
I'll never know. A real beauty, made to order. And I said: —
"That, Madame Margaritis, is my answer to you, given in

your mother tongue!" And I went back inside, slamming the door in her face! . . . ." '

— 'You don't mean it, Hecuba! You really showed her your backside?'

— 'And why not, if you please? I'd had about as much of her as I could take. There are some people you can't bring to their senses just with words. And, the fact is, from that day on she avoided starting rows with me. Every time we met at the front door she went as red as a beetroot and said nothing. She finally understood that she was no match for me and my backside. But I'm only telling you all this so you can understand the sort of terms we were on with our landlords when, one fine morning, completely out of the blue, my great lady of a daughter turns up and, without any preliminaries, announces — "I'm coming to stay with yer!". That was how she spoke. She was the only one of all my children who had picked up that dreadful Salonika accent. — "I'm coming to stay with yer!", she says, without so much as asking if I could have her or wanted to have her. I knew this time the landlady would have every right to be hopping mad. But even if it wasn't a question of the landlady, there was simply no room for her. The place we lived in, like I said, was very small. We'd only just managed to squeeze our own furniture in. But how was I to refuse? She was always complaining that we didn't treat her as a member of the family. You simply can't get on with Eleni. She's always flying off the handle and ready to misunderstand. She thinks the whole world is against her. — "Alright," I said, "come if you like. We'll be a bit cramped, but so long as we're easy going with each other we'll manage fine." About the landlady and the rows we had with her I said not a word. She would have thought I was saying it on purpose to put her off. At first we got along very well. The landlady didn't say anything, and Eleni herself was as well-behaved as could be. But not for long. We soon began squabbling over the slightest thing.

She'd start a row because I'd take Akis in my arms and sing him a little song my poor mama used to sing: "I have a son and I'm full of pride, he'll bring me a lovely bride; I've a daughter, woe is me, how can I find her a dowry . . ." She'd get mad because I didn't make a fuss of her daughter. God forgive me, I'd never seen an uglier child in my life. She had a head like a swollen pumpkin. — "What's it got to do with you?", I said, "aren't I entitled to make a fuss of whichever child I like? What's stopping you cuddling your daughter if you want to?" It made her furious. She said I had a weakness for boys, and it would be they who'd be my ruin one day. She said that I'd been the cause of Dimitris coming to no good because I'd spoiled him and pampered him, and that I used to beat her without any reason when she was little because I was jealous. Without reason, if you please! Why, if I were to sit down one day and tell you the things she did when she was little it would make your hair stand on end. — "You were jealous of me," she said. I, Hecuba, jealous of Eleni! Can you imagine! — "You were crazy and hysterical, that's why our father left you and went off with Frosso!" And, with one thing leading to another, we'd start a row you could hear all over the neighbourhood. Up to then neither the landlord nor his wife had said a word. But after she'd been staying with us for two months, he took me aside one day and, ever so politely, he said: — "Mrs Longos, you know I've never interfered up to now in the arguments you have with my wife. I know she's a bit difficult and touchy. Anyway, it's my rule never to get involved in women's squabbles. But on this business of your lodgers, Mrs Longos, I really think we ought not to overdo things . . ." I was so embarrassed I didn't know what to say. After all, God bless them there were three of them. — "I know, Mr Margaritis," I said, "but it won't be long now before her house is finished. There's only the plastering to be done. Have a little patience. As you know," I said, "her husband's died and left her with two orphans." What else could I tell him to work up his sympathy? – "It's my duty as a mother to help her . . ." And again I didn't say a word to Eleni about what had happened. I discussed it only with Polyxene. – "Why don't you make an effort to find another place", she told me, "am I supposed to take the responsibility for that too?" Poor Polyxene! She was always like the man of the house. She brought her wages straight home. And, as if that were not enough, I suddenly found out that Eleni was having an affair with the dentist upstairs! – "Wasn't it you who told me," she said with her usual impertinence, "to get off with some up and coming young man and marry him to give my children a father? So what are you so damned angry about now? . . ." Yes, Nina, on top of everything else, she had the nerve to jeer at me. – "Go tell that to the marines, you little tart," I told her. "Aren't there enough men for you in the world without getting mixed up with somebody living in our own house. How do you think we'll look when the landlady finds out? We'll never be able to lift our heads in public again!" But of course I had to swallow that too. Alright, I said to myself, we'll just have to wait and see what comes of it. Quite likely she'll manage to hook him, and it'll be the saving of her and of us. One day, it must have been about five or half past in the afternoon, Sophitsa came rushing into the house. "I can't stay long," she said, "I've got troubles with my Rena. I'll tell you all about it some other time. I just popped in to see how you were getting on. Where have you been all this time? Have you heard what happened to old Davikos, your landlord?" – "What?" – "You don't mean to tell me you don't know! Don't you ever read the newspapers?" – "When Theodore was here he used to bring home the 'Phos', but now he's gone we don't take it any more. We have to economise where we can. But tell me, Sophitsa dear, what happened to Davikos?" – "He set fire to his house to collect the insurance." – "Go on!" – "As I live and breathe! The whole top floor was burned to a cinder." – "Well I'll be blowed! You wouldn't believe it possible!" – "Well really, Hecuba," she said, "sometimes anyone might think you were a child of three. You know perfectly well what those dirty Jews are like. What do you expect of people who killed Christ on the cross? . . . ." There was a Christian family living on the upstairs floor, and they owed Davikos seven months rent. Not only that, but Davikos needed the rooms for his eldest daughter Alegra. She was on the point of getting married to a Jewish textile merchant, and they had nowhere to live. Davikos had already taken out three eviction orders against them but it didn't do any good. They were well in with the police. So he thought up the fire to get rid of them. He waited one night till they were all asleep, jumped into their kitchen through the fanlight, started the fire and walked out of the front door as large as life. He went across the road to the café, ordered himself an ouzo and sat there chatting with the customers to give himself an alibi. At least, that's what the insurance company's lawyer said at the trial. It wasn't long before smoke began to pour from under the roof. Davikos rushed into the road and began to beat his breast. — "My house is on fire! My house is on fire!", he shouted. Meanwhile, the people in the burning apartment and had woken up and, panic-stricken, they began throwing their furniture down through the windows into the street two floors below. Davikos's daughters rushed out of the house in their nightdresses, then they suddenly remembered their grandmother — Nona they used to call her — who couldn't walk by herself, and they began screeching away like the Jew-girls they were. The whole neighbourhood was up in arms. By the time the fire engines arrived the top floor was burning away like a bonfire. It was a miracle the fire didn't spread to the rest of the house. Next day, Davikos turned up at the insurance company office to make his claim and collect the cash. But the company sent an expert to see the house and he reported that it was a case of arson. So they prosecuted him. But the old Jew bastard got off scot free. With the insurance money he collected he not only re-paired the burned top floor and turned it over to Alegra and her Jew-husband, but he also bought her a plot of land out in the suburb at Harilaou. When Sophitsa had left I went and routed out Eleni. "Come on Eleni," I said, "get up. We'll go and have a look at the house and get a breath of fresh air. We'll start growing fungus if we stay in all the time." She hardly ever went outdoors ever since she had struck up with the dentist. We took the kids by the hand and began walking down towards the square. That same afternoon, as the devil would have it, Dimitris was out on leave—he was stationed at the Sedes Air Force base at the time. He went home, found the front door locked, opened it by his special system with a nail, went in and had a meal (there was some stewed aubergine in the pot), and left. It began to get dark and I winked at Eleni that it was time to go. Victoria had greeted us with all kinds of fuss and palaver. She was still madly in love with my son. She showed us the house and even made us some coffee, but I didn't want to stay any longer. Davikos might have come in at any moment. And I didn't want him to get the idea we were trying to get round his daughter because we were after his wretched house. Since it was July and steaming hot, I said: "Why don't we go and sit in the park for an hour or so?" — "Why not?" . . . On the way we passed the chemist shop where Polyxene worked and we called in to tell her where we would be, so that she could join us and we could all go home together. By coincidence, as we were sitting on the park bench, I was spotted by a woman I knew from way back, from the time I was still living with my fine husband. We got to talking about old times and sent the children off to play by themselves. — "Take your sister's hand," I said to Akis, "and off you go to play with the other children round the fountain. But keep your eyes and ears open now. The moment we call for you you're to come back at once!" — "Who's children are they?" — "My daughter's." — "What lovely little children they are! You must be very proud of them," she said to Eleni. Eleni preened herself, obviously pleased with the compliment. It was the first time I'd ever seen her take a pride in her children the way all mothers do, and to my great surprise (for she was usually too high and mighty to be pleasant to my friends) she chatted away as pleasant as could be. And what a lovely evening it was! A soft breeze blew in from the sea, and a gramophone played in the distance from some café. That was the time when "Rezenda" was all the rage — "Sweet Rezenda, in years long past and quite forgotten, please tell me why . . ." — and, as we chatted on about this and that, the time passed pleasantly till Polyxene came to fetch us. She bought us all an ice cream, we collected the children and set off all together for home in the sweetest possible mood. You can't imagine, Nina, how happy I was that evening! I just can't describe the joy I felt. I just couldn't get over the way Eleni was behaving so well. What's got into her suddenly, I asked myself. Coming with me to Davikos's and then to the park, without so much as a murmur! And so sociable, too! What kind of miracle was this! I simply couldn't believe it, and I crossed my fingers and prayed I wouldn't suddenly wake up and find it was all a dream. Dear God, I said to myself, I know I've sinned in my life, maybe out of sheer stupidity. And you've punished me for my sins. But enough's enough! I've suffered as much as I can stand. Please, dear God, let me grow old in peace; let me live in love and happiness with my children, without spite and hatred. There's no reason to be squabbling all the time with my Eleni. What is there to squabble about? The poor thing's had an unlucky life, just like me. She's not to blame. It was all that Frosso's fault, and her father's when he made her marry Babbis. But, after all, what's done is done. Dear Lord, let her catch the dentist now and not let her youth and beauty go to waste! If you won't have pity on her, at least show some mercy for her children. Those poor innocent babies . . . what have they done to deserve such punishment, why should they pay for the sins of the grown-ups? . . . . When we reached the house I went on ahead with the key to open the door. I was just going to put the key into the lock when the door swung open by itself! We rushed inside. I thought I'd faint clear away by the time I could find the matches to light the lamp. Eleni snatched

110

the lamp out of my hand and rushed over to the sideboard she kept her jewellery in one of the drawers. I saw her hand go to her face with the shock. – "The pendant!", I screamed. "Eleni! Child! don't carry on like that! Control yourself! Are you sure you've looked properly?" Blast you, God! So you won't leave me in peace yet! What kind of a God are you when you refuse to listen to a mother's prayers! Damnation on Davikos and the park! Why the hell did I have to go out and leave the house all alone? – "What shall we do now?", I said to Polyxene, "who can we turn to for help?" The pendant was a wedding present from her father-in-law, one of the best jewellers in Salonika. It was of solid gold, with a ruby the size of a hazel nut in the middle and little diamonds all around. In fact Eleni had just been thinking of taking it in for valuation. If she'd been offered a good enough price, she would have sold it to pay the builders to finish her house. Naturally, we all suspected Dimitris straight away. Eleni kept on fainting away as often as we revived her. I felt really sorry for her. I went straight out and began a round of his café haunts, one after the other. I went into every one and asked the owner and the customers if they had seen him. Nobody had. I was just on the point of going back home with nothing to show for my trouble when suddenly I thought of Darkie. She was a tart he used to go with from the time he was a boy of seventeen – on an unprofessional basis, mind you, because he tickled her fancy. Now she'd progressed in her career. She was a madam and had lots of girls working for her. The "house" was at the back of the fire station. She lived on the top floor, with a separate entrance. I knew all this from Dimitris himself. So far from being ashamed, he always liked to boast about his exploits with loose women. So I took the tram, got off at the Fountain, and asked the way to Darkie's house. The entrance was separate, but it had an open iron staircase and you could see everything that was going on down in the yard. I saw soldiers and sailors coming in and out and I thought I was going to be sick. I simply couldn't understand how they could bring themselves to queue up to go to bed with a woman who'd been in bed with somebody else five minutes earlier. Better I'd not lived to bring you into the world, my son, I said to myself as I stood waiting for somebody to answer my knock on the door. For your sake I've sunk so low as to come to a brothel! . . . . After a long wait, the door was opened by an old hag. You could see from her face what she'd done for a living when she was much younger. — "Tell your mistress I want to talk to her. I'm Dimitris's mother," I said. . . . But before the old woman could go inside, Darkie herself came to the door. She'd heard the conversation and came out. I've no idea why they called her Darkie. She was a pale pasty colour, with great rolls of flabby flesh all over her. Her face was painted and powdered like a clown's and she wore a sloppy dressing gown, red as hell's fire. God, I thought to myself, how can a son of mine bring himself to sleep with such a monster? — "Don't be alarmed," I said, "I've nothing against you, and I haven't come to make a scene. You've a fancy for young ones and you've got my son. Good luck to you! But just one thing I beg of you. In God's name, if you believe in God, I want you to tell me if he's here. I absolutely must see him if he is. It's urgent. Something's happened to his sister," I said. She seemed to be relieved. She stared at me hard and looked me over from head to toe, weighing me up. — "Wait a minute," she said and went inside. Then I heard muffled voices and, before very long, there was my son, in pyjamas if you please. They were too big for him (God knows which one of her fancy men they belonged to!) and he'd turned up the cuffs of the jacket and trousers. As soon as he saw me he smiled that guilty smile of his and opened his mouth to say something. But I didn't let him get a word out. — "You black-hearted rogue, you dirty dog," I screamed, "would to God I'd never lived to bring you into the world! Give me back your sister's pendant or I'll go this very minute and tell the police!" — "What pendant, mama," he says. Either he was innocent or he was putting on a splendid act. — "Don't you dare play the innocent with me, young man,"

I said. "I suppose you didn't break into the house this afternoon!" — "I opened the door with a nail," he said, "then
I ironed my tunic, ate an aubergine, gave Tyke some food and
left. I've no idea what pendant you're talking about. I didn't
even know Eleni had a pendant." — "Do you swear on your
father's bones?" — "I swear on your life, may you live to be a
hundred!" — "Never mind about my life," I said, "if you had
the slightest interest in my life you'd have mended your ways
long before this. Swear on the bones of your father!" — "You
really are a laugh," he said, "you know perfectly well that I
don't believe in swearing, but since you insist, I swear . . ."
— Then Darkie broke in: "If he says he didn't take it he didn't
take it!". Trying to teach her grandmother to suck eggs! As
if I couldn't tell when my own son was telling lies or telling
the truth. "Are you sure," she said, "did you have a really
good look? The same thing happened to me last year. I thought
I'd lost a golden bracelet and I suspected poor Grace of taking
it (Grace, if you please, was the old whore-madam who'd
opened the door to me). And it turned out to be sinfully unfair.
I went to a medium and she told me: the bracelet is in your
house; search and you will find it. So I did look again, and I
found the bracelet in the basket with the dirty clothes . . ." I
said nothing. I just looked at her as if to say: "Now tell us
another one." I hadn't the slightest intention of starting a
conversation with her. I may have set foot on your threshold,
you filthy old bitch, I thought to myself, but just don't get the
idea into your head that you're my equal. To tell you the truth,
Nina, it's not my habit to condemn a woman just because she
has a few men friends. I know perfectly well that some of those
prostitutes, when you really come down to it, are purer and
better than many a blushing virgin. But there are limits. She
was just too much for me to take. I couldn't help thinking she
was sleeping with my son and my insides simply turned over.
— "Get dressed," I told him "and come with me. I want you
to take an oath in front of your sister that it wasn't you who
took it. I can't face going back alone." — "Go on, Mimi, go with

113

her," said Darkie, as though we needed her permission, and pulled a long face. You see, we were spoiling her evening for her. He went inside and put on his clothes; then we took the tram back to the house. The children were asleep. Polyxene was lying down on the bed, but she was awake. Eleni was sitting on the sofa with a handkerchief in her hand. She looked like a mourner at the side of a corpse. But she livened up as soon as she saw her brother. She sprang to her feet and went for him like a tigress. Dimitris caught her by the arms and began to twist them. "Don't you try to get tough with me," he said, "or I'll spoil your beauty for you!" — "For God's sake let go of her," I shouted, "can't you see she's upset, what with losing her valuables? Eleni my child," I said to her, "your brother swears on his father's bones that he didn't even know you had the pendant. Have another look, dear; the devil may have hidden it on purpose to send us all this aggravation. Darkie told me she once lost a golden bracelet and turned the place upside down to find it; then she went to a medium and . . ." If her eyes could have shot poison at that moment I would have dropped on the spot. — "Medium, eh?", she screamed, "I'll show you! Medium indeed! I'll show the lot of you!" . . . And with that she tore out of the house, slamming the door behind her. I sank down on the sofa, utterly exhausted. — "You dirty rogue!", I shouted at my son, "not a day's happiness have I seen since the day you were born; the ikon of St Dimitrios wept the moment you came into the world. You'll always spread ruin and unhappiness wherever you go. Get out! . . . Get out and never let me set eyes on you again! Go back to that blood-sucking whore of yours! You ought to be ashamed of yourself, a strong young man like you sleeping with a hag older than your own mother! . . ." He got up and left. He could hardly have reached the corner of the street before Eleni came back with two plain clothes men. . . .

Next day was a Sunday. Polyxene stayed home and tried to console me, for I simply couldn't get over what had happened. — "Don't carry on like that," she said, "after all, you know your daughter. She's a schizo just like you are. When all's said and done, there's not much to choose between you. You're a pair of tough nuts, the two of you, and that's why you're always squabbling." Polyxene had always been the most logical and level-headed of all my children. She always tried to stay out of my fights with Eleni. — "What do you mean, that's why we're always squabbling, you little snot," I told her. "I suppose I took the pendant, or it's my fault if that ruffian came and broke open the door and let the thieves get in? Weren't we getting alone fine together all afternoon? And even if he did take it — may God cut off his hands at the root for it — was there any need for the bitch to bring the damned coppers back into my own house, questioning me as though I were a confirmed criminal?" — "You're making a mountain out of a molehill," she said. That's what she always told me, she always accused me of exaggerating. — "Dear Lord, dear sweet Lord," I said, "why did I ever agree to have that Eleni in my house? What am I to do now? What can I do for the best?" — "You can just sit tight and do nothing, and stop working yourself up into a state, that's what you can do!" — "And what if they arrest him and find out it really was his doing and they send him to the clink?" — "It'll serve him damn well right!" She wasn't a mother and couldn't understand what a mother feels. Maybe she'll become a mother one day, then she'll remember what I suffered. We sat down to eat. I ate and I cried. Try as I would, I couldn't keep the tears from my eyes. — "I simply can't understand what kind of a person you are," said Polyxene. "All I know is that when people are really upset they lose their appetite. You don't seem to have lost yours at all. So why don't you turn off the water tap and behave like a grown woman!" I was furious. She always used to accuse me of playacting. She still does. It's impossible to make her understand that the more upset I am the hungrier I get. It's the way nature made me, I can't help it. But she could never understand that. I almost started squabbling with her. Eleni had gone off with her children to eat at some tavern. When they came back, the kids went out to the yard to play until it was time for their siesta, and my daughter flopped down on her mattress — we hadn't put up a bed to save space — and began to smoke like a chimney. She stubbed out one cigarette and lit another continuously. My heart went out to her as I watched, but I didn't dare say a word. Eleni's like a wild jungle animal. You can see its stepped on a thorn and is in pain, and when you go to take the thorn out it turns on you and bites. Suddenly Tyke began to bark. She barked happily, like all dogs do when they play with children. I went out into the yard to bring the children indoors. From the time the landlady had stopped her grumbling I tried as much as I could not to give her cause for complaint. — "Come inside, children," I said, "it's midday and people are trying to get a bit of rest." But Eleni, who was looking for an excuse to blow off steam, shot up off the mattress and came out into the yard, kicking and cursing at the children: "Shoo! Go on, you little Babbis bastards, get out of here. Get on inside and keep your little mouths shut or I'll tear you all limb from limb! If it wasn't for you I'd never have had to ask for her charity!" Meaning me. — "What have the poor little kids ever done to you, you horrible witch, to deserve that kind of treatment. If you have to wallop somebody to satisfy your bloodthirsty instincts and get it out of your system why don't you lay into me, you fiendish bitch! Just you wait, you filthy cow, the day will come pretty soon when you'll be sorry for the way you've treated me and your children, but it'll be too late." — "Oh, I'll be sorry, will I? Alright then, I'll give them a really good hiding and we'll see if your prophecy comes true!" And she grabbed them off the sofa where they were sitting quiet as lambs and began pitching into them with kicks and punches in all directions. — "You murdering bitch," I shrieked, "leave the poor little fatherless mites alone in their misery! Call yourself a mother or a hyena? May God give you some of your own medicine, if there is a God, and beat you black and blue!" — "Oh, there's a God alright," she said giving me a shove that sent me sprawling on my back on the sofa.

"And since there is a God, he'll grant my prayer to see you peg out like a dog! I know what you want. You want to see me completely ruined, to see me begging for bread on the streets, so you can have the last laugh! But, don't worry, you'll never live to see the day! You'll never have the laugh on me! I'll not let you bring me to my ruin, as you brought our father to his! I'll live and I'll prosper, if only to see you bust!" . . . And with that she stamped off into her room and slammed the door in my face. – "Live and prosper, indeed!", I shouted after her. "Like hell you will. Oh yes, you can play the fine lady now, I'd forgotten, now you're to become the dentist's wife! Ha, ha, ha!" – "Mama," said Polyxene, "will you please calm down! Or are you determined to create more trouble?" – "Just leave me alone, will you? I'm upset and I've a right to speak my mind. When you're upset you like to shut yourself in your room and stop eating. It's my way to eat and to speak, and nothing you can do is going to change my habits. It's better to get it off our chests rather than keeping things locked up inside ourselves." – "But don't you understand that you simply make matters worse that way?" – "No, I don't. When you fall out with people you love, nothing's worse than keeping silent. If she was a stranger I wouldn't say a word, or at the very most, I'd lift up my skirts and show her my backside too, like I did to the landlady. But she's my daughter. How can I listen to the monstrous things she says without replying? Didn't you hear her say that I was responsible for your father's ruin?" – "And so you were!", Eleni shouted from her room, "you're responsible for the ruin of all of us! It was you who ruined that rogue of a son of yours, it was you who encouraged him not to give a damn for anything Frosso said, and that's why she had to throw him out of the house. But since you love him so much, he'll be your punishment from God! First you'll see him rotting in jail and then you'll peg out from the aggravation!" – "Oh really! Just listen to her talk!", I shouted back, "forgive her, Lord, she's stark staring mad and doesn't know what she's saying. Don't pay any attention to her!" – "I know bloody well what I'm talking about," she screamed, "ask your other daughter and see what she tells you. Don't get the idea, just because she's polite and doesn't say anything, that she agrees with you. Go on, ask her!" – "So it was my fault that your father deserted me?" I asked Polyxene. "Was it?" Polyxene said nothing. – "Yes it was," shouted Eleni again from inside. "It was all your fault, with your jealousy and your hysterics, as though he were the only man in the world to have a few girl friends! You had enough lovers yourself, didn't you! We know all about it, don't you worry! All Salonika knows about it!" – "I had lovers? Me? Name me just one! Go on, just one!" – "What about Papathanassiou!" – "What Papathanassiou?" – "Go on with you! The lawyer, of course! Don't pretend you don't know who I mean!" – " I had Papathanassiou for a lover! Well that's one for the book, I must say!" – "Well if he wasn't your fancy man why did he take on the case for nothing?" – "Because he hated your father on account of his politics, as you know perfectly well, and he wanted to get his revenge on him through me. But even if Papathanassiou was my lover, what has that to do with it? We kept company after your father had deserted me. I was alone and without a friend in the world. If I sinned, not just with Papathanassiou but with a hundred others, God will judge me for it. Can you name me a single friend I had when I was living with your father?" She didn't reply. – "Alright then," I said, "let's just skip all that. What's the good of raking over the past? The more you stir up the dung the more it stinks. So open your door now and let's talk to each other as mother and daughter should. Let's sit down together and consider what's to be done. I swear I don't hold it against you that you brought in the coppers. Whatever you may say, I still love you. After all, I'm still your mother." – "I have no mother!", she shouted from behind her door. "I have nobody. My own brother steals from me instead of helping me. Only one man in this world really loved me, and you killed him!" – "Loved you! Pardon me while I laugh!", I said. "If he loved you so much why did he marry you off to that drunken husband of yours? Eh? I've got you there! Why did he give you that Babbis for a husband? . . ." And suddenly the door opened and Eleni came tearing out like a tigress. She came for me with her fingernails, pushed me backwards onto the sofa and began to pummel away with her fists. Polyxene was in the toilet and came rushing out when she heard the commotion.—"Eleni!", she shouted, "shame on you, hitting your own mother!" She tried to grab me away but only got kicked for her trouble.—"Get away," screamed Eleni, "or I'll lay into you too. I've promised myself to give her a hiding she'll remember!" And with that she went back to work on me. The children squealed and sobbed as though it was they who were getting the beating. But the more they screamed the more furious she became. I made no resistance at all.—"Go on, daughter," I said, "punch away. Harder harder. That's right. It's what I deserve for the milk I fed you from my breast . . ."—"Poison!", she screamed.—"Go on, daughter, beat me, beat me. Don't be afraid. I'm not Eleni. There's no fear of my going to the police!". And my eyes flooded with tears like a fountain. Not from the beating, but from the sheer misery of it all. But nothing stopped Eleni. When she finally got tired of punching she went into her room and locked the door from the inside. With my hair all over the place, with bleeding lips and my eyes all puffed and bruised, I sat up on the floor and looked at Polyxene as though I were seeing a stranger. I felt as though I'd drunk a hundred gallons of wine. The poor girl went crying into the kitchen and boiled up some water for hot compresses. When I'd recovered somewhat and got my voice back, I said—"Come on, let's go. Since we can't turn her out of our house we'll leave ourselves." We walked slowly down towards the Square without saying a word. By instinct we walked towards Sophitsa's house. When she opened the door to us and saw how I looked she was flabbergasted.—"What on earth has happened?" she said, "how did you get into that state?"—"It's nothing, Sophitsa," I said, "don't worry. I fell down and banged myself on the doorknob. Be a love and fix me a cup of coffee without sugar. It'll revive me." She didn't swallow it, of course. She was nobody's fool. But she didn't say anything. She made us some coffee, gave us a spoonful of apricot, and we sat down and chatted for half an hour about the troubles she was having with her daughter Rena. She was sick of whoring but, try as they might, they couldn't get her off the police Register. But instead of recovering, I felt worse, as though I would choke. The house was stuffy and untidy. They'd had people in the night before playing cards and it hadn't been properly cleaned and aired. Suddenly I felt I was going to suffocate. If I'd stayed there another moment I'd have passed out. — "Come on, Polyxene," I said, "let's go. Bye-by Sophitsa, and thanks for the coffee. I'll come round one of these days to fix your coat and we can have a nice chat. . . ." We went out into the street. It would have been about five o'clock and the heat was still enough to fry an egg on the asphalt. The streets and pavements were bone dry, and the passing carts kicked up clouds of dust. The shops were still shut. The men were playing backgammon in the cafés. That fine son of mine happened to be sitting at one of them as we passed. He saw us and came out intending to speak to us. — "Walk on quickly!" I said to Polyxene, "pretend we haven't seen him." But he caught up with us. When he saw my face I could see the storm gathering in his eyes. It wasn't difficult for him to understand what had happened. Without so much as a word, he turned away and began running towards the house. I thought I would faint clean away. — "God help us now, Polyxene," I said, "he'll go to the house and murder her. It'll be the end of both of them. You've got young legs. You must rush and catch him in time!" She ran on ahead and I followed behind as fast as my legs would carry me towards the house. But just as we reached the corner of our street, struggling for breath, we were only just in time to see Eleni rush wildly out of the front door, barefoot, with her dressing gown torn to shreds, and run crazily up the hill towards the police station. Dimitris followed behind her. He

120

seemed absolutely calm and adjusted his trouser belt as he went. — "You bloody murderer!", I screamed at him. "You've gone and killed your own sister, your own flesh and blood! Go, and never let me set eyes on you again! He who lives by the sword, shall perish by the sword! . . ." And with that I went into the house, and as I made for the sofa the whole room began to whirl round like a top. My head dropped on to my chest and I fainted away . . .'

15

The next day Eleni collected her things and the children and, finished or unfinished, she moved into her own house. A few days after that, Hecuba also moved house again. After all the scandal and the police coming to the house she simply couldn't look her landlady in the face. In the new house they went to Polyxene took ill again and nearly passed away. The doctor had forbidden her to swim in the sea because she'd suffered from bronchial trouble for years.

— 'But you know what children are, Nina. Stubborn as mules. They always think they know best. One Sunday she went off with some girl friends to Carabournaki without telling me anything. They hired a boat to go diving from, and as she was getting ready to dive off, she slipped and hit her chest on a piece of iron sticking out from the front of the boat. They brought her home half-dead. I sent for the doctor: — "Quick," he said, "she's got an internal haemorrhage; get some ice at once!". And so we went on, ice and injections, ice and injections, and we just managed to snatch her from an early grave. But if you're poor you're not allowed to be ill. As soon as she stopped going to work, the weekly pay packet stopped too. I began doing odd sewing jobs, like I did the time my husband left me. But what was I to do first? Sewing or acting the nurse? I'm inclined to be a bit nervy, as you know. I simply haven't got the patience to sit for hours at the sewing machine like my sister Aphrodite does. And I didn't dare write to Theodore. I knew he'd found a job on the 'Acropolis' newspaper, but he was getting paid next to nothing. He couldn't keep himself and us at the same time. I sold a fur I had, the last relic of the things I had when I was still with my husband. But the money from that didn't last very long. I sold an old hand sewing-machine I had; that didn't keep us very long either. God knows what would have become of us if it hadn't been for Green-eyes turning up . . . One evening I was in the kitchen frying some sprats when there was a knock on the front door. I went to open the door, and there was an old man with frizzy grey hair and green eyes. — "Good evening," he said. — "Good evening. What is it you want?" — "Is this where Miss Longos lives?" — "Yes. What do you want her for?" — "I want to see her in person." — "In person?", I said, "I'm afraid you can't. She's ill. You can tell me anything you have to say to her. I'm her mother." But, of course, he couldn't tell me what he had to say to her, you know what I mean Nina. I showed him into Polyxene's room, but I was just boiling inside. My instinct was never wrong. I knew something fishy was going on. And, believe me, there was! As soon as he got to the bedside, he stooped down and then, if you please, he kissed her on the cheek as though he'd known her for years! Polyxene turned red as a beetroot. Well, well! I thought to myself, what's all this? So she's been getting to know people like this behind my back, and here am I completely in the dark! But I didn't say anything in front of him. After all, she wasn't a child any more. She was turned twenty-three that year. I didn't dare make a fuss right away and ask her what it was all about. I ran back to the kitchen to see if my sprats were burning. And when the mystery visitor finally left I grabbed her by the back hair and said: — "And now, if you don't mind, perhaps you'll be good enough to tell me who that was? Where did you meet him, and who does he think he is kissing you in front of me like that?" — "He's a notary from Kavalla," she said. "I met him when he came to the chemist shop one day to buy a truss." — "And just because he's a notary from Kavalla and has a rupture, does that entitle him to go around kissing all the girls he sees? You'll have to think of a better one that that, my girl!" — "Oh, please leave me alone," she said, "I'm a grown-up woman and I don't have to ask anybody's permission to do what I like and see anyone I like!" And she takes a five hundred drachma note, crisp and new, out of her bosom and waves it in front of my face. — "Just forget about the melo-

123

drama and the whys and wherefores, will you, and run along and pay what you owe to the grocer, will you!" – "Well, well!", I said, my hands going to my cheek, "so that's the way of it, is it? Well, my girl, if you're going to take the same road as that fine sister of yours, what's the use of me sitting here rubbing in linaments and looking after you? I might as well bury you straight away, and have done with it!" And that started off the row. She began to cry, and it brought on a bout of coughing and nausea so bad I could hardly bring her round again. Alright, I thought to myself, I'll just ignore it for the time being and we'll see what comes of it all. What else could I do? As the old saying goes: if you spit upwards, you spit at God; if you spit downwards, you spit in your beard. Whatever I did, it would do no good. Green-eyes was old, true, but she wouldn't be the first girl or the last to take an elderly man. If he really intended to marry her, as my daughter said he did, it wasn't such a disaster. But, meantime, I made sure that they were never left alone together for a single moment. Cerberus himself couldn't have been more careful. Not that they could have got up to anything very serious. She was ill, and her body stank from all those methylated spirits I'd been rubbing her with; and he was no gay young spark himself. All he did was to sit at the foot of her bed like a lazy tom and talk to her by the hour. That went on for about three months. Polyxene was almost completely cured and she'd be ready to go back to work in a month or so. One night I saw Eleni in my sleep. She was still a little girl in the dream, about the age when we were still living in the Bey's house. Except that the house wasn't exactly the same. You know how in dreams you seem to jump from one place to another and mix up the past with the present. The house I saw in the dream seemed to be on a hill full of cypresses, like in cemeteries, and I was there all alone. The maid was out and I went down to the cellar to get some oil to start cooking. And, instead of finding myself in the cellar, I found myself in an empty room which reminded me, God preserve us, of a tomb where they keep dead people's bones. The room was full of cupboards. Not just one or two, but hundreds of them. I began opening the cupboards, one after the other. I went on and on, opening the cupboard doors, and it was as though they would never end. Suddenly, I opened a cupboard which was apparently the last one, and standing there inside, upright on her feet with her hands crossed over her chest like a corpse, was my Eleni. I let out a shriek: "Help! help! Our Eleni's dead!" And I began to wail and tear my hair. But, instead of hair, I found myself holding fistfuls of seaweed, and then a mass of snakes. And as I went to rush upstairs to get out of danger, I saw her coming down a staircase, sprightly and flirtatious as you please, with a red ribbon in her hair. — "You ought to be ashamed of yourself, you little devil," I said, "giving me a turn like that! How did you get out of the cupboard without my seeing you?" And, as I turned to look back, there inside the cupboard was a priest with a long beard. — "When you see a priest in your dreams, it means bad luck," I said to Polyxene next morning. "I'm sure something's happened to her. I've never had such a horrible dream about her before." — "Nothing's happened to her, don't worry," said Polyxene, who was always making fun of me for believing in dreams and miracles. "You just ate too many chick-peas last night." But I was worried all day long, I just couldn't get it off my mind. Finally, I said to Polyxene: — "Don't be angry with me, Polyxene. I must just go and see how they all are. Just because Eleni's spiteful and she hasn't even bothered all this time to find out whether we're dead or alive, it doesn't mean that we have to behave like she does. I'll swallow my pride and go, not so much for her as for those poor children of hers. They must be starving to death now that the dentist has left her. My God," I said, "if only I could take the boy and bring him up for her, make a real man of him so that he can look after her in her old age, even if she never gave me a word of thanks for it. It would be an act of Christian charity. And don't start nagging about not being able to afford it. What's the difference if we cook for two or for three? Eh, what do you say?" She just lifted her arms as though to say: do what you like. — "Really, mama," she said, "I simply cannot understand you at all. You know perfectly well that every time, every single time you get involved with Eleni's affairs it only leads to trouble. Anyone would think you were asking for a fight. Is it really impossible for you to live without rowing with somebody?" — "Yes, impossible!" You can say what you like, I said to myself, as long as I take the boy. — "But can't you understand that it's a serious step to take? You can't just make a decision like that on the spur of a moment." — No, I don't understand. — "Well, then, why bother to ask my opinion? Go ahead and do what you like. But you'd better be careful of one thing: you're not to take the boy under any circumstances unless she gives him to you herself." — "What do you take me for," I said, "a gipsy? D'you think I'm going to pop him into a sack and run off with him? . . ." Then I got up and dressed to go out. Before very long there I was at Coulé-Café. It was bitter cold and the dirty slush from the snow had frozen on the pavements. You have to be in Salonika to realise what winter can be like — not like the winter in Athens where you can get by with a little coal in the brazier. There, if you don't have a big stove going full blast, it's simply impossible to live. After a while I reached the house. One of the rooms was still unfinished. A rag mat was hanging out of the window. By the front door there was an iron barrel full of caked old builder's lime. Really! I thought to myself, she's the limit. She hasn't even finished putting in all the window panes. Fancy, there she is living the life of a loose woman, and she doesn't even have enough money to live like a human being. It really is too much! If she can't even manage to do that work properly, why on earth did she go and leave her husband? . . . I knocked on the door. No answer. I looked in through the window and saw the children in bed, huddled up close to each other for warmth, playing with scissors and silver paper from cigarette packets. As soon as Akis saw me, he got up and came to the window. He stood on a chair and opened it. I gave him a kiss. —

"Where's your mama?", I asked him. — "Out." — "When will she be back?" — "This evening" . . . and he began to tremble with the cold and cough his heart out. — "Go on back to bed, child," I said, "before you catch your death of cold!" Calls herself a mother, I said to myself, leaving the poor kids in a refrigerator like that, without so much as a little brazier, while she goes street-walking. And my grandchildren, my very own grandchildren, left to live like the poor orphans in the fairy tale! . . . I just couldn't get over it. I stood there by the window for five or ten minutes trying to decide what to do. I thought about what Polyxene had told me: not to take the boy under any circumstances unless Eleni herself gave him to me. But I simply couldn't go back home without doing something, and, on the other hand, I couldn't just stand there in the bitter cold waiting for her. It might be ten o'clock at night before she got back. The door was locked from the outside and she had taken the key with her. And the longer I stood there listening to the child coughing away, the less sense there seemed to be in Polyxene's instructions. I went down the road to the kiosk and bought a bar of chocolate. Then I went back and waited another ten minutes. — "Come here," I called to Akis, "would you like to come and stay with me?". I don't care if Polyxene shouts her head off, I thought to myself; she's got no more brains in her head than Eleni. I'll take the child and to hell with it. — "Yes," said Akis. — "Alright, then," I said, "get up and get dressed!". He got up and got dressed by himself. He was still wearing the little overcoat I had made for him two years before and the sleeves were up to his elbows. As they say in the villages: the donkey grows up but the saddle stays the same size. I gave him the bar of chocolate. "Give it to your sister," I told him, "I'll buy you another." When I thought of the little girl staying there on her own, my heart bled for her. But what could I do? I simply couldn't afford to take both of them. It was a great help to her that I was taking just the one. At least it meant she'd be able to dress and feed the other one a bit better. — "Now kiss your sister good-bye," I told him.

"And you, dear, kiss your little brother. . . . Now stand up on the chair so I can reach you . . ." It was dark by the time we got home. I put him to bed straight away, stoked up the fire in the stove, put a few cups on his back to get rid of the bad blood, fixed him a good nourishing soup from a lamb's head I happened to have, and then I sat down on the sofa with the mandoline and began to sing softly to send him off to sleep. At that time "The Little Waistcoat" was all the rage:

> 'The little waistcoat that you wear,
> I sewed your love to gain;
> Each button is a bitter tear,
> Each stitch a prick of pain . . .'

—'I didn't know you could play the mandoline,' I said to Hecuba. 'You never told me so before.'

—'I used to play. . . . I learned to play at the same time as the children. I took lessons so that I could persuade Theodore to keep up his practising. But it's years since I held a mandoline in my hands. I don't have the concentration or the mood for such things nowadays. Come to that, I don't even have the mandoline. That son of mine came to the house one afternoon when we were out; he took a hundred drachmas out of Polyxene's drawer, and the mandoline. He left me only the thing you pluck it with. It's still lying around in the box where I keep all my buttons. . . .'

16

That was how things stood when they got a letter from Theodore telling them he had found a second job which paid him double what he was getting on the newspaper. He said he was getting along fine, that they shouldn't worry about him and that he was living with his aunt Frosso who waited on him hand and foot and even starched his shirts for him. He said he thought it was about time they made up their minds to go to Athens and that, till they could get fixed up in their own house, they were welcome to stay with aunt Frosso, who sent them her best regards!

—'Well, Nina, I read the letter and I read it again, and I simply couldn't believe my eyes. That wicked witch who'd stolen my husband from me, now she was stealing my son! And as for that son of mine, he was no better. How could he sink so low? Didn't he have the slightest bit of pride? Just because it suited his convenience, he was quite happy to live with the woman who'd destroyed our family. Simply because she starched his shirts for him! I tell you, Nina, I simply couldn't stomach it. I read the letters and the tears just flooded down my face. To think of it! The sheer cheek! Asking me to go and live with her! Me, Hecuba, go and live under the same roof with Frosso! Have you ever heard of a son making such a monstrous suggestion to his mother? I ask you! And even if I went to stay with her—let's suppose I could bring myself to do even that—what on earth would I want to go to Athens for? If that raving hypochondriac thought I'd go and keep house for him and be driven silly with his pernickety ways—oh, there's too much salt in the stew, or too much pepper, or why didn't you wake me up in time—then he had another think coming. In Salonika, at least, I had my friends—Domna, Sophitsa and old Marie—and I could always go to them and get my troubles off my chest. Poor old Marie! She'd shake her head sadly and say: "Ah yes, my dear Hecuba, that's the way of the world today; chamber pots have suddenly become rose bowls and shit is pure incense!" I also had my aunt Angela in Salonika, a cousin of my mother's who turned up out of the blue at the time I was still with my husband. Ever since I was left on my own I used to go and visit her quite often. She lived out at Holy Trinity, about half an hour away in the motor boat. We'd go every summer and have a free summer holiday. The food was simply wonderful. Yes, I had memories in Salonika. Every stone reminded me of something that happened in my life. It was there that I'd known my greatest happiness and my greatest misery. It was there that I finally opened my eyes and understood what a sham life is! And then you could get by in Salonika even if you were poor as we were. Things were really cheap. You should have seen the sprats, the shrimps, the mussels! Tons of them for next to nothing. Where would you find them in Athens, I'd like to know? And what sort of a life would I have led in Athens? A fine time I'd have had keeping company with Aphrodite and Miltiades. Another pain in the neck, he was! On his way back from Asia Minor he stopped in Salonika for a few days and we started a row as soon as we got to talking. He had the nerve to tell me as were were arguing that I was crazy and that Longos was quite right to leave me. That's a fine kind of brother to have! He's damned lucky to have the roof over his head and the morsel to eat he's getting from me now. — "No," I said to Polyxene, "that's not for me; he can keep his kind offer." Anyway, I knew she wasn't keen to leave Green-eyes and go to Athens. "Sit down," I said, "and write him a letter. Tell him the doctor says you can't be moved for the present." But, as they say, man proposes, God disposes. At that time Dimitris was stationed at a border post. They'd transferred him from the Air Force into the Army because he'd beaten up a Flight Lieutenant in a fight over some woman or other. One night he arrives out of the blue in Salonika and finds Green-eyes sitting as cosy as you please on the foot of Polyxene's bed. He wasn't slow on the up-take. He knew straight away how things stood between them. Without even saying good-evening, he dragged me into the kitchen and began shaking me by the shoulders demanding to know what was going on: — "What the hell do you mean, he's a 'protector', you wicked scheming bitch!", he screamed at me. "Do you realise what you're doing? You're putting her up for sale, you're selling her, that's what you're doing!" — "And what do you expect me to do, you ruddy delinquent!", I said, "did you want me to let her peg out for want of a bite of food? Did you want to see her dead? Instead of speaking to your own mother that way and getting up on your high horse, you miserable good-for-nothing, why don't you act like a man for a change and give us a helping hand instead of having me running off to visit you in one jail after the other?" And then, Nina, he grabs a dish off the dresser and smashes it down on the tiled floor. — "May your hands drop off your arms, you useless jailbird," I screamed at him. "Smashing my plates indeed! Why don't you try to be a real human being first and then you can buy your own plates to smash, instead of coming the tough guy with me!" . . . Then he grabs another dish (my best one this time, the one I used for the spaghetti) and he sent that flying onto the floor, too. — "Aki," I said to the boy (Polyxene had let Green-eyes make his escape meantime and was lying down on her bed quivering like a jelly from fright and distress) — "Aki," I said, "run out and get a policeman right away. Tell him we've got a murderer in the house!" I was really terrified. He's quite capable of finishing us all off, I thought to myself. But when he saw the boy was on the point of running off to fetch a policeman, he suddenly burst into sobs. He cried like a woman. He picked up his knapsack and, without saying a word, opened the door and left. I was so upset, I took it out on Polyxene. We had a real stand-up fight. For days I'd been on the point of saying to Green-eyes: either you marry her or never set foot on my doorstep again. The row with Dimitris reminded me of my duties as a mother. I couldn't forgive myself for speaking to him so harshly. I wept and beat my breast: "Forgive me, my son," I said, "I know it's not your fault. Nobody's to blame but me, me, me . . ." As if all that was not enough, we suddenly found out from a woman I knew who came from Kavalla that Green-eyes, who passed himself off as an old bachelor, was not only married but had two daughters older than Polyxene! And although she loved him, and for all the tears and heartache, even she finally understood that it was useless to continue going with him. And then, in spite of the help Green-eyes had given us, we were behind with the rent and the landlord was grumbling. There was only two ways out: either we had to pay up, or we had to find another house to go to. — "Unless we go to Athens," I said to Polyxene one day. The truth is, I had begun to get used to the idea. To hell with Salonika and all its advantages, I thought to myself. And to hell with my so-called friends. What had they done for me all these years? To hell with aunt Angela, and the mussels, and shrimps! I'll go back where I came from, back to beautiful Attica. After all, damn it, there's some sea there too! . . . So, we packed up our bits and pieces and sent them into store in a warehouse down by the docks. The few days we waited for the boat to sail, we stayed with Eleni. And we didn't have a single argument! . . . Finally, the day came when we were due to leave. The "Amfitriti" was to sail at nine o'clock at night. We made sure first of all that they'd stowed our furniture in a good place down in the hold. We found a corner on deck sheltered from the wind, near the funnel, and spread our rag rugs. When the bell rang for visitors to go ashore, I bent down and kissed Eleni and the little girl. — "At last," said Polyxene, 'you're behaving like a mother and daughter should, with a bit of love for each other." — "Bah!", I said, "don't you believe it! Eleni love me? That'll be the day!" I tried to make a joke of it, though I was really choked with the emotion of leaving! — "It's not me that doesn't love you," shouted Eleni, ready to start a fight as usual, "I love you alright, it's you that can't stand the sight of me and never could! None of you can stand the sight of me, and

132

now you're leaving me alone in Salonika without a soul in the world to care whether I live or die!" And she began to cry. "And watch out, monster," she said to Polyxene (she always called her 'monster' when she was being affectionate), "watch out for yourself down there. And find yourself a husband. But if he's to be like Babbis, then it's better you stay an old maid all your life! And make sure you drop me a line from time to time . . ." She bent down and kissed her son good-bye. — "Be a good boy," she said, "and do what your grandma tells you. But don't forget your mummy, either. Now kiss your sister . . ." — "What's the little one crying about?", asked the sailor who was hauling up the gangplank. — "He's crying because he's parting from his mother and his sister," I said, "but he'll get over it . . ." The lights of Salonika grew smaller and smaller until they finally disappeared out of sight. The moon hadn't yet risen. The passengers who had cabins had gone below, and the others were stretched out on the deck to sleep. After all the flurry and confusion of leaving, I felt the calm weighing on my chest like lead. Looking up at the stars and the sky, I remembered myself twenty years ago coming to Salonika on that hospital ship, full of hopes and dreams. And now I was going back like this. It made my heart bleed. I looked at the stars, at the red and green lamps on the bridge; I listened to the water splashing against the side of the ship in the dark; and then I felt an overwhelming loneliness, as though there were no-one on the ship, nor in the whole wide world, whom I could turn to, no one whose shoulder I could weep on and be comforted. . . . .'

And so they arrived in Athens.

Part Two

1

What wouldn't I have given to be there, somewhere where I couldn't be seen, when she met her great rival. And to think that Frosso's house was only three turnings up from ours!

—'Was she very beautiful, Hecuba?' I sometimes asked her. I always liked the way she would make a comic face to show her disgust, with her mouth twisted in a special way, full of sarcasm and disdain.

—'Ugh! She had nice eyes and a good figure, it's true. But, as for the rest, she was a real scarecrow and no mistake. And half her teeth were missing. I'd rather you didn't remind me of her, if you don't mind. It upsets me just to think of her. . . . That clever son of mine began giving me advice about how to behave to her while we were in the train on the way from the Piraeus to Athens. — "Now be careful what you say," he told me, "I don't want you raking up the past. I want you to be polite and dignified." I was simply furious. — "I don't need any lessons from you on how to behave, you little upstart," I told him, "it's I who brought you into the world, don't forget, not the other way round! And if you think that, before I've well and truly arrived, you can start laying down the law about what I must do and what I mustn't do, then mark my words I'll take the same boat and go straight back to Salonika this minute! . . ." We arrived at Omonia Square and took the bus. The furniture was to follow on with a lorry. Good Lord, I said to myself as we sat in the bus, how Athens has changed! Just look at those huge buildings, and all those cars, and the noise and the crowds! It was early morning and people were just on their way to work. — "That's Athens for you," I said to Polyxene, who was looking around her as though she couldn't believe her eyes. "This is where I grew up, not like you little provincials!" Suddenly, in a strange kind of way, I felt on top of the world. Everything seemed to be beautiful. I

137

had the feeling I wanted to kiss and hug everybody on the bus. Just by the bus-stop where we got off there was a flower stall. I looked at the anemones, I looked up at Mount Lycabettos with the church of St George on top, and tears came into my eyes. Frosso's house had two windows facing onto the street and two terra-cotta sphinxes with cactus plants over the front door. They've pulled that house down too, now, and put up one of those ghastly blocks of flats. Frosso lives out at Peristeri now, but in those days she was a real lady with a house in Kolonaki, if you please. Anyway, we went into the courtyard. She heard us and came out, with her kitchen apron, her hair all over the place, looking twice as old as when I'd last seen her. And she'd lost the rest of her teeth. As soon as she saw me she turned all the colours of the rainbow, red, yellow, green. She didn't know what to say, how to begin. But as for me, to tell you the honest truth Nina, I was as cool as a cucumber. I was feeling so happy at that moment that I was ready to forgive even Frosso. — "What are you standing there for like an idiot?" I said, "you have permission to kiss me. I don't mind. And wipe off that look of snivelling self-pity. If anyone ought to be sorry, it's me not you. Yiannis was the apple of discord. Well, we've eaten it now and we can forget about it!" — "We've grown old, Hecuba," she said, "the years have gone by and left us behind." — "Maybe you've grown old," I said, "but not me. I'm still young. Go on now, make me a cup of coffee, I've got a mouth like a kiln." It was only when I got into the drawing room and I suddenly saw his photograph, without being prepared for it, dressed in his uniform as an officer of the Macedonian Guard, it was only then that I felt upset. I've no idea how she managed to pinch it without my knowing when we were sharing out the furniture. Apparently she saw that I was shaken. — "Come on into the kitchen," she said. "My, my, you're a real beauty, aren't you," she said to Polyxene. "And what about this one here. Well, what do you know! He must be Eleni's little boy! And a fine little man he is, touch wood. I'd no idea he was so grown up! . . . If you'd arrived ten minutes earlier you'd have been in time to see the children. They've gone off to school. How's Dimitris? When shall we be seeing him?" . . . and so on, and so on. Really, Nina, anyone would have thought that absolutely nothing had happened. And the truth is that all the time we were with her she simply couldn't do enough to look after us. Her mother, that fiend of an aunt of mine who just stood by and gave her blessing while her daughter stole my husband, worked as housekeeper with some rich people near the Palace. She used to pinch the oil and butter and bring home great tinfuls of it. And by the time we'd found a house of our own to go to, we'd just about cleaned up her hen house. We had chicken for dinner every other day. Only once, I remember, we nearly came to blows, and that was on account of the children – her son was about the same age as Akis, perhaps a year or two older. They used to play together, uncle and nephew, like really good friends. Then one day, as bad luck would have it, they started boasting to each other, as children will: – "I've got a sword, you haven't" – "My drum is bigger than yours," and all that kind of thing. And suddenly Frosso's boy says to mine: – "My mother's called Mrs Longos!" – "And my grandma's called Mrs Longos!" – "No she isn't", says Fanis, "your grandpa left her and took my mama because she was prettier!" – "Ha, ha!", says my one, "she wasn't pretty, she was a witch and she cast a spell on him and stole him away from my grandma!" . . . . And so Fanis goes running off to his mother in tears and says: – "Akis says you're a witch! . . ." And Frosso gets hold of me and says: – "It isn't right for you to go telling the boy that kind of thing." – "And I suppose it's right for you to go telling your little bastards that Yiannis took you because you were prettier? Why don't you go and look at that lemon face of yours in the looking-glass," I said, "and then come and tell me which of us is the pretty one!" She began to answer back, but I didn't let her get a word out: "Oh, shut up," I told her, "for two pins I'll go straight round to the police and I'll show you which of the two of us is Mrs Longos, so don't try and come the lady over me! . . ." You see, after Yiannis died I hadn't gone on with the trial to get their marriage properly annulled. So she was still his legal widow. She got all upset and began crying, but there was nothing she could do about it. Anyway, it was just about then that we had found a house. In Kolokinthous Street it was, near my old haunts. We piled our things on a horsecart and we were just about ready to set off when I suddenly remembered the photograph. — "Wait there a minute," I shouted to the man with the cart. I ran inside, took the photo off the wall and gave it when I came out to Akis who was sitting on top of the bundles on the cart. Frosso changed colour, but she didn't dare say a word. Before getting up on the cart I bent over and kissed her. And I meant it! I swear to you, Nina, on the life of my Dimitris, and you know how much he means to me, I don't know what got into me at that moment. I suddenly felt I could cry. It was as though a whole chapter in my life was coming to an end that day and a new chapter was beginning, And I had so many worries on my mind, so much need of God's help, that I didn't want to make a new start full of hatred and spite. Suddenly it was as though Frosso wasn't the woman who'd stolen my husband and ruined my whole life. It was as though she, too, was the victim of some devil or other, and I felt sorry for her. But, naturally, I didn't let on. I pretended it was all in fun. — "Bye-bye, cousin," I said, "and thanks for the hospitality. You were a bit late, but you did pay it back! . . . Alright," I said to the driver who was waiting with the whip in his hand, "let's go. Alexander the Great Street!" . . . .'

That was in 1933.

2

One of the reasons Hecuba finally made up her mind to come back to Athens was the thought that, sooner or later, Dimitris would have to follow her there. She hoped the change of surroundings would do him good. In Salonika he'd come to feel that he was an outcast from society. All the police, the 'nicks' as he called them, knew him and waited for him to turn up like a bad penny. And once you get known to the police, they never get their hooks out of you. In Athens he'd be free of them and free of his friends, a bunch of hooligans who were driving him to ruin. He'd cut away from his past and try to start a new life.

— 'And that's how it turned out, Nina. As soon as he got his discharge from the Army he came down to Athens. Theodore found him a job straight away in an engraving works. Every Saturday I used to send the boy and Dimitris would give him a hundred-drachma note to help us along, and when the boy came back I'd cry and kiss the note for sheer joy at the thought that at last he was earning an honest living. But there was I, poor thing, happy that everything was going along fine and thanking God for listening to my prayers at last, when all the time the poison was working away inside him. The acid he breathed in at the engraving shop was gradually ruining his lungs. He came to the house one afternoon pale as a corpse and lay down on the bed. I was just going to take his temperature when he said: "Get me a basin, quick!" . . . I gave him a basin and he spewed up some black clots of blood and a greenish liquid, like bile . . . Theodore pulled all kinds of strings and managed to get him into the best TB clinic. It was still in the first stage and he came out after a year. But of course he couldn't go back to work at the engraving shop. He began mooning around the café in Omonia Square. He got mixed up with all kinds of crooked characters who taught him all the tricks he didn't know already, and soon he was ten times worse than he'd been in Salonika. Athens, you see, gave him a wider field of operations. As usual, he had the nerve to come and tell me all about his doings: how he sold a brass ring to some peasant, passing it off for gold; how he went home with some pansy and then left him in the lurch after blackmailing a hundred drachmas out of him; how he stole a prostitute's purse from under her pillow, and so on and so on.

— "Why, you dirty twister," I said to him, "haven't you got an ounce of self-respect left? Go on, tell me, is there absolutely nothing you believe in? Is that how I brought you up? Are those the ideas you got from me? And if they catch you, you little hoodlum, and you have another haemorrhage when they beat you up, you'll die, do you realise that?" — "Don't worry," he used to say, "they won't catch me!" I might have been listening to his father. — "Don't worry, I'm as hard to catch as a ghost in a haunted castle." But a thief's luck never holds for ever. A shop in Hermes Street found two or three rolls of material missing every so often. They changed the locks, but the rolls kept on vanishing into thin air. The police simply couldn't get to the bottom of the mystery. Finally a plain clothes man hid in the shop one night and caught the "ghost" in the act. A street-vendor who had his pitch in Aeolou Street had got friendly with the shopkeeper and got his permission to leave his barrow in the shop at night for safety. But, inside all the stuff on the barrow, it was hollow like the Trojan Horse. And that's where that clever son of mine used to hide. He'd come out at his leisure after the shop was closed, pick the materials he liked the look of, and in the morning his partner in crime would wheel him out of the main entrance in the barrow, under the very eyes of the shopkeeper. And nobody was the wiser. They sentenced him to twelve months. After nine months, he was out on good behaviour. But, on top of all his other faults, he got one more while he was in prison: he became a communist. He began spouting speeches about social justice and equality, he'd tell me all about the capitalists, and Marx and Lenin, and Dimitrov who learned German in forty days so he could defend himself in court without a lawyer. He even had the nerve to sit there drumming the communist lesson into little Akis, poisoning his child's mind with all that rubbish. – "Religion is the opium of the masses," he used to tell him. "All that stuff they teach you at school about Adam and Eve is just bible poppycock. God didn't create the world. The world created itself. Get some mud," he told him, "and put it under a big stone, and after a few days you'll see a mass of worms coming out. That's how people were created, bit by bit." – "You must be stark staring mad," I used to tell him, I was so furious; "at least you can keep your foul ideas to yourself." – "Oh no," he said, "this one seems to be a bright lad. He must be taught the facts of life. We don't want him going to waste like we did . . ." And he'd go on sermonising as calm as you please: Christ, he said, was a fakir. – "Tell me this," he said, "where was Christ from the time he taught in the temple at the age of twelve up to the time he was baptised by John the Baptist? He was in India. Proof? (that's how he talked) Proof? An Indian fakir came to Athens last year to give some performances at the Central Theatre. He said: crucify me and bury me, and in three days I'll rise up again like Christ . . . But these long-bearded priests had him chased out of town . . ." So you can see, Nina, with the political situation as it was then, with Metaxas just taking over, I trembled in my shoes every day at the thought that they might arrest him and send him into exile. . . .'

All this put me in mind of poor Dino. At that time he'd been dead hardly a year. As the years go by, my heart bleeds for him more and more whenever I think about him. But to this very day, I can't help a bitter smile when I think that, on top of all his other faults, he was a communist as well. Of course, we didn't find out until after he was dead. From the time father turned him out of the house we hardly ever saw him. We had no idea how he lived or where he slept at night. He'd never said a word to us about his politics, or even whether he had any. He wasn't the kind to say much or let people know what he was thinking. On that point, at least, I'm like him. Every now and again he'd turn up at the house when father was out, not to see us, but to squeeze some money out of poor mama. In fact, when he found out that I had got married and that Antoni was in the money, he used to come round more often. But even though mama was very ill at the time and I tried not to upset her, I'd no intention of letting her squander all her money so that he could go and get his morphine injections every day and commit suicide at my expense. I suggested he came and lived with us. I would have put a camp bed in the store-room up on the terrace, which was better than the downstairs rooms because it got the sun all day. I had discussed the idea with father and with Antoni and they both agreed.

— 'But on condition,' I said, 'that you agree to go into a clinic for a month or so to stop taking those drugs. What you do with the rest of your private life is your business. As long as we don't know anything about it. None of us will ever so much as hint about it, I promise you. But the drugs are something else. If you don't make an effort to stop, you'll ruin your health . . .'

But he didn't accept the offer. He preferred to go on living like a tramp. And he stopped coming to see us altogether. One day, uncle Stephen was walking through Klafthmonos Square and went into the public lavatory for a pee. Standing on the other side was Dino, unshaven and shabby as all those addicts always are. So as not to embarrass him he pretended not to see him and walked out looking the other way. But then he thought of the scene mama would make if she found out he had seen her little darling without speaking to him. So he stopped and waited for him to come out. He waited for a minute, then two, then five. But no Dino. How on earth can he have come out without my seeing him, thought poor uncle Stephen. So he went back in, and there was Dino standing in the same place, looking at his neighbour's thingummyjig. That was what we knew about Dino. That he was a drug addict and a pervert.

So when, in December 1937, a plain clothes security man came to the house and told us he had died in exile at Anafi from heart failure, I asked the man inside, in spite of the shock, to find out the details. — 'And why in exile?', I asked him. In my silly naïve way I assumed it had something to do with his drug-taking. When he told me he was a communist I simply couldn't believe my ears. Dino a communist! The idea was both comic and tragic! We just couldn't understand what kind of a communist he could have been. How could a debauched blackguard like him, without any kind of will power, pretend to be a communist which, so far as we understood, meant leading a life of sacrifice and iron discipline? Hecuba's son, at least, was a proper man. He may have got up to a few dirty tricks, like so many young people more's the pity; but at least he was a normal man. Nothing in skirts was taboo for him. Hecuba told me that she'd even caught him in the act one day with his cousin Gogo.

Gogo was the daughter of Hecuba's sister, the one who committed suicide. At one time she and her brother Rikis stayed with her for a while. He was a printer and worked a night shift. Once or twice, when he got back home, he caught her in the act. Once it was with an officer, another time with a sailor.

— 'He must have thought, Nina dear: what am I supposed to do first? Either I go to work to keep a roof over our heads or I sit at home keeping guard on Gogo's whatnot! So he came to the house one day and said: "Auntie, can we come and live with you? We'll pay for our keep, of course . . ." Well, the truth is that he wasn't any better than his sister. All his money went on the tarts in Socrates Street. That was the kind of woman that used to titillate his fancy. All the money he gave for the housekeeping every Saturday he used to take back during the week as a so-called loan. Polyxene, who was always the one who looked after the housekeeping money, used to grumble all the time. She kept telling me to get rid of them. But how could I turn my own sister's children out? I decided to be patient — till the day I caught my son in bed with Gogo. — "You shameless pervert!", I screamed at him, "as if the rest wasn't enough, you've got to have a bit of incest, too!" . . .'

At the time I met Hecuba, Rikis had set up house with some whore, and Gogo had been married for the past two years. Her husband was a plumber. Every time he was out of work, they'd both go over to their aunt's house and stay there from morning to night. And when they had kids, they'd drag the kids along with them.

— 'And Nina, you wouldn't believe it — not so much as an ounce or two of olives, just as a token!', Hecuba would come and tell me next day. Ever since the time she caught Gogo with her son, she simply couldn't stand the sight of her.

Theodore used to pull a long face, too, whenever he saw them. But for different reasons. He couldn't bear Stavros because he was low-class and never washed his hands before sitting down at table. But Polyxene liked him. They got on well together because they were both crazy about the cinema. He used to go and pick her up at the chemist's shop and they'd go to the double feature show late at night, when she didn't dare to go on her own. And when they got back at night they'd start laughing and joking, and Hecuba would come the next day and repeat what they'd said, as though she'd been terribly shocked:

— 'You know, mama, we'll take you with us to the Rosiclaire cinema one of these days. But you'll have to take your umbrella with you. — "And why would I have to take my umbrella with me," I asked in all innocence. — "Because the people in the balcony spit," they say. — "Aren't you the least bit ashamed of yourselves," I say, "shutting yourselves up in those stuffy holes just to watch all that rubbish on a white sheet, instead of going to a theatre and seeing something worthwhile, or at

-least having a beer at a café and breathing in some fresh air and watching a few people go by!" . . .'

—'Ah, but you don't understand how nice it is,' I used to tell her, 'that's why you talk the way you do. When I was Polyxene's age I used to come out of one cinema and pop straight into another! . . .'

She would just shake her head sadly and say nothing. Things are not what they used to be! . . . .

About that time, Dimitris had taken up with a nurse he'd met at the clinic. He used to bring her home to Hecuba's house as his 'fiancée'. Or they'd keep a watch to see when Hecuba left the house, and then they'd go in and have a fine old time. Hecuba was ready to forgive him almost anything: thefts, communism, blackmail, pimping, incest with Gogo, and so on. She often used to boast of his successes with women. Just so long as he didn't get seriously involved; then she went berserk. When she saw the romance with the nurse beginning to look serious, and when they began to talk of getting married, she was furious. She told him to stop bringing her to the house. And she started fighting with him on the slightest excuse: either because he mixed up his knives and forks with theirs and Akis might catch his TB; or because he sang common bouzouki songs and the child was picking them up (*'Remember the nights on the divan. The lovelight in your eye; Remember who was then your man, With the bouzouki lullaby'*), and so on, and so on. Finally, she got on his nerves so much that he packed up and left. After that, he didn't come back to the house. Or very rarely. And then only to cadge some money—Just the way Dino carried on with poor mama.

3

Suddenly, I lost track of her. What on earth's happened to Hecuba? What can be wrong? I kept asking myself. Not showing up for days on end, it's so unlike her! Antoni was inconsolable at losing his card playing partner. We sent Marietta round to her house and she came back and told us that the front door was locked and there didn't seem to be a soul in the house. One evening I happened to be passing by her house and at last I saw a light in the window, so I knocked on the door. It was Polyxene who opened it. What a lovely girl she is! I thought to myself. It was the first time I'd seen her. When she heard who I was, she said: 'Please come in and sit down' She was polite, but rather stiff and formal. She always was a cold type of person. Even now that she's my sister-in-law I don't feel as free with her or as close to her as I did to her mother. 'I'm sorry to disturb you,' I said, ' I know it's rather late to come bothering you. But it's days since I've seen anything of Hecuba and I was worried something might have happened to her.' I saw a frown pass over her face. – 'No, no,' she said, 'she's in Salonika. We had a letter from my sister yesterday. She arrived safely and she's fine . . .' She offered to make me some coffee, but I refused. It was about dinner time. So I said good night and left.

The mystery wasn't cleared up till four months later, by Hecuba herself, when she came back to Athens just as suddenly as she left. One day, Polyxene had given her a hundred-drachma note to do the week's shopping – oil, butter and so on. Then Dimitris turned up and, without knowing quite how it happened, she let herself be persuaded to 'lend' him the money. The row started when Polyxene got back and found out what had happened: – 'Holy Mary,' she ranted, 'why can't you put him six feet under so we can see the last of that plague of Pharoah!' Hecuba, who cursed him just as mercilessly, would go white with anger when she heard anybody else cursing her son. — 'Even if I was just a skivvy in the house, Nina,' she said when she came back and told me how it all happened, 'I'd have the right to spend a wretched hundred-drachma note for my own child. So I said to myself: alright, you ungrateful creatures! I'll go away and leave you to cook for yourselves and wash your own clothes, and perhaps then you'll appreciate what I do for you. So I put on my coat and went straight out . . .' — 'And how did you get to Salonika wihout a penny in your pocket?' I asked her. She smiled like a crafty child. — 'You remember that policeman Kalapothakis, the one I told you about that I got to know when they arrested Dimitris for stealing the first time? Well, I happened to know he'd been promoted in the meantime for good service. He'd caught some famous bandit or other in Macedonia and now, if you please, he was deputy chief of the Transport Section. I'd been thinking of going to see him for the past several days. So off I go down to Nikodimou Street and I say to the guard at the door: — "I want to see the deputy chief! Tell him Hecuba wants to see him and he'll understand . . ." And then, if you please, they show me into a grand-looking office. While I was waiting for Kalapothakis to arrive I kept thinking to myself: "Just fancy, just an ordinary lousy copper, he was, and look where he is now! Dear Lord, why couldn't it happen to my own son, instead of having him being kicked around from one jail to another under the thumb of these police bastards!" — "Well, well, look who's here! If it isn't old Mrs Longos," he says as soon as he comes into the room and sees me standing there. "Why you haven't changed a bit! God, it's been years and years since then! . . ." He called for two coffees and we sat down and began talking about old times. After a while, he says: — "Alright now, out with it. Tell me what brings you here to see me. I know you, you old rascal. You wouldn't have come to see me if you didn't want something out of me." And I told him: — "I want you to send me to Salonika, and no questions asked!" — "Bravo," he says, "nothing simpler! But I'll have to send you under escort, like we do the jailbirds!" And he began to laugh his head off. — "I don't give a damn how you send me," I say, "as long as I get to Salonika." Then he presses a button on his desk and an officer full of silver braid comes in and salutes by bowing his head because he's without his cap. "Get a travel warrant made out to so and so," he says, "to escort the lady here to Salonika tonight. And get on the phone to find out what time the express leaves." Then he came over and stood by me after I'd got up from the armchair. He put his hand on my shoulder and looked at me, shaking his head and smiling: "You're just the same as ever, the very same! . . ." And then he took the handbag I was carrying, put a hundred-drachma note inside, and handed it back to me: — "Have a good trip," he said. "Hecuba Longos, the woman who never says die! You're like Greece, you are. A little bit crazy, but you've a heart of gold. Go on with you now, take your little trip to the White Tower of Salonika, and when you get fed up and want to come back — well, just give me a little whistle! . . ." And next day, there I am large as life in Salonika. It seemed so funny after Athens. As though the roads were narrower and the houses smaller than I remembered them. I just couldn't believe that this was the town where I'd wasted a whole lifetime. . . ." And she began to cry. The idyllic life she was living — incredible as it may seem — with her elder daughter in Salonika was suddenly interrupted by a telegram from Polyxene: DIMITRIS ARRESTED ACCESSORY FOR MURDER COME QUICKLY.

4

Dimitris was in jail for five months in Syngrou Prison before his trial came on. All that time Hecuba was in a state of complete jitters and black pessimism. I'd never seen her in such a state, but now I realise it was a kind of premonition, a taste of the kind of sufferings she was to go through for the last time during the occupation. She stopped telling me all about her adventures, as though I'd grown too old to listen to fairy tales, or perhaps she'd grown too old to remember them. She was completely wrapped up in the present. She was much too worried about the future to sit telling stories about the past. She was always sad and silent. She'd lost her healthy colour, and snapped at everybody at the slightest excuse. Not at me and Antoni, of course; but every time she happened to be at home when aunt Katie or Mrs Cassimatis came in for a coffee (she couldn't bear either of them), and something was said that she didn't agree with, she'd go for them as though they were her worst enemies. Or she'd purse her lips sarcastically and stop talking altogether.

It was her brother Miltiades who caught most of her bad-tempered outbursts after they arrested Dimitris. Nervy and upset as she was, she began squabbling with him worse than ever. One afternoon she arrived at my place in high dudgeon. 'Just you wait and see,' she said, 'I'll teach that bloody brass-hat! I won't take the slightest pity on him. I'll just tell him to pack up and get the hell out of my house!' — 'What's the matter this time? What's he done again?', I asked her. — 'What do you think he's done! What he always does! He insists on interfering in the way I bring up Akis. He found out I went to father Nikos to hypnotise him and he almost murdered me. Can you imagine it! I don't dare do what I like in my own house without having him standing over me telling me what to do and what not to do! . . .'

In her state of despair with all the trouble she was going through at that time, she'd suddenly taken to religion again. But this time her God was a bit less primitive than the old one, a God whose apostles on earth were not saints, or monks or martyrs, but scientists, or scientists in a manner of speaking. Father Nikos was apparently a former priest, if he ever was a priest at all, and lived with a widow who was a button-hole maker. She made button-holes for small tailors and kept him in food and board so he could devote himself without material worries to his spiritual experiments. Just like holy Ephemia, Father Nikos was endowed with God's gift of being able to foretell the future — by the use of hypnotism. Suddenly, Hecuba had begun talking to me about tables that started walking, about speaking mirrors, about ectoplasm, mediums and such like. I used to laugh at her behind her back for the turn this religious crisis of hers had taken, but I never said anything to her face. I could see how much she was going through and I felt terribly sorry for her. Father Nikos tried several times to 'put her to sleep' so that she could 'go to God' and find out if Dimitris would get off. But she was a bundle of nerves, a sinner and a Doubting Thomas besides (she used to tell me so in tears) and she simply could not go off to sleep. So they decided to hypnotise little Akis, as he was an innocent child. — 'And who told your brother about it?', I asked her. — 'I did!', she said, banging her head with her fist, 'I must have been out of my mind!'. I told Antoni about it and we had a good laugh over it. The row she had with her brother was the last straw which broke the camel's back. Not because she told him to leave. She'd told him to go a hundred times before and he'd never taken any notice. But by now he'd had as much as he could stand. He just collected his things together and went straight off without another word, stopping just long enough for a last disgusted spit at the photographs of Constantine and Metaxas. Hecuba got some news of him later, and she came round to tell me about it with a sly smile: he'd set up house with a widow just outside Eleusis, the wife of an old comrade

of his who had been killed in the retreat from Sangarios. —
'Hmmm! That's the kind of man he is. He's always dreamed of
finding a woman to keep him in comfort. It's a fine thing, isn't
it? Just fancy! The hero of Bizani ending up by becoming a
gigolo. Ha!' — 'Well really,' I said, 'I don't know what you
find so shocking. Just because he's living with a widow it
doesn't mean he's become a gigolo.' — 'No, no,' she protested,
'don't misunderstand me. I don't want you to think I'm blaming him. In fact I'm delighted he's found a woman to pull him
together. I'd be the first to wish him well, the poor devil, if
they could get married and he could start a family.' — 'And
why can't they get married?' 'Ha! Really, Nina, sometimes I
think you deliberately pretend to be stupid. And lose her
pension? What would they live on then? . . .' That was probably the only time I saw her laugh during the time Dimitris
was waiting for trial.

5

'You stay right where you are,' Antoni said to me on the day of the trial, 'you're not to go anywhere.' — 'I must,' I told him, 'I simply have to go to give her a bit of courage. Mark my words, Antoni,' I said, 'if they find him guilty, she'll never get over it.' — 'Well alright,' he said, 'I suppose if you must go, you must (poor Antoni, he never refused me anything), but mind you don't come back home feeling ill, like you do when you see a sad film at the cinema!' — 'This isn't the cinema,' I said, 'this is real life!'. But, deep down, I knew he was right. My daughter may call me hard, heartless, cynical and I don't know what else, but in some things at least I'm as soft-hearted as a girl of twelve. Antoni knew it was the first time I was going to a trial in court. I'd seen lots of trials in the cinema, and I always read all the newspaper reports of the big murder trials and so on, but I'd never set foot in a real court-room, for all my determination to become a lawyer when I was young.

Dimitris was charged with being an accessory to a murder. He was supposed to have helped a friend of his to kill his wife's lover. He was in a very serious position. If he was found guilty, they could send him to jail for five or even ten years. But what made things even more serious was the fact that the victim happened by an unfortunate coincidence to be a sergeant of the police Crime Squad. His colleagues had sworn to get revenge and they were not nearly so vicious against the actual murderer, who had a clean record, as they were against Hecuba's son. You see, they knew him from way back. He was a thorn in their side they were determined to get rid of. One evening, according to the version Dimitris gave, he was sitting playing whist in a café in Omonia Square. At about eight o'clock, this man Gatsos walked in. — 'How did you know Gatsos?' — 'Well, I used to see him around the place, Your Honour. You see, I used to introduce customers to his shop. Ever since I got ill, I've been doing a bit of work as a salesman.' – 'And quite a few other things besides!', the Prosecutor chipped in with a poisonous little smile. 'You introduced customers to his shop, did you? Or' (and the smile faded from his lips) 'was it maybe that you sold him stolen watches? . . .' Cassianopoulos, an old friend of Theodore's who had agreed to defend Dimitris, and without taking a fee, stood up and began protesting very hard. A buzz went round the courtroom. It was chock-full, not so much with the usual bunch of idle curiosity-seekers (Theodore had spoken to his colleague on various newspapers and there hadn't been any publicity about the trial), but with the friends and relations of the various parties, especially colleagues of the victim, some of them in uniform and some in plain clothes. Every time Dimitris was questioned, they started making a terrible noise, as though they were following a prepared plan. – 'Just stick to the relevant facts,' said the judge finally to the Prosecutor. But he wasn't so easily put off. – 'The character and record of the accused in this case, Your Honour, are entirely relevant to the issues on trial. As I shall have an opportunity of explaining later to the members of the jury, the character of the accused . . .' – 'I don't see what connection there can possibly be between the business relations of the two accused and the murder, Your Honour,' shouted Cassiano- poulos in a fury. The Prosecutor smiled that sarcastic smile of his again. – 'You'll find out soon enough,' he said.

We'd all begun to suspect what he was getting at. At the beginning of the trial they had read out a long rigmarole with details of his previous criminal record, some of which Hecuba herself was hearing for the first time. She almost fainted clean away. Polyxene thought it was a good idea to take her out into the courtyard. She sat her down on a stone step and she stayed there until the trial was over. – 'All right then,' said the judge, 'so he came and sat down next to you. What then?' – ' "Hallo," he said. "Well, well, look who's here," I said. He seemed to be down in the dumps. "Is there something you

155

want?" — "I want to talk to you." — "Sit down," I said, "I'll be finishing the game in a minute or two . . ." '

Even if I didn't know he was Hecuba's son, I could have picked him out of a thousand just by his voice. He wasn't much like her to look at; he took more after his father. And anyway, it was almost impossible to recognise him with his head shaved almost to the bone. But his voice was an exact man's version of his mother's: the same pitch, the same intonations. When the game of whist was over and they were alone, Gatsos told him what it was all about: his wife had a lover and he needed somebody to go with him, so that they could catch her in the act and he could bring proceedings for adultery. — 'When was it exactly that he told you his wife's lover was a policeman?' — 'He didn't mention it at all, Your Honour. I found out next day at the police station.' — 'And do you expect the court to believe that?', said the Prosecutor. — 'In that case, Your Honour, I might as well sit down and say nothing . . .' He never replied directly to the Prosecutor. He just completely ignored him, and it made him hopping mad. Cassianopoulos saw what was happening and drummed his fingers nervously on the desk in front of him. Fortunately, the judge seemed to a patient kind of chap. — 'All right. Go on,' he said. — 'Well, Your Honour, to cut a long story short, I said to him: "And what's in it for me?" and he says: — "Twenty fives" — 'What does twenty fives mean?' — 'A hundred drachmas, Your Honour!' — 'Well say a hundred drachmas, then. We don't all spend our time at the cafés in Omonia Square, you know!' — 'I'm trying to tell you exactly what happened, Your Honour, that's why I'm telling it the way we speak among ourselves. But if you prefer, I'm quite willing to use all those long words we've been hearing from the Prosecutor . . .' From where I was sitting over on the left, I could see Cassianopoulos biting his lip . . . 'Well, as I was saying, he offered me twenty fives. I would have been a fool to refuse, now, wouldn't I? Ever since I got ill. . . .' — 'Never mind about being ill, just continue telling us what happened,' said the judge impatiently. — 'Ah, that's all very well, never mind about being ill. But if I hadn't got ill, Your Honour, I might easily not be standing where I am now. If you're going to treat me as a criminal and not as a human being I'll sit down this very minute and you can sentence me to a hundred years if you like, but don't try to kid me that you're giving me justice. . . .'

All the policemen who were in civilian clothes began making a buzz like a claque at the theatre. The judge banged on his bell. Finally the courtroom quietened down again and Dimitris continued telling his story: at ten o'clock they took a taxi and went down to a place near the fruit and vegetable market where Gatsos lived. They hid in a doorway opposite the house and waited for the victim to arrive. — 'How did Gatsos know that the victim would be paying a visit to his wife?' — 'He'd lied to her, Your Honour, and told her he'd be sleeping at his sister's place that night' (Gatsos confirmed this himself later). — 'Where is his sister's house?', asked the Prosecutor. Dimitris was on the point of answering, but Cassianopoulos jumped to his feet again to protest. — 'I fail to see the relevance of that question, Your Honour,' he said. Once again, the Prosecutor smiled that ironical smile of his. 'There are quite a lot of things my learned colleague for the defence fails to see, Your Honour, but we reserve the right to explain them in due course. If we didn't have serious reasons for asking the questions we wouldn't ask them!' — 'Answer the question,' said the judge to Dimitris, as though he were bored with the whole proceedings. — 'What question, Your Honour?' — 'Learned counsel for the Prosecution has asked you whether you know where the house of Gatsos's sister is' — 'In New Philadelphia' — 'So he went to all the trouble, did he, of telling you such an insignificant detail,' said the Prosecutor triumphantly, 'and yet he didn't bother to mention the fact that his wife's lover was a policeman!' — 'What has one thing got to do with another? I knew where his sister's house was long before, Your Honour. They had a party there one night and I went along.' The judge looked at the Prosecutor as if to say: don't overdo it. . . . 'All right, carry on,' he said to Dimitris.

They waited opposite Gatsos's house for half an hour or so. Finally, the victim arrived and rang the doorbell. Gatsos's wife opened the door, looked round to make sure nobody was watching, and let him in. Then they both went across to the house. — 'How long did you wait before you went over?' — 'Twenty minutes' — 'Is it true that Gatsos wanted to go straight away and you didn't let him?' — 'Yes, it's true' — 'Why?' — 'Well, it's a question of common sense, Your Honour! If he wanted to catch them in the act he had to give them time to get going' — 'I see. So you went in . . .'

With Gatsos leading the way, because he knew the house, and Dimitris following behind, they reached the door of the bedroom. Dimitris bent down first to take a look through the keyhole. — 'And what did you see?' — 'If I tell that, Your Honour, you'll be warning me again to mind my language' — 'There's no need for a detailed description,' said the judge sternly, 'just tell us what point they had reached. In long words if you like.' — 'I observed that they were engaged in fornication.' The judge could hardly keep himself from laughing: 'Yes,' he said, 'I can see you know quite a few long words when you want to. Now tell us what happened next. Just in ordinary language, if you don't mind.'

Gatsos gave the double doors a hefty shove and they opened wide. As soon as his wife saw him she began to squeal and shout for help. At the same time she was trying to cover herself with the sheet. — 'And what about the victim? What did he do?' — 'He went across the room to get his trousers. Then I heard two shots, and . . .' — 'When you were questioned before the trial,' said the Prosecutor, 'you claimed that the victim tried to take his revolver out of his trouser pocket.' — 'I said I thought he looked as though he was going to get his revolver.' — 'How could you possibly have thought that? You say you didn't know he was a policeman, so why should you assume that he carried a gun?' — 'Just instinct, I suppose . . . with all the years I've been floating around, I can smell a policeman a mile off . . .' — 'What was it you shouted out at that moment?' — 'Nothing' — 'What do you mean, nothing,' said the Prosecutor, 'Mrs Gatsos tells us that you shouted: "finish him off, the . . . the . . ." (he opened a file he had in front of him and read out) . . ."the sodding bastard!" ' — 'That's a lie! She's trying to make things easier for her husband so as to salve her own conscience. You'll be telling me before long that I shot her lover!' . . . 'There are lots of different ways of killing a man. For instance, you can encourage somebody else to commit the crime . . .' Cassianopoulos jumped to his feet again and began to protest more angrily than ever. Somebody in the courtroom had shouted 'Bravo' and the judge began banging on his bell and warned the spectators to stop expressing their feelings either for or against the accused, otherwise he would clear the court and continue the trial behind closed doors. — 'Well, as I was saying, I heard two shots and I saw the victim clutching his belly. "What have you done, you silly sod!" That's what I said, Your Honour. I never said finish him off the sodding bastard. I may be the worst man in the world, but I'm no criminal and I never will be! I don't have it in me. "For Jesus Christ's sake what have you done, you silly sod!" That's what I told him. I swear on my father's bones, Your Honour, I was taken completely by surprise. I had no idea he had a gun with him. I had no idea. . . .' But once more his voice was drowned in the pandemonium raised by the victim's police comrades when they heard him taking Christ's name in vain. Cassianopoulos was as white as a sheet. The jury shifted uneasily in their chairs. — 'I advise you,' said the judge sternly,' to stop using words that shock the religious feelings of the people here in this courtroom. Trial adjourned for ten minutes . . .' Phew!, I thought to myself, and about time, too. We all needed a breath of fresh air. The atmosphere in the courtroom had become stifling.

It was outside in the courtyard that I met Theodore for the first time. Polyxene introduced us. Hecuba wasn't up to that kind of thing just then. It was as though she had no idea of anything that was going on around her. She sat there with her fingers twined under her chin, the living image of sheer despair. I could read her like a book by then. While her son was standing trial in a real court of law, she imagined herself in the dock of some other, imaginary, courtroom. — 'Don't carry on like that,' I told her, 'you'll die of cancer like my mother if you don't stop worrying! After all, it wasn't he that killed the policeman. They can't chop his head off for what he did. You should have been inside to listen to him,' I said, 'he really put that Prosecutor in his place.' She raised her head and looked straight at me, as if to say: I know you don't believe all that. She was not a fool. Even though she hadn't been in court, she knew exactly what was happening, as though she'd been following every word. She knew, as we all did, that by 'putting the Prosecutor in his place' he was laying himself open to real danger, because it only went to support the theory the Prosecutor had already hinted at: that he was the real master-mind behind the crime. She knew how men's justice worked, and she knew her son's character. Then Polyxene arrived with a piece of Turkish delight and a glass of water. — 'Go on,' she said, eat it, it will do you good.' — Hecuba covered her face melodramatically with her hands. Polyxene offered the Turkish delight to me. — 'I don't want it, thanks,' I said, 'give it to the boy. I'd rather have a coffee.' Theodore had gone off for a moment, but he came back after a while with Cassianopoulos. What a difference, I thought as I saw him coming, between one son and the other! Dimitris may be handsome, but with his character what's the good of it! — 'Minos,' said Hecuba as soon as she saw Cassianopoulos, 'Minos, for God's sake, tell me . . . tell me . . .' Cassianopoulos spread his hands in a gesture of total resignation. 'You know very well, Mrs Longos,' he said, 'that I'll do everything I can. But I'm sorry to say that son of yours is making a thorough mess of things. I told him again and again to be respectful and say as little as possible. But not him! He's determined to show everybody how clever he is . . .' But when he saw she was on the point of passing out, he changed his tone at once. — 'Now, now, Mrs Longos. We mustn't carry on like that, must we? You promised to be brave' (more like a doctor than a lawyer). 'At the very most, he's likely to get six months. He's been in jail waiting trial for . . . how long is it? — seven months, isn't it? He'll be at home tonight. I'll bring him round myself, that's a promise. . . .' He looked around at all of us, as though he was asking our permission to leave. Then he disappeared down one of the corridors. Theodore took out a packet of cigarettes and was on the point of lighting up when he suddenly thought that maybe I smoked. He offered me a cigarette. Antoni didn't allow me to smoke, ever since that damned ulcer started playing me up. But I took one and, as he offered me a light, I caught him looking at me as though he was thinking: so this is the Nina who makes that wonderful moussaka! . . . When the time came for the trial to continue, I said to her: 'Aren't you going to come in at all?' — 'No' — 'Would you like me to stay and keep you company?' — 'No. Go on in, all of you, and leave me alone. Just pretend I don't exist . . .'

6

Two or three days before the trial Cassianopoulos had managed to get hold of a list of the jury's names, just in case we knew any of them. By some strange coincidence, one of the jurymen turned out to be our local grocer. — 'I'll go and see him!', Hecuba said to me, 'I'll fall at his feet and beg him . . .' — 'Do as you think fit,' I told her, 'but I doubt if it would do any good. That Bouchlos isn't the kind of man you can get round very easily. But there's no need to be ashamed of trying. If it doesn't work it doesn't work. More shame on him.' — 'Damn it all' she said, 'when you think of the money he takes from us every week! . . .' Poor Hecuba, I thought to myself, and my heart went out to her, how naïve you are! Do you think Bouchlos is going to listen to you just because you buy a pint of oil or a pound of beans from him every now and again?

And I wasn't wrong. She came round again that afternoon in a tearing rage: — 'The snivelling little bastard!,' she fumed, 'who does he think he is? The puffed up little nobody! He used to sell goat's cheese off a barrow, and now he thinks he's the Lord Almighty because they've put him on a jury! Even if he didn't mean it, what was to stop him saying: alright, Mrs Longos, I'll do what I can. But no, not him! Not his lordship the grocer-juryman! All I got was a long sermon about the sacred duty of a juryman and how he had to decide according to his conscience. I almost picked up the scoop from the sugar sack and laid into him good and proper. But I restrained myself. Just wait till the trial is over, I thought to myself, and I'll show you what's what, you pig! If you ever see another penny of mine may I drop dead on the spot! . . .' Now I could see him sitting in the front row of the jury-box, looking terribly self-important, with his pudgy hands crossed over his fat belly. And I said to myself: poor old Hecuba, you'll never really understand what monsters poeple are! When will you ever learn? . . .

Dimitris was in the witness box for a whole hour. But the stupid fool just ignored everything Cassianopoulos had told him. Instead of behaving as though butter wouldn't melt in his mouth, as Gatsos did, and saying: I realise I was foolish, I shouldn't have agreed to go with him, but I needed the money; instead of appealing to them to overlook his past and deal with him leniently, he began making a speech like a lawyer. And, because he wasn't a lawyer, he just made himself look ridiculous. The judge kept looking at him, as though he couldn't make up his mind whether to be angry or to feel sorry for him. Every time he heard him come out with some fancy long words, he smiled behind his hand. And he not only spouted away like a bath-tap; he had the full repertoire of dramatic gestures, too: he flung his arms wide open, pointed his finger threateningly, as though it was not he but the others who were on trial; he paced up and down, from the judge to the jury, and from the jury back to the judge, and every now and again he turned towards the spectators, like actors do in the theatre; he began to tell the story of his life from the time he was a child, just as Hecuba herself used to. Really, I thought to myself, there's no doubt he's his mother's son. But at least Hecuba is a woman. As a man, he ought to be more practical-minded. Does he really think he's going to get round the jury — a man like Bouchlos — by telling the story of his life! Poor Cassianopoulos clenched and unclenched his hands in a state of nerves. Obviously he couldn't tell Dimitris to shut up and sit down in front of everybody. So he kept finding excuses for passing close to him. Then he'd give him a nudge and whisper desperately in his ear for him to shut up. But Dimitris just ignored him. It got to the point where even we who were on his side and believed that he was really innocent began to get annoyed and lose our sympathy for him. The bumptious little nobody, we thought, having the sheer cheek to stand there making a speech! Instead of shutting his mouth and hoping to

163

get away with it, there he was behaving as though it was he who had a grievance! Cassianopoulos kept walking past him and nudging him in the ribs, but Dimitris was soaring in the clouds of his own eloquence. As he told his mother afterwards, he was determined to defend himself without the help of lawyers, just as Dimitrov had done. When she came and told me, I said to her: 'You ought to have told him that all he needed was the 'ov'! . . .' When he saw the jury looking at him, first with surprise and disbelief, and then with downright hostility, he began insulting them. He told them he knew they were determined to find him guilty and it was probably a waste of time appealing to them; that men who had pot bellies and wore clean white shirts couldn't possibly show any mercy for an outcast of society like him. But he didn't care, he said. One day things would change! One day justice would reign in the world! And then, even if it was after he was dead, his innocence would be recognised! . . . Either the judge had cottoned on to the desperate attempts of Cassianopoulos to silence his client, or he felt moved by sheer humanity to put a stop to this extraordinary act of suicide. At one point, he interrupted Dimitris and, with the gentlest voice in the world, he said it was getting late, that the lawyers and the jury were tired, and that the quicker he finished the better it would be for himself and for everybody else. And what do you think he answered? That the law gave him the right to defend himself as he thought best, and that he was shouting because he was the victim of an injustice. — 'Members of the jury,' he cried, 'I demand justice, I demand justice!' — 'He's stark raving mad,' Cassianopoulos told us when there was another adjournment and we went outside. 'He ought to be behind bars! And I don't mean prison bars. Mrs Longos,' he said to Hecuba, 'I've seen a lot of madmen in my time, but never anybody quite so schizophrenic as that. You really ought to take him to a psychiatrist . . .'

When the trial was resumed, the Prosecutor got to his feet and began outlining the whole story from the beginning. When he came to the part Dimitris had played in the affair, he went almost berserk, as though Dimitris was his personal enemy or had killed his father. He read out the whole of Dimitris's criminal record, pausing after each item and looking at the jury to emphasise the effect. And his final conclusion was that a man of that kind would naturally nurse a permanent grudge against society. — 'That is to say, gentlemen of the jury, a grudge against you, a grudge against law and order, and, even more of course, against the guardians of law and order! . . . How many times he must have thought, like some new Caligula, what a pity it is that all policemen haven't got a single head so that he could chop it off and put paid to all policemen in one fell swoop! . . . . Here was an opportunity not to be missed, an opportunity to take his revenge on all policemen in the person of the unfortunate victim, and indeed without taking any risk himself — or at least, so he thought, members of the jury . . . You have heard him in this court . . . We have all heard him. . . . With a cheap rhetoric imitated from inflammatory articles in the gutter press and a flood of words filled with hatred and intolerance — an eloquence, I confess, surprising in a man of his background — he has made it plain beyond a shadow of a doubt that it was he who stoked up the fires of Gatsos's natural desire for revenge against his wife's lover . . . . Certainly, he was guilty of adultery. But does that mean that he ought to pay for it with his life? Gentlemen of the jury, we are not living in the middle ages! It was Longos, gentlemen, who put him up to the idea of committing murder. Gatsos does not say so in so many words, out of a mistaken sense of loyalty. But we have every right to come to that conclusion from what has been heard in this courtroom. "Finish him off, the sodding bastard!". That's what he told him. "Go on, shoot him! Don't worry. I'm here and I'll be your witness, I'll prove you were under provocation and you'll get off scot free . . ." For he may not respect the law, gentlemen of the jury, but he knows it well enough. Oh yes, he knows it well enough! He admitted it himself in this courtroom. And you may well find it comical —

or shall we say outrageous, gentlemen—that this man who systematically flouts the law of God and the law of men with the same untroubled conscience, has the impudence, the sheer unmitigated impertinence, to stand here and claim the benefits of the laws of society he so scorns and desecrates . . ."Finish him off. Go on, shoot," he said . . . And in the person of this poor unhappy victim he takes his revenge not only on his relentless persecutors but on the whole of society of which they are the untiring guardians—that is to say, on me, and on you—just because we wear clean shirts! . . .' He finished by asking the jury to find Gatsos guilty of murder with malice aforethought but with extenuating circumstances, and Dimitris guilty of being an accessory before and after the fact.

Then poor Cassianopoulos got to his feet. He was as white as a sheet and his voice was almost inaudible as he said that it was getting very late and it was in the interest of his client to be as brief as possible. He begged them not to be swayed by the dismal picture which had been painted by the Prosecutor who, out of a sense of professional duty, tended to see every person charged with a crime as some kind of monster.—'He even dragged in Caligula, gentlemen of the jury!' And he turned on them a sad smile. Then, in a voice pulsing with emotion, he said: 'Gentlemen of the jury, I hand into your care a vase full of cracks . . . Tuberculosis . . . Misery . . . Dreadful ignorance of reality. . . . Handle the vase with care. . . . Don't shatter it to pieces . . .I beg you, not as a lawyer but as a man, hand it back in the same state you received it. . . . If you smash it to smithereens, how shall I find the courage to stoop and gather up the pieces to carry back to his mother? . . .' And with that he sank back in his chair and hid his face in the palm of his hands. When the jury retired to consider their verdict and we went out into the courtyard again, Hecuba kept fainting away as fast as we could bring her round again. And when the court reassembled after a while and the jury came out and found him guilty as an accessory before and after the fact and the court sentenced him to three years penal servitude – the same sentence as Gatsos got – then she began in real earnest to wail and beat her breast and ask us to give her a dose of poison to finish her off. But of course we did no such thing. Instead, we picked her up bodily, put her in a taxi and took her home, where we sat up late into the night with her as though it were a wake. There was only a twenty-five watt bulb in the hall, and that made it more depressing than ever. Cassianoppulos left later on and, to avoid having to sit up all night, I nipped back home and, walking on tip-toes, managed to find Antoni's sleeping pills. When I got back, we made her take a double dose after a lot of effort and soon, with the tears still running down her cheeks, she began to yawn. She rested her head on the divan pillow and, before long, she was sleeping as soundly as a baby. . . .

It was beginning to get light by the time I got back home. As I was undressing to get into bed I woke Antoni up without meaning to. 'What's the time?' he said. – 'Twenty to five' – 'What! You mean you've been out all this time!' – 'Be quiet, there's a good chap,' I said, 'there's no need to go waking up all the neighbourhood. I'm upset enough as it is. Turn over and go to sleep, and let me get some sleep myself. I'll tell you all about it tomorrow. . . .'

7

It was Easter after two or three weeks. On Holy Thursday I dyed some eggs and sent a few round to her with Marietta. I knew she'd be in no mood, in the state she was in, to bother about dyeing red eggs. On Good Friday morning she came round to the house and sat waiting in the hall for me, all alone, while I finished off something or other I was doing out in the yard. She began playing patience with a pack of cards and singing hymns from the Good Friday service: *'As an evildoer by evildoers you were accused, oh Christ our Lord, taking on your head the sins of us all . . .'* And then she began on that song that my poor mama used to sing on Good Fridays: *'Today the sky is dark, the day is black, today the wicked Jews seized our Lord Jesus . . .'* Suddenly the singing stopped and I heard some strange banging noises. I leaned in at the window to see what was happening and there she was banging her head on the wall! I ran inside, grabbed hold of her from behind, held her close to me and shouted to Marietta: — 'Quick get the doctor!' Boros came round almost at once and gave her an injection to calm her nerves. Then he wrote out a prescription for a syrup she had to take three times a day. For a time she seemed to have recovered. Then suddenly one day little Akis turned up and said: — 'My grandma's ill.' — 'What's the matter with her?' — 'Her legs have gone all stiff and she can't walk. She says please could you lend her one of Mr Antoni's old walking sticks.'

8

But prison turned out to be good for Dimitris. The regular hours and having none of the temptations of the outside world was just what the doctor ordered for a man with weak lungs. — 'You should see his rosy cheeks,' she used to tell me, laughing and crying at the same time, 'just like peaches they are! I don't remember him being so fit and well ever since he was a child.' To pass his time in jail, he made windmills and moneyboxes out of wood and coloured raffia. Or he read. He could never get enough books. One day Hecuba came round with a bit of paper in her hand and said: 'Look at this for me, will you Nina, and tell me what it's all about. You've had an education and read so many books yourself. Who on earth is this Max Nordau and this Freud he wants me to buy for him? If they're communist books he'll have them taken away by the wardens!' — 'Really, Hecuba,' I told her, 'sometimes I think it's a good thing you're around to give me a good laugh every now and again! What on earth are you afraid of? That book of Nordau's about conventional lies is one I remember my father used to read. As for Freud, he's a great psychiatrist. Don't tell me you've never heard of psycho-analysis and the Oedipus complex?' But as soon as she heard the word psychiatrist she didn't wait to hear the rest. — 'Psychiatrist! Well I never! And what would he be wanting with books like that?' It was all I could do to reassure her. — 'Stop being so damn suspicious like an old peasant woman!', I told her. 'Buy him the books, and if they confiscate them it'll just be too bad.' In fact I gave her fifty drachmas to help her out. Although we weren't too well off ourselves at the time, I used to help her as much as I could, for the sake of poor Dino's soul as much as anything. So she went down to the bookshops in Aesculapius Street and bought them. But before she took them to Dimitris she was silly enough to show them to Theodore. As soon as he saw them his eyes popped out of his head and he began shouting blue murder. He grabbed the books and burned them to a cinder in the stove. — 'Call yourself a journalist,' I sometimes say to him now to tease him, 'who ever heard of burning Freud! Even the servant girls have heard of him by now! . . .' Theodore is the nicest man in the world. I've no complaints, thank God. But, outside of his own work, his little account book and the sports pages of the newspapers, he hasn't got a clue about anything. He pokes fun at me when he sees me reading a serious book. Give him a blood and thunder thriller and that's all he asks for. And even those he prefers ready chopped up for him and served in the dark at the cinema. So that she wouldn't go to see him in jail empty-handed, I opened the cupboard with all those old books of poor papa's and gave her Darwin's 'Origin of the Species' and Emil Zola's 'Human Beast' to take to him.

9

In the autumn of 1939 Polyxene got engaged to a doctor. —
'And where did she meet him?', I asked Hecuba after the congratulations — 'At the chemist's shop' — 'I must say, those
chemist's shops are real marriage marts,' I said to her jokingly.
She looked at me blankly. 'Didn't you tell me about that
notary, that she met him in the chemist's shop as well?' —
'Shhh!' she hissed, pretending to be scared. 'Ssshh! Even walls
have ears! How the devil do you remember all that! I've forgotten it myself. I'll have to stop telling you my secrets. If ever
we should become enemies, you know enough about me to
hang me! But truly, Nina, you've no idea how I've begged and
prayed to God for a good boy to marry her! And He's listened
to my prayers at last, praise be. Let's hope He'll perform
the same miracle for Eleni, too, and she can leave that fat
slimy slob. The silly bitch had to go and get herself mixed
up with a married man. If only he was something to look
at, I might say good luck to her. But you can't imagine what
an ugly revolting monster he is, Nina. It makes you sick
just to look at him. God knows what she sees in him. He takes
her travelling, she says. But how long will he take her travelling, I'd like to know? That sort of thing soon wears off. The
day will come, make no mistake. I may be in my grave by
then, but you younger ones will still be alive and you'll see
If I wasn't right. He'll leave her flat, he will, and go back to
his wife and kids. And she'll be left all alone without a soul
in the world to turn to . . .'

Hecuba had the mistaken notion, just like my poor mama,
that all a girl had to do was to get married and all her problems
were solved overnight. Apparently she hadn't learned a lesson
from her own married troubles. Marriage was the only thing
she dreamed about for Theodore, too — but not for Dimitris.
She couldn't even imagine Dimitris getting married. But she

171

was in a hurry to marry Theodore off and get rid of him. 'Can't you help find sort of girl for him, Nina,' she used to say, 'so I can get some peace and not have to put up with his constant grumbling? But she must have a house of her own. I don't care what she is. She can be a widow, ugly as sin, old, hunchbacked, anything, as long as she's got a house! . . .' Although Theodore was only thirty-six or thirty-seven at the time, Hecuba was afraid he'd stay a bachelor for life. One day when I happened to be at her house, I asked her, out of sheer curiosity, how old Theodore was. She told me she wasn't sure whether he was born in 1903 or 1904. — 'Really, you're the limit!', I told her, don't you even know when your own children were born?' And she got her grandson to take down the ikon of St Fanourios off the wall. In a fine round hand, her husband had written in ink on the back the birth-dates of all the children — including the two from his second marriage. Beside Theodore's name was written: 3 September 1903. He was two years younger than me. *Two*. Not four, as that poison-tongued daughter of mine likes to make out!

10

From the summer of '38 Antoni's business began going downhill fast. His blood pressure went up from the worry, and he spent all day pacing up and down inside the house like a caged lion. 'Come on, Hecuba,' he'd say to her when she came, 'get out the pack of cards and let's see what's going to happen. Perhaps the cards can tell us whether business is going to pick up or not.' Hecuba would spread the cards on the table, as she'd learned to do from the Turkish women in Salonika: three rows of nine cards, and one face down on the cards which meant 'work', 'house', and 'bed'. That's the way she always told his fortune. But never the truth. We had a secret arrangement that she would tell him nothing but good, to keep his courage up. But when we were alone, she'd say sometimes: 'I'd keep your eye on him if I were you. That damned ten of clubs came up again today!'

And well might the ten of clubs keep turning up! It wasn't only his leg and his blood pressure. His heart was in an even worse mess. I simply shook with terror at the thought they might come and tell me one day that he'd dropped dead in the street. One day Boros stopped me in the hall as he was leaving: 'Ninetta,' he said—he always called me Ninetta, we're old family friends and we were on very familiar terms, in fact he was a bit keen on me once upon a time—'Ninetta,' he said, 'as your family doctor I'm going to ask you an indiscreet question.'—'Ask away!', I said.—'Tell me,' he said with a smile, 'how many times a month . . .'—'Stop!', I said, 'there's no need to say any more. I know what you're getting at. Really, Thanos, you must be pulling my leg! How many times a month? Once every three months, maybe, and that's if I'm lucky! . . .' As for him being incapable and all that kind of thing, I said not a word. There was no point in putting him to shame. Anyway, I knew it was all medical rubbish. Antoni's illness wasn't so much physical as psychological: he'd got used to having plenty of money in his pocket and spending it right and left, and when he saw the money giving out without being able to replace it, he began to give out himself. He'd already taken his suits twice to his cousin Fouriotis to have them taken in, and they still needed taking in some more. — 'Well, that's that,' he said to me in bed with a sigh the night Hitler invaded Poland, 'what I've managed to do in my life is done. From now on, the road goes downhill.' He knew that as long as the war went on in Europe, even if Greece stayed neutral, it was impossible for his business to pick up. — 'It's the young ones who are lucky now,' he said, 'they'll live to build from the ruins. We won't. We're finished.' To avoid paying rent for the storage yard, he decided to rent out the timber. We made do for a while with the money he got. But, you see, we always kept an open house. It isn't easy to change your ways of living overnight. We had a servant, and private school fees to pay for our Duchess. I was naïve enough to think that by keeping company with girls from good families she would learn how to behave. We began dipping into the money we kept in the Bank, the money we swore never to touch unless we were really desperate. I decided to get him to sell the piano. Nobody ever touched it. After four solid years of taking lessons, the silly little nitwit couldn't play so much as a tango with two fingers. What was the point of having a piano in the drawing room worth thirty five thousand drachmas just for an ornament? We could get by for at least six months with that money, time enough to see the way things were likely to go in Greece, whether there would be war or not. And although she hadn't so much as touched the keys in six months, when she saw the removers taking the piano out she made such a commotion and went into such tantrums that my ulcer played me up for days afterwards. The things she said to me and her stepfather! She carried on just as she does now with Theodore. She said I'd talked him into selling the piano because I was jealous of her and wanted to stop her making something of herself. Me! Jealous of her! After all the sacrifices I'd made, marrying a man twenty years older than me so she'd not want for anything! And when the examination results came out in July and she was told she'd failed, it was all my fault again because I hadn't hired a tutor, because I never once asked her how she was getting on with her studies, because I didn't love her, and all the rest of it. You monster, I thought to myself on Assumption Day as I was beating the egg whites for the cake, I'll never put myself out again for your Saint's day, and I don't care if they call me the worst woman in the world. It's not as if I ever got a word of thanks. She always used to say that I didn't make the cakes for her sake but just to show off.

Two of her classmates came round at about eleven o'clock, the only girls at school who would have anything to do with her. They came to wish her many happy returns, and I had to get rid of my kitchen apron and sit talking to them in the parlour keeping them company because Her Highness, for all that I'd been shouting for hours, had spent the whole morning slopping around like a slut and wasn't even dressed yet. As if this wasn't enough, I had a curious pain in my chest that morning. I've always been afraid, and I still am — call it some kind of presentiment or anything else you like — that I'd die of the same disease that killed my poor mama. Instead of sitting there being polite to visitors I ought to have been shut away in my room, not seeing anybody. My nerves were all on edge, probably because I never say a word to anybody when I'm feeling bad. I just keep it all bottled up inside me. You're lucky if you're one of those people who can cry and make a great big fuss, like Hecuba. But I'm quite different by nature. I do all my crying and shouting in my mind, in silence. So much so sometimes that the veins in my neck begin to swell and I turn almost black with frustration.

By about seven o'clock that evening our parlour was full of the usual visitors. Marietta took round the big tray with the ice-cream. Mrs Cassimatis had manoeuvred me into a corner by myself and was telling me all about the troubles she was having with her son. He'd got mixed up with some tart or other and was determined to marry her. I tried to listen to her, but my mind was a hundred miles away. The radio in the house opposite was blasting away at full pitch. I'd complained to Nota about it time and time again, but she took no notice. We had to listen to her radio whether we liked it or not. Mrs Cassimatis's son had set his heart on a tenth-rate so-called actress, one of those who dance in cabarets and night clubs. Wait a minute, I thought to myself as I half-listened to Mrs Cassimatis droning on, something funny's going on. I could see some strange comings and goings in the street outside: two or three neighbours had gathered outside Nota's window and were listening to the news on the radio. 'Excuse me a minute, Julia,' I said to Mrs Cassimatis, and I went to the window and shouted across to Nota: – 'What's going on?' At that moment the radio began playing the national anthem. I turned back into the room: 'Have you heard the news?' I said, 'A submarine has torpedoed the destroyer "Elli" at Tinos . . .' And suddenly I saw aunt Katie faint clean away. I knew Takis was an ensign on the 'Elli', but it just didn't occur to me at that moment. We found out afterwards that he hadn't come to any harm. There's no killing off a bad dog, as they say. At the time the ship was torpedoed he was strutting up and down on shore showing off his stripes to the girls. That's the kind of empty-headed cockerel he always was, and that's why I could never stand him. Anyway, when aunt Katie finally came round, and she was taken off by uncle Stephen and Irene, they all began to talk politics at the top of their voices. Cassimatis said the submarine must have been German or Italian, and Antoni, God rest his soul, insisted that it was British. Everybody was determined to have his say. But it didn't matter a damn to me what nationality the submarine was. Of one thing I was quite certain, and that was enough for me: that torpedo meant bad trouble.

11

On St Dimitrios' day we went to St Luke's at three in the afternoon for Polyxene's wedding. Her in-laws lived in Acharnon Street, in a two-storey house. Alexander's father was a doctor also. Polyxene's a lucky girl, I thought to myself in the taxi we took after the wedding to pay our respects to Cassimatis on his name-day. She'll escape at last from the dead-end of living with that Longos family. Fond as I was of Hecuba, and sorry as I was for all the troubles she had to put up with, I had to admit that her brother Miltiades and Eleni weren't altogether wrong when they accused her of being crazy and hysterical. It was because of her character that she'd suffered so much. And not only her, but her children also. Maybe she was unlucky, and maybe her husband was to blame as well, but her own way of carrying on had something to do with it. In fact, I used to tell her so later, during the occupation, when she went through one misfortune after another.

On our way through Omonia Square we stopped to buy a big bunch of chrysanthemums for Cassimatis. I usually made him a big almond cake for his Saint's day. It was a kind of tradition, just as they always brought a chocolate cake on St Anthony's day. But that year I simply wasn't in the mood to stand around baking cakes. I felt a strange kind of melancholy and my whole body was tired and aching. It wasn't just the cloudy autumn weather, or the international situation, or Antoni's health, or the way my daughter behaved to me. On top of all that, I had some trouble with my periods, for the very first time in my life. Although I was usually regular as clockwork, that month I was late for some reason. My nerves were more on edge than ever. I couldn't understand what was the matter with me. I felt I could start screaming at the slightest little thing. Damn it, I thought to myself, surely I can't be at the change already? Have I got so old without realising it? Have I wasted my whole life away already bringing up that bastard child of Fotis's? . . . .

At the Cassimatis's house there were more people than ever before. And, as you might expect, the men were soon busy talking politics. Cassimatis's brother Leo (we used to call him 'King of the beasts'), who worked at the Ministry of Information, told us they had found bits of the torpedo and it was of Italian manufacture. But Antoni stuck to his guns. God rest his soul, he could be so fanatical and obstinate when he wanted to. He said the British had deliberately used an Italian torpedo so as to turn Greek public opinion against the Axis and force us into the war, just as they did in 1914. — 'If Hitler wants Greece,' he said, 'why should he get the Italians to take her for him. He could come and do the job himself. Mark my words, the Germans aren't going to touch us. They're all Philhellenes. They learn Homer and Plato by heart in all their schools,' and so on and so forth till it turned eleven o'clock at night. — 'Oh, do be quiet,' I said to him finally, 'don't you realise you're working your nerves up and you'll need a double dose of sleeping pills tonight? You've got a very weak heart, you know, and it's about time you began taking care of yourself.' There was only one thing they were all agreed on: that, sooner or later, poor struggling little Greece would be in the war. You only had to look at a map to see there was no way of staying out. We're the bridge between the East and the West, you see, and we can never stay neutral.

12

But nobody expected we'd be in the war so quickly. When we heard the sirens going off that Monday morning we simply couldn't believe our ears. — 'Wake up,' I called to Antoni, 'there's an alert!' — 'Don't be silly. Let me sleep, will you. They must be practising.' And he turned over and went back to sleep. Every time he took sleeping pills the night before it took an earthquake to wake him up, — 'It's not a practice,' I said, 'I feel it in my bones. I'm never wrong about those things!'. Every time they planned to have a practice alert they used to put a warning in the newspapers. 'As sure as I'm standing on this spot it's a real alert. We're at war, you'll see if I'm not right!'. I jumped out of bed and ran to look out of the window. There was a great commotion in the street with people rushing around in all directions. From the distance you could hear the heavy drone of planes. — 'Italy's declared war! God help us all! Wake up Maria!', I called to Marietta. She seemed stunned by it all. 'Wake her up and tell her to get dressed straight away! We may have to go to the shelter.' — 'Are you going to the shelter?', I called across to Nota. But she didn't know. Nobody knew what to do or where to go. We were in a complete state of panic. It was as though the world was coming to an end. Antoni was sitting absent-mindedly on the edge of the bed, holding one sock in his hand. — 'Are you feeling alright?', I asked him. 'Would you like me to give you your drops?. And as I stood there in the middle of the hall completely at a loss, holding my head in my hands and not knowing what to do next, Marietta came and said: — 'The Sleeping Booby won't budge an inch! I went to pull the covers off her and she gave me such a kick . . .' And she burst into tears. The poor thing had three brothers. Two of them were already in the Navy, the other was in the '41 class and would be among the first to be called up. We must send her back to Andros right away, I thought to myself, her place now is with her mother and father. It's too big a responsibility to keep her here with us. I rushed to the Duchess's room in a rage and grabbed hold of her by the short hairs: 'Come on, you little bitch,' I screamed at her, 'the end of the world's come and you lie there like a dumb stupid animal. Get out of that bed this minute or today will be your last!' And as I went to pull the blankets off her she lashed out and gave me a hefty kick, too. So I gave her a real good pinch and a couple of four-penny ones across the face and I shouted at her: 'Take that, then! That'll teach you to kick your mother. You needn't think I'm like Hecuba who takes that kind of treatment from her daughter and doesn't do anything about it. Alright, if that's the way you want it. We're going off to the shelter. You stay behind if you like and I hope you peg out. I'll be able to say good riddance at last to the bad rubbish Fotis cursed me with . . .'

But just as I was coming out of her room the all-clear sounded. The little monster!, I thought to myself. The world seems to be made for unfeeling creatures like her. I went inside, and there was an Antoni changed out of all recognition, as though by magic. He was standing by the open window of the parlour talking with Koukis, Nota's husband. – 'We'll clear the bastards out!' he was shouting. 'We'll make mincemeat of 'em!' We'll shove them into the sea!' Well, well, I said to myself, and to think he's the same man who was saying only a couple of days ago that Hitler wouldn't let Mussolini attack Greece. But, of course, I didn't breathe a word. I thanked God he was taking it the way he was. I went over to the window also and felt tears coming to my eyes as I heard the radio playing military marches. It was the first time I felt grateful to Nota for keeping the radio on so loud:

'I'll be an airman,
High up above the cloud,
My wings above the mountain tops,
My country free and proud. . . .'

Antoni's eyes were brimming with tears. 'I'm going out to buy a radio,' he said, 'why should Koukis have a radio and not us?' I was about to say that it was probably a waste of money, that it wasn't the right time to be throwing our money away on inessentials. But I changed my mind. – 'Do as you think best,' I said, 'it's your money . . .' – 'Ah, Nina,' he said, 'what wouldn't I give to be young again.' I almost burst into tears myself. I left him and went back to the kitchen just to occupy myself with something. He'd brought home a couple of pounds of chestnuts the night before, the first of the season, and I put them on to boil. Well, I thought to myself, that's that. We've had whatever life had to give us. From now on . . . but I just didn't want to think about the future.

An hour hadn't gone by before Hecuba arrived, fresh as a daisy and full of beans. – 'Oh, Hecuba,' I said, 'what's to become of us all now? Where will all this end?' – 'Well, war's war,' she said, 'it's bound to end sometime. It's not the first war, or the last. That sort of thing doesn't bother me. It's other things I get worried about.' – 'You mean to say you weren't scared when you heard the sirens go off?' . . .'Scared? No, not me. I knew they were going to go off and I was expecting it. Theodore was on night duty at the newspaper last night, and they got the news on the telephone from the Ministry just as he was getting ready to come home to sleep. But he simply couldn't stay on. The poor boy was dead tired after working all night. He came home and told us the news, and then snuggled into bed and said: – "Mama, don't wake me up, not even if the bombs start coming down!" And being deaf in the one ear like he is, he didn't even hear the sirens.' I was amazed the way she was taking it so calmly. – 'But don't you realise,' I said, 'they're going to use poison gas bombs? They'll come and take our houses and our girls!' – 'Don't be daft!' she said, 'I'm surprised at you, and you calling yourself an educated woman! That's what they told us in the last war and scared the wits out of us for no reason at all. As for taking our girls' (she screwed up her mouth sarcastically) 'don't worry, they won't come to any harm. Nobody's going to hurt them unless they start wagging their bottoms. After all, the Italians are only people, just like us, they're not wild beasts out of the jungle . . .'

— 'What's she got to worry about,' said aunt Katie when she came round a bit later and I told her what Hecuba had said, 'one of her sons is deaf, the other's in jail, and her son-in-law's a doctor. He'll manage to fix himself up. But God help our boys!' Takis had been transferred to a small destroyer, Petros was stationed as a conscript somewhere outside Kozani, right in the line of battle. 'God help our boys!', she said and burst into tears. After a while, Akis arrived looking for his grandmother. 'She was here before,' I told him, 'but she's gone now.' — 'Well, well, if he isn't a little soldier!', said Antoni as soon as he set eyes on him. He was wearing the uniform of the National Youth Corps. 'How many Italians do you think you can kill? Have they given you rifles yet, or do they come later?' He'd been to his school that morning, but they'd sent all the children back home again. There were to be no more lessons till further notice. 'Our booby will be delighted!', said Marietta. So the boy went back home, put on his uniform and reported to his section headquarters. They were made to form up in a line and listen to a speech by the section leader. Poor kids! I thought to myself, as I listened to him telling us with his childish enthusiasm how they'd decorate the section headquarters with paper flags and pictures of the heros of 1821. What they only had to go through, what an unlucky time they'd been born into. . . . — 'It's a good thing we've got our flag out, too,' I said to Marietta. We'd put it out on the flagstaff over the front door for St Dimitrios' day and we hadn't taken it down yet. 'At least it'll save you climbing around to hang the flag out. It's an ill wind that blows nobody any good.' And suddenly I realised with a shock that I'd recovered my cool head and my usual sense of humour. What the hell, I thought to myself, it's no worse for us than it is for anyone else.

182

Now that I see Antoni taking it so well, I'm not worrying. What's to be will be.

After a while Hecuba came round again. 'Has that little rascal of mine been here by chance?', she asked. 'He's got the key to the front door and I can't get in, damn Metaxas and all his National Youth!' — 'Sit down there and take the load off your feet,' I told her, 'what's got into you whirling around the place like a spinning top? Sit down and wait for him. He's bound to come before long. Have you hung your flag out yet?' — 'Bah!' — 'And hasn't the policeman on the beat had something to say about that?' — 'Something to say? What's he supposed to say? I dyed an old sheet and sewed up a flag just before St Dimitrios' day, but I haven't got anywhere to hang it from, down in that semi-basement where we are. Our landlord upstairs hung one of his own out. One flag's more than enough I should say. . . .'

When the front door bell rang we thought it was Akis. But it was Erasmia. — 'Well, well, look who's here!' I said, 'where have you been all this time? What's to happen to us all now, Erasmia?', I said, more for the sake of something to say than because I was really interested in her opinion. 'Will you go to Cephalonia, or will you be staying on here?' She looked hard at me through those long curly eyelashes with that evil eye of hers and said: 'Often I've prayed to the Lord Almighty to bring down his fire and brimstone, like he did with Sodom and Gomorrah, to wipe out the sinners and the godless from the face of the earth, and now the Lord has heard my prayer. "*. . . And the Lord said I will destroy man whom I have created from the face of the earth; both man, and beast, and the creeping thing, and the fowls of the air; for it repenteth me that I have made them . . .*" ' I was so amazed I simply couldn't believe my ears. When I recovered from the first shock and took in the full meaning of her words, I was furious. Ask anybody who knows me, and they'll tell you what a patient and tolerant person I am. I've never liked squabbling and name-calling. Even when I get into a fight with my daughter,

I insult her more in mind than in actual words. But when I heard that black-hearted devil acting the great Christian, saying all those horrible things at a tragic time like that, I just boiled over with rage. Suddenly, I could see it all so vividly: the cruelty and inhumanity of self-righteous people, who like to think that they're saints, pure as the driven snow. Every thing I'd been bottling up inside me all those years suddenly bubbled over and I let her have it good and proper: — 'Aren't you ashamed of yourself, you miserable old cow,' I screamed at her, 'pretending to be so damn holy! If that God of yours has to torture and destroy us to make us believe in him, then you're welcome to him. Keep him, and good riddance! If that's your idea of Christianity, then I don't want to be a Christian. I'll change my religion and start going to a mosque with the Turks! You wicked bitch,' I screamed at her, 'I've put up with you and your stupid fanaticism long enough all these years! You've done enough damage in my family as it is. You cost me my mother's affection and you damn near took my husband away from me! Get off that chair this very minute and get out of my house! I've paid dearly enough for any-thing you've ever done for me. I owe you nothing, so get out! This minute!' I broke out into a hysterical kind of sobbing. But not a tear came. I almost fainted away. I went to lie down on the bed, gasping for breath. Antoni was in the bathroom and came running out when he heard the screaming to see what was happening. But he didn't try to interfere. He'd never seen me so upset before. Erasmia stood there for a moment looking stunned. She never expected such an outburst. But she soon recovered her poise. She went out into the shed in the yard, gathered up some sewing she'd left there, tied it up in a bundle and tucked it under her arm. But before she left she came back and stood outside the bedroom door and started off again like the Hebrew Prophet: — *"And the Lord rained upon Sodom and Gomorrah brimstone and fire out of the heaven; and he overthrew those cities, and all the plain, and all the inhabitants of the cities, and that which grew upon the ground; and*

Abraham looked and lo, the smoke of the country went up as the smoke of a furnace . . .'" — 'Come on, now Erasmia' said Hecuba, trying to grab her from behind to pull her out of the bedroom, 'can't you see the poor woman's suffering? Do you really think it's behaving like a Christian to be glad when you see death and ruin falling on your fellow men? Is that what Christ taught us? I should have thought . . .' But she didn't get time to finish. 'Don't you dare touch me!' Erasmia screamed, 'you're as bad as she is! I could see from the day I brought you here that you were taking her side against me, you ungrateful creature! But what can you expect from one of your sort!' — 'Now just you listen to me before you go too far,' said Hecuba working herself up to a fury. 'Just watch your words with me, my beauty, or I'll grab you by the short hairs and swing you round like a cat by the tail! . . .' But Erasmia paid no attention and turned back to me to carry on with her prophesying: ' *". . . For thus hath the Lord said, the whole land will be desolate . . ."* ' I had covered up my ears with my hands so as not to hear, but she kept on and on. — 'Come on, now, Erasmia,' said Antoni pushing her towards the front door, 'come on, that's enough now!' But, as she went, with Antoni pushing her from behind, she kept up her droning prophesy of disaster ' *". . . for this shall the earth mourn and the heavens above be black . . . the whole city shall flee for the noise of the horsemen and the bowmen . . . everyone that goeth out thence shall be torn in pieces, because their transgressions are many and their backslidings are increased. . . ."* ' and so on, till she disappeared out of hearing.

When I heard the front door close at last I burst out crying again. But this time because I felt guilty. I don't like hurting people, and I couldn't forgive myself for descending to Erasmia's own level. And at the same time I was worried in case the bitch should come between me and my husband again. But Antoni paid no attention to the row. He had other things on his mind. He went out and soon came back with a huge eight-valve radio under his arms. He plugged it in and began to twiddle the dials like a child with a new toy. Radio Athens was still playing military marches. Then it interrupted the music to broadcast the first war communiqué from the General Staff, the same one we had heard that morning on Nota's radio. Antoni got up suddenly and said to Marietta: 'Come on Marietta, let's go. Take that big empty oil can and as many shopping bags as you can lay your hands on and we'll go round to Bouchlos. . . . I'll lay in a stock of food for a couple of months,' he said to me, 'so at least we'll be sure of having something to eat. But I don't want you to go on digging into it now. Put the stuff in the cellar against a rainy day.' — 'Marietta ought to go back to Andros,' I said to him in a whisper, 'we can't keep her here now. When you get to Bouchlos phone up some agency and find out when there's a boat leaving for Andros . . .' And I made signs with my fingers to tell him that we owed her four months wages. — 'Alright,' he said, 'we'll see. There's still time for that.' And they went off together.

I stayed on alone with the Duchess. I turned off the radio which was beginning to get on my nerves, fed the dog, and went up on the terrace to get a breath of fresh air. The leaves of the poplar in our neighbour's yard were beginning to fall. When we first came to the neighbourhood it was just a tiny little tree. Now its half-bare branches reached almost up to our terrace. An autumn breeze gently fluttered the flags on the houses, the clouds had begun to break up and a pale sun broke through every now and again, as though the weather was somehow trying to express what everyone was feeling. Without knowing in the least why, I felt a strange sort of calm spreading over my body and through my heart. After all, I said to myself, I expect Hecuba is right. I expect we'll get through it somehow. What the hell, the worst that can happen is to get killed! So what?

13

It was Hecuba's optimism that had given me heart that morning. But the same afternoon she came round to the house again with red eyes, as though she'd been crying for hours. — 'What is it?', I asked, 'what's the matter with you?' — 'They've let Dimitris out of jail,' she said. She was so moved she could hardly get the words out as her breath came in chokes. 'He came home and had lunch with us! He put a couple of changes of clothes in a suitcase and went straight off to Salonika to report to his unit!'

— 'Aren't you pleased?', I said. And I remembered what aunt Katie had said: 'One thing's certain, they can't call him up with him being consumptive'. — 'Don't you see,' she answered, 'you read all those books of yours and you still can't understand. If he was in good health and they called him up I wouldn't worry at all. In fact, I'd be glad. A bit of discipline is good for people. As for the danger, well, I'd just make up my mind to it. After all, he's not the only one. But with his illness and his character, he'd have been a thousand times better off in jail. As least up to now I knew where to find him. I could go and see him as often as I liked and there was nothing to worry about. But now I'll be worried stiff in case they come knocking at the door to tell me he's got himself mixed up again in some dirty work. Up there in Salonika he'll start lounging around his old haunts again with those cronies of his; he'll be roaming the streets all night and taking up with those whore-bitches who sucked him dry all those years. Honestly, Nina, I can't take any more of it. I'm sick of my whole life. All I wish is that they get on with their bombing and poison gassing. The sooner the better. It's the only way I'll get some peace at last. . . .' — 'Go on with you, I don't want to hear you talk like that,' I told her, 'You know you don't really mean it. You enjoy life, I know you do, more than most of us probably. If you didn't you wouldn't get so upset when things go wrong. You've just got a fit of depression today and nothing seems worthwhile. But don't worry, you'll be as right as rain in the morning. . . .'

Poor old Hecuba! I said to myself. You really liked having him in jail, like people who shut birds up in cages on the excuse that they're protecting them from their enemies. But that Dimitris of yours isn't the kind of bird that sits quietly in his cage without trying to get out. He's an eagle, is that one! So let him go out into the world and take his chance, like the rest of us. How selfish mothers can be sometimes! I thought to myself after she'd left. I wonder, am I the same with my daughter? Am I being unfair to her? I stopped for a moment thinking, looking into my own conscience. I never liked to do things myself that I made fun of in others. God knows how much I loved her, how much I still love her, deep down inside. No matter what some children may say, a mother is always a mother. Blood is thicker than water. I always wanted her happiness. I hoped that she'd straighten out as she got older, and I might have someone of my own, someone to give me a glass of water in my old age. I never imagined the day would come when she'd regard me as her worst enemy! . . . .

14

The next day came. And the end of the world still hadn't arrived. Not only were we still alive and kicking, but we were a good bit livelier than ever before. Before it began to open new wounds, the war healed quite a few old ones: it shook us out of our lethargy, our life took on new meaning, we no longer lived without a purpose, eating and sleeping and excreting like animals. The danger aroused feelings we never knew we had in us. It brought people together. I'd never felt so close to Antoni as I did during those first few months of war. We may have slept side by side all those years, but we each lived our own lives, like strangers or sometimes even enemies. Now, for the first time, I realised how much he loved me and what a big-hearted man he was underneath his peasant ways. In bed at night he'd sigh sadly and say: 'What are we to do, Nina? The money in the bank is almost gone and all we have left is the timber'. And I told him: 'Oooff! Why worry? We're not the only ones. There are lots of people who have far less than we do, yet they're no happier and no unhappier than we are. Hecuba hasn't got a penny in the world except the little Theodore earns. And don't forget,' I said, 'the house is our own. If the worst comes to the worst we can sell it and all our belongings till things blow over and your business picks up again. You needn't think I propose to keep it all for my fine daughter's dowry, so she can give me some more of her poisonous tongue.' That made him furious. He'd sit up in bed and say: 'Now you just listen to me! I may not have much longer to live, but whatever happens, no matter what, I want you to give me your word that you won't sell the house. Otherwise I'll never rest quietly in my grave. I want to be sure that you'll never go in want for anything! . . .' And he'd burst into tears and roll over from his bed into mine (we slept in single beds, but we had them next to each other), and I'd caress him, not pretending as I used to, but with real affection of a kind I'd not felt for any man before, except for my poor papa, and I'd tell him: 'Please stop talking about dying all the time. If you love me don't say things like that! You can see now it wasn't your fault business was so bad. War was on the way, and people got wind of it. But you're such a silly-billy. Sitting there blaming yourself all the time and making yourself ill, convincing yourself that all the world was against you. Now you just look after your health, will you? That's all I want from you,' I said, 'you know I have nobody else in the world. If anything should happen to you I'll get no help from my relations. They'll just try to take advantage of me. And, as for my daughter, if ever she has me at her mercy it'll be better for me to commit suicide . . .' That's how I tried to cheer him up. It seemed to buck his spirits up and before long he was the same optimistic, lively Antoni I'd always known before he became ill. His health seemed to take a turn for the better, too. His leg didn't bother him nearly as much, his blood pressure fell almost to normal, and he hardly ever complained about his heart. I kept giving him his heart tonic out of habit, really, not so much because he needed it. His appetite came back, not so much as before, of course, but at least he didn't starve himself. It's funny, I used to think to myself, we had to have a war with the Italians for Antoni to get better. Life became more genuine, more sincere than it had been before. And somehow there was a different atmosphere. Every time there was a war communiqué announcing another victory in Albania, Athens burst out in blue flags and the streets filled with people as it used to in peacetime after a big parade. Half the men were in uniform, and alongside our men were the English, the New Zealanders and the Australians with those funny hats. Walking along in the middle of town it was more like Carnival time than war. As usually happens at times like that, a lot of people were having a wild fling, doing things they'd never dream of doing in peacetime. Let's live while we can—it may not be for long, that was the philosophy. All those first two or three months, November, December, January, we lived and moved at the pace of the military marches that came constantly over the radio. We might hear the national anthem being played twenty times a day, but every time it gave us a choking thrill of emotion. We were 'at battle stations' all the time. There was so much to be done, and it all had to be done by me. My darling daughter wouldn't so much as lift her little finger to help me. She just kept on reading her rubbishy novelettes – when she wasn't sleeping, that is. 'What on earth's the matter with you, you good-for-nothing slouch,' I used to shout at her. 'Have you been bitten by a tse-tse fly or something? I've never seen such an illness in my life! Perhaps I ought to take you to see a psychiatrist!' Unfortunately, I no longer had Marietta to help me. Three days after war broke out I sent her back to Andros. I collected all the old dresses of mine I could find, some old underclothes of Antoni's (for her father), and all the household bits and pieces I no longer used or had two of, and I gave them to her. After some hesitation, I put sentiment aside and gave her the old hand sewing machine of mama's which I'd saved as a keepsake. Somehow, I felt I didn't want junk in the house. Over the years I'd collected a huge assortment of rubbish. The cupboards were so full of it I hardly had any room to put the things I really used. On top of all that, although I knew how badly off he was for money, I got Antoni to give her three months extra wages as a gift, apart from the four months we owed her. I wonder whether she managed to buy herself a piece of land with it, or did she put it in a box, like most people did, until it was worth nothing at all? Poor Marietta, we'd gone through a whole lifetime together! She was a young girl when she came to us, and when she left she was a middle-aged woman. And unfortunately, in spite of all the promises we'd given her mother, we hadn't managed to find a good man to marry her. We'd tried to fix things up for her to marry a milk-man, but it came to nothing. I had a bad conscience about it. Poor thing, I thought to myself, she's gone through a whole lifetime working for us, the best years of her life, and now she has to start all over again at the beginning, learning how to feed the pigs and chop wood for the fire. Would she be able to stand it, I wondered, after the soft life she'd been living with us, with her nice clean room, her bath, her two square meals a day? The first few days after she left I felt as lost as the babes in the wood. I didn't know what to do or where to turn. It was lucky I had poor old Hecuba to lend me a hand. The two of us sat down one morning, without that beast in human form so much as offering to help her mother, and we cut up strips of paper for the windows. We stuck them with flour and water over the panes in criss-cross diagonals so the glass wouldn't fly and injure us if a bomb dropped close by. I never realised till then how many window panes we had in the house. We pasted and pasted and I thought we'd never get to the end. And that afternoon I went down to Aeolou Street and bought twenty yards of black dimity for the blackout. Hecuba sat down and sewed up the curtains and helped me put them up at the windows. Every time a crack of light showed at night a policeman would knock us up to complain. Apart from that, we cut up pieces of cardboard and put them round the chandelier in the parlour to dim the light, and some more round the ceiling light in the hall which used to burn all the time. That's where we used to eat, mostly. It was handy, close to the kitchen, and we used to sit there most of the time during the winter. It was small and easy to keep warm. It looked a bit like a knitting factory at that time We knitted woollies for the soldiers. We'd finish off the housework as quickly as we could and then we'd all meet in my house to knit vests, scarves and gloves for the soldiers — Mrs Cassimatis, Mrs Kontopoulos, Mrs Hamhoumi, aunt Katie with her Irene, Nota, Hecuba with her grandson, and myself. The poor lads were getting frostbite fighting in the ice and snow of the Albanian mountains. We knitted away like machines, competing with each other to see who would be first to finish a sleeve, a front or a back. We'd sit there knitting and telling stories or singing like weaving girls at the loom. At that time there were a lot of songs making fun of the Italians who, instead of invading Greece, were being pushed back almost into the sea by our lads:

'Our tent is full of holes and leaks,
No foot of ground we gain,
But don't blame us, just blame the Greeks
For all that bloody rain!' . . .

Sometimes I sing the song now and tears come to my eyes. I feel a strange kind of nostalgia when I think of those days.

Never in my life have I knitted with such gusto as I did then. I got to the point where I could finish a whole pullover in one day. The time passed pleasantly and we never felt the least bit tired. It was only that no-good daughter of mine who refused to do her share of the knitting, or at least help me with the housework. She'd begun a stupid little scarf a month back and she was still mucking about with it. She made one mistake after another, dropped stitches, and had to keep unravelling what she'd done and start all over again. And the worst of it was that I had to leave my own knitting to help her with hers, or she'd kick up no end of a fuss. She said I deliberately stopped her from learning how to knit properly so that I could boast about my own work. Even Hecuba's grandson had learned to knit. And very nicely, too, for all that he was a boy! He did a cable-stitch that was better than some of the women could manage. The truth is that we were most interested in speed, we didn't mind so much if it wasn't perfect. We'd watch him grab the great big knitting needles in his tiny hands and knit away, his tongue sticking out in concentration, as though he was born to it, and we'd burst out laughing.

Every now and again there would be an air raid alert on the sirens. But after the first two or three weeks we stopped going to the shelter. We knew they wouldn't bomb Athens on account of the ancient monuments. If they dared bomb Athens we'd have bombed their Rome to smithereens. And then again, Antoni used to take sleeping pills and didn't wake up very easily. And if he did wake up in the night, he was poorly next day. Not to mention my darling daughter who always slept as though she'd swallowed a dozen sleeping pills. God only knows what I used to go through to wake her up and get her dressed. Finally, I thought to myself: to hell with it! I don't care if it rains with bombs, I'm not moving out of my warm bed! I'd wake up when the sirens went, and all I would do was to prop myself up on the pillows and read till the all-clear sounded. I had a little bedside lamp that gave just enough light to see the page of my book. When there was no electricity, as often happened during an alert, I'd just lie awake in bed thinking: I'd think about the past, make plans for the future, until the all-clear went and I could go back to sleep. — 'You're absolutely right,' Hecuba said. She was furious with her Theodore. 'God help the woman he marries, Nina, I pity her from the bottom of my heart! (If we only knew!) I've never seen such a hypochondriac in my life. Whenever he's in trouble with his bosses at the office he comes home and lets it all out on us . . .' He insisted that they all slept in their clothes, with their shoes on, ready to run to the shelter as soon as the alert sounded. But Hecuba was not one to be chivvied so easily. She didn't argue with him about it, but when the sirens went off she'd say: — 'Take the child and go along, I'll follow you up in a minute. I just want to take the washing off the line. We don't want thieves coming in and stealing the clothes.' There were lots of cases of that sort of thing happening in those days. Then she'd just stay in the house doing the washing up or mopping the floor. — 'Why should I go to the shelter, Nina?, she said, 'I know perfectly well no bomb is going to get me. It's worrying about my Dimitris that's going to be the finish of me and nothing else!' — 'How did you know?', I said. — 'Oh I know alright,' she answered with complete conviction, and her face would grow as sad as could be. . . .

15

As I was saying the other day to Mrs Rossopoulos, you can't be sure of anything in this life. And you never know anybody's luck till you see how he finishes up. The ancient Greeks knew what they were talking about. There was one member of the family Hecuba wasn't in the least worried about, and that was her son-in-law. She knew he was well away from danger, and in fact aunt Katie was always hinting how lucky he was compared with her sons. And yet he was one of the first to get himself killed. When the war broke out, he was called up at once, two days a bridegroom, and sent as lieutenant to a military hospital in Patras. There was an air-raid, and, as he was running with a stretcher-bearer to pick up a casualty, a bomb fragment (touching wood) cut his throat from ear to ear.

When she'd buried him and come back to Athens, poor Polyxene collected her belongings and went back to live at Hecuba's house. Her in-laws didn't even suggest she went to live with them. Even when they found out she was pregnant, they never once made the slightest attempt to see her. Up to then they'd put up with her for Alexander's sake. He was their only son and they didn't want to upset him. But as soon as he was gone, they began turning up their noses at her. Who knows? Maybe deep down they blamed her for his death. People are terribly funny sometimes. And the poor girl found herself back in the same boat. Worse, really. He'd left her a bit of money and a small pension which meant she could live the rest of her life without going out to work for a pittance; but, on the other hand, there she was now with a bun in the oven and her heart, as they say, broken into little pieces. But, unlike her mother, Polyxene was one of those stoic types who never make a song and dance about their troubles, who never talk about themselves or confide in other people very easily.

Although she used to come to the house in those days pretty often with Hecuba, I never really got to know her very well. When she had a miscarriage at the end of February—if it was a miscarriage—the doctor ordered a change of climate. She decided to go and stay with Eleni—Eleni had gone to live at Kalamata meanwhile so as to be near her fancy-man—and it was almost three years before I saw her again.

16

At the beginning of December Antoni got a first-class contract quite unexpectedly. A major he knew — a man he used to play backgammon with at the café — put in a word for him and he was given a contract for some fortification works. Just where it was exactly, he never said — not even to me. Of course the major was well looked after. You can never get anywhere in this country without greasing a few palms. Usually contracts of that kind were awarded after a contest to the lowest bidder; but who was going to worry about little details like that in all the confusion at the time? The major had his palm very well greased indeed, I may say. But it was well worth it. Antoni cleaned up a sizeable lump sum and, God rest his soul, he had the good sense to go straight down to Sophocles Street and turn it into gold sovereigns. That's what saved us during the occupation. If it hadn't been for those sovereigns the house would have disappeared into thin air and we'd have died of starvation. He brought them to me done up in a paper bundle and told me: — 'Hide them away somewhere, wherever you think best. I don't even want to know where you put them. And don't touch them unless we get to the last gasp and there isn't a crust of bread to eat! . . .' He threw them down on the table as though they were Judas's silver pieces. His conscience troubled him for having taken public money at such a critical time for the country. I told him again and again not to feel that way, that if he hadn't taken the contract somebody else would. 'And you can bet your life,' I told him, 'that whoever else took the contract wouldn't be in the slightest bit bothered by his conscience.' But it was no good, he just wouldn't listen to me. To ease his mind he got the idea of putting his name down as a voluntary blood donor for the Red Cross, and of course I encouraged him to do it. I knew it would be good for his soul, and it would be good for his health at the same time. He needed to lose some blood at the best of times. So he began going down to the Red Cross in September 3rd Street once every ten days, and when he came back home he was always feeling spritely and cheerful. I always had a large bowl of yoghurt ready for him, and he'd sit down to eat it with great gusto. He was delighted to be giving his blood in the national cause.

It was only when he began taking all sorts of useful things from the house and giving them away for Frederika's 'Soldier's Woollies' Fund that we crossed swords. It was all very well. After all, I was as patriotic as anybody and was anxious to help; and I was helping—my hands were sore and calloused from all that knitting. But I'd no intention of letting him strip the house bare. — 'Considering what we can afford,' I told him, 'we're giving enough and more than enough. There are others who've got far more than we have and give far less! . . .' But he took no notice of me, any more than he did at Koroni and later in Athens at the time he'd fallen into Erasmia's clutches. One day the National Youth lads came down the street, as they often did, carrying an open blanket, and people would throw in anything they could spare: some gave woollen clothes, some books, some money. Unfortunately, I'd already given away all the old clothes I had to various people. The last of them I'd given to Marietta for her father. I couldn't think what to give them. The first time I gave them an armful of books, the second time a pullover of poor papa's and fifty drachmas. But when they came by a third time a few days later, I began to curse. It's getting to be too much of a good thing, I said to myself. As bad luck would have it, Antoni happened to be home at the time. — 'I've nothing at all to give them' I told him, 'anyway, I bet none of it goes to the soldiers; it gets snaffled by some smart operators, I expect! . . .' Then I remembered the old trunk I had in the wash-house. I hadn't opened it for years. I went up to the store-room and, among other things, I fished out an old leather coat of my father's. He used to wear it when he went climbing. Somebody will be glad of it to keep his bones warm, I thought to myself. But while I was up on the terrace that clever husband of mine had gone to the bedroom, taken half a dozen of his best undervests out of the drawer, fished his good brown suit out of the wardrobe, the two camel-hair blankets off our beds—the ones Fotis had brought from England—and given them all away. When I came down all unsuspecting, with the old leather coat in my hands, and saw the beds bare, I simply froze to the spot. That was one of our really slap-up rows. I cried and cried. I shut myself up in the bedroom and refused to open the door when he knocked. I really must nip this habit in the bud, I thought to myself, before it gets out of hand. To placate me he went down to Hermes Street and bought two new blankets, the ones we still have. Sometimes when I go to pull the blanket up to cover myself, it is as though I can see him standing there alive in front of my eyes. . . .

17

When our army captured Koritsa, he took us all down to Omonia Square to join in the celebrations — Irene, the Duchess and myself. I'd never seen such an ocean of people in my life. Where on earth do they all come from, where do they live, I thought to myself? There were marches booming out over the loudspeakers and flags flying everywhere. Our people were intoxicated with patriotic enthusiasm, the English and Australians were intoxicated with beer. God knows where those people managed to put all that beer! We could never understand what kind of stomachs they must have. They used to stop their lorries outside the Moriatis tavern and before long there wouldn't be a single bottle of beer left in the place — except for the empties, that is. They didn't drink the retsina. Sometimes you'd see them taking a sip just to try it, and they'd make a face as though they'd taken a dose of castor-oil. The Australians were the worst of the lot. You never saw them without a bottle in their hand. They were all very tall, sturdy men, but they had innocent baby-like faces. Even when they got up to doing things they shouldn't, they looked so sweetly guileless that you simply couldn't get angry with them. One day I heard a fuss going on in the street outside. I opened the parlour shutter to see what was happening, and there was an Australian, as tall as a telegraph pole, blind drunk and having a peaceful pee against our wall. It was broad daylight, but he didn't seem to be worrying in the least that everyone was looking at him. He just looked at me as though it was the most natural thing in the world, and calmly went on with the job. I closed the shutter as quickly as I could. I'd never felt so embarrassed in my life. I was telling Julia all about it, and she thought it was a great joke. — 'Honestly, Julia,' I said, 'as true as I'm standing here, there he was with his flies undone . . .' and all the rest of it. We'd known each other since we were girls together and we were very free with each other about things like that. 'You won't believe it, Julia,' I said, 'but I've had two husbands of my own and I never had the slightest idea that men could have such . . . such . . .' Julia wasn't slow to catch on. — 'I know what you mean,' she said, and I thought she would split her sides laughing, 'but it just happened that way in your case. It isn't only the Australians, believe me! You wouldn't believe what I had to go through with Cassimatis when we were first married . . .' — 'Now don't you go wandering off. Stick close to us!', I said to Irene and my daughter. We were mad to bring the girls down into this wild crush, I said to myself. If anything happens to Irene, aunt Katie will murder me.

It wasn't long before people began pushing and shoving worse than ever. Everyone was heading for the Town Hall, moving in a great big mass like lava coming down the side of a volcano. The policemen waved their clubs about in the air, but they simply couldn't control the crowd. They were carried along by the great human tide like everybody else. Women began screeching and I saw two or three who had fainted clean away. I was sure my stockings must be laddered to shreds. — 'Let's get out of this,' I shouted to Antoni. But he paid no attention. He'd tied a paper flag to his walking stick and he was waving it in the air like a banner. He carried on like a little boy. And, to be quite honest, it was impossible not to be carried away at the sight of such enthusiasm. Greece hadn't lived through times like that since the days of 1912 and '13. I thought of my poor father: like so many others, he used to dream of the Great Idea becoming a reality; but after the disaster of the Asia Minor campaign, he used to shake his head sadly and say Greece was finished for ever. How happy he would have been if he'd been alive now! If only we'd won in Asia Minor, how different Greece would be today, I thought to myself. We're not a bad people, we Greeks. Of course we've got any amount of faults: we're suspicious and poison-tongued, and it's not in us to say a good word or do a good deed for anybody. But it's being so poor that's to blame. Where there's poverty there's enmity, as the saying goes. Whereas, if we had Smyrna and Eastern Thrace we wouldn't have to be importing wheat for the very bread we eat . . . And suddenly, what I'd been suspecting for the last few seconds became a certainty: there was this filthy pig taking every opportunity he could to rub up against me in the crowd, and there was nothing I could do about it — I didn't want to cause a scandal; but suddenly, as though that wasn't enough, he had the nerve to put his hand up under my skirt. — 'Aah!', I shrieked. 'Antoni!' But Antoni didn't hear me. There he was waving his walking stick about with the flag on top, and by the time he cottoned on to what was happening the dirty devil had slipped away into the crowd and disappeared. — 'Alright, let's go now!' I said, and he understood from the tone of my voice that I wasn't prepared to stand there arguing. 'Let's get out of this at once, and the hell with Koritsa and with Greece. You'll never make decent human beings out of Greeks . . .' When we finally managed to worm our way out of the crush, using our elbows as hard as we could, we went to a dairy shop in Aeolou Street. The others had hot doughnuts and honey, and I just took a lemonade. I soon felt a bit better, but my good mood had gone. The dirty dog! I thought. And he seemed so prim and respectable! The beasts, there's just nothing they'll stop at!

But in spite of that unpleasant incident, it was a memorable afternoon. I'll never forget it. Unfortunately, we weren't due to celebrate many more victories like that one. True, we took Himara and Tepeleni later on, and even Klissoura which the macaronis boasted was impregnable. But, from the beginning of the New Year, our fighting spirit began to falter. We didn't say so in so many words, but we all knew in our bones that the Albanian War was one of those heroic but pointless follies that Greeks get involved in. Sooner or later we would have to give in. The British weren't in a position to help us, they had their own troubles. How long could we go on scaring the wits out of the spaghetti-mongers by making fierce noises, without anything to back up the troops? They might not be much good at fighting, but they had any amount of war materials and they were beginning to consolidate their position. Every day our lads would fight a bloody battle to capture a hill which, after a day or two, the Eyties would take back. Petros told us all about it when he came back.

And, as bad luck would have it, Metaxas died just at this critical moment. Some said he died of tonsilitis, others said it was his kidneys. Antoni was inconsolable. The day of the funeral he took us all to Fouriotis's shop — it was in Mitropoleos Street near the Cathedral — and we watched the procession from the balcony. We were both depressed and silent when we got back home. But not my daughter. She had an attack of verbal diarrhoea. She went on and on, deliberately to spite me. — 'Oh shut up, you unfeeling bitch!' I screamed at her. I felt I had come back from the funeral of all Greece, not just of Metaxas. It was only a couple of minutes after we got back home — I'd just plugged in the electric pot to make some coffee because my mouth was dry as a kiln, and I'd slipped out of my dress to put on my housecoat while the water was heating up — and there was Hecuba at the door. I could see from her face that she was upset. 'We've lost him' I said. 'Gradually, they're all going, one by one, Hecuba. If you'd come with us you could have seen the funeral from Fouriotis's balcony'. — 'Oh, you and your old Metaxas!' she said disgustedly, 'Who cares about him and all the other bastards who make wars. To hell with all of them! I've got troubles enough of my own. It's that son of mine again. He came down from Salonika today with that Jewess . . .' — 'What Jewess?' I said. Just at that moment I hadn't the slightest desire to stand there listening to Hecuba's troubles. Oooff! I thought to myself, everyone has their worries and their difficulties, but they don't make such a tragedy of everything. Are we never going to hear the last of Hecuba's disasters? The whole world was going up in smoke and all she could think about was her own petty worries. But then I suddenly thought, after all, she's come to me for consolation, it would be cruel to disappoint her. — 'What Jewess?' I said, trying hard to pretend I was really interested. — 'What do you mean, what Jewess? The Jewess, of course. That Victoria, the daughter of my old landlord. You remember, Davikos, the one I told you about who set fire to his house to collect the insurance money. They started going together again, she and that fine son of mine, as soon as he got up there. They decided to elope, and they arrived out of the blue today while we were having lunch, without so much as a telegram to warn us they were coming. You should have seen Theodore's face when he saw them . . .'

But I was no longer listening to her. My mind was a hundred miles away. With Metaxas dying, I suddenly felt afraid again about Antoni's health, more afraid than ever before. I'd been trying all morning to stop thinking about it. But it was no good. Please God, I whispered to myself, not that! Don't make me go through suffering like that! And all the time I was half-listening to Hecuba, as though in a dream, babbling away about a baptism or something. At that moment, I simply couldn't grasp what connection there could be between a baptism and Dimitris and Victoria. It was as though I was having a nightmare. I felt as though I had a slight temperature. I'd felt the 'flu coming on for the past two or three days, and my nerves were ready to break. My hand trembled as I poured the coffee into the cups. I took my first sip and rushed to the sink to spit it out. I'd put in salt instead of sugar! . . . .

18

It was only the next day, after we'd finished eating and I went to lie down for an hour or so and my mind, as usual, began to wander, that I suddenly recalled what had happened the day before, and I felt conscience-stricken. After all, I thought, when all's said and done, what's Metaxas to me? One man's dead, but there'll be ten others to step into his shoes. But Hecuba is one of us. As far as I'm concerned she's more important than a hundred Metaxases. I remembered the stories she'd told me about Davikos. At the time they'd seemed like fairy-tales, stories that would always belong to the past, that could never continue into the present or the future. And now suddenly they'd come alive again out of the past. — 'What's the matter with you, laughing to yourself like that?' said Antoni as he was pulling on his pyjamas ready to lie down on his bed. — 'Give me that novel on the tallboy, will you, to save me getting up,' I said. I was reading Anna Karenina. — 'It's true, you know Antoni, what the song says: "The first love never dies". Just fancy them taking up again where they left off, after all those years!' And as I said it, my mind went back to the days when I was a young girl, to Aryiris and Kifissia. I opened the book and tried to find my page. I'd left a marker in it, but that darling daughter of mine had the irritating habit of flipping through the pages of the books I was reading. — 'It makes me laugh to think what Hecuba's going to do now with a bride dropping out of the sky,' I said. Antoni got into bed and snuggled between the sheets. He was dead tired, and he was soon snoring away. If she really loves her son, I thought, finding it impossible to concentrate my mind on the story of Anna and Vronski, she'll sit quiet and say nothing. God help them if she starts grumbling and grousing like she did with that nurse. The quicker they get married the better. Marriage is sometimes the only thing that saves wild young men like Dimitris: it gives them a sense of responsibility, makes them more mature, better balanced, even changes their whole appearance sometimes. Let's hope the same thing happens with Dimitris. And, after all, why not? As long as the Jewish girl has a little sense in her head, and Hecuba minds her own business. But will she? . . . .

I wasn't very reassured when she came round again next day and I asked her how things were going. 'What do you expect?' she said, in that grumpy tone of hers, 'It's a mess. She's had a letter from that father of hers, the big Archkike himself, and the old skinflint says she's to go back home at once. Tell me, Nina, what am I to do! I just don't know what's best. Sometimes I think it'll do him good to get married. It'll bring him in off the streets. He's turned thirty this year, and it's time he started to think about raising a family. And they love each other like two little turtle-doves. It makes me sick to see them billing and cooing together. It seems so funny. I just can't get used to the idea, my little boy with long curls and sailor suit being so grown up that he can kiss a girl that way in front of me. I don't care what he gets up to behind my back, but really, in front of me like that! . . . That's no way for a grown up man to carry on, Nina. After all, you can't live on cuddles and kisses. My son's been accustomed to living fast and free. He can't possibly go back to working at the engraving shop. He worked for three months up in Salonika and he almost had a relapse. You'd be horrified if you saw his handkerchiefs. And she doesn't know a trade either. She used to do a bit of sewing, but she doesn't seem to want to go to work. She brought a bit of money with her. But how long will that last? If she could persuade that skinflint father of hers to part with her dowry they could sell her share of the house in Tsimiski Street and they could buy a house of their own down here, to save them paying rent, and use the rest to open up a little shop and earn enough to keep themselves. I could move in with them and help bring up their children. But if he cuts her off without a penny, what then? What happens if he gives it all to Alegra, like he threatens to?' – 'And what about your grandson?' I said, 'what will you do with him?' – 'My grandson can go back to his mother. I've mothered him long enough, it's time she had a taste of a mother's joys. I'm sorry to say he's getting to be a real little roughneck himself, as pigheaded and disrespectful as his mother. You know the old saying: you pick up apples under the apple tree. He's not like the Akis you used to know. The other day he threw his silver cross into the dustbin, the one I gave him and he's worn round his neck ever since he was a baby. And last week he went off with some young louts on a walk as far as the monastery at Kaesariani, at least that's what he told me. When he came back he had a snake skin about six feet long. Said he found it among the rocks. I just can't cope with him any more, Nina, he's too big a responsibility . . .' – 'When can I come round and meet the bride?', I asked her. – 'Come any time you like,' she said. But when I called in for five minutes next day on my way back from the dentist, Victoria wasn't there. She'd gone up to Mount Lycabettos with Dimitris. – 'They've suddenly become great nature-worshippers!', said Hecuba, twisting her mouth into that sardonic smile of hers. 'They don't dare get up to any funny business as long as I'm in the house, and they start pulling long faces when they see I've no intention of going out. They seem to think I ought to let them turn the house into a brothel. Anyway, I've told them straight to their faces: either she gets baptised and they get married, or they can get out of my house, the both of them. I just can't stand him any longer. Every time I see him looking at her as though she was the only woman in the world, I feel I could be sick on the spot. To think of it! My Dimitris! He used to have women buzzing around him like flies, and now he's gone and got himself hooked by that Victoria! I really can't get over it. . . .'

Well, well, I thought to myself on the way back home.

there's certainly a storm blowing up there! And I wasn't wrong. The storm came in due course, but meantime I found myself involved in much worse storms of my own, and I had no time for other people's. Oh, what I've gone through in my lifetime! . . . .

19

We all knew Hitler would come to the rescue of the spa-ghetti-mongers soon or later. — 'Let's face it,' Hecuba told us several times, 'there's no getting round it, it's like the old prophecy told years and years ago: one of these days a horde of blonde monsters will come down into Greece from the north riding great iron birds spouting fire and brimstone from their beaks . . .' I'd laugh at her for being so simple-minded. In her own way, though, she was only saying what we all had in our minds. But people are strange creatures. Even though they expect something to happen, it always comes as a bit of a surprise. When we heard on the radio that Germany had de-clared war on us, Antoni turned all colours of the rainbow. Please Lord, I said to myself, please don't let him have a heart attack. What worried me more than anything was that since he heard the news he hadn't opened his mouth to say a single word. Was it that he felt guilty for having been on their side for so many years, or was it that he realised, as we all did, that this was the real thing, that all the heroics and triumphs of Albania were things of the past? Up to a point, we'd managed to get the better of the Italians. After all, they were people not very different from ourselves. But for years and years we'd been told that the Germans were like machines. What chance did we stand with them? The military marches they played over the radio that morning sounded to us more like funeral marches, like the death-song of the women of Zalongo before they threw themselves over the cliff to defy the Turks. — 'Please turn off the radio,' I said to him. 'Why don't you go down to the café and have a chat with some of your friends? It'll do you good to get out for a bit.' When he left I began read-ing the newspaper. The front page headline, in thick black type, said: GREECE FACES UP TO OVERWHELMINGLY SUPERIOR ENEMY FORCES IN DEFENCE OF

NATIVE SOIL . . . It was like reading an obituary notice. I threw the paper down on the table. At about half past one, just as we were finishing lunch, Nota came over from across the street and told us about the damage the Stukas had done in a raid on the Piraeus. Her cousin had gone down to see what had happened to his shop and found it a mass of smoking ruins. From inside the kitchen I caught her eye and signalled her to be quiet, nodding my head towards Antoni. 'He's not been himself ever since this morning,' I told her as I went with her to the front door. 'If only he would talk and get it off his chest I wouldn't worry. It's this silence of his that terrifies me. And what's got into that damned dog, howling away like that all day long!' – 'I expect she's been scared by the sirens,' said Nota. – 'Bah!', I said, 'she's never whimpered like that before. Frieda! Come on here, there's a good dog. What's the matter, girl, what's all the whimpering about? Well, bye-bye for now,' I said to Nota. 'What's the matter, love,' I said to Frieda, 'come on, now, stop crying and I'll give you a nice big bone.' But she wouldn't so much as sniff at it. She just tucked her tail between her legs, like she did when I scolded her, and curled up at Antoni's feet. – 'The dog's ill,' I said, 'do you think she's eaten something poisoned. Aren't you going to lie down and have your rest?' – 'Alright,' he said, 'but make sure you wake me up at four o'clock. It's my day for the Red Cross . . .' – 'What, with all those alerts going off, you must be mad! It won't do any harm if you miss one day. One way or another, the war won't last very long now.' I realised straight away that I'd put my foot in it. It was as though I'd told him: 'They don't need your blood now.' – 'Before you get undressed,' I said to my darling daughter, 'pop round to the dairy and get a large yoghurt, or two small ones if he hasn't got a large.' – 'Oh, leave me alone,' she said with her usual impertinence, 'I'll go later on.' – 'You'll go now!', I told her, 'once you get into that death-bed of yours I'll need a crane to get you up. Go on now, and get a move on! . . .' She didn't even answer me. Instead, she picked up her cheap novelette and plunked herself down on her bed. –

'You're nothing but a human monster!' I screamed at her, 'haven't you got a ha'porth of self-respect? You've no school and you don't even lift your little finger to help me in the house. Do you expect me to go and get the yoghurt? Don't you care the slightest little bit for your poor father's health? Do you want to kill him, is that what you want?' — And what do you think she said? — 'He's not my father, my father's dead.' — 'Shut up, you little beast,' I hissed at her between my teeth. 'Shut up, he might hear you!' And I gave her a good hefty pinch. 'Who do you think has been feeding you and clothing you all these years, you ungrateful bitch? Why don't you go and stay with your grandmother, and find out how long she'll put up with you? I curse the day I ever brought you into the world! Oh yes, you're Fotis's daughter alright! What else could he have fathered except a good-for-nothing slut like you!' In a tearing rage I went to put on my coat to go for the yoghurt and there was Antoni sobbing his heart out. — 'For God's sake,' I said, 'what's the matter now? Anybody would think you were the only one who took the side of the Germans.' He must have heard her, I thought to myself, and I could have gone back and torn her to pieces with my teeth. 'That's war for you,' I said, 'there's no need to take it so much to heart.' — 'I'm a failure, a complete failure,' he said, wiping his eyes. But they soon filled with tears again. 'Everything I've tried to do in my life, everything I've dreamed of, everything I've believed in, nothing's left. It's all dust and ashes. There's nothing to live for any more! . . .' — 'And what about me?' I said, 'don't you think of me at all? Am I nothing to you?' . . . . I kissed him and stroked his hair. — 'Go on now, go and get some rest,' I said, 'you'll see, everything will turn out alright . . .'

He went into the bedroom and lay down on the bed without taking his clothes off. — 'Aren't you going to get undressed?' I said. — 'No! Just give me an aspirin, will you, or make it two . . .' — 'Here you are,' I said with a sigh, 'but don't ask me for any more till the end of the week. You know aspirins are the worst possible thing for your heart . . .' He nodded wearily, as if to say: what does it matter now . . . And when I went to the kitchen to take back the glass, I suddenly felt terribly lonely, as though I were the only person left alive in the world, as though the world was coming to an end. I bit my lip to keep from crying out, threw my coat over my shoulders and went out.

On the way back I knocked at Hecuba's door. – 'Come on in,' she said, giving me a broad wink, 'come in and meet my future daughter-in-law. Victoria, this is Mrs Nina that I was telling you about.' – 'How do you do,' I said. Her eyes were red and swollen, and she was twisting a handkerchief nervously in her hands. As she was sitting there huddled up on the divan, she turned her head towards me and looked at me blankly as though she didn't see me. – 'I won't come in just now, Hecuba,' I said, 'I've left Antoni all alone in the house. If you've nothing better to do, come round and see us later on. He's down in the dumps again today. As if the little surprise packet from the Germans wasn't enough to be getting on with, we've been having some more bother with my daughter. I'll tell you all about when you come . . .'

Shortly before four o'clock Antoni started getting ready to go out. But as soon as he saw her he took off his hat and sat down again. – 'Come on,' he said, 'get out the cards and tell me my fortune!' – 'If I could tell people's fortunes, Antoni,' said Hecuba, 'I'd start off by telling my own. But even if I could tell your fortune, what would be the use? We can't change the blasted thing! You say you're feeling low. If you think you've got troubles, what should I say? That Jew-devil Davikos came down from Salonika last night, and he threatens to kill them both, may he rot in hell, him and all those Jew Iscariots who betrayed Christ for thirty pieces of silver! If only God would send a plague to wipe all of them off the face of the earth, every single one of those dirty sheeny villains! You've never seen such fanaticism! They're the most fanatical people in the world! That's why they keep getting themselves thrown out everywhere and they don't have a country of their own . . . You're a little bit depressed,' she said, turning up the closed card she'd put on top of the King of Spades, 'but it's nothing to worry about. You'll soon get over it . . . Now that's a strange thing . . . Are you by any chance thinking about a journey? You've got some money coming to you. Well, as a matter of fact, your cards are absolutely first-class today. But as for you,' she said turning to me, 'you're in for some bad news I'm afraid! Really, I wish you wouldn't insist on me telling the cards. Sometimes, you know, they come true and then I feel bad about it . . . Well, as I was saying, Davikos arrived at the house like a bull on the rampage. Victoria had stretched out on her divan and we were sitting there chatting away. I opened the door all unsuspecting to see who it was knocking like that, and as soon as he saw her, he just shoved me out of the way and walked past me into the room. Then they started on that Jewish jabber of theirs. I didn't understand a word. She got up from the divan, threw herself at his feet and began crying and pleading with him like a child asking to be forgiven. Well, well, I thought to myself, what's going on here?—"Perhaps you wouldn't mind stopping all that sheeny double-talk and speaking plain Greek," I said, "so I can find out what's going on in my own house?" '

—'Well, I'm off,' said Antoni, 'See you later. I'm going down to the Red Cross. Bye-bye, Hecuba . . .' And as I saw him out to the door, he said:—'Don't forget to water the flower pots. The gardenia leaves are turning yellow.'—'I've told the Duchess a hundred times since yesterday,' I said, 'but she won't do even that much for me.' He left, and I heard the front door close gently. The hinges were rusty and squeaked a bit. We'd not got around to oiling them ever since Marietta left. But it wasn't long before he was back. He got as far as halfway up the outside corridor and shouted: 'Hecuba! did I remember to say good-bye to you? . . .' We both went to the kitchen door. 'Of course you said good-bye,' I said, 'have you forgotten already?—'Oh well, good-bye again, then,' he said, I won't be long.' — 'Good-bye Antoni!' shouted Hecuba after him.

— 'What's the matter with him?' she said when the front door finally closed again. — 'God knows, Hecuba,' I said, 'I really don't know what's got into him! I'm not surprised the cards said I'd have bad news. I'm that depressed I feel I could put my head in a gas oven! You should have been here this morning when he heard the Germans had declared war. He turned all the colours of the rainbow. I always told him it would happen, but he'd never listen to me. I'd like to see what he's going to say the next time he sees Cassimatis. He thought they'd leave us alone just because they admire the ancient Greeks! But never mind that now. Tell me what happened finally with that Davikos. — 'What do you think happened? He gave her three days to go back with him to Salonika. He told her what hotel he's staying at, and he said he'll wait for her there. And now she's weeping and wailing and doesn't know what to do for the best. She loves Dimitris, but she doesn't want to break off relations with her father, and I don't altogether blame her. To be perfectly honest, I feel really sorry for the poor girl. But, after all, it's not my fault. Tell me, why should I have to go through all this aggravation on top of all my other troubles? It's not fair.'

Suddenly we heard a neighbour calling me from the street. 'Mrs Nina, Mrs Nina!'

— 'What the devil does she want, shouting like that?' I said to Hecuba. We never had much to say to each other. I avoided her because she was such a great gossip. I went out to the front door, cursing away under my breath for ever coming to live in such a cheap little neighbourhood. — 'What is it you want, Mrs Lola?', I said. — 'Quick!' she shouted, 'Mr Antoni's had a dizzy spell and he's fallen down in the street!' — 'Oh my God!' I whispered, and, just as I was, still wearing my house-coat, I began running down the hill. But I didn't get very far. I'd run no more than a dozen steps when I saw three neighbours turning the corner carrying him by the feet and shoulders. We took him to the house, laid him on his bed and called for Boros. He shut himself up in the bedroom with him, and when he came out there was no need for him to say anything. I could see it in his eyes: Antoni was gone! . . . I felt everything going black around me. — 'Nina!' I could hear Hecuba's voice like a faint echo in the far distance. 'Nina! Don't take on like that! Please, Nina! Say something! Don't keep it all bottled up inside! Scream! Cry! . . . .'

Part Three

1

The day Victoria disappeared, Hecuba had been at my place all morning altering two dresses I'd had dyed. When my poor husband passed away I found I hadn't a single black dress to wear. With all those deaths in the family, one after the other, I'd got sick and tired of wearing black. I didn't even want to have the spooky things hanging in the cupboard. So I gave them away to various people. I'd given the last one to Polyxene after Alexander died, a really lovely black crepe it was. I preferred not to think it might come handy for me one day. I'm a practical sort of person about most things, but when it comes to people dying I'm completely useless. I made the same mistake with the business about our family grave. I kept on getting reminders about paying the tax. We hadn't paid anything since the time poor papa passed away, and I kept on putting it off. I didn't want to ask Antoni for the money in case it might upset him and put bad thoughts into his head. And when we telephoned next morning to the cemetery and asked them to open the grave, they told us: 'You've lost your burial rights.' Poor uncle Stephen did everything he could. He begged and pleaded, but it was no good. 'Unfortunately, it's out of our hands,' they said, 'we've had an official notification,' and so on and so forth. Finally he had to dash round to the tax office to pay the overdue taxes so he could show the cemetery people the receipt. We only just managed to get him buried late that afternoon. He'd taken so many different drugs and medicines while he was alive that, touching wood, he'd begun to swell up and smell pretty bad. God save us all, what a nightmare it was! If it wasn't for having Hecuba to stand by me and console me I'd have gone out of my mind. As for that fine daughter of mine, she didn't even have the decency to act as any child would to her mother at a time like that. Not a single kiss, not a single word of comfort. Not once did she come and say: 'Don't worry, mother, everything will be alright.' And it's a good thing she didn't dare. At that moment, I couldn't have stood the sight of her. I remembered the aggravation she'd given us and I boiled with anger. She killed him off, I thought to myself. She killed him off, and now she's happy. — 'Take her,' I said to Hecuba when I came out of the faint and I'd recovered control of myself, 'take her and leave her with aunt Katie. And tell uncle Stephen to do just what we did with papa and mama. He'll know what I mean. And on your way back buy me a couple of packets of black dye. I've nothing black to wear at all!' My mind suddenly began to work as clear as a bell, as though it wasn't my own. The neighbours will hear that I'm sending for black dye and they'll say (I thought to myself) that I'm a heartless woman who can think of nothing but her clothes and that I didn't love him at all. But I didn't give a damn what they thought. What do those silly gossiping creatures know about me and Antoni, about the joys and sorrows we went through all those eight years we were together? They'll be asking themselves why I'm not crying and wailing, as if a person couldn't suffer agonies of pain without ranting and hysterics! . . .

Now, a fortnight afterwards, I began asking myself for the first time whether maybe they were right, whether I really was heartless and had no real love for him. Papa used to say that the death of someone we love is like a cut from a sharp knife — the pain comes later when the wound gets cold. And he was right, as he was about so many things. I know it now. But at the time I didn't know that a fortnight wasn't enough for that kind of wound to grow cold, that years and years would go by before I really understood what I'd lost and before I'd shed real tears for him. All those days soon after he died, I caught myself several times thinking about those gold sovereigns: at least I have the sovereigns, I thought to myself and then I would pull myself together. Nina, I'd tell myself, how can you be so hard and calculating, you a daughter of the

Aravantinos family! There's your husband's corpse still fresh in the grave, and all you can think about is the gold sovereigns! It upset me so much I couldn't sleep at night, and when I finally dozed off I'd get the most horrible nightmares. It's only now that I realise what a terrible state my nerves were in, and how human and natural it was, really, to think the way I did at the time. Everything had happened so quickly, it was all so sudden and upsetting, that no woman in my place would have behaved any differently. It wasn't like the death of mama or papa. It was a waking nightmare. I remember the night we sat up with the body in the parlour – aunt Katie, uncle Stephen, Hecuba and me (the others had gone to the shelters earlier in the evening). I looked at him in the light of the candles – we had to burn candles for there was no electricity – and I listened to the distant but clear rumbling of the explosions down in the Piraeus. I hardly knew who or what to cry for: for him, who'd escaped from a wicked lousy world, or for ourselves who were still alive and facing God knew what kind of future. I sat there talking to him in my imagination: if a bomb were to fall on us this minute, I said, you'd be the only one it couldn't harm, Antoni! And I turned my face away. I just couldn't bear to look at him. His features had changed so much, he wasn't any longer the Antoni I knew.

At three in the morning the house suddenly rocked to its foundations, as though the end of the world had really come. It was like an earthquake. In spite of all the strips of paper, the window panes smashed to pieces and one of the candles went out. We all thought a bomb had fallen on the next-door house. And, as though by pre-arranged plan, we all fell on our knees waiting for our turn to come. But several agonised seconds went by without another explosion. We read in the newspapers next day what had happened: a Stuka had dropped an incendiary bomb on a British ammunition ship and, instead of towing it out to sea at once, the fools had left the ship burning alongside the wharf till the flames reached the ammunition in the hold and the whole bag of tricks blew sky high, taking half the Piraeus waterfront with it. How could I cry for Antoni when we ourselves were living in that kind of hell and didn't know whether we'd be dead or alive next day? And, of course, the change of surroundings had something to do with it, too.

Straight after the funeral I went to aunt Katie's house and when she asked me next day whether I wouldn't like to stay on there, I gratefully said yes. I just couldn't face the idea of going back to that house. It would have been like shutting myself up in a tomb, with only my daughter to keep me company. And such shattering events were happening every day (the Germans had reached as far as Thermopylae) that I simply had no time or inclination to think about the dead. I realised that if I wanted to keep myself alive, myself and that monster I was saddled with, I had to leave sentiment aside and be practical. – 'What's happened to that future daughter-in-law of yours?' I said to Hecuba, more to break the silence than anything. It was getting on my nerves and I felt the need to hear a familiar human voice. 'I thought you told me the other day that she'd come round with you to give us a hand?' Hecuba lifted her head from the dress she was tacking, spat out a bit of cotton that had stuck to her lip, twisted up her mouth sarcastically and imitated Victoria's la-di-da way of talking: 'Oh, she had a reely spli-i-ting headache, and she just h – a – d to lie down, you see' – 'And what about your son, what's he up to?' Her face turned dark and expressionless. 'I haven't the faintest idea. He used to come and tell me all about his exploits, everything in detail. Now he doesn't say a word. Ever since he came down from Salonika with her he's not been the same old Dimitris. Last night he got home at two in the morning. There it is, you see, he has to get up to all sorts of tricks to keep the spawn of Davikos in the style she's accustomed to! I'd hoped that pagan old Shylock would get used to the idea and resign himself to it. But I'm very much afraid that my hopes will remain mere hopes.' – 'I wouldn't be in such a hurry, if I were you,' I said. 'Give him a bit more time to come round. Just wait and see, things will straighten themselves out . . . '

After the row in Hecuba's house, Davikos had gone off to a hotel, determined to wait there for his daughter. But when the war news came next day, he abandoned his daughter and rushed straight back to Salonika. Since then, of course, he hadn't given a sign of life. There was no transport and no post between Salonika and Athens. So the whole business remained up in the air. Hecuba brought her round to my place once or twice, but I never managed to bring her out of her shell. She'd sit in her chair with her arms folded and her head to one side, looking like a martyr determined to get through her ordeal. But, as we found out later, that undying Hebrew flame was burning away inside her all the time. When I asked her something she'd reply politely, but she never opened that enormous mouth of hers to speak unless she was spoken to. Her whole attitude seemed to say: what on earth am I doing here, sitting and listening to this Nina and her aunt Katie? I happened to fall in love with Dimitris. What have I got to do with these people? I don't know them and I don't want to know them. — 'For the last two or three days,' said Hecuba, as though she'd been reading my thoughts, 'she's hardly said a word to me. She seems to think I ought to let them carry on together under my own roof.' — 'I don't see why you can't close a blind eye,' I told her, 'after all, they're young people. What do you expect them to do?'

I really can't understand, I thought to myself, why you take it all so much to heart. Is it worth making so much fuss and getting so upset? One of these days we'll all be dead. That's the way I see it. True, I sometimes take things to heart and upset myself for the slightest thing. But at least I wake up every now and again and realise how much wiser those people are who don't give a damn about anything. That was the thought that had occurred to me that day a dozen times over, and I'd taken an oath on the bones of my father that I'd never say another word to my daughter. Let her get on with it, I thought to myself. Let her lounge around as much as she likes, read whatever she likes, on her own head be it! It wasn't up to me to mend the ways of the world. The main thing in those difficult days was to survive. I'd given the house to three different house agents to find a tenant, but I still hadn't found anybody suitable. They all wanted to rent it unfurnished. And what would I have done with all the furniture? Aunt Katie's house hadn't room for so much as a single extra chair. Fraulein Ober had one of the two front rooms, and the parlour and dining room furniture were crammed into the other. Aunt Katie had given us her own bedroom for the time being, and she slept with uncle Stephen in Petros's room. But we all hoped that, God willing, Petros would soon be home again. A friend of his had come back and told us he was still alive and that he'd seen him somewhere near Larissa.

At about six o'clock, Hecuba went off with her grandson. I cleared the sewing out of the way and prepared a few meat balls ready for frying later. Then, I remember, we sat down in the hall and listened to the radio. It was almost time for the news. Suddenly, there was a knock on the door. I opened up. It was the boy who'd come back again. – 'Did my auntie Victoria come by?', he asked. – 'Why, isn't she at home?' – 'No. And her trunk has gone, too. Uncle Dimitris is crying and rowing with my grandma . . .' – 'Hecuba's future daughter-in-law's disappeared,' I said to aunt Katie when the boy had gone and I'd shut the door. 'She's taken her trunk and all her belongings and they're looking all over to find her. I told the silly woman to close a blind eye, but she wouldn't listen to me. It serves her right.' – 'Shsh!' said Irene, with her ear glued to the radio, 'be quiet, I want to listen! . . .' – ' . . . The harsh realties of war,' said the voice, 'oblige us to leave Athens today and to transfer the capital of our state to Crete. Men and women of Greece, do not be dismayed . . . we will always be by your side . . . proud of your Greek heritage, you will resist the violence and the lures of the enemy . . . happy days will return to Greece again . . . long live the Greek nation! . . .' – 'Who was that,' I asked Irene. – 'The King . . .' Aunt Katie wiped the tears from her eyes with her apron. Uncle Stephen got up and went out on the verandah. They played the national anthem, and the Prime Minister Tsouderos began to read his

224

message to the nation. Damn it all, I said to myself, when will we Greeks ever be left in peace? Do we have to go on for ever crying and mourning? What an unlucky people we are! After all, the Jews are supposed to have gone through all their suffering because they crucified Christ. But who did *we* crucify? Why has God cursed us like this, why will he never let us lift up our heads? . . .

At that moment Fraulein Ober's door opened and she came out into the hall, pale as a ghost and with her hair all over the place. She'd been going downhill pretty rapidly for the last two or three years. She always used to go to Germany every year to spend Christmas with some nieces of hers, but she'd had no heart to go back to Germany since Hitler invaded Poland. Her father was a German, but her mother was Polish. She hated Hitler even more than we did in the worst days of the occupation. Every time I heard my poor husband, God rest his soul, sounding off about what a fine chap Hitler was, as though he were some kind of new Messiah, I used to tell him: 'You ought to go and listen to Fraulein Ober; she'll tell you what sort of a man your Hitler is . . .' She used to go to people's houses to give German lessons. In fact she even gave a few lessons to my genius of a daughter at one time, but not for very long. The princess found German 'terribly dry' so why should I waste good money? But ever since 1939 her health had not been so good, and she couldn't get about very easily. Two or three children used to come and have their lessons in her room, but even they stopped coming as soon as the Albanian war started. Aunt Katie and Irene kept their distance from her. Every time she was ill and couldn't go to the restaurant to eat, they'd take her a plate of food to eat in her room and throw it down in front of her as though she were a dog. The truth is, it wasn't so much because she was a German, but they'd begun to get fed up with her. She'd been in their house seven years. But, just because the situation was what it was, it seemed to me that they ought to treat her with extra special kindness, and I'd told them so a dozen times. I could see that she was suffering more than us. It's not exactly pleasant to have spent half your lifetime in a country and to love it as your very own, and then suddenly find yourself, through no fault of your own, living in the enemy camp. She stood hesitating in front of her door for a moment or two. She said something to Irene (in German), but Irene was fed up with running errands for her and replied (in Greek): – 'Alright, I'll bring it later . . .' I noticed how upset it made her, and her lips began to tremble as if she was going to cry. Suddenly, quite spontaneously, I felt the need to say something to her, to let her know, even indirectly, that I didn't look on her as an enemy. And, just as she was on the point of going back into her room, I said, laughing: – 'D'you know something, Fraulein Ober, I wouldn't be a bit surprised if I started learning German, too, in my old age. I'll come to your room for lessons and it'll be a nice way to pass the time for both of us. You'll see,' I said, 'in six months I'll be talking German like a house on fire!' She stopped short for a moment, and when she understood what I was trying to do, she tried to smile at me, as though she wanted to say "thank you". Then she went into her room and closed the door. And then suddenly, without the slightest warning, all hell was let loose! My daughter pounced on me like a tigress, trying to tear me to little pieces. – 'Aren't you ashamed of yourself,' she screamed as loud as she could, on purpose to make sure the old woman heard, 'aren't you ashamed of yourself, wanting to learn the enemy's language! Just wait and see. If they set foot in Athens I'll go straight out into the street and spit on the face of the first one I see! And to think that we put up with German cows in our own homes!' – 'Shut up, you silly little bitch!' I said between my teeth, trying to control myself. 'Shut up, or the poor old woman will hear you! Would that I'd never lived to bring you into the world – you she-devil! Get into your room at once or I'll beat the living daylights out of you! I've had about as much of you as I can take! . . . ' But she wouldn't go into her room. She kept on and on about it, till aunt Katie had to interfere. – 'Now you just listen to me, Maria,' she said, 'who we have in the house and why we have them is our business. Let's say it's because we're hospitable people; if we weren't you wouldn't be here right now . . .' And, shaking with indignation, she stalked off into the kitchen. – 'Monster!', I turned on her and shouted, taking hold of her by her back hair and giving her a good shaking, 'here we are hardly settled in, and already you've got me squabbling with my aunt!' For the truth is, I didn't like that hint about hospitality one little bit. Hospitality, indeed! A lot of rubbish that was! We were paying more than a fair price for what we were getting in her house, and if it wasn't for me helping them during the occupation, they'd have died of starvation. 'Monster!' I screamed at her, 'so you've suddenly become the great patriot, have you? When you could have done something practical to help, you preferred to sit there on your arse reading your trashy novels. Two months it took you to finish one little scarf! And what a mess it was when you did finish!' I was so upset I hardly slept a wink all night. I heard her snoring away in the other bed, and I could have gone over and strangled her. Lord, I said to myself, what a happy woman I'd be if I hadn't had that bastard child of Fotis's!

2

Next day I got dressed at about eleven to go round to get the latest news about Hecuba and get a breath of air at the same time. Apart from the once or twice I'd gone round to the house to get some things I needed, I'd not been out at all since Antoni died. I'd begun to get bored. Aunt Katie was never very pleasant company. She was altogether different from poor papa. And now that she was worrying about her sons, she was more boring than ever. She'd just sit there on the verandah and sigh away for hours on end, but she'd never open her mouth to say a word to pass the time of day. Not like old Hecuba. She could keep you amused no matter how upset and worried she was. In fact, that was when she was at her most entertaining. The poor thing! I thought to myself, fancy having that happen out of the blue at a time like this, with everything topsy-turvy and nobody knowing what may happen the next day! But maybe it's all for the best. One way or another, she'd never have made a go of it with Victoria. I'll take her a couple of tins, I thought. We'd had a visit half an hour before from the two Englishmen we'd met at the Hamiltons to say good-bye to us. They'd been to the Hamiltons first, and then come on to us. A general retreat of the troops from Greece had been ordered, and they were getting out as fast as they could. Ever since that morning, they'd opened up their stores and were giving the food and other stuff away so that the Germans wouldn't get it. So they arrived in a half-ton truck full of tinned food and all kinds of things, even things like those sun helmets they wear to go big-game hunting in Africa. They knew we weren't the kind of people who'd have gone scrambling among the crowds to get a few tins of food. Up to then, thank God, we'd not been short of anything. They took half the stuff to the Hamiltons and brought the other half round to us. Tom was a bit stricken with Irene. – 'Well, hello, Tom,' I called. And then, in what English I could muster, 'H-how are yew.' I'd begun to speak a word or two of English and could say a few simple things. I had a book called 'English Without a Teacher' and I used to glance at it from time to time. Tom began talking away like a multiple machine gun, and I couldn't make out a single word. 'Not understand,' I said. – 'Won't they sit down while I make them some coffee?' asked aunt Katie. Sometimes she was so simple-minded it made me mad. – 'Really, mama,' said Irene, 'you talk such nonsense sometimes! Coffee! Can't you see the poor boys can't stop for a single second. The Germans will be here any moment!' Tom looked at her, trying to tell her with his eyes what he couldn't say with his lips. He was red as a beetroot with the emotion of it. 'Good-bye, Reenie,' he said – he always called her Reenie. – 'What lovely fellows they are!' said Mrs. Hamilton who was sitting on her balcony and saw me as I came out. 'My Bertha is just madly in love with that Freddie. When she comes home from work and finds out he came to say good-bye and she wasn't here, she'll die of disappointment. Only last night they were swearing to love each other for ever . . .' That was the way she talked. Anyone who didn't know her would think she didn't care if her daughters had a hundred lovers. but we became friends later and I got to know her. In fact it was in her house that I passed some of the most tolerable evenings of the occupation. In fact, a more devoted wife and more careful mother of her children you couldn't hope to find. What made her different from other Greek women was that she wasn't in the least bit mealy-mouthed. She was simple and straightforward about everything. And she wasn't one of those who make out that a woman's virtue starts from the waist downwards, who put on puritan airs and graces in front of people and get up to all sorts of wickedness behind their backs. Her husband was English, and I expect that was something to do with it. Willy was a chief engineer at the power station, which was owned by an English company. He'd been in Greece almost thirty years. They're all in London now.

— 'Poison's what you ought to have brought me, not corned beef!' said Hecuba when I gave her the tins. 'It won't be long now, Nina, mark my words. I'm not long for this world, I just can't go on like this much longer!' — 'What's the matter now?', I asked, 'have you found that future daughter-in-law of yours or not?' — 'Dear Lord in heaven, may I never be cursed to set eyes on the Jew-bitch again! May she roast in eternal hell flames, the whore-devil! He's gone, Nina! Dimitris is gone! I've lost my son! . . .' And she started to tell me what had happened: when Dimitris saw that Victoria had vanished into thin air he began to cry and threaten to commit suicide. At that moment Theodore came home from the newspaper and when he found out why they were all out of bed and carrying on that hour of night, he blew his top and laid into Dimitris with his tongue good and proper: 'You silly little bastard,' he bawled at him, 'when will you ever grow up! Call yourself a man? If you had an ounce of guts and self-respect you'd go and shoot yourself! . . .' And with that Dimitris got up and left in the middle of the night. The next morning he went back to get his clothes. — 'If you'd come a bit earlier,' she said, swaying her body back and forth in sheer despair, 'you'd have been in time to see him. He was calm as calm could be, and he had a broad smile on his face as though he was having a sweet dream . . .' — 'You mean to say he found her?' I said. I hadn't cottoned on yet. And when she told me you could have knocked me over with a feather. — 'No! You don't mean It. Hecuba. Oh, you poor, poor thing!' I didn't know what to say to comfort her. The same as Dino, I thought to myself. Better if he'd gone and cut his veins once and for all, rather than do *that*. — 'Really, Hecuba,' I told her, 'anyone would think you had some kind of magnet, it's just one trouble after another!' I knew it would do no good if I told her what I was thinking, that she had only herself to blame for everything. It'll only make her feel bitter, I told myself. If I thought for a moment it would teach her a lesson, I'd have given her a real piece of my mind, even if it meant she would never speak to me again. But my poor papa was right when he used to say that people simply won't learn from their mistakes and go on suffering for it all their lives. Come to think of it, I told myself, I'm not much better myself. But at least I thought it was my duty to give her some practical advice. – 'Don't lose a single moment!', I told her, 'have a talk with your elder son and take him to a good nerve specialist, even if you have to drag him there, before it's too late for him to stop.' I knew of some cases of people who'd had serious operations and had become morphine addicts afterwards. But I knew it could be treated. 'If you have to,' I told her, 'put him away in an asylum . . .' And then for the first time, I sat there and told her all about poor Dino. Up to that time I'd never been open with anybody about the details of my private life, not even with her. Unlike Hecuba, I didn't like the idea of washing the family's dirty linen in public.

On the way home I passed by the English stores. People were crowded round the doors, pushing and shoving to get in and take anything that was left. A few hoodlums had grabbed hold of a jeep and were stripping it like vultures tearing at a corpse. As I went up the hill towards the house I felt a terrible emptiness inside me. If you'd asked me at that moment what I believed in, I'd have said: nothing! . . . When I got to the house I felt as exhausted as if I'd walked for miles. I kicked off my shoes and lay down on the bed. The Duchess was stretched out on the other, scratching her head happily like some halfwit. Then she began singing through her nose, pretending to be a baby, although she knew how much it got on my nerves. I gave her a sideways look without saying a word. The unfeeling bitch! I thought to myself, she doesn't even remember how much she upset me last night. I lit a cigarette. I'd begun to smoke regularly again ever since Antoni died. – 'Oh, so we've begun on the fags again, have we?' she said with a kind of sneer. 'Just shut up, will you,'

I said, ready to slap her silly if she said another word. I'll not have you telling me what to do and what not to do! Go on, get out of here! Go and park that fat behind of yours somewhere else! What harm have I done in my life to deserve you? Will God Never let me see the back of you? . . .'

3

It was about a week after the Germans marched into Athens that Petros got back at last. He'd been walking for three weeks, poor lad, sometimes finding some food to eat, and sometimes not. I suddenly heard his voice behind me as I was sweeping the yard: 'Hello, cousin!' — 'Petros!' I shouted, and began to dance round him and make a commotion so that aunt Katie, who was in the kitchen at the time, would hear. If she'd seen him suddenly without any warning she'd be liable to die of heart failure. I tried to put my arms round him, but he wouldn't let me. — 'Don't touch me!', he said, 'I'm full of those lovely little crawling animals! . . .' But aunt Katie wasn't to be put off by a trifle like that. She fell into his arms and began to weep her heart out. For a whole week afterwards she kept searching herself for lice. — 'What's happened to that pot-belly of yours, Petros?', I asked him. Petros was always on the stout side, like his father. I was very fond of him. He wasn't in the least bit stuck up and cocksure like his brother Takis. He had a heart of gold. It was his kind heart and human feelings that had made him a communist and let him in for all the troubles he went through. He wasn't the same kind of communist as Dino and Hecuba's son. At bottom, he was more of a Christian than any of us. — 'You gave us a real turn, Petros,' I said, 'arriving like that out of the blue. We thought we'd never see hair or hide of you again! How many days have you been on the go?' What on earth is she doing here, he must have been asking himself all the time, seeing me in their house as though I belonged there. — 'And why the black dress?' he asked me. — 'It was Antoni,' said aunt Katie. And, as he held me by the arm, I could feel him giving it a little squeeze. — 'And how's Takis?' he asked, 'Oh, Takis,' I cut in before aunt Katie could start her moaning, trying to make a joke of it: — 'Takis is doing fine, he's become a historical researcher, no less!'. In fact they'd seconded him to a Ministry and he sat there translating some secret documents or other that the Jerries were interested in. 'You ought to see him, Petros,' I said, 'without his uniform!' I was on the point of saying 'like a plucked turkey-cock,' but I stopped myself in time. 'He's like a new man,' I said. Aunt Katie didn't take kindly to jokes about her beloved first-born. As far as she was concerned, the demobilisation of Takis was equal to a death sentence. A few days before, she'd ironed all his uniforms and put them away in a trunk, shedding bitter tears, as though she was burying her son and not just his uniforms. Only she knew what sacrifices they'd made for those damned uniforms. For years she'd been obliged to wait hand and foot on Fraulein Ober; and Irene had to abandon her plans to become a dentist. Uncle Stephen, you see, had been fool enough to sell the café and go into premature retirement, all because the high and mighty Admiral was ashamed of having a café proprietor for a father. He kept grumbling that it would harm his career. It didn't matter so much about selling the café. After all, they'd have sold it sooner or later anyway. Petros may not have had airy-fairy ideas like his brother, but he wasn't the type to sit behind a café cash-desk keeping count of the coffees and clocking the billiard games. He was a studious kind of person and wanted to become a teacher of Greek literature. No, the worst of it was that instead of investing the money they got from selling the café, as Antoni advised them to do, or buying the bit of land at Batsi as Aunt Bolena suggested, so at least they'd have an income from the olive oil, they went out and bought themselves a French period-style drawing-room suite (it was about as French as I am!) and an English style dining room suite, not from just any shop, if you please, but from Varangis, no less! And it wasn't for Irene's dowry, as aunt Katie tried to pretend when I told her off about it, but just so that the high and mighty Mr. Takis could swank to his Kolonaki friends. And now all those sacrifices were buried in a trunk, with a ton of mothballs, and who could say when – if ever – they would see the light of day again!

That was the day I saw my first Germans. Just before my poor husband died, I'd begun having some fillings done to my teeth. I'd stopped going to the dentist since, at first because I just couldn't be bothered with that kind of thing, and later, after the Germans arrived in Athens, because I didn't dare go down town by myself until things sorted themselves out a bit. I thought it would upset me no end when I saw them. I sat on the bus looking out of the window sadly onto the streets which had been buzzing with life just a little while before. Now they were dead and deserted. The few people I saw seemed to be hypnotised as they walked along. Even the noise of the traffic seemed muffled and strange, as though someone had put silencers on the motor horns and the engines. But when I saw my first Germans I didn't feel the urge to spit at them, as my darling daughter said she would. The first thing I felt was more like pity than fear or hatred. It wasn't for a long time, till we went through all we did during the occupation, seeing children with their bones sticking out like skeletons roaming the streets like packs of hungry wolves, the corpses in the municipal carts, the hostages being rounded up, the executions, before I realised what beasts were hidden behind those angelic expressionless faces. That afternoon my curiosity got the upper hand. They seemed to be more like visitors from some other planet, rather than invaders. The first one I saw at close quarters was stretched out on the wing of his car eating an orange, peel and all! His skin was chocolate colour from the hot Mediterranean sun, as though he had a white father and a negro mother. Around his neck, inside his green military tunic, he wore a red handkerchief. Two or three kids stood around him, gaping. For them he was like a strange creature quite different from anything they'd ever seen before. One of the children was saying something to him, but he was suddenly finding out that the language he'd always used to express himself to everybody was absolutely useless. He stood there looking puzzled and almost scared, as though he were face to face with a great impenetrable mystery. I took it all in with one glance as I passed. In spite of myself, I smiled.

After the dentist I planned to go to visit Hecuba's son in the nerve clinic. Victoria had turned up long before and she and Hecuba had kissed and made up. Lots of tears of forgiveness were shed and they all agreed that Dimitris would go into a clinic, as I advised them, and cure himself of taking drugs. When he came out they were to be married. I knew she'd be annoyed if I didn't go. But when I finally got through with the dentist it was six o'clock. I'd no intention of being out on the streets after sunset, so I decided to go straight home.

And, as it turned out, it was a good thing I did. Hecuba came round the next day and told me Dimitris had come out of the clinic and invited me to go to Victoria's baptism. They planned to get married a fortnight after she was baptised. I went alone. Petros was ill in bed, and aunt Katie didn't want to leave him by himself. As soon as he'd recovered slightly from his ordeal he went down with an obstinate streaming cold, a really bad one. Irene had the curse, and she never went to church, she said, when she had the curse. Anyone would think God wasn't responsible for that just like everything else. As for my daughter, she didn't feel that the baptism of a twenty-five year old girl was worth going out of her way to see, certainly not if it meant interrupting her lie-in and her latest Marie Corelli. The fact is, they didn't put her into the water naked as I imagined they would. The priest just made the sign of the cross over her three times, waved the incense over her head, cut off a tuft of her hair with a pair of scissors, read the Gospel of the Epiphany, and there it was. From then on her name was Fotini—'the enlightened one.' I'd been used to calling her Victoria, and calling her Fotini didn't come very easily. It struck me as being in rather bad taste. But not Hecuba. It was Fotini this and Fotini that, and when she was feeling specially affectionate, as she was quite often at that time, she'd even call her Fofo. To avoid any chance that they

236

might start their old squabbles all over again, Hecuba set out by herself and found them a place with one room and a kitchen in her neighbourhood, so that they would be independent but she could still pop round to do their washing. At the time she was baptised, 'the enlightened one' was already pregnant. Hecuba treated her like a piece of fragile china and wouldn't let her lift a little finger, so to speak. They got along so swimmingly together that they agreed it was an unnecessary luxury to have two separate places. So they decided to move back together to save money. Ever since their marriage, Dimitris's mysterious 'business' activities hadn't been going at all well.

It was Akis who told me all this. Hecuba stopped telling me her secrets, and, as time went on, she came round to the house less and less often. Sometimes she went completely out of my head for weeks on end, just like Mrs Kontopoulos and Mrs Cassimatis. There were lots of reasons: she and aunt Katie had always disliked each other. – 'What's the point of coming?' she used to say at the beginning when I asked her if she'd forgotten me, 'I've no business in that house. When you go back to your own house I'll come . . .' Then again, the house was on a steep hill and she was still troubled by the nerve pains in the legs she'd had ever since Dimitris's trial. But these were only excuses. If Hecuba really wanted to come and see me, she'd have come. She wasn't the kind of person to be put off by obstacles of that kind. The truth is that our relations had changed a great deal by that time. Antoni's dying, which had brought us closer together than ever for a short time, later began to make us drift apart. She never told me so in so many words, but from the way she behaved and the stream of hints she used to throw out, I realised that she felt I hadn't mourned enough for him, hadn't shed enough tears. The funny thing is that she'd agreed with me hundreds of times before that strict mourning may have had some meaning in the old days, but today it was nothing but a theatrical sham; that you don't mourn for people by wearing black, you mourn for them in your own heart. And yet now she was criticising me for not

wearing a black widow's veil! And anyway, how could she
know what I really felt about poor Antoni's death, seeing that
I wasn't sure what I felt myself? After all, when all's said and
done, I wasn't under any obligation to put on a show of feelings I didn't have. I no longer had people who could tell me
what to do and what not to do, and I certainly wasn't going
to have Hecuba laying down the law to me like a mother-in-
law! Then, I could tell she didn't like the idea of my going to
visit Mrs Hamilton . . . not because she used to play cards,
but out of sheer jealousy. She came round to see me once or
twice when I happened to be over the road with Cleo and she
didn't like it one little bit. Cleo went out on the balcony and
called to her to come up and sit with us. She was always simple
and easy-going like that. But Hecuba just screwed up her face
in that sarcastic way of hers and said no thanks very much.
She thought Cleo was a loose sort of woman, not fit for my
company. She often used to say that prostitutes were sometimes purer in heart than so-call respectable women (if you
could imagine poor Cleo being a prostitute!), and now she was
siding with her natural enemies, aunt Katie and my daughter,
and taking every opportunity to attack the poor woman.
Naturally, it irritated me. But now that I look back, I realise
that the main reason why I began to grow cool towards her
was that while I was struggling to forget the past, to forget
Antoni, Hecuba reminded me of him constantly, by her very
presence even when she didn't mention him. When I saw her,
it was as though I was seeing him. I couldn't help remembering
that his last words were to her: 'Hecuba,' he'd said, 'did I remember to say good-bye to you?' And although I realised it
was silly to be jealous of a dead man, in my heart of hearts I
never forgave him or her. I often used to think with anger
and sorrow at the same time, that I'd spent nearly ten years
by his side, and that there was always a third person standing
between us all that time, stealing something of Antoni from
me. Somebody he preferred to my own company. At the time
it didn't worry me so very much, but as time went by and the

idea began to sink in, it made me more and more furious. Nobody knew as I did, even if I never admitted it even to myself, what his death meant to me. It was only after I'd lost him that I realised that, such as it was, our marriage for me was a return, a temporary return more's the pity, to my days as a young girl, to the carefree irresponsible days of Kifissia when I'd put my hand in uncle Markoussis's pocket and take as much money as I could hold in my fist. Antoni may not have been the world's greatest lover, that's not so very important for a woman, but he was a real man in every sense of the word. By his side I felt like a little girl held in the strong comforting arms of her father. I came down to earth with a bump when I lost him . . . Those are the reasons, more or less, why I began to drift apart from her.

But the last straw was when she began hinting about marriage with Theodore. She didn't say it in so many words. She just talked around it, vaguely, but not so vaguely that I couldn't see what she was getting at. And she was hurt by the way I answered, or rather by the way I didn't answer — I just pretended not to understand what she meant. I could see from her eyes that she was hurt. But who can blame me for it? The very idea that I might marry her son seemed at that time laughable and even revolting. Not only was he much younger than me, not only was it impossible for me to imagine myself a bride, but, when all was said and done, I thought to myself, what has he got to offer me? I had the house, the sovereigns, the timber. I'd no need of a gigolo. If I'd wanted a gigolo I could have found myself a handsome young one. Why should I marry Theodore, bald as he was and deaf as a stone? I just wouldn't think of it. Twice was enough. I wasn't fool enough to try it again. . . .

Every now and again I used to get some news of her from her grandson. He used to come to see me quite often and he was always complaining about her. He'd reached the age when it was natural he should rebel against her tyrannical ways. He told me she used to pinch some of their bread ration (the so-called bread they used to give us at the times — more like sawdust, really) and give it to Fotini on the quiet. After all, she was going to lay her a fine red egg, give her another Dimitris (it never even occurred to her that Fotini might have a girl); and that she poured more oil over Fotini's plate, and so on. It was from Akis that I also found out the latest about Dimitris. He used to take him and Fotini to the cinemas with the biggest crowds. Then he'd put them in the balcony and go and sit in the stalls himself. His wife would sit there crying to herself all through the film, and when it was finished he'd take her handbag and fill it with the loot: wallets, spectacles (for the sun or short sight), golden chains, brooches, lighters, and even tails from fox furs which he'd cut off with a razor blade. So, in spite of all Hecuba's secrecy, I know enough even about that period of her life to fill a book, as the saying goes. And then there were certain things she couldn't hide from me, like Victoria's imaginary pregnancy. It turned out to be a gastric condition. It was one of those depressing days in the winter of 1942, I remember, when she came round one afternoon to tell me the news. I found it so comic I nearly burst out laughing to her face. But when I saw her crying for the loss of a life which had never existed, not even as a foetus, I couldn't help feeling sorry for her. I felt something of our old friendship stirring inside me. I persuaded her to stay and eat with us to get it off her mind a bit. Then it got late, too late for her to be out alone in those dangerous days. So I said: — 'Why don't you spend the night here with us? It won't matter if you don't go home just this once.' After Fraulein Ober died, aunt Katie had given us her room and we'd plenty of space to spare. I put a mattress down on the floor for her, and she slept the night through without stirring, even if she wouldn't admit it next morning, like a weary child who's been wandering in the world and finds himself back home at last. . . .

4

One of the reasons I started to play cards was to stay awake at night and sleep for as much of the daytime as I could. Sometimes I slept till four or five in the afternoon. I used to swallow luminal tablets as though they were peppermint lumps. At that time sleep was the most harmless narcotic you could have to close your mind to a tragedy which, no matter what you did, you could do nothing to prevent. I knew that even if I were to open my cupboards and share out all the food I had to those who were starving, it would do nothing to save anybody and we should die of starvation ourselves. Every day I would listen to the eternal sing-song appeal: 'take pity on me lady, I'm hungry, my insides are falling out from hunger.' No matter how often I heard it, it never failed to upset me. I would feel a nervous pain in the stomach, even though I knew the beggar was often getting more to eat than we did. I used to think of the thousands of Greeks who were dying from lack of nourishment and my heart wept for them, not because they were dying — we all die sooner or later — but because of the way they were dying, like beasts, after hunger had stripped them first of every semblance of human dignity. The worst thing of all was that we became like them. Even those of us who had enough food to keep body and soul together were losing our human feelings. Every time I saw someone dying, one of those who used to collapse on the pavement before your eyes every day of the week, and I passed by as everyone else did without stopping, I felt disgusted with myself. It terrified me to see how hard and unfeeling I had become. In desperation, I started playing cards, like a drunkard who drinks sometimes to forget that he is a drunkard. My empty-headed daughter, of course, who had not the slightest pang of conscience about her own heartless character, never understood and never will. She used to call me the 'merry widow' and said I was a card fiend like my father. I see red to this day when I remember it.

Another reason I began playing cards was that I no longer had as much to do as I used to when I was in my own house. It was a way of passing the time. Aunt Katie never let me do anything in the house. Not that she worried about me getting tired, but because she was so fussy and wanted everything done her own way. I didn't enjoy reading as I used to. Somehow it no longer gave me the same kind of consolation. The books I read all seemed somehow dull and unreal. They made me impatient and irritated. As for my old love, the cinema, I just never felt in the mood to go. You had to fight and shove to get in the queue for the box office, then you had to fight and shove to find a seat, and after all that there was good chance of going back home full of lice. It wasn't just the revolting job of digging them out and cracking them one by one with your thumb-nail or soaking your hair in paraffin as I once had to do. It was the danger of catching typhoid. A block of flats in our district was put in quarantine at one time, and nobody in the flats was allowed out even to get their food rations. The food was brought by the Red Cross. They used to leave it outside the front door as though it were a leper colony. As for the buses, well I can't just describe what they were like. They made you curse the hour you decided to move outside your own house. If you didn't feel up to walking, you'd have to get on one of those gas producer affairs, when you could find one, and you'd get back home as black as a chimney sweep. Up to that time my relations with Mrs Hamilton were limited to a few words to pass the time of day from one balcony to the other. And even then I felt I was doing something I shouldn't. Aunt Katie used to pull a face a mile long. She didn't speak to her at all any more, just because she used to entertain an Italian in her house – Fiore he was called, from the block of flats opposite that had been requisitioned by the Italians. She simply couldn't understand that not all Italians were alike. Fiore was a good lad: he hated Mussolini and the war as much as we did, perhaps more. She accused her of having him as her lover, but I'm not blind nor simple-minded and I never saw anything the slightest bit suspicious going on, even though I was in and out of her house all the time. She used to let him come, not caring that he was an enemy, because she saw him as she would any young lad who was far away from his home and his mother. We found him very good fun to be with. He'd learned a bit of Greek, and he'd sit there for hours telling us about Italy and his home town of Padua. He was a law student, but he would have made a much better clown than he would a lawyer. And, let's face it, he used to bring us a bit of coffee every now and again — real coffee, not ground chick-peas. And only those who have tasted chick-pea coffee will realise what that meant for us! She invited me over one afternoon to have some coffee, and although aunt Katie pulled her long face again, I pretended not to notice and went. The next time she asked me over she happened to have some other visitors. We started on a little game of poker, just to pass the time, and it was really rather pleasant I must say. From then on, every time she asked some people in for cards (and it began to happen more and more often) I would be there among the first. In the world of aces and kings I could forget unpleasant realities for a while. I knew that staying up all hours of the night was the worst possible thing for my ulcer which, strangely enough, continued to bother me in spite of being forced to give up animal fats and live on a diet which made any number of people much healthier during the occupation than they'd ever been before. But I didn't give a damn. I just took aspirins by the dozen, and almost every night I'd slip over to Cleo's house.

It was a small group, but very select and pleasant company. They were all people who were stoically eating their way through fortunes it had taken them a lifetime to collect, for none of them were the kind of people who could cooperate with the Germans or live off the black market: Doratos was a former judge, Mrs Melas was the widow of a factory owner, a friend of Willie's, Mrs Caravidas had some land in the Peloponnese. She was the merriest of all. I simply couldn't understand how she could keep so cheerful with people dying all around us like so many flies. But I can see now that being able to forget from time to time and having a good laugh was what saved us, otherwise we would have gone mad. Every time they were setting off to come to Cleo's to play cards, she'd throw her husband on the bed and pull out two or three hairs from his you-know-what — for luck, she told us. — 'It's a wonder you've got any hair left there at all, Aris!' we used to tell him. He was a great lump of a man, as placid and simple-minded as you please. He had a passion for changing his seat at the card table every few minutes. He would pay you to take your chair, and when he had a good hand his face would beam with satisfaction. You could tell it a mile off. So naturally, every time we saw him smiling to himself we all threw our hands in and he never won a single pot worth having.

It was then that I noticed for the first time how much more level-headed women often are than men. One evening I played off a hand with Doratos, after the others had dropped out, and I took six sovereigns off him. He was flirting with me at the time. He was a widower himself, and Cleo wanted to marry us off. But I let her know there was nothing doing, and I began to treat him rather coldly. He was bidding up his cards obstinately, determined to make me throw in my hand, as though his male vanity was at stake. But I just kept following him as cool and calm as you please. You could never tell from my expression what cards I held when I was playing poker. What the devil can he be holding, I thought to myself, to be pushing up the bidding like that? But don't you worry, you old goat, I said to myself, I'll take this pot if it's the last thing I do, just wait and see. Not for any other reason, but just so you understand who it is you thought you could make gooey eyes at. Flirt with me would you! Well, if you think I'm going to saddle myself with a third bloody weight on my back, you've got another think coming! Either he's trying for a flush, I thought to myself, or he has threes, but anyway they can't be three

244

aces. I had two covered aces in my own hand. We were playing stud. Finally the last card was dealt, and I got a third ace. — 'It's you to speak,' I said. I didn't show it, but I was trembling like a leaf. After all, I didn't have so much money that I could afford to risk such a big loss. Instead of seeing me, he said: — 'One sovereign!'. That was a lot of money, considering the small game we were playing. — 'Everything you've got on the table!', I said. He came with me. He had three kings. He almost had a heart attack on the spot. Ah, what good times we used to have! Cleo, who wasn't so terribly keen on cards (Willie was the passionate card player of the family) used to get up from the table every now and again and bring us some almond paste she'd made, or some cake made with raisin syrup — not a hope of sugar in those days! We always used to put aside a small part of the pot for the house. Then, at ten o'clock, we would turn on the radio and listen to B.B.C. We would hear the news from the African and the Russian fronts — the real news, not the ridiculous propaganda the Germans served up in the newspapers. All radios had been sealed a long time before. But Willie, in spite of being a British subject (he'd spent two months in a concentration camp at the beginning of the occupation, and still had to report once a month to the Kommandatur) wasn't one to be put off by things like that. He had hidden a radio set in the little room on the terrace and he'd bring it down every night wrapped in a blanket like a baby. Poor Willie, poor Cleo. How I miss them now!...

5

But that night we'd decided not to play cards — to 'let the pack cool off' as the saying goes — and to go to bed at a human sort of hour. But in spite of taking three luminal tablets, it was almost one o'clock in the morning and my eyes simply wouldn't close. Habit is a bad thing. And it was one of those moonlit August nights when it seems a pity to sleep, when life seems beautiful in spite of everything! From the block of flats where the Italians lived I could hear one of those lilting gentle songs of theirs that was all the rage at the time: 'Dormi, dormi bambina, mentre io veglio per te . . .' it's as though he's singing it for me, I thought to myself. Except that I was no longer a bambina, God knows! The truth is, they had really lovely voices. You could go on listening to them for ever. — 'Instead of us going to Italy,' I said to aunt Katie, 'Italy has come to us. Would you ever had believed, aunt,' I said, 'that you'd have so many tenors from the land of tenors singing you serenades? . . . .'

With the Greeks it was different. When I heard them singing it was anything but pleasant. And some of those so-called 'light' songs that were the rage at the time were so absurd it made me sick to listen to them. Light-headed, I called them, not just light.

> 'You're so tiny and tender,
> Your waist is so slender,
> I long to caress and embrace you.
> But you're just out of school,
> I'm a silly old fool,
> And I haven't the courage to face you. . . .'

A silly old fool indeed! Well, you can say that again, I said to myself, and I shuddered at the mere thought of this doddering old slobberer who was daft enough to sing of his cheap yearning for a girl young enough to be his daughter. It was all very well for the Italians to sing about cuore and amore; after all, they were the conquerors – for the time being, anyway – and they were entitled to sing as much as they liked. But for the Greeks it would have been far better to behave a bit more seriously, maybe not to stop singing altogether, but at least to show a bit of dignity and self-respect. It goes without saying, of course, that my daughter, whose only real hobby in life was to disagree with me about everything, used to say I was a fascist. Me, Nina, a fascist! As though the stupid idiot had the slightest idea what the word meant. . . .

Suddenly I heard some shots. The Italians must be killing cats, that was my first thought. People used to say that the Italians regarded male cats as first class food, whether it was true or not I don't really know. I asked Fiore what was happening, and he just gave us a quizzical smile without saying anything. Well, that's the end of quite a few little pussy-cats, I thought to myself. Some more heroic victims in the cause of King and country! But when I heard some more shots, this time much closer, I began to get worried. My mind went at once to Willie's radio. I wonder if Fiore has given us away, I thought, and poor Cleo will find herself in real trouble. Well there it is, you can't really trust an Italian. But it will teach her a lesson. Nobody says she oughtn't to let him come to her house. But, anti-fascist or not, it's sheer madness to be so open and unreserved with him. Recently I'd begun to feel sure that Fiore was a spy deliberately planted by the Italians to find out what we were up to. It must be a patrol they've sent to find the radio, I thought to myself as I heard more shooting, this time from just below our balcony. I'd hardly had time to collect my thoughts when I heard the iron gate opening, hurried footsteps across the yard, and then the tell-tale squeaking of the kitchen door which overlooked the back of the house. I jumped up trembling with fright and ran to wake up uncle Stephen and aunt Katie. As I came out into the hall I ran slap into Petros looking wild and desperate. – 'The Germans are after me!' he said. I just froze to the spot and my hand went to my cheek. I didn't know what to do. 'Quick' I said, 'up in the store-room. Hide quickly!' God, I said to myself, they'll kill us all! Nina, get ready to join your father! At that very moment there was a loud banging on the door. They were pounding it with their fists and kicking it with their heavy boots, fit to break the door down. Uncle Stephen came out pale as a ghost and opened the door. In rushed two Germans wearing their steel helmets and with their fingers on the trigger of their machine guns. With them they had three of our own traitor bastards in uniform. They lined us up against the wall with our hands in the air while they searched the house. It wasn't long before they found him, handcuffed him and dragged him out of the house by brute force. When they'd gone aunt Katie began to wail and moan. We went to the kitchen to make some coffee. Willie and Cleo had woken up with all the commotion and came over to keep us company for a while. But we couldn't just sit there all night bemoaning our fate. — 'Go on now,' I said to aunt Katie, 'go and get some sleep, or you'll be dead tired in the morning. Tomorrow's a new day. Go to sleep now and first thing in the morning we'll think of something.' I simply couldn't keep my eyes open any longer. Those damned luminal tablets had begun to work at last!

6

Early next day uncle Stephen began scouring the whole of Athens to find an old friend who was hand in glove with the Germans. At last he found him. Together they hurried over to the Kommandatur and they soon found out what had happened: they'd been caught printing EAM resistance leaflets and Petros had managed to escape while the others were being rounded up. They were holding him for the time being in the Gestapo headquarters. But a week later they transferred him to the Averoff jail, which was close to where we lived, and I decided to go and see him. They didn't allow visitors, or very rarely, but people used to go round to the back of the jail and one prisoner would call another and they could talk to you, or at least talk in sign language, from the top of some high steps behind an iron bar grating. But it turned out to be impossible to get Petros. We found out later that he was in an isolation cell.

But to my great surprise I saw Hecuba and Victoria there. They'd come to see Dimitris. – 'Caught you!' I said. She turned round and looked startled to see me there. 'What are you doing here?' she said. I told her. – 'Well you are a devil,' she said, 'It's impossible to hide anything from you!' And she smiled. She seemed to be pleased to see me. In fact we hadn't seen each other for nearly two months. 'Come home and have some chick-pea coffee with us,' she said, 'you'll just die when I tell you the news . . .' For a split second, for all that she was terribly thin from lack of food and she'd aged at least ten years in the last couple of years, I seemed to see a flash of the old Hecuba I used to know. – 'You remember,' she said (all this as we were walking back to her house), 'you remember what I always used to tell you, that my sister Aphrodite would pay for all her sins. That slut of a daughter she doted on so much was bound to come to no good. Well, it's happened and serve her right!' Hecuba smiled that devilish sarcastic smile of hers. — 'My niece Gogo came round the other day (she's got her own troubles, too, poor thing; her husband's gone off to the mountains with the Resistance and left her alone with the two kids to look after), well she came round and told me the news: the little tart went and eloped with an Italian, and he plucked her little cherry, if you please. And just when my sister was hoping to marry them off and patch the thing up without anybody being the wiser, he got orders to move to the Russian front. It's very unlikely he'll ever come back. They say you just can't imagine how cold it is out there. They just freeze to death. And now she's been left with second-hand goods for sale, and she just can't get over it. I went over there the other day to see them. She didn't dare try to hide it from me. She must have thought to herself: she must know something, coming to see us after all this time. — "Ah, I'm in such bad trouble, sister. Sit down and I'll tell you all about it. It's like this. . . ." And so on, and so on. To tell you the honest truth, Nina, I felt sorry for her. But at the same time I can't pretend I wasn't pleased, even if it's a sin to say so. I always said Evanthia would be the ruination of her. God was bound to punish her for the dirty way she treated us. And wait till I tell you the latest about holy Ephemia! . . .' — 'What?' I asked. The fact is I was more interested in holy Ephemia than I was in Aphrodite; she was a piece out of my past. — 'She's dead,' she told me, 'just rotted to pieces. They didn't know where to grab hold of her. And as soon as she died her louse-tube* opened and she was eaten up by the lice.' — 'Go on with you, Hecuba,' I said, 'surely you don't believe that old wive's tale!' — 'Of course I believe it. . . .'

Victoria listened without saying a word. I had shot her one or two sidelong glances, but her face was quite expressionless. Only her big eyelashes opened and closed slowly like the wings of a bird exhausted after a long flight. When we had nearly

---

* A Greek superstition. Those who lead wicked lives have a chest full of lice, which break out as soon as they die.

250

reached their house she suddenly spoke up. — 'Mother,' she said, 'I'm going off, you know where.' She was always a bit formal and stiff when she spoke to Hecuba, like calling her mother instead of mama, except when they were having a row. — 'Where's she going?' I asked. — 'To the devil,' she said, 'and there's no coming back from there! . . .' She opened the door and we went in. Then, as though she couldn't keep up the play-acting any longer, she suddenly burst into tears, biting her lips in despair. — 'Oh Nina,' she said, 'if only you knew what an unhappy woman I am. Mark my words, this can't go on much longer. My Dimitris isn't for this world very long. It's the end of all my hopes and dreams, and I'll tell you this here and now' (it was though she was making some kind of threat), 'I'll tell you this,' she said, 'if I lose him I'll not live myself. I'll die like my mother when she lost Achilles! . . .' — 'now, now,' I said, 'don't go on like that. Take a grip of yourself. Just be patient until this filthy situation blows over. The war can't go on much longer. All we have to do is to hang on and we'll live to see better days! . . .' But even that afternoon she still tried to hide from me the real reason why Dimitris was in prison. She told me he'd beaten up an Italian. But I found out later from Akis that they'd caught him selling drugs to a poet who later committed suicide — I don't remember his name. And if he was caught selling drugs, I thought to myself, he must have started taking them again himself. But I pretended to swallow what she told me about the Italian. Beating up an Italian in those days wasn't a disgrace; on the contrary, it was an act of heroism, and Hecuba, as far as I could see, was doing her best to believe in a lie, any kind of lie. Not because she wanted to hide the truth from me, but because she herself was scared to face the truth. She spoke the words with her lips, but in her heart of hearts she simply wouldn't, couldn't bring herself to believe that there was no more hope, no hope at all, that everything really was at an end. . . .

It was about four months before I saw her again, except once when I bumped into her for a moment down at the market where we both happened to be buying pine cones to burn in the kitchen stove. About that time Theodore left for the Middle East and her grandsom went off to Kalamata. He went to stay with his mother. Hecuba and the boy simply couldn't get on together any longer. She used to love him dearly, but now, in her constant state of nerves and irritation, she took everything out on him. They'd begun to fight all the time. When Polyxene came to stay in Athens for a week or two she saw what was going on and decided to take him back with her. Hecuba was left alone, just with Victoria — Dimitris was still in jail. They'd transferred him to a hospital prison because of his consumption. From then on we began seeing each other rather more often.

7

For a time, in fact, we lived through some of those pre-war honeymoon days all over again. Squabbling with her grandson all the time used to keep her occupied. But now he was gone, and she began coming round to see me quite often. Either she would call for me or I would call for her and we'd go down together to the journalists' co-operative where she used to get her food rations. She had no use for her rations now, and I used to take most of them. I used to give Cleo anything I could spare. It was a pity to let them go to waste. People weren't dying of starvation in the streets any more, as they did in 1941, but the food was still awful and terribly expensive. There was a huge black market and prices went higher and higher every day. I no longer dared to exchange more than one gold sovereign at a time. Before you could spend it, the millions of drachmas had become billions — or rather the billions, millions. But of course I didn't go with her just for the food. It wasn't just because I wanted to suit my own book, as that ungrateful monster of a daughter always said. I went more for the company than anything else. We no longer played cards as often as we used to, in fact the card-playing group had begun to break up. I felt I needed to get out a bit to get a breath of air. Anybody who spent four years living under aunt Katie's roof would know what I mean. And, when all's said and done, we may have drifted apart a bit, but I was still very fond of her. We used to go and stand in the queue, chatting with the wives and mothers of other newspapermen. It was a pleasant way of passing the time, and we heard all kinds of interesting gossip and all the latest war news. After the fright we and the Hamiltons got that night with Petros, we no longer dared to listen to London. For the first time in my life I saw people at close quarters who had only been names up to then: poets, writers, and so on. You could hear the man behind the counter shouting: – 'Mr Varnalis, will you come and take your cauliflower or not?' It struck me as so funny to hear such a famous poet being talked to like that! I'd never read any poems by Varnalis. In fact, I never cared much for poetry at all. For me it somehow seemed to be the symbol of everything that had kept me apart from Aryiris. But of course I'd heard of him. Just fancy, I thought to myself, poets eat cauliflower too! It was stupid of me, I know. After all, I wasn't exactly a child, and I hadn't been brought up entirely out of contact with cultured people. My poor papa knew all sorts of intellectuals: he knew Palamas in person, they were students together at the university. In fact he'd presented papa with a collection of his poems, with a very flattering dedication. I remembered it that day when there was all that fuss with his maid. Hecuba and I had gone together to the greengrocery depot in the Pappos arcade to get our vegetables. The sky was clouded over, and the first drops of rain began to fall. As we moved under the shelter of the arcade out of the wet, some clever dicks (and there's always some of those to be found in Greece) began leaving their place and pushing to the front of the queue. The people left at the back began shouting and cursing. God preserve us from newspapermen when they open those great big mouths of theirs, I thought to myself. Some of them were really dreadful people. I remember one called Chiroutsas, the nastiest slimiest kind of man I'd ever set eyes on. But, quite suddenly, the noise and the squabbling stopped. There was dead silence. It was as though the scruffy vegetable stall had suddenly turned into a church by the wave of some magic wand. The people in the queue began to stand to one side to make way for an ordinary young working girl to go to the front. – 'How is Mr Palamas?' asked one journalist, and by the way he waited to hear the answer you'd have thought the salvation or ruination of Greece depended on it. At that time Palamas was at death's door. Then the journalist also stood aside to let her pass, with such a show of respect that you might have thought she wasn't just his maid, as I later found

254

out, but the poet himself. No, I wasn't brought up in unrefined surroundings, but it was the first time I found myself at such close quarters to a world I'd always dreamed of entering. And in those surroundings I was discovering, also for the first time, a new Hecuba – lively and witty as always, but with a totally different air about her, on a much higher social level than I'd ever thought possible. The journalists spoke to her respectfully and asked for news of Theodore with real interest. She behaved as though she was completely at home among all that difficult crowd of snobby intellectuals. One day we were waiting our turn sitting on a ledge outside the depot. Sitting next to Hecuba was a woman of really huge proportions wearing one of those old-fashioned hats smothered in artificial violets. I was racking my brains trying to remember who she was. I knew I'd seen her somewhere. As for the hat and the violets, it seemed so curious. We'd all of us by that time given up fripperies such as hats and stockings. Hecuba had got into conversation with her and was telling her some long story. – 'Do you know who she is?' I asked her when we came out. I knew by then, because I'd asked the woman next to me and she'd told me who the fat lady was. – 'What do I care who she is?', replied Hecuba, smiling contentedly. Of course I'd always admired Hecuba's gift of the gab, but when I saw her talking to the great Spanoudi, the most eccentric and brilliant music critic of the day, as equal to equal, I began to think that maybe I'd underestimated her a bit. When poor Antoni was still alive I used to receive her in my home, but although I was fond of her I never regarded her as my social equal, I don't mind admitting it. Now I realised that I wasn't altogether right. After all, what was Antoni when you come to think of it? A contractor mucking about all day long with cement and scaffolding. Of course we had more money than Hecuba. But money isn't everything. I remembered the way I'd behaved to her when she hinted about me getting married to Theodore, and I felt ashamed of myself. Not because I'm snobbish in any way, as that clever daughter of mine likes to say, but I knew, apart from anything else, that even if Theodore was in a position to guarantee all the things a woman wants to be sure of when she marries at my age, it was simply unthinkable that I could become Hecuba's daughter-in-law and Dimitris's sister-in-law. And anyway, even if I'd been given the chance of marrying Prince Charming himself, straight out of the fairy tale, I'd have said no thanks very much at that particular time.

But in the meantime I'd begun to see things a bit differently. And who can blame me for it? My daughter's insufferable behaviour towards me was getting worse all the time, and I doubted very much if I could count on her to give me a peaceful old age. Even now, when I'm still young and able to stand up for myself, she makes my life a misery, I thought to myself. Imagine what will happen when I get old and she can do what she likes with me! She'll tear me to little pieces! And then, I'd begun to feel terribly lonely. Marriage may have its drawbacks, but, when all's said and done, it's a great thing to be able to go to bed at night with your man beside you and tell each other all your worries and troubles. What a pity! I thought. If only he was free of family obligations, it would probably be the ideal solution. He may not have very much money, but I've got plenty for the two of us. I still had quite a few gold sovereigns left, the timber which I could easily hire out as soon as conditions improved, and I had the house as well. About a month after the Germans marched into Athens I had found a tenant at last: a black marketeer from Thebes who rented the place furnished. The rent was coming in regularly, and I'd no need to marry an old man and have to nurse him all the time. But of course I didn't breathe a word of this to Hecuba. I never let her guess the slightest thing. In fact, I soon enough forgot all about it myself. I put it out of my mind as something totally improbable and impractical. It's only now that I sometimes look back and realise that our marriage when he got back from the Middle East wasn't nearly so sudden or strange as it seemed at the time to my relations, and even to me.

8

I remember I'd knitted a green cardigan for Cleo and I was waiting for Hecuba to come round and sew on the sleeves for me. But she hadn't shown up for more than a fortnight and I decided to go round to her house to see how she was. She'd been on my mind for several days. I knew that, except for those nerve pains of hers, she was always in bursting good health. But, for some reason, every time I thought of her I pictured her lying on her death bed. The front door of her house was open, and as I went down the little flight of steps it was impossible to mistake the sound of a really first-class row going on. She must be squabbling with Dimitris, I thought. I went into the hall, and I could hear the raised voices coming from her bedroom. I stood there undecided what to do. I could hear Dimitris's voice quite plainly, and he was saying things which made me think the best thing to do was to leave straight away. I'm not such a prude or hypocritical puritan that I'm easily shocked. But there's a limit to everything— 'No!' he was shouting at her, 'I don't propose to screw you! I know that's what you've been wanting all these years, but that's just too bad! . . . It's Victoria I'll screw, and you can bust with envy for all I care! I'll screw her ten times a day if I feel like it, and in future we'll leave the door open so you can take a good look at us, if it gives you any pleasure. You can drool away to your heart's content! . . .'

Good God! I thought. Can things have reached such a point between them? And I was just on the point of slipping out as silently as I'd come when the door of the bedroom suddenly flew open and Hecuba rushed out with her hair all over the place, her dressing gown in shreds, and half her dangling livid-looking breasts hanging out. It was only at that moment that I realised how much she'd aged since the time I first met her, a plump and healthy-looking woman in her fifties. She froze to the spot as soon as she saw me, as though she'd seen the Medusa or my ghost. But when she finally realised that it was me, Nina, she slumped against the door as though she'd escaped from a thousand devils and could breathe in safety at last. — 'Nina!' she said, 'Nina! Did you hear what he said to me? Have you ever heard anything like it in all your born days? And it's not the first time. I've never told you. I'm ashamed for him. . . . He beat me, Nina . . . You're my witness . . . My Dimitris, the boy in the sailor suit, beating me, his own mother. . . . Just for a woman, for a filthy bitch of a woman . . .' And she began to choke and sob. I helped her into the kitchen. — 'Don't go on like that,' I said, 'try to take a grip of yourself. Come and wash your face . . . Really, Dimitris,' I told him as I went back into the hall, 'you ought to be ashamed of yourself. Honestly, I never expected a thing like that from you. I'd never have believed it if she told me. I'd have said she was exaggerating. And there was I with the impression that you were a gentleman! Can't you see what you're doing to her? She's as thin as a rake, poor thing. You'll kill her if you go on like that!' — 'Don't worry!' he said, 'she won't die. She'll kill me first!' — 'Do you really think it's right to talk like that?' I said. 'Even if she's in the wrong, it's no way for a man like you to behave, a man who's read a few books in his life. The least you can do is to think of all she's been through for your sake.' — 'That's what she likes,' he said. 'She likes to suffer. She likes me to swear at her, she can't live without fighting. It's her bread and butter. She deliberately eggs me on . . .' As he talked he was trying to fix his pyjama trousers. The fly was open in front and his privates were showing. — 'I've had as much of her as I can take, Mrs Nina,' he said. And the truth was that he looked like a skeleton himself what with the drugs and not having enough food. The veins of his neck stood out so much they seemed to be on top of his skin instead of under it. — 'She opens our door without knocking! I don't even dare to make love to my own wife! She's trying to play on our nerves. She'd rather see me dead than living happily with the woman I love! She won't even give us our proper food rations! We're starving, Mrs Nina, we're absolutely starving! . . . '—'That I just don't believe,' I said. But something told me it was probably true. I knew her through and through. She was capable of being kind and generous to a fault, but, if she wanted to, she could be as malicious as the devil himself.—'I don't believe it,' I said, 'I know she loves you more than her own life . . .' He shook his head impatiently.—'What's the good of standing here talking to you . . . you can't possibly understand . . . you don't know everything that's happened . . .'—'That's where you're wrong!' I told him, 'and it's just because I know her. . . .'

But he didn't stop to listen. He went into his room and closed the door in my face. I heard him talking quietly to Victoria. Meanwhile, Hecuba came back from the kitchen, washed, freshened up and feeling much stronger. She bent down to pick up a comb which had apparently fallen from her hair after the struggle, re-wound her bun and pinned it into place. Her face was burning as though she had a fever, but her movements were slow and deliberate as though nothing untoward was happening. She sat down on a chair and for a few seconds she said nothing at all. She just sat thinking. Then, as though she had just arrived that moment at her final decision, she said:—'I don't want him any more, Nina. I can't stand that drug fiend in my house any longer! As far as I'm concerned, he's not my son any more! . . .' From inside the bedroom we could hear Dimitris talking softly again with Victoria. Hecuba's eyes flashed with anger. She turned towards the closed door and shouted:—'I don't want you any longer. You're not my son any more. If you've got an ounce of self-respect in you you'll pack up your rubbish this very minute and clear out! . . .'—'Quiet!' I said, 'that's enough now . . .' —'No! Nina, believe me I know what I'm doing. I've had just about enough of him, I can't stand any more.' And she turned towards the bedroom door again. 'As far as I'm concerned you don't exist. Die! Peg out, you dirty bastard! Daring to lift a hand against a mother who's spat blood for you for all these years, who hasn't known a momen't happiness since the day you were born, who fell out with her husband and her children for your stinking sake! . . . .'

When she saw that Dimitris wasn't answering, she turned to me and said: — 'Nina, I want to die . . .' She said it so simply but with such determination I felt goose-pimples all over. She wasn't play-acting for once. This time her heart was in it. It wasn't just words. — 'Come on now Hecuba,' I said, 'don't take on so. Pull yourself together, just be patient for a while! Don't imagine you're the only one with troubles. We've all had our nerves torn to shreds. God knows how I manage to keep myself from going overboard. We're all hoping better days will come soon. Don't you see, the Italians have surrendered already. It won't be long before the Germans have to give in too. They'll be made to pay with their blood for all they've done to us. We've got through so many storms all these years. Don't you think it's a pity to give up just when we're almost safely in harbour? When peace comes, God willing, and things quieten down and you have your children round you again in your own home, it will all seem like a bad dream. Just think of those millions of people who've lost their lives these last three or four years. Don't you think you're lucky, touch wood, that at least you're all alive and well. . . .'

She stared hard at me and began drumming her fingers on the table. We sat there just looking at each other without saying a word for a moment or two. — 'How about coming back and spending the night at my place,' I said. 'I'll put a mattress down on the floor for you like I did last time . . .' She just shook her head. I sat there for a while, but I just couldn't think what more to do or say. The way things were, the Almighty himself couldn't have done anything to help. I got up and picked up the parcel with Cleo's cardigan. — 'Are you sure you don't want to come back with me? Would you prefer me to stay here with you for the night? You look as if you've got a temperature.' She gave me one of her grimaces. — 'Don't worry,

260

she said, 'there's nothing the matter with me. When my time comes to go I'll let you know. . . .' I was so upset by it all that I had the worse nightmares of my life that night, filthy sinful kind of dreams: I saw my poor papa naked, and Antoni crying as he did the first night we were married. I saw Dimitris, or rather a beggar I took to be Dimitris, covered with lice. Suddenly he began to get smaller and smaller, till he was just a little ball no bigger than a walnut. Then Hecuba appeared on the scene, half-naked, with a mass of golden bangles on her arm and her hair down to her shoulders. She had a tambourine in her hand and she began to dance, like the painted ladies on the hurdy-gurdies. . . .

A few days later she came round and told me in a matter-of-fact kind of way, as though it was the most unimportant thing in the world, that Victoria had disappeared like the first time, But this time, no matter how hard Dimitris looked, there was not a sign of her anywhere. He was told later that she'd been seen in Salonika, and he rushed up there to find her. But it was too late. The Germans had rounded up all the Jews and sent them off to Poland. When he finally reconciled himself to the fact that he'd lost her for good, he came back to Athens and started taking drugs in real earnest, not just to forget his troubles like before, but like a man who jumps head first from the top of a tall building. When they caught him for some petty theft and shut him up again in the prison hospital, he'd had three bouts of blood-spitting, his teeth had begun to fall out, and he was dirtying his pants like a small child. God save us from a fate like that! — 'That's the end of him,' I said to aunt Katie, 'just the same as Dino went. It's a shame, he wasn't really a bad chap! . . .' Aunt Katie made a wry face. I knew what she was thinking. But I didn't feel it was up to me to pass judgement on people, I didn't dare ask the whys and where-fores. I just thanked whatever god it was who took pity on mama and made her blind with cataract so that she didn't see Dino dying on his feet. No matter what you are told, it isn't easy to imagine the reality unless you see it with your own eyes.

9

Hecuba had spent half her life worrying continuously about losing her son. But now that it was almost certain he was near the end, she just wouldn't believe it. Now that there was no hope for him at all, she waited more hopefully than ever for God to perform a miracle. She believed it was all for the best that things had turned out as they had, with Victoria and her evil influence out of the way for good and all. Now they could start all over again where they'd left off on the day war broke out. It was all for the best that they'd put him in prison again, and a prison that was really a sanatorium at that. There he'd be out of reach of the drugs, out of reach of the whores who were sucking his blood, out of reach of the Germans and the EAM (it seems he'd got mixed up with the EAM, too). When, God willing, the war ended and he came out of prison, they could start a new life. That was how she thought about it, and I don't altogether blame her. After all, we all had more or less the same dreams. Everybody was convinced that if only they managed to survive they'd be eating off gold plate for the rest of their lives

At that time, the Spring of 1944, it was Polyxene she was more concerned about than Dimitris. She came round one afternoon with a letter in her hand and gave it to me to read. Polyxene had written to tell her she'd become engaged. Her fiancé was a major in the gendarmes. Both Polyxene and Eleni described him in the most glowing terms. But Hecuba didn't share their enthusiasm; she didn't know whether to be pleased or sorry. — 'Naturally, Nina, I want to see her well set up in life. After all, she's a widow (even if they haven't told him so) and I suppose I ought to be glad someone's turned up to take her. But did it have to be a bloody policeman, I ask you? It's just my bad luck. How do you think I'm going to break the news to my Dimitris? "Really mama," he'll say, and

262

he'll be quite right, "really mama, aren't there any other men in the world? Did she have to go and get herself engaged to one of my persecutors?" . . .' – 'Don't jump to conclusions before you see him,' I said, 'they're not all of them monsters!' But she shook her head doubtfully. In one paragraph of her letter Polyxene said they wouldn't get married on any account until Sotiris (Sotiris he was called) was sure of getting his transfer to Athens. It looked as thought the Germans wouldn't be in Greece much longer and he was afraid of reprisals from the ELAS resistance. – 'God knows what kind of a bastard he is, Nina! Not to mention the other stupid nonsense!' – 'What other nonsense?' – 'He went and got hold of Eleni's fancy man and made him swear on the life of his children that Polyxene was a virgin. What could the poor man do? He swore. But imagine what kind of a peasant brute he must be to have ideas like that! They told him I'm ill so Polyxene would have an excuse to come up to Athens for a few days to go to a doctor and get herself sewed up, the sort of thing I've always thought so absurd. . . .'

A week or two later Polyxene did come up from Kalamata. She got to Athens after all sorts of adventures just impossible to imagine, apparently. At least I can imagine them now, but at that time we still had no idea what the rebels were doing. I knew Mrs Cassimatis's son was 'in the mountains,' as they said. But none of us really knew what it meant. They grabbed her, she told us, just outside Tripolis. They took her off the bus with all the others and insisted on finding out what she was doing in Kalamata and why she was going to Athens. She was forced to tell them the truth. When she came out of the clinic, she came round to my place one afternoon with Hecuba, and we all sat out on the balcony chatting and drinking coffee – the two of them, Cleo and myself. She seemed a bit thin, but quite happy. We began talking about the stupidity and narrow-mindedness of men, and the cunning tricks women had to get up to pull the wool over their eyes. I told them about the time I went to see a gynaecologist when I was forced to patch things up with the father of that fine daughter of mine, and I got him to twist my womb round. You can't ever be sure. No matter how careful you are, however particular about counting the days, you're liable to get caught just once. And once would have been more than enough. I hadn't the slightest desire to bring any more bastards of Fotis's into the world!

10

Two months went by. One afternoon I went round to see her and found her bending over the ikon of St Fanourios. She was trying to change Polyxene's date of birth. She'd been born in 1910 and Hecuba was trying to change the nought into a six. She was in one of her good moods. — 'Come and see what I'm doing,' she said. She could hardly stop herself from laughing out loud. — 'Really you're the limit!' I laughed, 'aren't you afraid you'll be punished, making forgeries on an ikon! You ought to be ashamed of yourself!' — 'What can I do?' she said, 'there's no other way out. It would have been better if she'd told him the truth in the first place, but now that she's lied to him I don't want to give her away. Those damned coppers are always snooping about, putting their noses into everything. I wouldn't put it past him to turn St Fanourios round one of these days and see her real birth date. Sooner or later, of course, he's bound to find out. There's nothing hidden under the sun. Just so long as he doesn't find out now when they've only just got married. Did I tell you? Yes, they're married! They'll be here in a fortnight or so. He finally managed to get a transfer to the gendarme headquarters here.' — 'Congratulations!' I said, 'long life to them both.' — 'The same to you!' she said, 'it's high time you got married yourself, you know. Why don't you find yourself some nice chap and get yourself hitched? You've not much time to lose, my girl. It's no good waiting till your daughter puts you into the old-age home....' I helped her change the nought into a six. Her eyesight was none too good and her hand shook. But no matter how hard we tried to make it convincing, you'd have had to be blind not to notice it was a forgery.

Before I left we made an arrangement that I would call for her the day after next and we'd both go to visit Dimitris in jail. She hadn't breathed a word to him about the engagement

—she didn't want to upset him without reason. But now they were actually married she couldn't very well keep it from him any longer.—'I just don't know how he'll take it, Nina,' she said, 'I just tremble at the thought of it. But no matter how he takes it, he won't dare make a scene in front of you . . .' I very much wanted to go with her to see him, not so much for his sake as for poor Dino's. But the day we had arranged to go, I woke up with a terrible pain in the stomach. I sent Irene round to her house (the Duchess, of course, wouldn't even do a simple errand like that for me) to tell her not to expect me and we'd go another day together. But she went on her own. What happened between the two of them she never told me, but it seems they started fighting through the prison bars. To teach him a lesson she didn't go to see him again for a week. Prison rations at that time were a starvation diet. Usually she would take him food from home every other day. When she finally decided the punishment had lasted long enough and she went round to the jail with a tin of chick-peas, they told her he'd been dead for three days.

11

It was early in May, about three or four in the afternoon, and we were on our way back from the sanatorium cemetery. She'd ordered a wooden cross from a carpenter two or three days before, painted it herself, and carried it herself all the way out to Holargos. I begged and pleaded with her to let me carry it, but she wouldn't let go of it. She was like a wild hungry dog when you try to snatch a piece of meat from its mouth. I saw her struggling and panting with the weight of it and I thought my heart would break. In two weeks she'd got thinner than she ever was even at the time of the worst famine in '41. Her back was stooped, her face had a wild look, and even the locks of her hair, which used to blow about softly in the slightest breeze, looked like matted clumps of fine wire.

First we went to the prison to get a warden to come with us to show us where they'd buried him. When he left we lit a little fire of dry branches and pine cones to make some embers to burn the incense she'd brought with her. I don't think she spoke more than two or three words all afternoon. I expected her to start wailing and beating her breast. But she didn't, and the complete silence scared me.

To leave her alone with him for a while, and anyway because the smell of musk incense always made me feel suffocated and depressed, I walked off a little way into the thyme bushes and camomile flowers. It was the first time I'd been outside of Athens since the beginning of the war. I'd almost forgotten nature existed. I felt tears coming to my eyes as I breathed the sweet smell of the thyme and looked out at the gentle curve of the hills, 'pillows on which Hymettus rested his feet like a Byzantine Emperor', as I had once written in an essay when I was at high school. My breast seemed to swell with a feeling of well-being I had almost forgotten existed in life. For a fleeting moment it seemed that the clock had been turned back twenty-five years, that I was eighteen years old again, lying among the thyme close to Aryiris, listening to him reciting poetry to me:

Oh, how the dream of beauty blinds our sight!
As though but once in life we drift astray. . . .

God! I thought to myself as I wandered back, how time has flown! I've gone through a lifetime without knowing real happiness. Now, even if the war ends quickly, what good will it do me? I've had my time. I've grown old bringing up that ungrateful spawn of Fotis's. . .

When I got back to the place where I'd left Hecuba, I found her sitting on the ground with her head to one side, like Christ on the cross, her hands resting listlessly on her knees, as dumb and tearless as before. I helped her get to her feet, and we started back through the sanatorium's pine wood. I have always thought pines are the most beautiful trees in the world. When I was little I used to lie down under the pine trees on uncle Markoussi's estate. I used to love to roll on the soft bed of clean dry pine needles. Now, as we walked through the pine wood, I thought to myself how lucky it was, for all the merciless cutting of trees during the last two or three years, that there were still a few trees left standing in Attica.

As we were walking along I saw a bench by the side of the path. 'Let's sit down and rest a while,' I said. I knew she was dead tired after walking all that distance carrying the heavy cross. We sat down and I took my shoes off to air my feet a bit. 'Ah, what a lovely breeze there is here,' I said, taking a deep breath of air. 'We ought to be thankful, Hecuba, that they've left us a few trees. If the war had gone for another couple of winters there wouldn't be so much as a single pine cone left . . .' It's time, I thought to myself, to drag her out of that depressing silence of hers. If she goes on like that she'll get ill or go mad. Much better for her to break down at last and cry her heart out. Just fancy, Hecuba not crying! It seemed so strange. But I never imagined for a moment that what I said would raise

268

such a storm. Suddenly, she began to shriek and scream. All the tears she'd been holding back so many days came out in a flood, as though some dam had broken: – 'My son! My child! The pine trees live, my son! They live and breathe! It's only you who's dead! I've lost you for ever! . . .' I just let her cry to her heart's content. And when we got up to start walking again, her face had lost something of that wild expression it had before. She'll forget, I thought. Whether she wants to or not, she'll forget. Time is a great healer. When my poor papa died I thought I'd never get used to the idea that he was gone. But after two or three months there were moments when it seemed that he had never existed.

12

Of course it wasn't at all a suitable time for Polyxene and her husband to come to Athens. — 'It will do her good to have some company and things to keep her busy in the house like before,' said aunt Katie who, for the very first time, had begun to feel sorry for her. — 'You're quite wrong, aunt,' I said, 'you just don't know what she's like. In the state she's in at the moment she can't possibly bear to live with other people. She can't even stand seeing people around her, let alone live in the same house with a newly married couple.' In fact I knew she couldn't even put up with her cat. — 'I hear the damned cat miaowing when she's hungry and I could cheerfully strangle the little beast,' she told me. 'Do you happen to know anybody I could give it to?' Finally she tied the cat up in a sack and left it in a doorway a few streets away. But the little devil was back after a couple of days, and she didn't have the heart to get rid of it again. She thought the cat had come back because she loved her and was sorry for her. The cat, she said, understood her better than most people. That was a dig at me. She had never really forgiven me for not going with her to the jail that last time when she had a fight with Dimitris. But I pretended not to hear what she said and changed the subject. My heart bled at the thought that, after all the people she'd been used to having around the house, she'd come down to living alone with a mangy little cat for company. Not that she was ever really happy even when she had people round her. Her life had always been a constant whirlwind. But Hecuba's ideas of happiness were not the same as most people's. There may have been moments when even she must have craved for a little peace and quiet, but deep down it was that whirlwind which kept her happy.

The first thing she said to Polyxene, even before she kissed her or welcomed her new son-in-law, was: 'Well, you've got your wish, daughter. I've buried him for you. Why don't you take a red handkerchief and start to dance?...' Polyxene came and told me about it. She asked me to advise her how to placate her mother. The truth is, she was in a very difficult position. So far from wanting to dance with a red handkerchief, the poor girl felt terribly guilty about Dimitris. I could sympathise with her because I had gone through exactly the same thing with poor Dino. Many was the time I had the strange notion that he had died to take his revenge on me. As long as she was in Kalamata she simply couldn't believe that Dimitris was gone for good. She consoled herself with the delusion that it might have been one of those petty annoying little tricks he played on them so often through the years. But when she arrived in Athens and came face to face with the reality, she knew there was no more room for self-deception. It was a great shock to her.

But no matter what she did or said, she simply couldn't persuade Hecuba that she was really sorry about her brother's death. She wore black, even though she was a bride of only a few weeks. But Hecuba just put it down to hypocrisy. Not a single day went by, whether Sotiris was present or not, without Hecuba dragging up some incident out of the past, like the row over the hundred drachma note. She would break into bouts of wailing and breast-beating in the middle of meals, she'd look at Sotiris fit to kill every time he forgot himself and made a little joke, and so on. It was so bad that Polyxene, quite naturally, began to lose her patience and to curse him dead as much as she did when he was alive. She wouldn't have minded so much if she'd been alone. She'd learned her mother's ways over the years. But there was Sotiris, you see. What had the poor man done to deserve it, finding himself suddenly forced to live in a house smelling of death from morning to night? It was the first time he had married, and the first time he'd come to Athens. He'd imagined it all very differently. The poor man wasn't even allowed to laugh or kiss his wife for fear of upsetting Hecuba. It wasn't fair on him, being obliged to mourn for somebody he'd never so much as seen in his life and who, according to his way of thinking as a policeman, wasn't worth mourning for anyway.

At the beginning he did everything he could to act the part of the affectionate son-in-law, but Hecuba no longer had any use for anybody's love or affection. And certainly not from a man she regarded as indirectly responsible for the death of Dimitris, a 'bloody copper' as she called him, one of those 'monsters' who had persecuted him without mercy all his life and finally driven him to his death! . . . That's how she thought. And things got worse and worse because Sotiris was one of those people who are bursting with good health, who laugh and talk at the top of their voices, who simply fill the whole house with their presence as soon as they come through the door. But he didn't need to laugh or talk. The mere fact that he was alive was enough to get on Hecuba's nerves. Just to breathe in her presence was a provocation, with her Dimitris six feet under.

—'A worse beast than him I've never come across in all my life, Nina,' she used to come and tell me. 'How on earth could a daughter of mine agree to marry a man like that? What could she possibly see in him? The other day he grabbed her head between his two hands and dribbled spit into her mouth with a great slobbery kiss—may I not live another day if I'm telling a word of a lie, Nina. It just makes me sick to think about it. And the more the great big brute sees that it upsets me, the more he does it, just to spite me. And as for that bed of theirs at night, it's just past belief, Nina. Creak-creak-creak, all the time. He's younger than she is and she's not too strong, you know. He'll knock her out in no time at all, just you mark my words. To think of it, my Polyxene, the girl I brought up so sheltered and refined, after having such a fine lad like Alexander, making love with that . . . that . . . orang-utang! I don't care what you say, Nina, I just can't get over it! . . . 'Oh, go on with you now,' I said 'fancy spoiling your beauty sleep over a stupid thing like that! After all, you can't very well tell them what to do and what not to do in bed. When all's said and done, as you know perfectly well, no woman has ever come to any harm from *that* . . .'

But I was just wasting my words. As she herself said, no matter what I said she couldn't get over it. Naturally it wasn't long before they started squabbling, and then having really violent rows, with the two of them swearing away at each other in the most vulgar language you can imagine, with poor Polyxene in the middle, not knowing what to do or whose side to take. When she took Sotiris's side, Hecuba threatened to spill the beans and tell him about her first marriage, about what she really did in Athens when she was visiting her 'sick' mother, and so on. And when she took Hecuba's side, begging Sotiris to make allowances and swallow his anger, she was offended. She'd far rather have a flaming row than be scorned or even pitied. She didn't want her daughter's help, she didn't want her to take her side, she didn't want her compassion, in fact she didn't want to see any more of her or her husband and she threatened to turn them out of the house. When Polyxene came and told me about it, — 'What can I say, Polyxene my dear,' I told her. 'I'm very fond of her, as you know; but I do understand how difficult it must be for you. On the other hand, if you go off and find yourselves a little room of your own somewhere, as you say, it's not really a solution either for you or for her. She'll be all alone again, with only the cat to keep her company. She won't live very long if that happens. The best solution, if you ask me' (and I didn't say it just for the ease and comfort of Sotiris — it may not have been entirely his fault, but his behaviour was inhuman, you simply couldn't treat an unhappy broken old woman the way he did — I said it for the good of Hecuba), 'the best solution, if you ask me,' I said, 'would be to send her off to Eleni for a while. If times were better I'd have her myself, really I would, and I'd take her to Andros for a month or so. I could do with a change of air myself. But the way things are right now, the only solution is to do what I say: send her to stay with Eleni. The change of surroundings will do her good, and most of all she'll be able to see her grandson again. I don't know what she's told you, but I know it cost her a lot when he left her and went back to his mother . . .'

Polyxene wrote Eleni a letter and she came to Athens straight away. I didn't see her at all. The day I happened to call at the house she was out somewhere. At the beginning Hecuba didn't want to go. – 'You really must go,' I told her, 'the change will do you the world of good. I only wish I could come with you. It would give me a rest from having to see the bitchy face of that darling daughter of mine . . .'

I must have been terribly naïve to imagine that a change of surroundings would save her. For her, the earth was no longer anything but a little globe, the same all over, in which Dimitris was buried; and no matter where she went, she would always be walking on his grave. However, she finally agreed to go. One reason was that every time she had a row with Polyxene she would discover new virtues in Eleni. Another reason was the thought that, if she went, she might be able to bring her grandson back with her. As it proved later, it was her last effort to find a purpose, any kind of purpose, to make her life worth living. For all that she was constantly saying she wanted to die, she had far too strong an instinct for life to give up the struggle all that easily. Just as a drowning man grabs at a straw, she seized on the idea that it was her sacred duty to save Akis from his mother's clutches, even against his own will.

But her plans to kidnap him, as she had done the other time in Salonika, didn't work. What happened exactly, I don't know, except for what Eleni herself told me when she came to Athens after the December rising in '44. It was almost two months since she'd left, and I was under the impression that she was still in Kalamata when Polyxene arrived suddenly one afternoon and said: – 'Mama's very ill and she wants to see you'. – 'And when did she get back from Kalamata?' – 'Almost three weeks ago.' – 'Really, Polyxene, you should

274

have let me know. What's the matter with her?'—'I don't know. Up to yesterday the doctor was saying it was 'flu. Yesterday she went into a coma. I called a specialist and he found she had urea. Apparently it's quite far advanced. . . .' Her eyes filled with tears. I realised that things were serious. —O my God, Polyxene, that's awful. I simply can't believe it,' I said and I felt my knees giving way under me.

I threw a coat round my shoulders. It was September and already a bit chilly. The sky was clouded over and it had been threatening rain for hours. As soon as we got into the hall I was hit by a dreadful stink of medicine and sour bile. Polyxene had lit an old paraffin lamp. We hadn't had any electricity for three or four days. People said the Germans had cut it off deliberately. The bastards were finally packing up and leaving and they didn't want people to watch their movements. You were only allowed out in the streets up to seven o'clock in the evening. Every now and again, you could hear the muffled sounds of gunfire in the distance. As we found out later, they were trying to cover their retreat. The resistance troops had come down as far as Thebes.

Hecuba was lying propped up on three or four pillows to ease her breathing. She was just a shadow of her old self. If I'd seen her without knowing it was Hecuba, I'd never have recognised her. From her mouth there was a heavy rumbling sound like a loud snore. I took hold of her hand. She breathed a deep plaintive little sigh and opened her eyes.—'Who are you? . . .'—'It's Nina . . .'—'Oh, so you've come? . . . Thank you for coming . . .'—'What do you think you're playing at, Hecuba,' I said, trying to sound as natural as I could to hide the way I was feeling, 'fancy being back so long and not even sending me a word! . . .' She didn't answer. 'How do you feel now?'—'You seem to be all blurred . . . I've such a headache . . . But I'll get over it . . .' Suddenly she waved her hand impatiently towards Polyxene who was standing beside me, as though she wanted to get rid of her. Polyxene left the room in tears and the two of us were alone together.—'Nina . . . I don't want to die . . . You remember when I told you I wanted to die?. . . . Well I don't want to now . . . I want to live to see my son. . . . He's probably the only one of my children who loved me a little bit . . . He was a loud-mouth, I know. . . . But he never said a hard word to me. . . . God bless him. . . . But if I die . . .' – 'Sshh!', I said, 'you're not going to die. In a few days you'll be right as rain! . . .' She tried to smile, as if to say: you don't really believe that. – 'But if I die,' she said again, 'I want you to promise me that you'll tell him every-thing . . . give me your word that you'll tell him every-thing . . .' – 'What do you want me to tell him?' – 'Everything they did to me . . .' – 'I promise . . .'

Her face relaxed. She sank back on the pillows as though a great weight had gone off her mind, and she began the same rumbling snore. Outside it was quite dark. I remembered that the curfew started at seven. I tried to disengage my hand from hers ever so gently. But apparently it upset her. She opened her eyes again and tried to struggle up on the pillows. – 'You mustn't tire yourself,' I said, 'lie down and rest . . .' She pulled a face impatiently and dragged me by the hand closer to her, as though she wanted to whisper a secret in my ear. – 'Nina . . .' – 'Yes, I'm listening,' I said. – 'Nina . . . there isn't any God! . . .' For a few seconds she stayed there in the same position, half sitting, half lying down, supporting ing herself on my arm, looking at me with a questioning expression in her eyes, as though she was appealing to me, asking me to tell her she was wrong. I didn't know what to say. Anyway, at that moment I couldn't have got a single word out. A sob had stuck in my throat and it was choking me. I would have liked to tell her the things I had thought about so often those last three or four years when we'd all lived so close to death, but I didn't know where to begin. It would have been pointless anyway, utterly useless. I would only have upset her, and she'd have departed from this world with the unhappy feeling that she was wrong, whereas I knew she was right. The God she meant, the one we'd been taught to believe in as children, the one poor mama and Erasmia thought they knew, that God didn't exist of course; and it was far too late for her to get to know the other God, the real one. I pushed her gently down on to the pillows, and this time she didn't resist at all.

13

Petros stayed in jail for eighteen months. Three times he was due for execution, and once, in fact, he was taken to the firing range just outside Kaesariani. Every time we just managed to save him from the jaws of death. Thanks to that old friend of uncle Stephen's. He'd helped him out of trouble at the time when he still had the café by giving him money to get his wife to a hospital, and he happened to be the rare sort of man who remembers other people's kindness and tries to pay it back. But the amount of money they spent, the agonising moments they went through—and I with them—simply can't be imagined.

When we finally managed to get him out of prison he insisted on going off to join the resistance in the mountains. But Takis shouted blue murder, and aunt Katie implored him not to go. I had my little say, too, and finally we persuaded him to go to stay in Andros for a while with his aunt Bolena, so that he could get out of the way of the Germans and they could forget all about him while he got his strength back. His health had been badly affected by the physical and mental suffering he'd gone through in jail.

But as soon as the Germans packed up and left he came straight back to Athens, and of course he got mixed up again with the EAM: he used to round up the members of their youth branch and spend hours giving them indoctrination courses. Well, I used to be in favour of the EAM myself, but I gradually realised like everybody else that there was a wolf under the sheep's clothing. With my very own eyes I'd seen servant girls and the whores of Socrates Street shouting for the 'rule of the people' and 'down with virginity'. And when the communist rebellion broke out later and they began rounding up hostages just like the Germans and slaughtering innocent people with jagged tomato tins, I'd seen enough. I knew Petros himself was incapable of hurting a fly, but every time he tried to find excuses for them I used to fly off the handle and give him a real piece of my mind: – 'And if you think I'm a bloody reactionary,' I used to tell him, 'why don't you run and denounce me to your comrades, and to those little tarts you have on your side? I wouldn't put anything past any of you. That Lenin of yours taught you not to respect anything, not to spare even your own mother in the great cause! . . .'

Petros used to smile when he saw me getting worked up like that. He just found it amusing, and he didn't hold it against me. In a little while we'd be friends again. There were times when even I had to admit that he was right about some things, that lots of things in Greece were far from perfect. And Petros agreed, although he never admitted it in so many words, that I was right when I said that slaughtering people wasn't going to make things any better, that bloodshed would only lead to more bloodshed.

Although Petros was a man and knew what was going on and what he was talking about, he wasn't a fanatic. At least you could talk to him. But not that freak of nature I had for a daughter! She was capable of taking sides with the devil himself to spite me, and she had the nerve to put her oar in when I was arguing with Petros and stick up for the communists: – 'Let them slaughter a few of the bastards!' she would shout, 'it'll serve them right!' It made me feel quite ill to hear her. Sometimes she got on my nerves so much I would sit there shaking with sheer aggravation. She upset me so much one day that I grabbed her by the neck and nearly choked the life out of her. – 'You little she-devil!' I said, 'Who asked you for your silly opinion? You haven't the slightest idea what you're talking about! If they only slaughtered little monsters like you I'd say they were bloody heroes, but unfortunately it's the innocent people they're murdering.' – 'Were you with the EAM?' – 'No. I wasn't' – 'Right then, over there!' Any member of the EAM with a personal grudge could put his enemy's name on the blacklist, and that would be the end of him. We'd hardly stopped thanking the Lord for escaping the clutches of the Gestapo, and here we were shivering with fright for fear of being picked on by our own murderers. And they were ten times worse than the Germans. As the old saying goes: who gouged your eye out so deep? – my brother. . . .

– 'And just because they're playing the game of the capitalists and don't know what side their own bread's buttered on, does that mean you have to slit all their throats?', I said to Petros. 'Don't talk to me about the French Revolution,' I said. It would make me wild when he began on his phoney plausible arguments. 'I've read some history, too, you know. In the French Revolution it was the aristocrats they sent to the guillotine. They didn't slit the throats of ordinary innocent working class people with jagged vegetable tins. Just wait and see,' I told him, 'it's as certain as day is day and night is night, with all those filthy atrocities of yours the people will turn against you and the rebellion will come to a sticky end, and all that bloodshed will have gone for nothing. But there's one thing I want to tell you, my lad, and get it well into that thick head of yours: don't stick your neck out too far. If the other side get you on *their* blacklist and the situation changes, you'll be done for good and proper!' – 'You're my cousin, aren't you?', he said laughing, 'I'll come and ask you to save me.' He was joking, of course. He didn't imagine the day would come, and very soon at that, when I really would save him.

One afternoon he was on his way home to wash and change his clothes. It was a week since we'd seen him and we didn't know whether he was dead or alive. In those days there was heavy street-fighting going on all the time. Athens was divided into two sectors. One was held by the ELAS, and the other by the British and the National Guard. We were in the middle. Some blocks of flats were occupied by the communists and others by the nationalists. The machine guns chattered between them night and day, like birds twittering from one tree to the other. As he ran towards home, ducking into one doorway after another, he suddenly felt a stabbing pain just below the knee. He lost his balance and fell over. He dragged himself into a doorway and some friends of the family found him there when the shooting stopped. They put him in a cart they found outside a greengrocer's shop and took him off to the Yeroulanos clinic. Then they came to the house and told us what had happened. Aunt Katie happened to be ill in bed at the time with pneumonia. Uncle Stephen had gone downhill very badly the last two or three years and could hardly drag his feet along. We hadn't seen Takis for three weeks. He had telephoned a message to the Hamiltons that he was well and was living at the Grande Bretagne hotel. He'd been seconded to General Scobie's staff because of his English. — 'Don't breathe a word to your mother or to your father,' I said to Irene, who was simply paralysed with panic. 'Put your coat on and we'll dash round to the clinic and find out exactly what's happened . . .'

Thank God, it wasn't very serious, as we thought at first it might be. They'd already removed the bullet, but it had broken the bone through and through. And the worst thing of all was that there wasn't a scrap of plaster in the whole clinic, not a single scrap. — 'For God's sake,' I said to the nurse, 'you don't mean to tell me that there isn't a handful of plaster to be had in the whole of Athens!' She shook her head. — 'Of course there is,' she said, 'but as long as this situation lasts there's absolutely nothing we can do. I've got seven patients with broken arms and legs and they're all in wooden splints . . .' For a moment I thought of going back home at once and setting off to find Kallinikos who sold building materials. He used to be a friend of poor Antoni's. But my heart sank when the nurse explained that it had to be a special kind of plaster. But just as she was on the point of leaving, I had a brainwave: — 'how about the plaster they use for making statues?' I said, 'will that do?' — 'Yes, that would do,' she said, 'but where are you going to find it?'

I grabbed Irene by the arm and we went out, straight up the hill towards Kolonaki. When we got to Aesculapius Street we were stopped by some national guards. — 'Halt!' they said. They searched my handbag and gave us both a good feel, searching for weapons – at least, that was the excuse! – 'And where might you two girls be going?', they asked. Usually they let people through to go shopping in Kolonaki. It was the only place you could find any food. But nobody was allowed through after sunset. By now it had got quite dark. – 'Come on now, be good fellows,' I said, 'don't turn us back now! Do we look like a couple of comrades, I ask you?' And I explained what it was all about. One of them laughed. He seemed to find it funny. – 'Alright, you can come through,' he said, 'but don't tell anybody we let you . . .'

We got to Athina's house and banged on the door. She lived in Spevsippou Street. I had met her at Cleo's place. She was a real card maniac. I didn't know her husband but I'd heard he was a sculptor and a teacher at the Fine Arts College. – 'you must be raving mad!' she said when she'd shown us into the drawing room and I'd told her what I wanted. She was a very jolly type of person with quite an air about her. You could tell from her eyes that she'd always enjoyed her life and still did. She wasn't a stupid little ninny like me. – 'I don't know what to say, my love,' she said and took a long puff at her cigarette through a holder a yard long. 'Telis is a dear sweet man, but heaven help me if I interfere with his work. He won't even let me set foot in his studio, and when I send the maid in to sweep it for him he stands over her like a Cerberus in case she touches anything.' – 'There's no need for you to go,' I said, I'll go myself!' – 'Well, yes,' she said, 'but what if he needs the plaster? The other day he told me he was starting on a new piece of sculpture.' – 'Really, Athina,' I said, 'you can't be serious thinking about some silly piece of sculpture at a time like this! Be logical! After all, you're a woman and you ought to understand these things. The whole world's going up in smoke. What counts now is to survive. There'll be time for sculpture later! You might as well make up your mind to it,' I said, 'I'm not moving from here without that plaster. I'll just sit here on the floor until you get sick and tired of me.' She pulled a bit of a face, but she could hardly refuse me. She took us to her husband's studio and I filled a big paper bag full of plaster I scooped out of the sack with my hands. I was wearing my black astrakhan, and by the time I finished I was white all over, like a miller's wife smothered in flour.

We put the paper bag in a shopping basket and started going down the hill back towards the clinic. But when we got as far as Sina Street we heard some hand grenades going off. — 'Better leave it till the morning,' I said to Irene. We started up the hill towards the French Institute, cut through the pine trees at the St Nicholas church and went back home.

First thing next morning I left Irene to look after her mother, took the bag of plaster and started down Harilaou Tricoupi Street. The clinic was bang in the middle of the neutral zone. The communists held the area down from the church of Zoodochou Pigis, and the National Guard were in control from Mavromichali Street upwards. The state Chemical Laboratory was full of English. I found the door of the clinic closed. I banged hard and the door began to open cautiously. Through the crack of the opening I suddenly saw the nose of a revolver poking out. — 'Alright, get in!' said a voice, 'and act as though nothing was happening. If you try to do a bunk I'll shoot . . .' I thought I would faint away on the spot. I went inside and found myself faced with about a dozen communists, looking like ferocious bandits, with great big beards almost down to their knees. Most of them were wearing military tunics dyed black. As we found out later, they'd arrived a couple of hours after we left to get the plaster. They wormed their way along a dry sewer which came out in the yard of the clinic and took the place over. But they were hiding for fear of being spotted by the British in the Chemical Laboratory and being attacked with mortars. They had two lady comrades with them, each of them with two bandoliers of bullets criss-crossed over their tits and wearing khaki trousers. I don't think there's anything more revolting than the sight of fat-bottomed women in trousers. One of the women took my bag of plaster and opened it to see what was inside.

She searched my handbag and then put her hands up under my coat and searched everything down to the hems of my clothes. You filthy little tart! I thought to myself, looking at her cheap permanent wave plastered down with brilliantine like oiled rat-tails. And her armpits stank to high heaven. You filthy little tart, daring to search me! I wouldn't have you in my house even for a skivvy! . . .'

But I managed to pretend that I was perfectly cool and composed. I even seemed to be smiling. I realised I needed to do some play-acting. – 'Who have you come to see?' asked one of them. From the way the others looked at him it was obvious he was the leader. He stared straight into my eyes as though he was daring me to see who would flinch first. – 'I've come to see Mr Emmanuel,' I said. He gestured to one of his 'comrades' to give him a notebook he was holding. He opened it, closed it, and looked fiercely straight into my eyes again. – 'I'll have to send you to the firing squad!', he said suddenly. 'You've been sent by the English to do a reconnaissance . . .' He spoke slowly and deliberately, but that made it feel all the more like standing in front of a judge in court. – 'Well, that's the giddy limit!', I shouted. 'Just listen to that! I've been sent by the English, he says! You must be out of your mind! I don't like the damn rotten British any more than you do. If it wasn't for them Greece would be far better off today than she is, and that's a fact!' – 'Don't speak so loud . . .' – 'If you don't believe that I'm on your side, just ask my cousin, he'll tell you!' – 'Who's your cousin?' – 'You don't have to ask me. Just get on the phone to your headquarters, and they'll soon tell you who and what Mr Emmanuel is! . . .' He looked hard at the coat I was wearing. – 'And there's no need to look at my coat like that,' I said, 'you can't judge people by a lousy coat.' In fact it wasn't a 'lousy coat' at all, it was the very best astrakhan. – 'Anyway,' I told him, 'in Russia everyone wears fur coats! . . .' At last I saw his lips break into a smile, as though to say: you're a sly one, you are! I began to have some hopes. – 'Can I see the nurse for a minute to give her the plaster?' I said. – 'You can see her for as long as your heart desires, today, tomorrow, the day after tomorrow . . .' He made a sign to the lady and gentlemen comrades to let me pass and turned his back on me. – 'Hey! where are you going?', I said, 'what do you mean, today, tomorrow, the day after tomorrow? Do you mean you're going to keep me here? I've got a home and a family. They'll be worrying about me.' He turned and looked at me. – 'Let's say, for the sake of argument, that I let you go. How do I know you won't go and tell the English that you've seen us?' – 'Here we go again!' I said. 'What do you want me to swear on? I give you my word, I tell you. Send one of the boys here, or go inside yourself and ask my cousin to tell you who I am. His room's the fourth on the right. To tell you the honest truth, I don't take much interest in politics myself. Anything that's good for Greece and for the workers, that's good enough for me.' He looked me up and down, trying to make up his mind. – 'Alright,' he said, 'you can leave the plaster and go.' But before I had time to breathe a sigh of relief, he added: – 'But if the English attack us I'll hold you responsible and I'll execute your cousin in his bed!' – 'But he's a communist!' – 'I don't care if he's Stalin himself!' – And he turned his back on me again.

I stood there rooted to the spot. Then I began to think. I'm between two fires, I thought to myself. I didn't want to fall into their hands, but on the other hand I could hardly leave Petros in pawn and just take myself off. The British might easily find out from somebody else that the communists were in the clinic and start an attack. I could see from the way he spoke that he meant what he said. Communist or no communist he'd execute him without batting an eyelid. For people like them the success of the rebellion was far more important than one communist intellectual with a broken leg. And how would I ever face aunt Katie? She'd never stop blaming me as long as she lived. I grabbed the bag of plaster and started off towards Petros's room, struggling to keep my tears back. I could have screamed out loud with rage. Fancy me, Nina, falling into that murderer's hands and being forced to swear that I was on their side! . . .

I stayed in the clinic for a week. I ate the hospital food, mostly plain lentil soup, and slept on two armchairs with only my fur coat to cover myself with. It's a miracle I didn't catch pneumonia. Even before I shut myself up in the clinic, they'd torn down and burned anything that would burn for warmth. They'd even stripped some of the shutters from the windows. At the same time I was bleeding badly: what with being so upset, my monthlies had come on earlier than usual and the blood just wouldn't stop. The doctor gave me some drops to take, but they made it worse rather than better.

I woke up on the eighth day very early, stiff with cold and worn out after a restless night. Straight away I noticed a change in the atmosphere. I jumped out of bed and went into the corridor, bumping straight into an officer of the National Guard. — 'They're ours! They're ours!', I began shouting, wild with joy. I hugged him and kissed him, and the tears rolled down my face. I was simply hysterical with relief. I rushed into Petros's room. But no Petros! My enthusiasm collapsed like a pricked balloon. — 'Where's my cousin?' I asked the nurse, imagining the worst. — 'Don't worry,' she said with a smile, 'I've let him go to the lavatory by himself . . .' I breathed a sigh of relief. But it wasn't another ten seconds before one of those anti-communist 'X' organisation men came in, with a carefully trimmed moustache and a ridiculous beret on his head. — 'Are you Emmanuel's cousin?', he asked. From his face and his voice you would have sworn he was a drug addict. It's one lot of ruffians worse than the other, I thought to myself. At least the communists do what they do because they believe they can change Greece a bit for the better. But what does this stinking little stool-pigeon hope to do? What does he believe in? — 'No!' I said. I had a feeling he was up to no good, and my instinct was never wrong. 'I'm here to visit my brother,' I said. 'His name is Longos, Dimitris Longos . . .' It was the first name that came into my head. I shudder when

I think about it. He looked at me suspiciously. At that moment Petros appeared in the doorway. My blood ran cold. — 'Dimitris!' I shouted, looking hard at him so that he should catch on. 'Tell the officer here your name. He doesn't believe me when I tell him your name is Dimitris Longos . . .' Petros was confused for a moment, but he wasn't a fool. He soon understood what was going on. — 'Yes, that's right,' he said, Longos is my name.' He said it with all the casualness in the world, as though he was bored stiff, and stretched out on his bed. — 'I should try upstairs if I were you,' I said to the X-officer, 'I think there's somebody called Emmanuel in the same room on the second or third floor . . .'

The officer went out and began running upstairs, taking the stairs two at a time. — 'Quick!' I said to Petros, 'get up, there isn't a minute to lose! If you can walk to the lavatory you can walk home . . .' His room was on the ground floor. He held on to my shoulders and, somehow or other, we managed to get to the front door. The officer I had kissed in my fit of enthusiasm was standing outside talking to an Englishman. When he saw me he smiled and brought his hand up to his cap in a salute. — 'Thank you, thank you,' I said, and I smiled at him as naturally as I could. But I was trembling from head to foot in case the X-man came down and caught us. All my instincts told me to run as fast as I could. But I was forced to keep pace with Petros as he struggled along on his broken leg. I thought my nerves would snap with the strain. When we got home and I felt safe at last, I fell on the bed and broke into a hysterical flood of tears. I just couldn't stop. I hadn't cried so much for years.

Five days later, or maybe six, Theodore arrived back from the Middle East.

14

Sotiris was one of the first to be taken by the communists. Even before poor Hecuba had returned from Kalamata, the gendarmerie had requisitioned a house in Halandri for him. On St Barbara's day, Polyxene left him ill with 'flu at home and went down to the square to do her shopping. When she got back she found the house empty. A neighbour told her what had happened. 'If I were you I'd leave straight away,' she said, 'I heard them say they'd be coming back.' Like a mad thing she ran off, over the Tourkovounia hill, cutting through by Galatsi, until she got to poor Hecuba's house to stay until things sorted themselves out. At that time the house was completely deserted. The communists had taken the landlord and his family. He had collaborated with the Germans. She came to see me three or four times and we sat chatting over some coffee. I tried to console her, poor thing, she was as thin as a rake with all the aggravation. No matter how stoical and self-controlled you may be, the breakdown is bound to come one day. It wasn't exactly roses and honey for the poor girl. She'd lost her first husband when they'd been married less than a month, she'd lost her brother and her mother inside three months, and now they'd taken her second husband and it was quite likely she'd never see him again . . . But, the way things were, when Theodore came back he at least found Polyxene in the house. He'd learned the news about Dimitris and Hecuba from some journalist colleagues of his who'd gone to the Middle East soon after the liberation.

It was at that time also that my own house was left empty. My black-marketeer tenant stayed in hiding all through the rebellion, and he only showed up again when the communists had left Athens. But although there was no longer any danger, he decided to move to another house. Strictly speaking, I ought to have found another tenant immediately, for we badly needed the rent to keep going. But I was so fed up with aunt Katie and her impossible ways that I said to hell with it. I don't care if I die of starvation, I must get out of here, I must get back to my own home! . . .

The house seemed so strange to me for the first two or three days, as though it was no longer my own. Every house has a special smell of its own, and it was not the one I remembered. It was quite a few days before I finished putting things back in their right place and creating an impression, at least, that everything was like it used to be. But it still didn't feel like peacetime. Before we had time to celebrate after the Germans packed up and cleared out, the rebellion had started. It was only now, for the very first time, that we began to feel the war was really over. Food began to appear in the shops, and we felt like new people as soon as we greased our insides a bit. People threw their houses open and welcomed the victors back from the Middle East with open arms, without giving a damn who or what they were. If you had a son, a brother, a cousin or anybody you knew among those who'd come back, they'd turn up with their comrades, and what with the tins and beer and stuff they brought, and the food we could get on our ration at the grocer's, we managed to throw parties of a kind and pass the time pleasantly enough. Theodore was very friendly at the time with a naval officer and a sergeant of the Rimini Brigade. I used to invite them, Polyxene, Cleo and Willie with their Bertha, Takis with Irene, and we'd eat and dance to the gramophone. And when Sotiris finally came back after being a hostage, pale and thin but still alive, the atmosphere became really gay and carefree.

Theodore had begun to make up to me, a little smile here and a little word there. But I pretended not to catch on. Let's wait and see what he'll do, I thought to myself. I could see he was trying to get me alone, away from the others, but I avoided it. To be quite honest, I didn't much like the way he'd never asked me a single thing either about his brother or about his mother. He never mentioned them at all, as though they had never existed, although the truth is, of course, I wouldn't have breathed a word of what I knew even if he had asked me. In spite of the promise I'd given her, I was determined never to open my mouth. The best thing, I told myself, was to let the past alone. It wasn't right to set him against Sotiris. Their relations in any case, as far as I could see, were not the friendliest. They had absolutely nothing in common. Every time Sotiris opened his mouth to make one of those daft country-bumpkin jokes of his, Theodore would pull a long face and puff out those great lips of his in exasperation. Polyxene hadn't said anything to me, but I could see it wouldn't be very long before they had a row. Sotiris had no intention of sharing his wife with her brother, and Polyxene couldn't wash and iron Theodore's shirts for him. In any case, they were only living temporarily in Hecuba's house. Sooner or later they'd have to go back to their house in Halandri.

As you might expect, they soon came to the conclusion that the best solution for all concerned was for Theodore to get married. Suddenly I saw their attitude towards me beginning to change: Polyxene was ever so warm and affectionate, Sotiris began to call me 'sis', and Theodore was all over me, more so than ever before. Funnily enough, it was Eleni who made the proposal. As soon as things quietened down a bit, she came up from Kalamata for a few days to see them. When I first saw her I felt the same thing as I felt later when I met her aunt Aphrodite. Fancy! I thought to myself, is it really possible for such a nice pleasant-looking little woman to be the monster her mother made her out to be? One evening I asked her to stay overnight to keep me company. The Duchess had her own room now, as she did in the old days. Sometimes at night I felt so scared, being all alone. We went to bed and put out the bedside light. But neither of us could go to sleep. We started chatting. I began asking her all sorts of things about Hecuba. Eleni hadn't needed much persuading when I asked her to stay the night, but it wasn't just for my bright blue eyes. I realised she stayed for a purpose, and I had no doubt at all what the purpose was. But the mere thought of what she was going to say made me uncomfortable, as though I were an eighteen-year-old. Every time I felt she was getting ready to come out with it, I stopped her by asking another question. — 'But tell me, Eleni, what really happened down there in Kalamata?', I said, 'why did she leave so suddenly? Did you have a row or something?' Eleni heaved a deep sigh in the dark. — 'I can imagine what she must have told you!' she said. 'God forgive her, she never could stand me. She used to turn my very own son against me, telling him I was the worst woman in the world. The day she left there'd been a man with a barrow pass by the house selling fresh figs. It was August. I went out and bought a couple of pounds and, as we were sitting there in the yard, I gave her and the kids two or three figs each. But she got the idea that I'd given more to Anna because I was supposed to love her more than Akis, and she started a row. But it wouldn't have led to anything if it hadn't been for Akis himself butting in: — 'I can't see what you're making such a fuss about, grandma,' he told her, 'if I want some more figs the plate's there, I'll just take some! . . .' And she was so offended because even her beloved grandson hadn't taken her part that she tried to commit suicide. You see, she'd come with the idea at the back of her head that she'd take him back to Athens with her . . .' — 'And what about the pendant? Is it true that poor Dimitris took it?' — 'So she told you that as well, did she? Yes, of course he took it. The police found it at some fence's place. He'd sold it for next to nothing. God forgive him . . .'

Although it was dark and I couldn't see her face, I could tell she was being sincere by the way she spoke. — 'Well, never mind all that now,' she said, 'let's change the subject. They're dead now, let them rest in peace. It's much better to talk about the present and the future. There's something I want to tell you . . .' O-oh! I thought to myself, here it comes. — 'I'm not such a great one for talking as my mother was,' she said, 'I'm a bit of a country bumpkin. I wasn't brought up in Athens and what I have to say I like to say straight out without any trimmings. We've discussed it with Theodore and with Polyxene, and we'd be glad to make you one of the family!... Don't give me your answer straight away. Think it over yourself, and let me know tomorrow morning.'

I blessed the darkness for covering up my confusion and my blushes. But I had no need to think it over. I'd thought about it, not once but a hundred times, in the last few days, and weighed all the pros and cons. I knew perfectly well what an outcry there'd be both from my daughter and from aunt Katie, and from many of my friends, but I'd no intention of arranging my life to please other people. I had no hopes left whatever of my daughter. Hecuba was right: if I was left at her mercy, she'd make my life a misery, she'd eat me alive. Then, on the other hand, my gold sovereigns had gone – we were eating our way through the last of them that month. I'd sold half of the timber, and the other half had been stolen during the rebellion. All we had left was the house, but either I had to rent it again and continue to live like a refugee in one room, or I had to sell it and live on the money I got for it. But that, whatever that monstrous freak of mine said, I had no intention of doing. Not so much for myself, but in her own interests, so there'd be something left for her when I finally closed my eyes. With her stupidity and her lazy good-for-nothing ways, she'd soon end up begging on the streets if she was left alone, without so much as the house to depend on. And then, I thought to myself. Theodore may not be exactly anyone's idea of Prince Charming; in fact, now that I'd got to know him better I could see that poor old Hecuba was right: he was a bit selfish, obstinate and narrow-minded. But, on the other hand, I wasn't exactly a raving young beauty myself. – 'What is there to think over?' I told her. 'Anything I can tell you in the morning I might just as well tell you now: the only difficulty I can see is that he'll be wanting children, and I can't have children any more . . .' The haemorrhage I'd had while I was in the clinic had turned out to be the last. – 'I wouldn't worry too much about children if I were you,' she said, 'the fewer Longos offspring in the world, the better for everybody! . . .'

15

A month after we were married, we went to Hecuba's house
— he and Polyxene and I — to share out the things. We had no
need of the furniture. We agreed with Theodore to give it all
to Polyxene. We took just a few picture frames to hang on the
wall, one with a photograph of Hecuba, one with a photograph
of my father-in-law — the one where he's dressed as an officer
of the Macedonian Guard, and an oil painting of King Constantine — the one that used to hang side by side with the photo
of Metaxas and made her brother Miltiades spit on the floor.
We also took a thick red woolen blanket, the pair of the one
Dimitris stole, an embroidered tablecloth, and a big seashell-
ashtray with a picture of the Acropolis painted on it. — 'You
must take those brass shell cases of uncle Miltiades!' said Polyxene, who thought they belonged to Theodore as of right. —
'Shell cases! Do me a favour and get them off my hands,' I
said to her in a whisper to prevent him hearing as he went in
and out from room to room. 'Do me a favour and get them off
my hands, I've got enough rubbish to cope with. Why don't
you send them to Eleni? . . .'

Standing on a chair, I began taking down the ikons off the
wall and handing them to Polyxene one by one: the St Dimitrios, the one poor Hecuba said had made a cracking noise
when her son was born, the St Fanourios with the forged birth
date of Polyxene's on the back, and the St Anastasia the
Healer. Now, after all those years of rubbing with brasso and
soda, the 'Hecuba' had begun to fade, too. . . . I remembered
the story of the miracle: 'Dear Saint Anastasia, I cried, you
who predicted my ruin, couldn't you prevent it from happening? But what could the poor Saint do, Nina? What could
God himself do? I had been warned. It was up to me to open
my eyes and take some action. . . .' Poor old Hecuba! She was
no fool. She knew all her own faults. But her nerves weren't
very strong. I always used to tell her: 'Your nerves aren't

strong at all, you ought to go to a doctor and get him to give you some sort of bromide, you really must make an effort to calm yourself.' But she never paid any attention. Some people have the seeds of their own destruction inside them. For all her cleverness, she was simply incapable of facing up to reality with calmness and logic, and that's why she always made such a mess of things.

But I wasn't in much of a mood that day to sit there thinking about the past and about dead people. And then, her death was still very recent. Sometimes I had the impression that she wasn't dead but only gone away somewhere on a long journey. I hadn't begun to cry for her yet. In fact quite often – like when Antoni died and all I could think about was the sovereigns – I caught myself thinking all kinds of cynical and selfish thoughts: Oooff! I thought to myself, it's a good thing she's dead. If she were still alive I wouldn't be married to Theodore, and even if he's no great prize, the truth is I don't know how we'd get along without him! It's only after all these years that I've really begun to mourn for her, that I've really begun to realise that, apart from poor papa, I've lost the only other person in the world who really understood something of what went on inside me, who taught me a thing or two in this life. That's why I get so mad now when I hear that beast in human form insulting her.

Just as I was getting down off the chair holding the last ikon and the red ikon lamp, I heard a loud sobbing noise from the kitchen. I exchanged a glance full of meaning with Polyxene. – 'Don't go in,' I whispered to her, 'leave him alone to cry as much as he wants.' It was the first – and last – sign on his part that he knew, so to speak, that his mother and brother were no more! That's the strange, closed-in kind of character he has. In fact when he came back into the room there was nothing in his expression to suggest a man who had just been crying his eyes out. And when we got back home he was more cheerful than I've seen him on almost any occasion since. Poor Hecuba! I said to myself, you used to say that when they'd lost you they'd come and scratch at your grave with their fingernails. But that was one more of your delusions. The truth is that the living forget. When you're dead, you're dead, and that's that.

As soon as we got into our kitchen he began sniffing the air and wrinkling up his nose to guess what I had cooking in the oven. It was really comic. — 'It's your favourite dish, baldie,' I said. 'Baldie' is my nickname for him. To think of it! And I've always made fun of men without hair. He rubbed his hands gleefully, like a child. He's just like Antoni, God bless him — always thinking of his stomach. I piled his plate with as much moussaka as it would hold and he sat and wolfed it down as though he hadn't eaten for a week.

16

Six years have gone by since then—almost seven. If I said I was happy with my life, I'd be telling a lie. True, in spite of all his shouting and his peculiar ways, Theodore is a good man. But it's not easy making do on a bare monthly wage. As for my daughter, she's turned out even worse than I expected. She never loses an opportunity to upset me and make my life a misery. Often, inside me and all round me, I feel the same terrible kind of emptiness I felt when we were waiting for the Germans to march into Athens. And I think to myself: is this what we fought for? Is this the end of so much blood and suffering? Sometimes I sit and think that maybe Petros was right after all. Maybe, for all their faults, it would have been better if the communists had won in '44. Who knows! Perhaps our lives would have changed a bit for the better. Whereas now—it's the same old story all over again: the poor are still hungry, and all they're allowed to do about it (and as a great concession, at that) is to wail about their bad luck, singing those bouzouki songs you hear so often that they drive you mad:

'*A lousy world, a lousy life, a lousy damned society. . . .*'— yes, they wail about their bad luck. What else can they do? They certainly can't change it. And then you have to put up with all those Americans (and even some Germans lately!) coming to the country, and gaping at us as though we were animals in a zoo.

But, when you come to think of it, people are never happy. The main thing is to be alive and in good health. And thank God, to the great disappointment of my daughter, I feel more lively and full of beans than ever. Actually, I've dyed my hair. My husband doesn't mind, so I don't give a damn what my daughter or anybody else says.

The other day I had a letter from Cleo. Poor Cleo! She never forgets me. They've left Altrincham and live in London now. Bertha's married an airline pilot and they have a little boy. Willie's taken his pension and plays golf all day long, Cleo says. If only I were a bird! I'd fly straight over to see them, and we'd sit down and play a little game of poker like we did in the old days. I've missed it so much. And it would be a chance to see what the rest of the world is like. Is it so different from Greece as they say, I wonder, or is it all much of a muchness?

But what's the point of wondering? It's all a midsummer night's dream as far as I'm concerned. Now that the rebellion's over it's easier to travel abroad than it used to be. But as long as I've got this all-devouring Medusa to feed and clothe, there's not a hope of putting a single penny aside — not even for a fortnight's holiday on the beach in Greece somewhere, let alone London and Paris! And anyway Theodore isn't much of a one for travelling. He's not like his mother in any way. As a member of the Journalists' Union he can travel anywhere he likes in Europe for next to nothing. But not he! He won't move a step out of lousy Athens. He's such a dull stick-in-the-mud, and as time goes on he gets even worse. Just when I was thinking I might get to know some worthwhile people, he went and left his job on the newspaper. Cut himself off completely from journalism. He was fed up with it, he said. Couldn't stand the people. Now he just works mornings as an office clerk, and every afternoon he goes and sits for hours at the same café poor Antoni used to go to, playing whist with the pensioners. Or he goes off to play backgammon with Irene's husband. Instead of keeping in with his own circle of friends, he prefers my relations. So much so that sometimes I say to him: — 'I really can't make it out, Theodore, didn't you ever have any friends of your own?'

It's all I can do to get him to come to Halandri from time to time. But, to be perfectly honest, that's not so much because he finds it a long way to go but because he simply can't stand being in the same room with Sotiris.

The last time we were there, he got up suddenly, put his hat on and left — because he saw Sotiris wearing his pyjamas over his underclothes.

'What's it to you?' I said to him when I got back home. 'Why worry what Sotiris does? Let him go to bed in his uniform if he wants to! You don't go to see him, you go to see your sister.'

Of course we all know Sotiris is a dreadful peasant, and sometimes his habits make you sick. But, I ask you, is that a good reason why Theodore shouldn't go to see his sister and make her cry? The fact is, I'm much more tolerant about that kind of thing. It takes all sorts to make a world, and I can get along with everybody. Sometimes I take the bus and go up there by myself, to get a breath of fresh air and get away from my daughter for a while. I don't care what Theodore says. All I know is, bumpkin or no bumpkin, Sotiris is a very good husband to Polyxene. She twists him round her little finger. She's luckier than any of us. His only regret is not having any children. — 'If I'd knowed yew couldn't have no kids, I wouldna married yah. I'd a gorn back home and gotten one of the girls back there, that could have me some kids! . . .' When he says that Polyxene winks at me. Of course, she can't very well tell him: I've got proof that I could 'have you some kids,' it's you that can't. — 'It's not my fault,' she says, 'you ought to have tried me out before you married me! . . .'

17

Eleni lives in Athens now. Her daughter met an engineer, before she'd properly finished high school. He was from a very good family, and he fell in love with her and married her, just as she was, without a dowry or anything. They all live together in the Plaka, in a fine old house near St Saviour's church, and they have a fine little boy. But I hardly ever see them now. Eleni acts very coldly towards me. She's angry because we didn't send her any of Hecuba's things, as if it was up to me to decide, or as if it was the treasure of Ali Baba or something! Twice I told Polyxene that she ought to send her something, just so she'd have some kind of keepsake of her mother's. I really can't understand why she puts the blame on me.

But I do see quite a lot of Akis. He comes at least twice a week and has a meal with us.

— 'And even if you hadn't married my uncle,' he says. 'I'd still come and see you. We're old friends, we are . . .'

Sometimes I look at him and I simply can't believe he used to be the skinny little boy who sat there knitting scarves and balaclava helmets for the soldiers. He's quite a grown-up young man now, tall and handsome. Of course, like all the Longos family, he's got a bee in his bonnet. Instead of choosing a proper respectable career, like a doctor or an engineer or something, and earning a really good living, he insists on becoming a painter! The year before last he started going to the College of Fine Arts, and last year he took second prize in his class. I'm not saying he isn't talented. At least with the pictures he paints in school—old houses, landscapes, still lifes and that kind of thing. They're really quite nice, and you can understand them. They have some meaning, so to speak. But every now and again he comes and shows me some of that modern rubbish he paints by himself at home. And that's when I draw the line and give him a good telling off.

Not that I'm an expert, but I pride myself on knowing something about that kind of thing. When I was a young girl I used to go quite often to exhibitions of painting at the 'Parnassus' gallery. Papa was a bosom friend of the painter Thalia Flora-Caravia. She always sent us invitations to the opening of her exhibitions, and she went on sending them for two or three years after poor papa died. That was painting if you like! Not like those daft concoctions they call painting today. — 'Just explain something to me, Akis,' I tell him, 'am I barmy or are you? How can a nose possibly come down there underneath the chin?' — 'That's the way I see it,' he says. Or he says: 'That's the way you'll look when you're dead.' But most times he doesn't bother to answer me at all. He just shakes his head with a pitying kind of smile, as if to say: what's the good of trying to explain to old fogeys. . . .

On one of those pictures, full of black, yellow and blue splotches, that he had the nerve to send to the Zappeion Panhellenic Exibition, he put the title: 'A dream: my grandmother'! Theodore, mainly because of Maria's poisonous tongue, has forbidden all of us so much as to mention Hecuba's name. You can imagine how furious he was when he found out. It was two months before he spoke to Akis again. Of course I can understand the boy's feelings. He remembers her more than any of us. It was she who brought him up and was more than a mother to him. How she loved that boy! 'It's my child's son,' she used to say, 'so he's twice my son.' And I remember once when she was telling us about how she stopped Eleni from having the abortion, she turned round to him and said: — 'And if it wasn't for me, young man, you wouldn't be alive right now . . .' I happened to mention it to him the other day. — 'Do you remember, Akis?', I asked him. He remembers. And it makes him sad. He hasn't told me so in so many words, but I know what goes on in his mind, and I know he blames himself for leaving her all alone in Athens and going back to his mother. If he hadn't abandoned her like all the others, if she'd had somebody to keep her busy, somebody to cook for, maybe she'd have eaten properly herself, and then perhaps she wouldn't have got that urea, and maybe she wouldn't have died. . . .

The other day I was reading in a magazine all about hypnotism, and I remembered the story about Father Nikos and how it all led up to her turning her poor brother out of the house. — 'Was it really true, Akis?' I asked him, 'did Father Nikos actually hypnotise you?' — 'Are you kidding?' he said, 'I just pretended to be hypnotised.' — 'And what did he ask you?' — 'Well, let me think: he told me to go up to heaven and ask God if uncle Dimitris would get off. "Do you see Him?" he said. — "Yes, I see Him" — "What's He wearing?" — "A long red Grecian tunic; He's sitting on a golden throne, and the throne seems to be riding on top of a mass of white clouds like cotton wool . . ." — "Is He alone?" — "Yes. He's alone." — "Ask Him: will my uncle Dimitris get off?" I didn't know what to say. — "He doesn't speak," I told him. But the silly old goat insisted. — "Ask Him again," he said. "What did He say? Will he get off?" — "Er-er, yes! He'll get off!" He began to pray. And when he finished praying, he said: "Now I'll count up to three, and as soon as I say phhh! you'll wake up and you won't remember anything of what you've seen! . . ." '.

18

Aunt Katie went too, and we buried her on St Gabriel's day. When I got back from the cemetery I went up to the terrace to be alone for a while. I didn't cry for her. For all that she was eight years older than my father, she lived for sixteen whole years after he died. If I feel sorry for her at all, it's because she didn't really live — not as I understand living. She was never troubled by her conscience, never had the slightest doubts about anything. Hecuba may have gone through the trials and tribulations of a Job, maybe she was a bit neurotic, but at least she was a real live person. She was one of those people who leave something behind them when they're gone, one of those people you don't easily forget. Whereas aunt Katie lived and died like a pudding. Her only regret, and she didn't even take that very much to heart, was that she couldn't see Petros once more before she closed her eyes for good. Takis tried through the General Staff, and Theodore through some people he knew at the Ministry of the Interior, to arrange for a permit to come home under escort from the Makronissos island where he was exiled with the other communists, even if only for a few hours. But it was impossible.

I leaned my elbows on the parapet and looked across absent-mindedly at Nota's honeysuckle. It had begun to blossom. The poplar in the next-door yard, which had reached the level of our terrace in 1940, had pushed up another six feet or more and completely shut off our view of Mount Lycabettus. I idly studied the poplar's leaves and noticed for the first time how strange they are: like double-sided material. Rotten old trees! I thought to myself. Poor Hecuba was right about them. They die and come to life again, die and come to life again. It's only we that die once and for all. . . .

— 'You'll peg out!' That's what Fotis's bastard child told me today. 'You'll peg out, just like your washerwoman of a mother-in-law! But Eleni's alive and doing very nicely thank you!' — 'My mother-in-law,' I told her, 'may have pegged out, and pegged out all alone, but not for the reasons you may imagine with that narrow little mind of yours. Everybody pegs out, and alone, if it comes to that. As for Eleni, she may be alive, but as to whether she's doing nicely, I'm not so sure she'd agree with you. But even if she is, I wouldn't mention myself in the same breath as her if I were you. Oh, you needn't think I mean that you're better than she is, just because of the kind of life she's led. Quite the contrary. If only you were like her, yes, even like her! When she was younger than you are now she'd married, had two children and left her husband. And a good thing, too, the kind of bastard he was! And she had the guts to face life with a bit of courage, all alone. She wouldn't have deigned to live as a burden to her mother and her step-father like you! If you've got a spark of self-respect in you,' I said, 'why don't you do the same? I don't mean exactly the same as Eleni, of course. You'd earn precious little money with that ugly mug of yours. But at least you could find your-self an honest job, in a shop or a factory, anything just so long as you brought something into the house. It's high time after all the years I've been feeding you and clothing you. And don't be in too much of a hurry to bury me,' I said, 'you never know, it may end by me burying you! I've a strong constitution, you know, and I might live to be a hundred. I pray to God my husband lives to a ripe old age too, so we can grow old together and I can take him by the hand and we can go for walks in the park like all the other old folk do.' Unfortunately the doctor found he had a touch of diabetes recently, and what with his greedy habits I'm not too optimistic about the chances. I hope and pray I'm spared yet another bitter experience in my life. . . . 'But if, God forbid, anything happens to him, and the clergymen decide, like I saw in the newspapers, to allow a fourth wedding, then I may very well take a fourth husband yet. Not for anything else,' I said, 'just to make you bust!'

Red Dust Books:

Sights: Three Novellas
Anna Holmes $1.95 paper

Mathis at Colmar: A Visual Confrontation
Linda Nochlin $5.00 hard cover
                                               $3.00 paper

Indrani and I
Anne de Viri $4.25 hard cover
                                               $1.95 paper

Elizabeth Newt
Harold Fleming $4.25 hard cover
                                               $1.95 paper

Green Seacoast—an autobiography
George Buchanan $4.25 hard cover
                                               $1.95 paper

Ornashious—a novel
John O'Hare $4.25 hard cover
                                               $1.95 paper

The Park
Philippe Sollers $4.25

Sentimental Talks—two novels
Daniel Castelain $4.95 hard cover

Law and Order
Claude Ollier $4.95 hard cover

Red Dust 1—New Writing
Christine Bowler, Lyman Andrews, $4.95 hard cover
  F. W. Willetts $2.50 paper

Recordings:

Reconstruction of a Me and Letter to a Cold Place
M. Younger Roberts $5.95

To be published:

Red Dust 2, 3—works by Simon Vestdijk, Alan Burns, Babette
Sassoon, T. Fallon, and Bruce Woods.

Behind the White Screen—Sotiris Spatharis

History of/Reflections on Film—Ken Kelman

The Byzantine Wall Paintings of Crete by Konstantin Kalokyris,
with photographs in black and white and color by Farrel Grehan.

Red Dust, Inc., 218 E. 81st Street, New York, N. Y. 10028

Paris
7-